K.C. BARNES

The Narrator

First edition

ISBN: 979-8-9937853-0-1

Cover art by Jordan Clevenger

This book was professionally typeset on Reedsy.
Find out more at reedsy.com

To 24-year-old me.
We did it!

&

To the audiobook readers who love having their dark and spicy romance
read to them while multitasking.
The Narrator is waiting for you...

Introduction

Reader discretion is advised.

"The Narrator" is a dark romance novel that contains sensitive material which may be difficult or triggering for some readers including:

- Stalking: Online/Real Life
- Vulgar Language
- Consensual Non-Consent
- Mask Play
- Marking Kink: The intentional practice of leaving hickeys, scratches, or bite marks on a partner.
- Mental Illness: mention of depression in thought.

Violence: (not between the couple)

- Hostage Situation/Extortion
- Torture: Includes physical/psychological torment.
- Graphic violence and gore: Explicit and detailed depictions of violence and injury.
- Death/Attempted Murder
- Gun violence: Using a gun to hold someone hostage
- Dismemberment: Depictions of cutting off fingers with a sharp object.
- Depictions of blood and bones breaking.

Natalie

"The way he looked at her when he saw she was wearing another man's jersey! 'If you don't take that off right now, I'll rip it off.' Sir! My jaw was on the floor!" Kayley squealed as she held up her copy of "Naughty and Ice" by Tilly Brand. "Five stars!"

"You rate every book we read five stars." Riley jumped in. "You just finished it last night, let it simmer in the brain for a second."

"Fine." She rolled her eyes as she picked up her wine glass. "What would you rate it?"

Riley shrugged her shoulders. "Three and a half stars for sure. I like the plot and the spice was spicing but the end where she's so in love with him she threw out her life long promise to not have kids, to have a kid with him."

I scrunched my nose. "Yeah, I agree. I get when you love someone so much you see yourself having a child with them and you've thought about having kids one day. But, don't make her throw out her promise and completely change her because of a man she fucked for a month."

"Ugh." Kayley groaned as she swung her legs over the armrest of her chair. "You're getting too hung up on the details. Besides, it was in the epilogue so it doesn't count."

"It so counts!" I argued.

"Natalie. Please." Kayley continued. "When you're having sex do you focus on the tip or the entire shaft?"

Blake raised an eyebrow. "True." Her face indicated her thought process before she brushed away the thoughts and shifted under her blanket on the couch. "Honestly, as long as the magical button gets pressed I really don't pay attention to the rest."

"Please stop calling it a button." Riley pressed her eyes shut and turned her head away from her sister-in-law sitting next to her.

"We're talking about smut books here, you can say G-Spot." Kayley giggled as Blake's face turned red.

Blake, Riley's sister in law, who only reads academically, is the newest member of our book club The Spice Shelf. Where we get together every couple of weeks or so to talk about the latest and greatest, smuttiest books we can find. It all started when Kayley turned on a spicy audiobook during our girl's trip a few years ago and the rest is history.

"You're telling me, this man, that *voice*, narrates romance novels, *spicy*, romance novels?" I looked over at Kayley sitting in the passenger seat.

"Oh yeah, Dean Craven is by far one of the best narrators out there and he has an entire list of books he's narrated over the years. I'm telling you, this man will make you leave porn faster than your vibrator vibrates." She reassured me. "Not to mention, he's hot as fuck! Take a look at his Instagram."

From that moment I was hooked. Not just because of his voice, I mean, it's a fantastic bonus, but the plots and stories started peaking my interest. Not to mention helped me find things about myself that I never knew were there. Before we started this book club I only ever thought of masks being used for medical staff or for superheroes and villains. Now, when I see a man in a motorcycle helmet or a mask in horror movies my face gets hot. Thanks to all the video edits I've found of masked men on the internet using one of Dean's lines.

Plus, audiobooks are a great way for me to get through my TBR list that's currently stacked to the ceiling. Since work has been picking up more and more I haven't had a moment to just sit down and read a physical book in a long time. Kayley has given me flack for it but mainly because she thinks I "work too much".

When you work in the media, the news never stops, especially in pop culture media.

So of course when my phone suddenly pings with a message from my boss, I immediately take a deep breath before reading it to prepare myself.

Brock: *"Hey Natalie. It's Brock. Ell Wyms and Tanner Brunswick got engaged. We're going to need all hands on deck tonight and tomorrow morning. Could you rally the team together and ask if anyone would be willing to switch shifts? If they work over two hours they can take two hours off their shift the next day."*

"Son of a bitch." I muttered.

"What's wrong?" Riley asked as she set her glass of wine on the coffee table.

"It's Brock. That pop star Ell Wyms got engaged to Tanner Brunswick and it's an 'all hands on deck' situation." I mocked with a low tone.

"It's always an 'all hands on deck' situation with him." Kayley rolled her eyes.

She works on the same team with me at World Entertainment Media. Generic as hell, I know, and trust me the content we make matches the energy. She's just there to get her first five years of experience and leave. Not that I blame her, I've definitely had more moments as of late to dip out early because of Brock. He's a higher up, and my boss, therefore his job consists of making the CEO, CFO, COO, and other C acronyms happy. And, of course, we can't forget chewing out managers, like me, for every single mistake even if it was caused by a system *he* and other higher ups created.

That man's voice makes me want to jump out of my skin and itch my bones. He is the definition of having nothing better to do than work. And of course, he expects everyone to do the same thing. He's also a big fat liar and his only talent is talking his way out of any situation and redirecting the blame straight to myself and my team.

I shuddered at the thought of Brock's voice and threw back the rest of my wine as I typed back.

"Thanks for the heads up. On it."

While I dislike a lot of people in upper management and the overall environment of a knockoff Google lounge, I do like the work to a certain extent. I mainly manage a lot of the social media accounts, each one with its own niche and audience. Movies, cooking, history, celeb gossip, all the way to daily hacks.

When I was first hired I thought about how cool it was to publish movie review videos, but then as I watched more and more of the content they created I realized it was garbage. I went to Brock a few times to try and help make the content better, more engaging, and actually connect with our audiences, but being a woman in her mid-twenties at the time talking to a middle aged man at a company owned by more middle aged men, I suddenly had "no idea what I was talking about". From then on, I quickly learned that my thoughts and opinions meant nothing to them. Which made me into the person I am today: overworked and drastically underfucked because of my fear of failing and loyalty to paying my bills.

Are there days where I wonder to myself why I'm helping this company put out trash videos on the internet, every single fucking day. And, I know I don't want to spend my entire career listening to a middle aged white guy man-splain how social media works to *me*. A literal content manager. So, for now, I'm just going to stick it out and take their money until I find something better. My toxic trait is thinking it'll just fall into my lap one day and I can finally say "goodbye forever and *fuck you* Brock".

Recently though, since I have a higher position, I've been getting more experience working with our voice over talents. Which has peaked my interest and slowly pushed finding that one-way golden ticket out of there to the back burner. So far it's been a great change of scenery to my day to day tasks. I send the script over, they read it, and if we want something changed or there was a mispronunciation I send it back for a pickup until we can get it perfect. Plus, Brock has very little jurisdiction over that department, since he knows nothing about it and instructed me to "see what worked best".

"Wait." Kayley suddenly sat up. "Tanner Brunswick is engaged? As in my *insanely hot golden retriever actor husband?*"

She pouted her lower lip as I gave her sorrowful look.

"Say it ain't so, Nat... please don't take him away from me." She pleaded as the wine helped her with a little theatrics.

"What did you expect, Kayley?" Riley chimed in, putting her elbows on her knees. "They've been dating for, what, five years now?"

"Five years too long. Everyone loves Little Miss Pop Star. But I see right through that shit. There's nothing behind those eyes but greed and secrets. Dammit." She whined. "Tanner and I were supposed to find each other, elope, and move to England together." Kayley stared at her wine as she swirled it around. She watched the red liquid as though she was waiting for genie to pop out and grant her three wishes all having to do with Tanner. She sighed like a damsel. "Men. I swear."

Blake dropped her hand from her cheek as if she was over Kayley's dramatics. "Weren't you just giggling and screaming about how a hockey player was threatening to rip off her jersey because it wasn't his?"

"That's different." She snapped. "Fictional men would *never* betray me like this." Kayley threw back the rest of her wine as she saw me glued to my phone.

She groaned and rolled her head around dramatically. "Let me guess. 'Shift Switch'."

"Yup." I frustratingly popped. "I sent a message to the entire team. Hopefully Ben and Miranda can work this Saturday evening and we can have Megan take over Sunday morning-"

"BORING." She drew out as she threw her head back in a tantrum. "Let's get back to this book before you have to go hide away in your cave."

"It's not my 'cave' it's my room." I point to her room that's just off the living room with my phone. "Don't act like yours is any better. Miss Gamer." Kayley shoots me a childish look as I grin knowing her cleaning day isn't until Sunday and her room is a disaster at the moment.

"You guys are so lucky you get to work from home." Riley snuggled up in the corner of the couch sharing the blanket with Blake. "I have to leave my poor kitty and hubby at home to go deal with assholes who think the uniform is sexy and when I put the handcuffs on them they say 'kinky'." She stuck out her tongue and mocked in a male voice.

"Gross." Blake scrunched her nose.

"Okay, ladies, ladies." Kayley announced as she stood and wobbled for a second. "I believe it is time to give 'Naughty and Ice' its official rating." She held up the book displaying it like Vanna White.

Everyone went around and gave their rating out of five. Kayley gave Blake a look after she only rated it two and half stars. The overall consensus is an average of three and a half stars besides Kayley's constant protests.

"So what made you rate it a two and a half?" I questioned as I picked up the empty wine bottles.

"Sports just isn't my thing." Blake shrugged as she folded the knitted blanket and threw it on the back of the couch. "I get the possessiveness and the sweaty abed men on ice, but eh. Seems basic."

Kayley scoffed from the kitchen. *"Basic?"* She muttered as she pointed to Blake with her pink rubber cleaning gloves. "Did the new girl just call this book... *basic?*"

Riley and I quietly chuckled and nodded.

"Yeah." Blake continued as if she was stating the obvious. "I mean. It seems like they fell for each other pretty easily. There was no begging, pining, and a lot of the sex seemed a little, I don't know. Vanilla."

"Vanilla?" Kayley looked like she was about to have a stroke.

I grinned as I put the wine bottles in the recycling bin. "Oh girl," I called back, "Just wait until we get into some dark romance."

"What's classified as *dark* romance?" She questioned.

"Sweetheart." Riley held her hand as we all remained silent. "I will pray for the next man who comes into your life after you're introduced to dark romance."

"What are you into if you think *this* is vanilla?" Kayley rasped as she made her way back into the living room with her wet gloves still on.

Blake tried to think. "I don't know, never been with a man who's willing to try anything outside missionary or cowgirl. Which is why I've never really read these books. They all blend together, and do the same thing. However," She held up the book and flipped it back and forth. "I do know he'd have to put in a lot more work than this Grant guy did."

Kayley's eyes remained wide. "The man literally ate her out in the locker room so he could still taste her on his lips during the game."

Blake scrunched her nose as if she was disgusted. "Yeah, because getting eaten out in a locker room where it smells like man sweat, blood, tears, snot, and god knows what else is totally 'hot' and 'original.'"

Kayley turned to Riley and I with a shocked expression and a hand out pointing towards Blake. "Someone help me out here?"

"Blake," Riley giggled as she lightly put her hand to her forehead, "these books are like movies, the characters never get cavities, never get allergies, and locker rooms don't smell like ass. It's all a part of the fantasy."

"I understand that. It's just not where I'd like to be taken to for a fun time." She replied.

I lifted my shoulder. "Okay. Understandable. How about this? Where would you like to go for a 'fun time' in a fantasy setting?"

"Somewhere a little more private," her eyes began to stare off as if she was picturing it. "Because if anyone dared to catch me in any state of undress he'll pluck their eyes out so they can never see again, put them in resin, and gift them to me as Christmas ornaments."

We all stayed still and silent for a moment.

"While that was… oddly descriptive." Riley shook the thought from her brain. "I think you're going to love dark romance."

"Agreed." I nodded and smiled at her creative description. While I don't think she was serious about every detail in the fantasy she painted for us I'd pick up that book. Kayley was still shocked into silence as I tried to shut her gaping mouth with my finger under her chin.

"Is she okay?" Blake pointed at Kayley.

I waved my hand in front of her. "No. I think you broke her. I'm impressed." I pursed my lips. "Normally she's numb to these things." I turned to Riley. "I think that deserves an award of some kind."

"Next month's pick?" Riley lifted her shoulders. I nodded as she continued. "Since you're new to dark romance we'll give you a curated list and you can pick from there?"

"Sounds good to me." Blake smiled.

"Christmas ornaments?" Kayley whispered. "That's genius!"

Natalie

Luckily I was able to get through the next couple weeks with only thinking about stuffing a sock in Brock's mouth eleven times. Yes, I counted. Which, during times like these with a high amount of content, is a record breaking low.

Thankfully, within the lulls and very few breaks, I was able to start the next book Blake picked for book club. "House of Mischief" by V. E. Summons. A dark romance about a filthy rich family whose past is sketchy as fuck but with three brothers who are sexy as fuck.

This one follows the middle brother who has a knack for causing mischief, obviously, and according to the eldest brother and father, has to get his shit together and marry into a rival family. He tries to scare her away in every single way possible but he has no idea the kind of twisted things she's hiding behind her pale skin and pretty green eyes.

This definitely piqued Blake's interest, and since the audiobook is narrated by none other than Dean Craven himself it immediately had my vote.

"You shouldn't have come here.'" Dean's voice lightly brushed my ears. *"You have no idea what you're getting yourself into, Princess.'"*

"'I have no idea what I'm getting into?' She replied with a disgusted look on her face. 'You do realize our fathers are in the same business. Or are you so out of touch that you forgot what your daddy does for a living?'"

"Oh shit." I muttered.

"'Hm.' I lick my lips as I slowly approach her. She looks so innocent it makes me want to corrupt her. To destroy her, until nothing is left but lust and tears staring back at me.

"'That mouth of yours is going to get you in trouble, Princess.' I pull on her lower lip with my thumb and forefinger. 'Say something like that again, and I'll fill it until you're unable to breath.'"

"She smacked my hand away. 'Don't call me Princess.' She replied. She's trying to act all tough to throw me off. Cute. If anything she's just an innocent brat who hasn't had a big enough cock in her mouth to make her realize there are dire consequences to her actions."

"'I'll call you whatever I want, Princess. You're mine now. There's no going back. Your precious daddy sold off his only daughter to me, on her 25th birthday no less, for a business deal, because that's all you're worth to him.'"

My thighs began to shift as my body temperature began to rise. "Right on cue." I whispered.

"I could smell the fear coming off of her as her pink bottom lip twitched. Getting under her skin was too easy. This will be fun."

"'You have no idea what you're talking about.' She whispered back. Her chest rising and falling as she breathed heavily, making her breasts hit my chest. That little brat."

"I leaned down to whisper in her ear, and the faint smell of lavender hit my nose from her hair making my dick pulse. 'I think I know exactly what I'm talking about. Princess. You're mine now. From the hair on your head, to your cunt, all of you... is... mine.'"

A shutter went through my entire body as I opened my eyes. His voice was so smooth it felt as if he was whispering to *me*.

"Holy shit." I muttered to myself as the butterflies in my stomach kept flying around.

I paused the audiobook and slipped off my headphones. I needed a second after that one, *holy fuck*. This was a newer audiobook of his and it sounded *different*. I don't know how to explain it, but compared to the rest of his work it just seems *raw* in a way. As if he was speaking to someone directly. Maybe he's just that talented? Maybe it's the book? I don't know. Whatever it was it made me need a moment to breathe.

I really don't understand how I got to this point. I've listened to probably over a hundred audiobooks and *this man* is the only one that gets me hot and bothered every single time without fail. I really shouldn't be listening to Dean's voice while I'm at work, but he's the only one that can make days like this seem bearable.

I wiped my hand down my face as I stared at my computer in my room. Thank god it was Friday at 4:55 P.M. because if I get any more stories about Ell and Tanner's engagement I was going to lose it. I took a moment to breathe and center myself as the beginning of a migraine started to pound in my head. I looked over at my water tumbler and thought for a moment. Shit, when was the last time I drank water today? Suddenly, my hopefulness came to a very stark halt as Brock messaged me asking for a call.

"Seriously? It's 4:57." I huffed. "If this ends up being short enough to be a message or an email I'm going to be pissed." I whispered to myself.

The dreaded ring from our messenger rang and I picked up my Bluetooth headphones.

"Hey Natalie. Apologies for the late call. I was swamped today, but I wanted to catch ya before you left for the weekend."

Swamped? I wouldn't call coming in late because you had a groomer's appointment and then taking a long lunch with the CEO while my team and I set up the entire weekend with twice the amount of content than usual, *swamped*.

"Any-who. We need you to come into the office on Monday."

"Okay, what for?" It wasn't uncommon for me to get called into the office from time to time, but that usually meant there was an important change or meeting of some kind. Definitely something I'm probably not prepared for.

"We have a new VO joining the team and I want you to show him around the office and get him acquainted with our processes." Brock cleared his throat. "The higher ups wanted to try this 'new direction' so he's a bit different from the other VO we have on standby. Since you've been working with our other VO's as of late, and live close by, you'd be a great fit."

Or Brock didn't want to do it himself and everyone else was "too busy". While I'm also busy, there was a part of me that didn't want to say no since this will finally give me a break from Ell and Tanner content.

"Okay? Sure, yeah. No problem."

"Perfect. I'll give ya the details on Monday."

"Sounds good. See ya then." I didn't want to pry any further since it was currently 5:02 P.M. and I desperately needed some me-time and probably some water.

I hung up and ripped off my headphones for a moment and stretched. I love working from home, but damn it really takes a toll on your brain and back. Then again, when I get to work I have a hard time stopping for anything which includes standing, sometimes eating, and filling up my water. Kayley thinks one day it'll kill me and she'll find me slumped over my desk with my fingers still typing like some sort of work zombie. I roll my eyes every time, it's not like I do it on purpose. On normal days I tend to use my standing desk more and take moments to stretch or get some food. But, these past couple of weeks those good habits were tossed out the window.

I took a final deep breath as I logged off for the day. It's finally the weekend and I can just lounge in peace while listening to Dean's sweet and savory voice.

Before I could even put my headphones back on, Kayley burst into my room. When I agreed to be roommates with her in this house, I knew she wasn't one to shy away from anything, but seriously a knock would have been appreciated.

"Jesus, Kay!" I clutched my chest as I turned to her.

"Did you hear?" She jumped onto my bed with a huge grin on her face.

"My heart stop? Yeah!"

"No! We're getting a new VO!"

"I did. I just got off the phone with Brock." I sat back in my chair and swiveled to face her.

She folded her legs and propped her chin in her hands as if we were at a slumber party. "So? Who is it?"

I lifted my shoulders. "No clue. Brock said he'll give me the details on Monday. Apparently, I'll be the one showing him around the office."

"You're going into the office?" She questioned.

"Yeah, Monday." I reiterated. "To give this poor VO a boring tour of our outdated audio booths, tiny set, and snack counter filled with expired protein bars and stale coffee." I narrowed my brow at her. "Why are you so chipper?"

She bit her bottom lip as if she couldn't wait to tell me. "Only because I got a juicy detail from Helen in HR. Apparently, it's someone who's semi-famous."

"Semi-famous?" I lifted a brow as I scoffed in disbelief. "Seriously?"

"Yeah, but that's all the little tease would give me. Apparently, if I want to know who it is I'd have to come in on Monday and 'see for myself'." She rolled her eyes. "She sounded giddy about it too."

"Must be a VO for ads on TV or something." I tried to think. "Brock did mention that the higher ups wanted to try a 'new direction'.

Wonder how they can afford someone 'semi-famous'."

It's no secret that the company has been losing money over the past year and half. Cutting our equipment down in half, multiple accounts within the programs we pay for suddenly down to only one person having access so it's cheaper. It doesn't seem to be affecting staff which is great, but if we keep on this decline layoffs could be coming sooner rather than later. I've tried to present Brock with ideas, but he said everything is fine and it doesn't, and will not, affect my department so I "shouldn't worry about it". After a little frustrated rant with Kayley I've put the thought at the back of my mind. Excuse me for trying to make our content better to get sufficient views so we can get paid, Brock.

"They must be getting desperate if they're going for a marketing tone." Kayley put her chin in her hand.

I shook my head. "No, it'd be more for the monotone than the marketing. But, I doubt they'd head that way, that'd just make our content even more boring than it already is. I guess I'll find out on Monday."

"And you'll have to tell me all about it." She jumped off my bed and headed downstairs into the kitchen.

"Wait. Kayley Lockwood not going into the office to flirt with the new VO?" I followed her as I teased.

"Nat. I'm going to be gone all week, remember? Family vacay. You approved it." She gave me a weird look as I suddenly remembered.

"Right." I slowly shut my eyes. "I completely forgot."

"Girl. You really need to take a break. This job is burning you out faster than a candle snuffer." She handed me water from the fridge.

"I know, I know." I unscrewed the cap from the bottle and sat on one of the stools at the counter. "But, the team needs me, we've been swamped with top priority scripts. I can't just leave while we're already going to be down a person." I pointed at her.

"Fair enough." She stood at the other side of the counter and looked down at me with her gray blue eyes and curled blonde hair flowing down like a waterfall over her shoulders. "Once everything dies down, promise me you'll take at least a few days off." She begged.

"You know I like to save up my PTO for the holidays." I sipped on my water trying to avoid her eye.

"Nat." She leaned on the counter as she pinned me with a stare to wear me down. "How much of your PTO do you actually use during the holidays?"

I lifted my shoulders. "I take the week from the 23rd to the 2nd of the new year. Depending on how the weekends fall."

Kayley licked her top lip. "And how many days of PTO is that?"

I paused for a moment as I gripped the cap on my water bottle again. "Six days." I muttered.

"Out of the 2 weeks we get for PTO." She shook her head as she stood tall. "Seriously, Nat, it's not going to kill you to take a Friday and Monday off here and there. Take a long weekend for yourself. You more than anyone at the company deserves it."

I pressed my lips into a thin smile. "Thank you. For your sake, I'll consider it."

"Great! Now. Down to brass tax. Have you started the book yet?" Kayley shot a wicked grin.

"I'm on chapter four. Her father just handed her over to the 'Lord of Mischief.'"

"Oh girl! Just wait until you get to chapter eighteen. More like Lord of Eating Out." She grinned and swooned.

I raised my brows and shot her an intrigued look. "Girl, trust me, I'll get through the rest tonight and tomorrow. The audiobook is only fifteen hours long." I glanced down at my phone to see a notification from Instagram.

I could feel Kayley watching me as I tried not to smile at my phone.

"Let me guess. Your smooth and velvety boyfriend Dean Craven is the narrator?" She ohh'd and ahh'd. "Is that why you voted for this book?"

"He's *not* my boyfriend, and it's not the only reason." I pointed my finger at her. "I've seen some of the reviews in passing and after hearing Blake's thoughts on the last book I knew she'd be interested, which is why I added it to the list."

I clicked on the notification to see that Dean posted to his story. I've been following his Instagram ever since Kayley introduced him to us on that girls trip a few years ago. He had a decent following back then, but since a couple of his projects went viral and the constant rise of masked men taking over the internet, his following grew exponentially. Now, I'm one of hundreds of thousands of people liking his photos and videos. While not all of it his content is thirst traps this man can make anything look sexy. Have I stared at his accounts more times than my own, probably. Is it considered stalking when you google him, follow his career, and listen to anything and everything he's in even if the script isn't exactly the greatest thing that's ever been written? According to Kayley no, and according to Riley it's just collecting intel. However, that hushed voice in my brain that sounds suspiciously like Dean calls me *"his dirty little stalker"*. Especially, when he pops into my fantasies during my more intimate moments.

I blushed as I stared at the mirror selfie where his face was covered by his phone wearing a black hoodie and sweatpants. He's given hints like these on social media about his appearance, but he's never revealed his whole face. Which somehow, some way, makes him even sexier. Even without revealing his true identity I know this man is fucking gorgeous. He's only posted one closeup of his icy blue eyes, filled with desire and passion as he looks at the phone instead of the mirror. His comment section was absolutely unhinged.

Me being one of them, commenting, "holy hot damn who needs a vibrator when you have those eyes and that voice!"

That was the bottle of wine talking, but I still meant it. And, freaked the fuck out when I saw he liked it the next morning. When Riley couldn't get a hold of me because my phone was shut off, she found me sitting in the back yard with bare feet intertwined in the blades of grass.

She gave me a questionable look while Kayley cackled on the patio. "She said needed to touch some grass because she went wine-drunk-feral on the internet."

"Ah," Riley folded her arms. "Been there."

I couldn't help but stare at the photo on his story. Dean tends to have that effect on me. No matter what he's posting I'm dialed in. The dark aesthetic filter made the tattoo peaking through the cuff of his sweatshirt pop as he sat in what looked like an airport and the mirror pillar gave him a perfect angle to take a photo. His hand looked like it dwarfed the phone, I wouldn't doubt he's at least 6'3". Given the angles and positions of his pictures he was definitely over six feet tall, dark hair, and toned. Really, toned.

"Oh, I know that look." Kayley snatched the phone from my hand and tilted her head. *"Damn."* She tapped her thumb twice on my phone.

"Kay!" I snatched my phone back to find she sent a burning hot face emoji as a direct message from the story.

"What? You'll thank me later!"

"For what? My embarrassment when he sees the notification thinking I'm another feral woman drooling over his story!"

"You are a feral woman drooling over his story." She shrugged. "Besides, I'm sure he gets tons of those messages, he probably won't even see it right away. Especially if he's flying right now."

"He posted it two minutes ago."

"Relax! Take a chance! You've been following this man for years, you're obsessed with his work. Why not try to reach out? You never know what could happen."

"He could block me and I'll be embarrassed for the rest of my life."

She gave me a deadpan look. "C'mon you're being dramatic. He probably mutes those notifications anyway. I would if I had that big of a following. But still, you never know. Maybe he'll look at your profile, see how gorgeous you are, and fall in love with you. Just like Tanner and I will."

I look at her through my eyebrow. "Now look who's being dramatic? Shouldn't you be packing by the way?"

"I already did." She replied after taking a drink of her water. "I'm just waiting for Justin to pick me up."

"You're leaving tonight?"

She put both hands on the counter as if to brace herself to give me a lecture. "Seriously. Take. A. Day. Off. I told you about it when I sent in my request." We both turned as the front door opened and Justin walked into the living room.

"Hey girls, what did I say about keeping this door locked?" Justin is Kayley's over protective big brother. With ashy brown hair, strong jawline, blue eyes just like Kayley's, and muscles covered in tattoos. The man looks like he rode his bike straight out of a dark romance novel. I've known Kayley for years and all four of her brothers have a similar look to where you can definitely tell they're family, but each one has their own personality.

Justin for example can be terrifying, and definitely fits the profile of the protective, doberman, eldest brother vibe. If he doesn't like you or you screw him or his family over you're dead to him. Sometimes from a certain look in his eye I think he means that literally. I've only seen him get pissed a few times and holy hell I was terrified and I was just in the vicinity.

He also has no sense of boundaries when it comes to his siblings, which includes me now apparently since I cut ties with my family years ago and Kayley took me in as her quote "long lost only sister". He works in the family home security business that they don't seem to talk about much while I'm around. Which is on par for the course because every time I meet with their parents they seem more family oriented than family business oriented. I tried to remind Kayley how lucky she was every time we visited but she just rolled her eyes at me and scoffed. I get it, growing up with all brothers probably wasn't her first choice, but I told her she was still lucky to have a family that looked out for one another. "I'll remind you of that statement when we live together." She grinned.

To this day she won't let me live it down. I began to see why she got so annoyed with her brothers shortly after we moved. Especially Justin. He thinks he can barge into our house whenever he feels like it. Once, I snuck out of my room to grab a midnight snack in only a t-shirt that barely covered my ass and the motherfucker was sitting there on the couch reading one of Kayley's books. He was so quiet I didn't even see him.

"Evening, Natalie." His low voice called from the other side of the room.

I jumped, almost dropping my cereal. "Jesus!"

"Close. Justin." He kept his eyes on the book as he flipped through the pages.

"Justin, what the hell are you doing here? How did you even get in?"

"Door was unlocked." He closed the book and flipped it to see the back. "You and Kay really need to get a security system. And start locking your door. Anyone could've walked in here." Justin huffed as he read the back of the book. In that moment I could see why Kayley and Justin always but heads and argue every time they're in the same room. And, why she didn't want a security system from her family's business.

The memory made me shutter. There was something about Justin that scared me a little bit. Not in a bad way, he'd never hurt me or his family, but like he holds some dark secrets that he refuses to tell anyone. As if he's involved with something darker than he's letting on. He's never threatened anyone within our circle of friends nor has he ever really given me a real reason to fear him. If anything he's always made sure we were protected in one way or another. Apparently, that night I found him on the couch, he was waiting for Kayley to say good night to her date out in the driveway. Once Justin got tired of waiting he scared him off within two seconds. Which later turned into a screaming match that was semi-entertaining.

"I knew you were coming jackass." She huffed. "Now that I think about it, I should've kept it locked."

"That would require you listening to me, which would be a fucking miracle."

"Whatever," She rolled her eyes. "I'll grab my suitcases."

"Seriously, Kay. Plural?" Justin replied.

"Duh. Do you even know me?" She shot him with a disgusted look.

"Unfortunately." He groaned.

As her brother reluctantly loaded the last suitcase in the car Kay grabbed her purse and turned to me standing near the doorway.

"So." Kay threw on her jacket. "What kind of party will you be hosting while I'm away? A keg party? Orgy maybe?"

Justin paused in his tracks as he stepped onto the porch. He gave a disgusted look at his sister for saying the word 'orgy'.

"No, and definitely not. I think I'll just catch up on reading, work, laundry, maybe invite Riley and Blake over at some point." I followed as she walked out the door.

"Ugh. You bore. You sound like an old woman." Kay rolled her eyes.

"Eh. It'll be nice actually, have some peace and quiet with no one barging into my room." I replied looking directly at my roommate.

"It may not be so quiet." Justin interjected. "I saw a group of cleaners leaving the house next door. Looks like someone's renting out the Airbnb this weekend."

Kay and I gave him a confused look. Maybe that's what it is, he does seem to know a lot about the neighborhood. No doubt he did his research when we moved here. He probably did a deep dive on me too years ago, making sure I wasn't a threat or something.

"I don't remember telling you that Mrs. B turned that house into an Airbnb." Kay crossed her arms and faced her brother.

"You didn't have to." He returned a stare as if to communicate silently to her.

"You know what, never mind. I don't want to know." She turned back to me and gave me a hug. "I'll see you next Sunday, don't have a party without me. If you do record it so I don't miss anything."

"Offer still stands." Justin turned from the house next door to me, talking about his offer for me to join them.

"I'm okay, it's a *family* vacation, even if I didn't need to work I wouldn't want to intrude." I explained.

Kayley gave me a matter of fact look before gripping my shoulders. "How many times have we been over this? You *are* family. You are never an intrusion. You should come with us. You'd have a great time, and be a fantastic scapegoat to stay as far away from my brothers as possible."

Justin rolled his eyes at the offense. "Looking forward to spending time with you too, little shit."

Kayley kept her blinking eyes on me. "Please for the love of god come with me." She half joked.

I couldn't help but laugh. "I'm okay. While I love you and appreciate that you both think of me as family, I wouldn't mind just having a week to myself."

"Ugh. I envy you." Kayley whispered before she let go of my shoulders.

"Call Riley if you need anything. She's on duty tonight." Justin followed up. "If those new neighbors give you any trouble, lock your door and call her. If she doesn't answer for some reason, call me." He nodded over to the house next door. It's fairly similar to ours, a little nicer since Mrs. B spruced it up. And, from what I heard, makes a killing from it.

Kay rolled her eyes as she gave me one last hug and took off. Leaving me alone on the porch taking in the evening air.

Dean

After what felt like the longest trip from Chicago to Indianapolis all I wanted to do was to get the hell out of the airport. Apparently, fate had another plan when some poor overworked middle aged woman, who was probably late for her flight, ran straight into my chest and spilled her coffee all over me. Since I was staring down at my phone checking my notifications instead of paying attention to where I was walking, I probably deserved it.

She apologized for nearly burning my abdomen and thigh, and scurried off in a hurry after making sure I was okay.

I told her it was fine and went straight to the nearest restroom to change. While I am exhausted, overstimulated, and a social battery at one percent, a spilled coffee from a woman who looked as though she had ninety nine other problems, wasn't that big of a deal. I wasn't going to be her hundredth problem of the day when I was fifty percent of the problem. I have other clothes I can change into, and I don't need to add to that poor woman's suffering already.

As I made my way through the airport in a fresh pair of sweats I finally found my poor little brother. Covered head to toe in sweat pants, sweatshirt, hat, medical mask, and sunglasses. Hunched over next to a McDonald's that sells their chicken nuggets at double the price.

I pulled out the chair next to him, making the metal scratch on the floor. Probably thinking I was just some random person he jumped almost falling to the ground as I sat across from him.

"A little overkill don't you think?" I tapped the brim of his hat as he recovered himself.

He clutched his chest. "Easy for you to say, faceless Instagram."

I chuckled. "It's not my fault you decided to become a famous actor and get engaged to the most popular pop star on the fucking planet."

"Keep your voice down." He groaned as he tried to hide his face.

"For god sake we're in Indianapolis, I doubt anyone is going to recognize you right off the bat."

"I've already had a few close calls. One person recognizes me my holiday is screwed." He tried to hush. "Can we just go, please?" He begged. "If I see one more checkered racing flag I'm gonna lose my bloody mind."

We both stood as I grinned and squeezed my brother's shoulder. "Nice to see you too, Teddy."

My little brother Theodore Roberts, or Tanner Brunswick now, got his break in the movie industry as a child actor back home in England. Mum and Dad wanted me to do the same, but I wasn't the biggest fan of the lights, the glitz, the glamour of it all. So, instead, I chose voice acting. I had a natural knack for it, then as I got older I found my niche in the audiobook industry. When I started reading within the romance genre my career really took off.

The minute I started gaining more of a following I scrubbed all of my accounts, used an American accent paired with colored contacts for work, and created a new last name for myself. After going all in on the sultry, mysterious, bad boy, who reads romance books for a living on my social media pages, I went viral. Which at times I enjoyed, but it's also nice not having people follow me everywhere I go with cameras. Like someone who's easily ten steps ahead of me now.

So, to this day, I've kept my identity a secret. After watching what my little brother went through his entire life, and what he's currently going through, it only solidified my decision. Not only does that help amplify the reader or watcher's experience but it gives me freedom to walk outside without packing on layers like my brother is currently doing in seventy degree weather.

We quickly, on Teddy's part, grabbed our bags and headed towards the rental car park. Of course, he practically ran to the car as soon as we got our keys because the poor lady at the desk was squinting her eyes at him as if he looked familiar.

After he ran as if he stole something she asked me if his name was Xavier, some ex of hers. I shook my head and laughed. She looked confused and then concerned with his behavior after I said no. With a drained social battery, no more fucks to give, and possibly a third degree burn on my torso I said, "He's fine, he's just a little uncomfortable because he shit himself on the plane. Have a great day," and left the counter leaving her speechless.

I should probably tell him to relax, this isn't L.A., and that he has nothing to worry about, but what's the fun in that?

"Dude slow the fuck down." I called after him, walking at a leisurely pace. "I know you need to wipe your arse but if you run too fast it'll only get worse."

Once we finally made it to the car I tossed the bags in the back and slipped into the driver's side. While I was here for business, Teddy was here for a break. When he heard I was heading to Indy he thought it'd be the perfect opportunity to get away and have a brotherly trip together for a month.

A fucking month.

I love my little brother, but I'm not sure I can handle him for 30 days. Let alone a week. He peeled off the hat, hood, and mask as he took in a deep breath. Yup. Still happy I took the secret identity route.

"Better?" I asked, seeing the beads of sweat on my brother's forehead.

"Not really." He huffed before peeling off his sweatshirt. "I haven't taken my phone off airplane mode yet. To be honest, I don't think I want to."

I took a deep breath for him as I drove us out of the car park. I can only imagine what he's going through. Not only is Ell the bitch in sheep's clothing but when they got together my brother's popularity soared through the roof. After they announced their relationship he was offered more movie deals than he had ever dreamed of. He had a career before Ell, but as soon as they got together, he was front and center as America's Prince Charming.

A part of me thinks he's still with her because he's afraid of what might happen to his career if they call it quits. Not only would she drag his name through the dirt like she has with every other ex, but all of her followers would shun him from the film industry for breaking up with "America's Pop Star Sweetheart". All of his deals would be thrown out the window along with his reputation.

"I don't blame you." I groaned. "What did Ell think of your month-long holiday?"

He shrugged. "She was fine with it. She left for her Europe tour last night."

I paused and thought for a moment. "You didn't tell her, did you?"
He stayed silent.

"And let me guess." I went on. "She's gone for at least a month?"
He nodded.

I clicked my tongue. "Can I ask you something?"
"No."

"Too bad. *Why* are you still with Ell?" The question has been poking in the back of my brain since year two of his relationship when I found out how they actually met. It was all apparently choreographed by her agent at the time by putting Ell and Teddy in the right room at the right time. While that may sound like an innocent set up, Ell had chosen Teddy because it would be "great for appearances", setting up one of UK's finest with America's Sweetheart. Teddy of course didn't care because they ended up "falling in love with each other anyway". While that may be true on Teddy's end I can see Ell feels nothing when she looks at him. All she cares about is her career, *her* image, and as of late I've been getting hints from Teddy that he realized the truth. That is until I found out they got engaged online and I was immediately dumbfounded with a swift phone call from Mum right after. While we weren't expecting a break up any time soon, we didn't expect *that*.

"I've seen you two in a camera-less room together." I continued. "She ignores you. Excludes you from conversations-"

He cut me off. "Why are you asking me this?"

"Because I care about you, and I want you to be happy."

"Bullshit." He snapped. "You just want to be right. When I brought her home for the first time you said it wouldn't last. You tried to sabotage our relationship when her agent got drunk and told you she put us in a room together. You just want to say 'I told you so.'"

"I wouldn't call pulling you aside to talk 'sabotage'." I narrowed my brow at him after I made a right turn. "Is that why you've been with her for five years? To prove your older brother wrong? That's not exactly a great foundation for a relationship, Teddy."

"Of course not, and who gave you the right to poke into my relationship in the first place?"

"When *you* hijacked *my* work trip." I huffed. "Clearly, something is wrong and I'm more than willing to help you. But, you need to talk to me."

He shook his head. "You can't help me with this okay, I just wanted to spend some time with my brother before the wedding craziness.

Okay? Don't make me regret it."

Teddy was always a stubborn little shit. I could tell something was on his mind, but clearly he wasn't ready to open up or talk about it yet. Thankfully we have an entire month for that.

Fucker.

"You know what, fine." I continued as I kept my eyes on the road. "I'll drop it, for now. Just remember, *you* hijacked *my* trip so if you don't tell me by the end of the month I will bring Mum into this." Mum feels the same way I do, and I know for a fact if she found out what was going on, she wouldn't hesitate to be on the next flight out.

Teddy rolled his eyes thinking I didn't see the dramatics behind his sunglasses.

"Fine." He whispered. "What are you doing in Indianapolis anyway? It's one of the most boring cities in one of the most problematic states. Marijuana isn't even legal here for medical or personal use."

"Glad you're enjoying the trip so far." I stated sarcastically. "If anything, this is probably the best place for you to lay low. No one would expect *you* to come to Indiana for a holiday."

"Whatever." He snapped. "You didn't answer my question."

"I told you on the phone, it's for work."

He kept his curious eye on me. "I thought you did most of your work in your home studio?"

"I do."

"So why are you here? I thought the whole point of your brand was the 'secret identity' thing." He stated with air quotes.

"It's called wearing a face mask, using an American accent, and having the privacy of a sound booth. My identity will remain a secret, and they know how important that is in my contract." I spat back. "That's all you're getting unless you'd like to share a little tidbit about how you're *still* with Ell."

Teddy licked his teeth behind his lip as he stayed silent and turned his head away.

"That's what I thought."

He wasn't wrong. However, I wasn't about to confess to my little brother that I was actually here with an ulterior motive, to fuel an intense obsession of mine. One that's been plaguing my mind for almost a year now. A curvy blue eyed brunette, who commented on one of my posts, and found out she sent me an emoji through my Instagram story after I landed causing me to ignore my surroundings.

After I liked her comment I looked through her profile and found her to be one of the most gorgeous women I have ever laid my eyes on. So, like any sane person would, I created a burner account and followed her. Then, after I binge watched all of her videos I found out that not only is she the most beautiful woman I have ever seen but the kindest and most thoughtful. The more I saw her on my feed, the more I wanted to learn about her, the family that she cut off a long time ago (for good reason), her friends, her exes, her job, her little book club, her love of audio books.

Everything.

Next thing I knew, I had my notifications set with her profile, so I could watch her new videos when she posted them, look at photos people have tagged her in, and blackmail the useless internet scums of the earth that left terrible comments on her posts.

One of which I found lived fairly close to me, and paid him a little visit in the dark alleyway of the bar he frequented.

"Hello, Gerry." I called out from the shadows.

He jumped out of his skin with fright as he turned to face me. His tie was loose, shirt stained with beer, sweat, and barbecue sauce from the bar food he just consumed.

"Who's there?" He whispered.

Oh yeah, he's drunk off his arse, which will make this a lot more fun.

"You've been a bad boy, Gerry." I slowly push off the brick wall taking slow calculated steps.

"No, no, wai- wait!" He stuck his hand out as I cocked my head. "My payment isn't due till next week man! I can give you a portion now but-"

"Oh, Gerry, Gerry, Gerry, you think I'm here for your gambling debts?" I laughed as I approached the now shaking piece of shit. "No, no, no, you can keep your money." I rounded him so he didn't have any chance to escape. "You're going to need it for the plastic surgery when I'm done with you."

Before he could question me I pinned him to the brick wall by his throat and pulled out my phone to read the disgusting comment he left on my girl's gorgeous photo of herself in shorts and a tank on a hot summer day. I made a shushing sound to make sure he was listening.

"Does this sound familiar?" I questioned as he whimpered and choked. "'All of that cellulite is disgusting, no one wants to see that! Go to the gym you fat bitch!'" My anger took over my entire body as I threw him to the dumpster leaving a small dent in the side.

I stretched out my neck. *Don't kill him, don't kill him.* I tried to tell myself as I saw nothing but red. I grabbed his shirt to make him look at me.

"Lo-look man... I- I'm sor-sorry," He cried out. "I didn't know she had a boyfri-"

"You're sorry?" I tilted my head to make sure I heard him right? I couldn't help but chuckle. "No you're not. Scum like you never apologize. They only say sorry for getting caught and when the consequences catch up to their actions. You meant every single word begging for any kind of attention she would be willing to spare you. Did you cry yourself to sleep when she blocked you?"

"Wh- what do you want from me?" He whimpered.

"What do *I* want?" I pointed to my chest and chuckled as he pulled at my wrist trying to make me loosen the death grip I had on his shirt. "I want my girl to live in a world where if she chooses to grace us with a beautiful photo of herself, she can do so confidently, without cockroaches like you crawling into her comment section to put her down." I gritted out as he began to cry. "You know what I do with men who shit on my girl's posts, Gerry?"

He shook his head violently as I leaned close enough to smell the beer and piss.

"I. Break. Them."

Gerry is now living on the other side of the country with a fucked up nose even the top plastic surgeons couldn't save, half of his teeth, and a gambling debt deadline so close to his salary he shits himself every time it's due. Gerry isn't the only one I've paid a visit to, and there are many others that somehow get fired from their jobs, or their relationships destroyed because of their behavior on my girls feed. I'm the consequence they don't see coming.

Which brings me to Indy. My agent asked me three times if I was sick when I asked if World Entertainment Media was looking for some new VOs. I wasn't a big fan of their content, especially with the way they talked about my brother. Not to mention, after doing some digging, I found some not so nice reviews from some former employees about the company. Not only do they work their employees to the bone, but the company seems to have very little concern when it comes to the treatment of their employees.

My blood was boiling as I read every single one. Knowing that someone as wonderful and kind as her works at a place like this?

Absolutely the fuck not.

While I could drag her bosses out and give them exactly what they deserve, I had to do this one the smart way. Her job is her lively hood, and I couldn't do something so drastic without meeting her first, and give her the option to take the first punch of course. Random men saying disgusting things on the internet is one thing, her boss, a totally different beast that requires a bit more consideration.

So, I had to find a way to meet her that didn't involve walking up to her door saying, "Hi, I think you're the most gorgeous woman I've ever seen in my life. Your workplace is shit, you should leave, I can make them pay for their negligence. Also I read those spicy books you like so much *for a living*, wanna have dinner and try out some of your favorite scenes?"

Totally not creepy.

So, again, like any other sane person, when I found out they weren't hiring I called the CEO directly and stated how much their company was missing out in the book industry. If they did movie and TV show reviews, why not books? Especially when it's voiced by a popular narrator like myself.

Of course, the more I talked about the industry the more he was foaming at the mouth for it. So, I booked a flight to Indy the next day, and paid a very large chunk of change for an Airbnb that happened to be right next door to her.

Was it a little far to book the Airbnb *next door*, maybe, but I didn't care. Again, this woman has been on my mind for a long time, and I had to see what her everyday life was like, to see her in person, and make sure she wasn't overworking herself. After looking at all the work she's done for this mediocre media company, she definitely has and they don't deserve a drop of it.

Was I willing to risk my secret identity for this woman, who I've never met in person, and who only knows Dean Craven not Dean Roberts? If that's what it meant to see her even for a short amount of time, then I'd risk it all over and over again.

Teddy and I stayed silent for the rest of the ride as we pulled up to the house. I flicked my eye next door and saw Natalie sitting near the front window with headphones on and a book in her hand. I've been waiting a long time to see her in person, and now that I am, it's even better than I imagined. Even though she's just sitting there doing something so simple as reading a book, she's just as beautiful as all of her dolled up selfies. A few of which totally aren't on my phone at the moment. What I wouldn't give to make her tea, kiss her head, and wait for her until she's finished and tell me all about what she just read. And, of course, reenact some of her favorite scenes in the bedroom afterwards if she wants to.

Teddy snapped me out of my trance. He's lucky I didn't break his fingers for that.

"What's with you?" He asked.

"Just making sure we're at the right house." I swallowed hard as I pulled into the driveway. "Once we get settled, I'm getting groceries." I shut off the car and opened the door to get out. "Is there anything you want in particular?"

Teddy quickly followed. "Ell's put me on this no sugar, no fat, no sodium, no gluten diet."

"So, a can of air?" I teased as I grabbed our bags out the back. "That should last you a month right?"

He gave me a snarky look. "Funny. This is probably my final month of freedom so I'm going all in. Steaks, pasta, pizza, pies, crisps, fizzy drinks, anything that would piss Ell off."

I stopped in my tracks and narrowed my brow. "Are you sure you don't want to talk about it?"

"Positive." He groaned angrily as he aggressively took his bag from my hand. I shook my head and closed the car door when I saw a cute nosy little neighbor looking out her window at me. She quickly retreated when she saw me catching her snooping on our conversation.

"Don't worry, sweetheart. It won't be long now." I smirked as I made my way up to the porch.

The Airbnb was nice, it's a very simple layout with, what looked like updated, modern fixtures. Since the house looked fairly similar on the outside to Natalie's I'm assuming it has a very similar layout just flipped.

Teddy didn't seem as impressed. With fame, came high expectations. One thing I hope to help him with during this long month. We grew up in a modest home, nothing extra fancy but we also didn't have any trouble splurging here and there. Somewhere along the way, Teddy lost a lot of that humbleness.

I started to unpack upstairs after pulling on Teddy's hood to peel him away from the master bedroom, and pushing him into the room across the hall.

Little shit.

Thinking he could hijack the master bedroom when he invited himself on *my* work trip.

Absolutely not.

The bed gave me a direct line of sight to a window that peered directly to another window next door. If that was Natalie's room I'm so fucked. I peered through the curtain and sure enough there was Natalie returning to her room with a load of laundry. Dressed in a hoodie and leggings with her headphones still on. She paused folding her clothes as she grinned and her mouth suddenly went agape. I chuckled. She's definitely listening to an audiobook right now.

Through my research on Natalie, that's her favorite way to read. And, come to find out, *I'm* her favorite narrator. I couldn't help but be proud of that fact, my girl loves listening to my voice. Plus, as evidenced from her comment, she has come to my voice. If I have anything to say about it, I'll be the only voice she'll ever come to.

My cock began to pulse, as if seeing her immediately set me off. I kept the main curtains open while having the inner sheer ones just barely shut to not make it too obvious. It was only fair that if her window was open, so was mine.

I immediately started the shower to clean off the smell of the plane, airport, and coffee. There was a reason why I built my own sound studio at home. I'm not the biggest fan of air travel, and I only step on a plane for people I care about. My parents, my brother, and now Natalie. The only reason I didn't drive was because I wanted to get here quickly.

I wiped my hand down my face as I stood under the hot water. Now that I'm here I'm not sure where to go next. I haven't had a serious relationship in a very long time, let alone *a* relationship. I've had sex, sure. But, not since I discovered Natalie. She's all I've thought about, and I can't picture anyone but her when I need a release.

She posted a picture of herself in a bikini on a beach one summer that revealed her thigh tattoos of vines that traveled along her thick thighs all the way up to her hips and curved around her hip bones. Her skin was sun-kissed with sunglasses, a sunhat, the biggest smile on her face, beaming with confidence as she showed off every single curve, with a wine cooler in her hand. What I wouldn't give to leave outlines of my teeth all over her, to mark her, and show the world that she's mine.

My imagination has run wild for far too long. What she looked like without that bikini, what positions she would prefer, what kind of kinks she has. If she wants me to crawl through her window and fuck her to tears until she calls out my name, or does she want to take control, blindfold me and suck on my cock until she hears *me* call out *her* name?

Now I'm so hard I can't see straight. I fist my cock as I hiss a curse at myself. This woman has the tightest grip on me and she hasn't even met me yet. What will I be like when we're together? She's already affected my recent projects to where they've become more raw, more *real.* What will it be like when she's near me everyday? She'd have me wrapped around her finger that's for certain, and I'd be the happiest man in the world. She'll never have to worry about a thing. Anything my girl wants, she'll get. Pizza on Fridays, done. Coffee and flowers every morning, done. Cut off the fingers of any man who makes her feel uncomfortable, fucking done.

I come in no time flat as I picture gripping her curves with her thick thighs wrapped around my waist as I thrust deeper and deeper inside of her. Making her scream out my name as she comes and her cunt pulses and clenches against my cock.

I curse myself again. I need to gain control of myself if I'm going to be face to face with her on Monday. I can't just grab her and fuck her right on the desks... although... *no. No. NO.*

I wrapped a towel around my waist as I walked back out into the bedroom feeling a million times better after getting the stench of airport off of me. I took a small peek to see if she's still folding her laundry. I grinned to find her laying on top of her folded clothes with the same book from earlier back in her hands facing her open window. The scene is so simple yet charming I couldn't turn away and noticed which book she was reading, "The House of Mischief".

I've narrated a lot of books across all kinds of sub genres. Contemporary, Western, Billionaire, Dark, Fantasy, even Monster romances, but that one in particular is one of the darker ones I've read. It's not the darkest, but it's definitely up there. And, judging by her biting her bottom lip with a small grin, I'm guessing she's enjoying it. I couldn't help but smile as I watched her lightly kick her feet. Looks like my girl has a thing for dark romance, I can definitely work with that.

I walked over to the side of the bed and started putting away my clothes as I dried off. From a distance I caught my girl trying to sneak a peek through my window. I tried to suppress my grin as I walked to the end of the bed with my back to the window. Suddenly, I could use a stretch from the very long hour and ten minute flight. I could feel her stare as I stretched my arms as if I was trying to stretch out my aching back that one day *will* be filled with her nail marks.

Natalie

I've lost all focus from my book as I stared like a peeping Tom at the man next door. Holy hell, this man was so handsome I could weep. He's toned enough to show that he worked out and took care of himself, but not too bulky as if he made going to the gym his *entire* life.

His back, arms, and shoulders are covered with black and white tattoos, his dark hair still wet from the shower he just took, and from what I saw earlier the face of a heart breaker with a wicked grin. Probably amused after he caught me staring at him through the window like an idiot. Of all the Airbnb guests we've encountered, he was by far the hottest and most intriguing. From what I heard earlier, he had a British accent, which made him even more attractive and another man who did not seem to be in the best of moods. With the way they bickered he's more than likely a sibling or one pissed off friend.

Suddenly, I realized I was blushing and painfully aware of how hot the room just became. Here I am listening to my favorite narrator with the sexiest voice on the planet whispering filthy, unspeakable things in my ear while looking at a man who's *very* attractive.

I need to calm down.

The thought flew right out the window when his towel began to loosen and I could start to see the peak of his round ass. I was so stunned I couldn't look away, if he turned around I'd die of embarrassment.

"You're staring again Princess," My audiobook continued. *"You're not prepared for what I have in store for you if you keep staring at* him *like that."*

The way his tattoos moved with him as he stretched, relieving any aches and pains he had from his travels. What I wouldn't give to help him relieve it. Now, I'm painfully aware of how long it's been since I felt another man's body against mine.

"'Like what?' She finally blinked as I flicked my eyes to hers."

"'Like you're trying to fuck him from across the room.'"

"'You don't know what you're talking about.' She whispered with a slight hesitation in her breath."

His still wet skin reflected the light showing the small groves of his build and the outlines of his tattoos. He shifted the towel lower, lower...

"I leaned down to her ear." Dean's voice went low. *"You. Are. Mine. And I will fuck every thought of him out of your pretty little head to make sure you remember that. Don't. Test. Me.'"*

My trance was suddenly broken when I heard my phone start to ring. I threw off my headphones and kicked off a few pieces of folded laundry as I stumbled my way over to grab it. I answered when I saw it was Kayley facetiming me.

"Heyyy." I frantically began to speed walk out of my room ignoring the sudden gush of wetness between my thighs. "What's up?" I made my way to the kitchen to get as far away from that man as I could before I had the cops called on me for watching my neighbor *undress*.

"Hey?" She narrowed her brow at me in the passenger seat of Justin's car. Looking as though they were stopped at a gas station. "Why are you all hot and sweaty, did you work out?"

"What?" I shake my head. "No."

She grinned. "Did you get to chapter eighteen?"

"Yes." I tried to use that as an excuse even though I was in chapter sixteen. "Yes, I did. Damn it is, wow."

"Ha! Knew it. The part where he shifts the eye cover to her mouth for her to 'stay quiet'. Oh. My. Fucking. God. So hot! Anyway, sorry for interrupting your toy time, but I wanted to call and make sure you weren't working."

"What makes you think I'd be working on a Friday night?"

She rolled her eyes. "Because I know you, okay, despite how much you hate the company you're always there to answer Brock's call."

"I don't *always* answer his call." I set her up on the kitchen counter

"Yes you do." She argued. "So do me a favor, block his number for the weekend and have some me-time. Go out with Riley if she's off, go to a park, go for a walk with your location shared."

"I'm good, thanks. The furthest I'll be going this weekend is the porch."

"So you can spy on the guests in the Airbnb?"

My face began to feel flushed as I remembered the absurdly handsome half naked man next door.

Kay began to gasp as she saw my face. "Who is it? Do you know them? Are they hot? They're hot aren't they?" She practically squealed as she pulled the phone closer. "Dammit, the one time I take a family vacation."

"You'd rather have a minuscule chance of sex with a stranger than spend time with your entire family who you haven't seen together in over a year?" Justin spoke up in the background.

"Mind your business." She spat back.

"Relax." I responded. "From what I can tell so far, it's two men, and they're..." I hesitated, "British."

"British?" She squeaked. "Are you fucking kidding me? J, drive me home. Now!"

"Fuck no." He spat.

"I'll keep you up to date if anything new arises." I reassured her.

"You promise?"

"I promise."

She huffed. "If you talk to them, try and convince them to stay until I get back."

I chuckled. "Yeah, I'll get right on that." After seeing that man in the window there was no way I was going to introduce myself to him. I'd go red, easily cave, and then apologize for the breach of privacy. Although, to be fair, who leaves their curtains open, in a neighborhood they don't know, and walks in front of it half naked.

"You better." She replied. "I have to go. You better send me updates."

"I will."

"And pictures. I need pictures, Nat. Do you hear me?" She gets so close to the phone I can see only her forehead and eyes.

"Seriously?"

Her eye began to twitch. "There are British men staying in the Airbnb next door to my house, that could literally turn into a plot in one of our books, does it look like I'm joking?"

"Jesus. Fine, your majesty, I'll try to get pictures. As long as you bail me out for stalking."

"Worth it. Thank you."

"Don't fuel her toxic habits and behaviors, Nat." Justin responded in the background.

Kay groaned as she turned to give her brother a death glare. "Nat I'll call you later, I have a brother whose nose needs to be broken."

"Good fucking luck demon spawn." He replied.

I tried to contain my chuckle as I said goodbye to Kay and good luck to Justin. The call ended with a fist in the air, "Come here motherfuc-"

I love her, but I'm so glad I didn't grow up with her as a full blooded sibling. I set my phone down, took care of my sudden pent up gush from earlier, and began to make some tea. Once I was finished my phone pinged again with text. I turn it over to see it's from Brock.

Dammit.

I set my phone back down on the counter as quickly as I picked it up. "No. No. It's Friday after 5 P.M."

Another ping echoed throughout the kitchen, as if to taunt me. I squeezed my eyes shut as I tried to ignore it. How can I relax knowing that my boss is texting me on a Friday night. Working in the media I always have to be prepared for the worst. A celebrity death, a celebrity scandal, a midnight showing of a box office movie.

It could be anything from news to one of my team members making a minor mistake that Brock just has to tell me about while I'm off the clock. I sighed as I reached for my phone again and opened the text.

Brock: *Hey Natalie. It's Brock. Just wanted to send you this for Monday so I don't forget. Wouldn't hurt to review it a little over the weekend so you know what to expect.*

I sighed with a bit of relief. "Well at least it's not a breaking news thing. That can be a Sunday night problem." I stuffed my phone back in my pocket and took my tea back upstairs with me. I took a *small* peek out my window to find that the curtains are still open but he's nowhere in sight.

That's when I heard a car door open and close and found him leaving the house. This was typical of every guest's routine. They get in, get settled, probably shower, and head out for food or groceries. However, most guests keep all the windows sealed shut. This guy didn't seem to have a care in the world about that part.

Clearly.

At least while he's out I can enjoy the evening air for a minute on my porch. I sat on the swing after I made sure his car was out of sight and took a moment to breathe. Our neighborhood was a nice little collection of older homes on the north side of Indy. It was quiet, other than the occasional nosy neighbor, there wasn't much going on up here. Some of the neighbors threw a fit on social media when Mrs. B put up her house on Airbnb, but given she's very selective about her guests, we haven't had much to worry about and the chatter slowly quieted down when nothing bad came of it.

So far.

I leaned my head back as I took in the small September breeze. It was still warm enough to be considered summer but there were some chilly days here and there. And tonight was one of those nights. I love these kinds of evenings where the sky is clear, stars are shining, and the cool breeze is just warm enough to not need layers.

I jolt my eyes open when I hear a car start to pull up and instantly relax when I see Riley stepping out of her police cruiser with a smile on her face. Riley's a bad ass and getting closer and closer to detective status. That's her endgame, and her amazing husband Rob supports her in every way that counts, and always has dinner ready for her when she gets home. They are the cutest couple. It's sickening sometimes, but I'm so happy she's found someone who makes her happy and supports her in every way that counts.

"Hey, Nat!" She walked up to the porch as I stood to give her a quick hug.

"Evening officer, what brings you this way? Is everything okay?"

"Oh, yeah. Everything's fine." She waved her hand as she leaned against the porch pole. "I was on my way home and thought I'd stop by."

"Gotcha." I nodded. "How was your shift?"

"It was fine. Got to tackle a home invader today."

I couldn't help but chuckle as she held a grin on her face. "Nice."

"Oh. I don't know if you saw, but Kayley texted in the Spice Shelf group chat earlier." She pulled out her phone.

I rolled my eyes as I stood across from her. "I haven't, but I'm assuming it's about them." I pointed at my chest to point at the house behind me to insinuate my neighbors.

"Yeah, actually." She looked at me confused.

I nodded. "Yeah. She's freaking out because I made the mistake of telling her that they're two British guys." I tried to whisper.

Her eyes widened. "Really?" She paused for a moment as she pulled up the chat. "Yeah that'll explain why she said: 'I can't believe Nat gets to live out my fantasy', 'Nat seriously send me pictures of the hotty totties next door you're a life saver if you do', and 'Pleassseee'."

I rolled my eyes. "Sounds about right."

"She's just pissy because she's stuck with her family for a week." She shook her head as she chuckled. "Have you seen them yet?"

I blink at her. "Not you too."

"No. No. I'm just curious to know what they look like so I can keep an eye out. Plus, I can tease Kayley about it later. Drive her nuts while she's away."

We both chuckle at that. "She'll kill you after she tortures Justin for the rest of the week."

Before we finish up our conversation. I suddenly see Riley's eyes flick to a car that's pulling in the driveway next door.

I stay firmly put and fight every urge in my body to turn around. I heard a car door shut as Riley's eyes went wide and hid in front of me to give me a mouthed, "Oh my god."

"Yeah." I whispered.

"Ohhh. Kayley is going to be so pissed." She tried to keep a whisper.

"Apparently, there's another one too. Not sure if he's a sibling or friend or what, I didn't get a good look at him since he had his hood up." I whispered back.

"Hmm." She began to think and suddenly raised her eyebrows. "We might get an answer to that."

"Why?" I straightened.

"He just spotted my cruiser, and is sending a serious look of curiosity and concern our way." Riley raised her brow at me.

I knew exactly what she was thinking as she flicked her eyes back to me. "No."

"Yes. C'mon, you haven't dated in how long? And now a very handsome 6'3" British guy, who looks to be in his late twenties early thirties, with no ring, is staying next door to you." She paused. "Give me one reason why not?"

"Okay, first of all your ability to profile people from a distance is insanely impressive and a little terrifying. Second, I look like shit, there is no way in hell-"

"Hi there!" Riley leaned over and waved to my neighbor.

"Oh you did not just-" I whisper yelled.

"Evening officer." A British voice called over. "Everything alright?"

I slowly turned to see the man I saw stretching with only a towel on earlier. His hair was dry with a little bit of fluff to it, his hazel eyes were piercing as he looked over at me. My heart began to race and butterflies flitted across my stomach, as I watched him stuff his hands into the pockets of his dark jeans. His black t-shirt had just enough give to keep things to the imagination but fit well enough you could see a few outlines. The short sleeves clung to his shoulders and upper arms as his tattoos shifted when he tensed and flexed his arms.

"Oh, yeah." She waved. "Just visiting a friend." The subtle warning in her tone wasn't lost on me. While she was a social butterfly she was protective of every single person in her close circle. Judging by his calm demeanor Riley's tone didn't seem to scare him off or cause him to retreat. Which is usually her first test when scouting out potential partners for us.

"I'm Officer Riley Bradley. This is Natalie." She pointed to me.

I gave a subtle wave and a small grin. "Evening."

"Nice to meet you, Natalie." There was softness to his tone. Great, he's charming too. "I'm Dean. My brother Teddy is inside, apologies, he's a bit of an introvert."

"So is Nat." She gave me a smirk as she approached the front yard to get closer.

Riley, you're getting an earful after this I swear to every god in existence.

"Where are you and your brother visiting from?" She continued as I reluctantly followed closer. Here I was meeting an extremely handsome, well put together guy and I'm wearing leggings and a hoodie. God I could die right now.

He stepped closer and my heart responded by beating faster. Up close he's even more devilishly handsome, because of course he is.

"My brother lives in L.A. and I'm in Chicago, but we're both from London." He flicks his eyes back to me and I nearly have a heart attack at the sudden eye contact. Something about him seems familiar, but I can't quite put my finger on it.

"Wow." Riley nodded.

Suddenly I went to speak and I had no control over my words. "So, what brings you here then? Business or pleasure?" I instantly regret saying that after he subtly looks me up and down. As if the word pleasure raised an alarm for him. He smiled at the ground.

"A little bit of both." His eye met mine again and now I'm pretty sure my heart is trying to escape as the butterflies fly faster. "It's my first time in Indianapolis," He continued. "So, I'm hoping to do a little sight seeing while I'm here."

"Well," I chuckled as my mouth kept running. "Unfortunately, you won't find too many here. Don't get me wrong, there are some cool places, but not as many as Chicago."

He shrugged. "I'm sure a great tour guide might be able to help me with that."

I caught Riley's eyes widening. "Yeah. You know, Natalie grew up here, maybe she could show you around when you're free."

My heart stopped and the butterflies came to a halt.

"Really?" He grinned as he raised his eyebrows.

I began to stutter. "H- how long are you in town for?"

He breathed sharply. "A month. Maybe longer. It all depends on the business portion of my trip."

His hazel eyes stayed on me as a small grin tugged at his lips. God, he *is* charming. A little *too* charming, there's no way this man doesn't have a girlfriend or a significant other of some kind. The thought quickly faded as he handed his phone to me.

"Input your number? So we can set up a time."

I slowly took his phone, trying not to show how inexperienced I am at… *this*. "Sure."

As I put in my number Riley turned in her lips as she realized her work here was done, and slowly tried to slip away so she didn't have to feel my scorn. I quickly caught her arm as I handed his phone back.

"Brilliant, thank you. Now, if you ladies will excuse me, I have some perishables to put away." He stood tall. "It was nice meeting you, Officer Bradley. Natalie." He looked over at me. "I hope to hear from you."

"Nice meeting you." Riley gave a small wave as I nodded and tugged her back to the house.

Once we got back in the house I shut the front door behind me and leaned against it. Letting all the air out of my lungs in a sigh of relief.

"Girl." Riley stated.

"Nuh-uh. Don't *girl* me! What the hell was that?" I tried to whisper yell as if he could still hear us.

"I helped you get a date." She shrugged. "You're welcome!"

"No… no ya didn't, giving a tour of *Indy* is not a date."

She narrowed her eyes on me. "What's going on with you? I can see why you'd blush and get flustered a bit since he's hot, but this,"

She waved her hand in front of me, "is intense."

She was right to a certain extent. I breathed slowly and sat on the couch as she joined me. "Okay, before you stopped by, I *saw* him…"

"Saw him… what?"

I rubbed my hands together not knowing how to explain this. "I saw him through his window, after he got out of the shower. In a towel."

She couldn't help but laugh.

"Riley! This is so not funny!"

"I'm sorry," She laughed, "is that why you got so nervous? Because you saw him half naked through his window?"

"Well, yeah. I invaded his privacy. I mean, I *looked,* Riley. If Kay didn't call me, I'm pretty sure I would've seen more than that." I squeezed my eyes shut as the memory replayed in my head. "Who leaves their windows open like that after taking a shower?"

She shrugged as she joked. "Maybe he wanted you to look?"

I paused and gave her a deadpan look. "I'm serious. It didn't help that I was listening to one of the most filthiest chapters in 'House of Mischief'."

"Wait- wait, you were listening to Dean Craven while a hot half-naked British guy stood in the window across from you?" She began to laugh again. "Holy shit, this is gold."

"Well, now thanks to you, I have to give him a tour of Indy while trying not to picture him *shirtless.*"

"Oh c'mon. You'll be fine. Hey, maybe if you're lucky you'll get to see more." She licked her teeth.

I side eye her. "Yeah because giving a tour is so sexy." I pushed off the couch to stand up.

"Relax, Nat. By the way he was checking you out I have no doubt that he's interested." She paused. "Even if he's only here for a month, I think you'd kick yourself if you didn't at least give it a shot."

"Please. With my luck I'll find out he has a girlfriend who's out to kill me."

Riley rolled her eyes as she stood. "That's when you look him up on socials, do a little research, family, friends, exes, that kind of thing."

"You mean stalk him?"

She shrugged. "It's not stalking. It's called, gathering intel, or a light investigation for your sanity and safety if you will. It'd be foolish to trust a man you just met."

I gave her a curious look. "Is that what you did with Rob?"

"Of course." She didn't hesitate. "His background was clean, great job, all of his answers to my questions on our dates aligned with what I found. That's when I knew he was a keeper, that and well, he's the sweetest most caring man I've ever met in my life." She paused thinking about the early days of their relationship. "Oh, that reminds me, I gotta get home. Are you gonna be okay by yourself?"

I walked with her to the porch. "I'll be fine, officer. If I need anything I'll call you."

"Good. Be sure to send updates in chat, I can't wait to watch Kayley go nuts."

I leaned against the porch post and waved as she took off towards home. Which luckily wasn't too far. Her and Rob live in a suburb five minutes down the road, which is extremely convenient for girls nights, book club meetings, or just to hang out. Things have slowed down a bit since Blake moved in with them.

Rob's sister has been through a lot within the past few years and to top it all off her apartment complex caught fire and she lost everything last year. Rob and Riley being the amazing people they are didn't hesitate to offer up their home to her for as long as she needed. Now, she's acquainted with our friend group, slowly gaining her groove back, and after six months of begging (on Kayley's part) she joined our little book club. According to Riley, she's really enjoyed it so far and has helped her regain some confidence in herself and life in general.

I understand more than anyone what it feels like when you need a place to escape to. For me, it's books, TV shows, and movies. I love storytelling in all forms and how it transports me to another world even if it's only for a couple of hours.

I took one last long deep breath of the fresh air and made my way back inside. It has been a long ass day, and I've had quite enough excitement for one night. The first thing I do is shut my curtains. I don't need any more temptation for the night than I already had. I turned on my lamp for a bit of mood lighting and finished putting away my laundry while listening to my book and finally making it to chapter eighteen.

"You think after what you did last night you deserve to come?" Dean's voice growled. *"I kept my hand to her throat as I hooked my fingers into her wet cunt with the other, and my thumb pressed firmly to her clit."*

"Think again, Princess. You are mine. Therefore, this cunt is mine. If you try to run away with him again, I will hunt you down, I will bring you right back here, and I will fuck you in his blood to remind you exactly who you belong to."

"I could feel her arousal coating my fingers as I made the slightest movement with my thumb over her clit. Making her legs tremble. My little Princess is loving every second of this."

"Is that what you want, Princess? For me to kill your prince so you can fuck the monster in a pool of his blood?"

My face ran hot again. Not only because of the audiobook, but because the scene that's playing through my head has a certain handsome neighbor suddenly attached to the voice that's whispering in my ear. If he was at my front door right now it'd be embarrassing how quickly I'd give in and try to climb him like a tree.

I paused folding my clothes for a moment and closed my eyes while listening intently.

"I slipped the mask covering her eyes to her mouth. The fabric slipped between her teeth and muffled her little whimpers. She shook her head to say no as I stared back down at her with a wicked grin on my face."

I squeezed my eyes tighter and listened closer for a moment.

"'Don't lie to me. Your cunt is begging for it. For me. Tonight, you're going to be screaming my name, begging me for that sweet release.'"

I put my hand to the side of my headphones.

"'Tonight, you're going to regret ever trying to step foot off of my estate.'"

What if…

"'Tonight, you are at my mercy.'"

I turned to my window with the closed curtains. I shook my head as if to throw the thought away completely.

No. I'm losing my mind. There's no way.

Dean

First thing on the list of things to do, is buy her new curtains. Even while they're closed I can still see right through them when the lights are on. I can't have anyone who plans to stay here in the future have any kind of access to her room. Knowing that there's a possibility of someone looking through her window in the past makes me clench my fist so hard my knuckles turn white.

My first encounter with Natalie face to face was unexpected in the least. I thought I had way more time to prepare, maybe meet her as Dean Craven first. However, that thought was thrown out the window when I saw a police car in front of her house. I was so focused on every possibility, and ready to take down whoever attempted to harm her enough to call the police, I didn't register it was Riley. Not until I got out of the car and saw her standing on the porch.

To be honest, I didn't really have a plan of attack when I decided to come down here and meet her face to face. All I knew was I had to see her as soon as I could, and make sure she wasn't overworking herself. I partially blame my brother for that, he had to go and get engaged to the most popular pop star on the planet, which makes my girl's job an absolute hell.

I panicked for a moment when she had her headphones on again with a thoughtful look and peering at her curtains. As if she was currently piecing together that I'm the one who's saying all those filthy things in her ear right now.

I handed over my work phone to her so she could put in her number, since I already had it saved in my personal one. At this point I didn't care if she found out I was Dean Craven, but I didn't want to scare her off knowing I had her number saved already. I've spent months debating whether or not I should reach out to her. Too many times I've stared at the blank text box wondering if I should pretend that this was a wrong number.

Second thing to do, make *Brock* take down their employee's personal contact info from their main website.

I quickly stepped away from the window as I heard my brother's footsteps approaching. He turned the corner with a box of hair dye in his hand and a questionable look on his face.

"Why did you buy a box of hair dye?" He chuckled. "Did you spot a few gray hairs already?" He tossed the box at me.

"I'm 31 not 50." I threw the box back at him. "It's for you."

"Why did you buy me hair dye?"

"Because you're not staying locked up in this house every single day for a month. If we end up going somewhere I don't want to walk around with someone who puts on twenty layers and looks like they're on the run."

Especially now that Officer Bradley has me clocked on her radar. From what I could tell she's good at her job, and I definitely don't want her red flags to be raised.

"It worked fine in the airport."

"I haven't got a clue how. Being covered up like that you probably attracted more eyes than if you just wore sunglasses."

"Don't patronize me."

"I'm not patronizing you. I just don't want you to spend this entire getaway locked up in a house. If you wanted to do that you might as well have stayed home." I sighed as I collected my thoughts. "I only bought it as an option. It's fine if you don't want to use it but you're not walking around with your hood, hat, glasses, and mask, it draws more attention than you think. Plus, you look ridiculous with blonde hair."

He shrugged as he scrunched his nose. "Ell likes it."

I paused and crossed my arms. "Remind me why you're here again?"

He licked his teeth behind his lip. "Can I use your shower so I don't stain the tub?"

"Knock yourself out." He ran past me and paused at the window. "Huh. Cute neighbor."

Oh hell no. "Off limits, Theodore." I stated in a low growl. Probably a little more intense than I should've but I don't give a fuck. Especially, when it comes to what's mine.

He gave me a confused look. "Jesus. What's got you riled up?"

"The last thing you need right now is cheating rumors that will make Ell fly over here and turn my work trip into a nightmare. So, I'll say it again. Off. Limits." And the last thing I want to do is kill my little brother for gawking at my girl.

I closed the curtains as he rolled his eyes. "You're no fun."

"I'm not the one with the whole world watching my every move." I said as he flipped me the bird and closed the bathroom door.

Fucker.

I peeked through the curtain one more time to find she's gone for now. At least I don't have to worry about Teddy sneaking another peek at her.

I made my way downstairs to make dinner and try to come up with a plan. As of right now, I have no idea if she knows that Dean Craven is the new VO that will be visiting her home office. Now that we've met earlier than planned I need to decide how I want to reveal my double life to her. On one hand, I don't want to lie to her. She already has some suspicions about me as it is. The way she narrowed her light eyes at me earlier definitely stated she could recognize me from somewhere but couldn't pinpoint it. If I lie, either way she wouldn't want anything to do with me when she found out the truth. And, I don't want her to have any reason to doubt me or not trust me.

I paused as I pulled out my phone to text her.

Dean: *Hey, it's Dean. Are you free tomorrow for a tour?*

I took a deep breath as I hit send, I waited for the bubbles to appear and disappear then appear again.

My Girl: *Sure. What's a good time for you?*

Dean: *9 AM too early? Lighter traffic.*

Once again the bubbles appear and disappear.

My Girl: *I don't know...the traffic between your place and mine could get bumper to bumper really fast*

I smile down at my phone.

Dean: *I'm an early riser so I'll head out early just to be safe*

Is the wink a little too much? Probably.

The bubbles appear and disappear at least four times, I could practically feel her face getting warm through the screen. My heart beat faster as I thought about her rose colored cheeks when she looked at me. She's so goddamn cute, I feel like I'm a teenager all over again with a crush. She makes me act like one too when I can't keep my dick from rising every time I see or think about her.

My Girl: *Sounds like a plan, I'll see you at 9*

My heart doesn't slow down as I look at the texts. A part of me still wanted to crawl through her window and curl up next to her. How did I handle being so far away from her? Now the thought of leaving to go back to Chicago makes my stomach turn. I've had a little taste of her now, I can't go back. Jesus, if this is how I am after one conversation, what the hell am I going to do after our first date, after the first time we sleep together.

Fuck, I'm gonna be a menace.

At this point, I've decided to let the cards fall where they may. The last thing I want to do is build our relationship on a lie about who I am and what I do for a living. That doesn't mean I'm ready to tell her about how I've been obsessed with her for almost a year now. I still haven't figured out how to tell her about that bit.

If I want to have a life with Natalie, she needs to trust me and get a taste of both Dean Craven and Dean Roberts. Which is why I booked the date for tomorrow and, if it goes well, see if she'll have lunch with me as a thank you. Before she finds out who I really am.

That was one of the issues I would always run into when I dated in the past. I was afraid to show them both sides. Not only because I wanted to keep my identity a secret and one pissed off ex would expose me to the entire world, but because I knew there was never going to be a balance. One would always like one more than the other. I quickly found that out when one of my exes from the early stages in my career wanted me to use my American accent all the time. From that point on I knew it would only get worse from there.

I care about Natalie so much, and I have to be willing to trust her with this part of my life if she's willing to trust me too.

I straightened as I heard my brother come downstairs. I turned to see him with wet dark brown hair looking more like the little brother I know. I picked one that was as close to his natural hair as possible. There are a lot of motives behind this trip and one of them is to bring my brother back to reality, back to himself again.

"Feel better?" I took in the look of calmness and relief on his face. For a moment he doesn't look like the scared little shit I saw at the airport.

"Not gonna lie. Yeah. Much."

"That's good. Ready to talk about what's been bothering you?"

He gave me a deadpan look. "Are you going to ask that every day we're here?"

"I wasn't. But, now that you mention it, it sounds like a good idea."

He sighed as he sat at the table. I set the pasta dish I prepared down on the table and sat across from him.

"If I tell you, will you please let it go for the rest of the trip?" He begged.

I thought about it. "Depends."

"On?"

"How bad it is. If I need to call a few lawyers. Or Mum."

"Dean, do not bring Mum into this."

I shrugged. "I'm sure she'd be more than happy to destroy whoever hurt her youngest son."

"Look. I just don't want to end up talking about it the entire trip. Alright? I'm only telling you this so you can leave me the hell alone."

"Well, if you were trying to do that you wouldn't have joined me on this trip." I shook my head. "Look, you're clearly running from your life in L.A. and I'm guessing you joined *my* trip because you didn't want to be alone. I can help you but you have to tell me what's going on and be *open* to my help."

He took a moment to think before wiping his hand down his face. I could tell he was debating on telling me what he was about to say.

"I don't love Ell anymore. Okay. You were right. I haven't been in love with her for a while."

I nodded as I set my silverware down, resisting my brotherly urge to tell him I was right.

"Fuck knows what happened." He continued. "She was different when we first got together. She was sweet and kind, we would have movie nights and date nights. But, now, we schedule our dates when we know the press is nearby. I walk the red carpet with her and put on a smile, act like we're happy and then we're silent on the way home. I thought proposing would be the answer, to bring back the spark, to remind us of why we're together. Even if we were put into a room by her agent, that didn't change what we had." He hung his head. "But, she found the ring and planned the entire engagement."

"Wait." I paused him. "She planned her own proposal?"

He sighed. "She said she wanted it to be perfect."

I bit my lip, trying to keep all the words I wanted to say inside. "Okay."

"I know, it sounds nuts."

"Then why did you go along with it?" I questioned.

"Because when I thought about leaving her, all of the PR nightmares came together at once. She'll create a heartbroken breakup song that'll be a hit, her millions of fans will send me hate, her and her followers will drag me and my career through the fucking mud." He paused. "I-I just don't think I could handle that and dealing with losing what I had with Ell. And, you can forget about having a relationship again after that, because I'll forever be known as the guy who broke up with Ell Wyms." He sighed as he gathered his thoughts. "Any snarky comebacks? An 'I told you so'?"

I shook my head. "No. Sounds like you have enough on your plate already."

"Seriously?"

"Yeah." I leaned on the table. "I'm the last person to be taking dating advice from. But I will tell you this. I want you to be happy Teddy, whatever form that takes, bring it on. Right now, you're not happy. The way I see it in this situation you have a choice to make. You can either, live in a loveless marriage while maintaining a successful career with the possibility of an even bigger, nastier, divorce. Or, you break up with Ell, take some time for yourself, let the PR nightmare pass, and work hard to rebuild yourself stronger than ever. Maybe even find someone else you care about even more."

"Are you finished?"

Little shit.

"Yes. Now, eat, living on canned air is making you lose your muscle mass."

"Whatever." He rolled his eyes before poking at his pasta. "Thank you." He muttered.

I let out a small quiet chuckle, a little brotherly connection, we're off to a good start. Teddy and I were close growing up, and I can't help but feel a little regretful for not being there for him as much as I should have for the past five years. He's still my brother, and I'd do anything for him, even when he's with someone like Ell. Hopefully this can be the first step in mending our relationship.

After Teddy finished the dishes we both closed ourselves in our rooms for night to sleep off the busy day. Except, of course, I couldn't sleep knowing my girl is right next door, probably fast asleep herself.

When I peered through the window, I found that her room wasn't completely dark. Her side lamp was still on, she's not under her covers, and her laptop is open in front of her. She looked so peaceful, I could watch her sleep all night.

I looked at the window realizing I still have a clear view of her from my bed. It's not as clear as I would like it to be, but it's just enough to where I could see the outline of her. Dressed in from what I could tell are her pajama shorts and an over-sized t-shirt. The t-shirt laid gently on her curves while her shorts were short enough I could see a good portion of her thigh tattoos.

Fucking gorgeous.

I couldn't help but panic a little when she woke up, thinking she could see me watching her. Thankfully, it was dark enough outside she wouldn't be able to see through her curtains on her side. With how sleepy she looked I doubt she would even notice if she could. She did a small stretch and closed her laptop to get ready for bed. She paused, looked over at her nightstand and thought for a moment.

Is she doing what I think she's doing? She laid the laptop back on her desk and dug something out of her nightstand.

I sit straight up when I see her pull out a vibrator.

A fucking vibrator.

Natalie

When I woke up from my dream of an unapologetically beautiful neighbor I was left with pent up energy. I quickly shut my light off and shut my door, as if anyone was here.

I've imagined Dean Craven's voice and mysterious face in my fantasies before. But, now, why does my imagination immediately paste my neighbor's face? And, why does it work so well?

I got back into bed, switched on my vibrator, put my headphones back on, and put on some soft music. I've listened to Dean a lot today, so I let my imagination take hold and imagine he's here with me. Dressed in all black, in his mask with messy hair, and sleeves rolled to see his tattoos.

The vibration on my clit made my back arch. He watched as he crawled onto the bed. My eyes still closed as I imagined him taking his mask off, and it's... my neighbor.

Surprise, surprise.

He explored my body, caressed my curves, dug his fingers into my hips and said, "You're so wet for me."

"Yes." I whispered to him. I'm so immersed and dazed I can't tell if I say it out loud. I sink my nails into my thigh as if he's digging his fingers in.

My back arched again, as I threw my head back a sudden breeze came through the window that sent chills through my body.

My whole body stiffened when I felt a hand on my mouth that wasn't mine. My eyes flew open to see a dark figure dressed in all black, icy blue eyes, messy dark hair, with a woodsy scent that filled the now hot air.

Am I dreaming?

Did the vibrator short circuit and now I'm in my personal heaven?

He took off my headphones and leaned close as he hovered over me. I could feel the heat radiating off of him. If this is a dream, this is getting way too real. My breaths became quicker as he got mere inches away from my face.

"Be a good girl, Natalie. And, I'll help you finish what you started." My body froze, and my chest tightened. I know that voice…

Dean?

I must still be dreaming.

"You get so wet and needy when you think about me." His mask muffled his low voice. "Don't you?"

His voice was like velvet on my skin, so smooth that I caved into my body's needs.

"Yes." I let out.

I'm not sure if it was the sudden fear and thinking that there is a real person in my room, or the fact that he lightly brushed his fingers down my body. Feeling every inch as he traced around my tattoos. But, I've never felt more… special. Every move he made was calculated and gentle as if he was consuming every single inch of me, wanting to take advantage of every second. This is nothing like I've ever experienced.

"Nobody can make you come the way I can. Can they?" His icy blue eyes are pinned to mine, making my entire body shutter again.

"No." I muttered.

I let out a sharp breath as he softly but firmly grabbed my wrists and pinned them above my head.

"Keep your hands where they are." He stated. "Move them. We start over. Understand, *Princess*?"

God, his voice makes me weak, his low growl matching my current read which makes this even more intense.

He slid the back of his fingers from my chest, my stomach, my hips, and put himself in between my thighs as I obeyed. He wrapped his arms around them keeping me in place as his fingers tightened and tensed as if he couldn't let go. He leaned his head against my thigh giving me a very lustful side eye.

He looked as if he's possessing me, claiming me, and drinking in all of me as I begged for him. *This* was my fantasy. Down to the sight of him. And, I'm… Oh god, just his touch gets me so close to the edge.

"A beautiful sight, Princess. Your body is beautiful. *You* are so beautiful." His fingers on my inner thighs inch closer and closer. "Close your eyes for me, Princess."

I let out a soft moan as he pressed his thumb to my clit. I almost burst from the sensation alone. He followed up a satisfied groan.

He prowls back up to face me.

"Am I going to have to blindfold you, or are you going to be a good girl and do as I say?" He flicked his icy eyes to me as I nodded.

"Good. Now, close your eyes." He rubbed his thumb on my bottom lip. "The only screams I want to hear are the ones you make when you come on my face. Do you understand, Natalie?"

Again, I'm melting under his touch. His hand shifted and caressed the side of cheek with his thumb gently brushing back and forth.

"Yes." I muttered under a shaky breath.

I have no time to think logically, as his fingers explore me. God, I haven't been touched like this for so long. His hands and fingers were magic as they explored my body.

He shifted his large body further and further down. I closed my eyes, feeling every touch, every grip, every… the feeling of his lips and tongue as he licked me up and down made my heart stop.

Holy fuck.

I kept my eyes closed as he commanded. Even if I wanted to open them, I can feel he's buried himself to where I couldn't make out any noticeable features even if I wanted to while he devastatingly devours me.

He pushed my thighs to the sides of his face as if he was ready to be locked here forever. His fingers dug into my thighs gripping them tighter. The movements of his tongue were slow as if he wanted to take his sweet time taking me in and tasting me as if I'm going to be the last meal he ever had. He dug his tongue deep and slowly licked up taking in every single drop, sensation, and twitch as the pressure began to build and build.

"Dean…" I muttered as my thighs shook. He sucked on my clit again making my muscles tense up, as if he was satisfied that I called out his name. Waves crash over me, once, twice, three times. He didn't want to stop as if this feeling was addicting to him and he couldn't pull away while I'm white knuckling the headboard to make sure he doesn't stop. He placed his hand on my stomach and the other across my thighs like a belt as if to steady me and himself. I felt like I was going to pass out, I've never had this many in one sitting.

"Oh fuck, Dean!" I called out again as I'm seeing stars behind my eyelids and shattered under him a fourth time. God his tongue was otherworldly. Before I knew it, he already put his mask back on and crawled back up to me.

He brushed his thumb along my jaw and moved up to wipe the stray tears that I didn't realize were there.

"Open your eyes, Princess."

I obeyed to see his body hovered over me with a possessive aura as he looked down at me. Taking in the sight of pleasure on my face, all because of him. He lightly brushed a few hairs from my face and brushed my cheek with his thumb once again.

"Absolutely stunning." He whispered as he took in the sight of the mess he created of me.

I reached out to touch the side of his face. He caught my wrist, held it for a moment, and pressed his mask-covered lips to the palm of my hand. "I really don't want this dream to end." I whispered.

His eyes softened as he pressed his face into my palm once again. "I know, Princess. With time, I promise."

The last thing I remembered, before I passed out from exhaustion, was the feeling of his warm lips on my forehead.

When I woke up from a *very* blissful sleep, I slowly rose out of bed to turn off the alarm I set for seven. I suddenly jolted up and looked around the room. The dream I had last night felt very, *very*, real. I've never had an erotic dream *that* intense. Because, that's what it was, a dream. A very real, very intense dream.

My eyes suddenly widened as I looked over at my now cracked window. "No."

I peaked through and saw Dean's curtains still open to show him sleeping face down with back muscles on full display. I looked down to see the vines on the trellis slightly disturbed.

"Oh no, no, no. I definitely had my window closed last night. Right?"

I immediately shut the window fully and lock it. "What if someone *was* here?" I frantically began to search around the house. There was nothing out of place that I could see. I even checked Kay's room with a metal hanger in hand. I forgot to grab my bat upstairs and it was the first thing I saw in Kay's room. It won't do much damage but it will do enough.

Nothing.

Everything was as it was before I went to bed.

Should I call the police?

"And tell them what?" I began to tell myself as I paced in the living room. "The guy who broke into my house gave me the best set of orgasms I've had in my entire life. Also, he sounded like my favorite audiobook narrator. What does he look like? No clue."

Then suddenly paused. "What if…" I storm off back to my room and peek through my window again. He's gone.

Dammit.

"There's no fucking way." I whispered to myself and took a few deep breaths. "Calm down." I whispered to myself. "It's just your wild imagination mixed with hours listening to 'House of Mischief'. You left the window cracked, the disturbed vines on the trellis was an animal. You listened to half of that audiobook yesterday, your imagination just took over. He had an American accent, your neighbor has a British accent. That's it. End of story."

I took one final breath to start getting ready for the not-date tour I have with my hot temporary neighbor. Flashes of the dream entered my mind, the way his tongue worked around my clit like magic. Gripping my thighs and pressing a strong hand on my stomach as if steadying himself for dear life. Without a doubt the best dream I've ever had.

Unless it wasn't a dream. It could've been my neighbor. My intrusive thoughts tell me.

No. No. NO.

I already established it was a dream. So, why do I feel disappointed? What's wrong with me… I should be terrified, I should be getting a security system, yet here I am hoping it happens again so I can find out if it was real or not. His tongue certainly felt real. His hands on my thighs. His lips on my forehead.

"The only screams I want to hear are the ones you make when you come on my face. Do you understand, Natalie?"

I stood under the warm water and snapped out of the vision before my hand began to roam.

"God, how am I going to get through this day?" I quickly switched the water to cold before getting out, because honestly I'm willing to try anything to cool me the fuck off. I wrapped my towel around me and walked back to my room to pick out an outfit.

"Okay, what do I wear, to take a very good looking British man, with hazel eyes, on a tour around Indy." I paused and sighed. "That is not a date." I raised a brow, but if he is single would he be interested in me? I love my curvy body, but would he? Riley said he was checking me out last night. I shake my head. I'm not going to overthink this. Just wear something nice but casual.

I finally settled for some jeans, a cute tank loosely tucked in, and a crop jacket to finish it off. If this isn't a date why am I so nervous? How could I tell if he's flirting, not flirting, interested, not interested. It's been so long since I've dated, I can't remember. Will I just know? I groaned as I headed back to the bathroom to finish off my hair. I curled it, pinned two sides up, and brought out my face framing pieces.

I'm getting ready like it's a date. Fuck, why am I so in my head about this? "Don't worry about the date thing," I told myself, "Find out more information about him first, then make your conclusion. That's what a normal person would do.

After I finished getting dressed the time was 8:55 AM. Perfect. I tied on my shoes and suddenly paused when I heard a knock at the door. I looked at my phone, no messages, it's still 8:55, who is that? I opened the door to find someone I was not ready to see yet.

"Dean?"

"Morning. Sorry, I'm a little early. The bumper to bumper traffic was lighter than expected."

He's dressed in dark jeans with a dark gray Henley underneath his leather jacket. Because of course he has a leather jacket. His eyes were bright, and I could see a little more green in his eyes with his dark hair styled.

I shook my head and let out a small chuckle. "Right." I forgot he did say he was going to be by a little early. "C'mon in." I motioned. "I was just about to make some coffee, would you like some?" As he stepped by his clean cologne filled my nose and immediately I knew I was in for a long ass day. Dammit why does he have to smell good too? I relaxed when I realized it wasn't the same scent as last night and forgot my tiny theory that he was the one who snuck into my room last night. Yup. Definitely, definitely a dream.

"Sure."

"How do you take it?" I closed the door behind us before heading over to the kitchen.

"Black, thank you." He took a look around the living room for a moment. "You have a lovely home."

"Thank you. It really helps when I have my roommates door shut." I quipped as I started up the coffee maker.

"You have a housemate? I hope I'm not disturbing them." He inched closer to the kitchen.

"Oh no. She's out of town for a week." I leaned against the counter as he looked me up and down with a quick flit of his eyes. Is he checking me out? Jesus, Nat. Make it out of the house and get to know him first! "You said you were staying here with your brother? Teddy, right?"

He hung his head for a beat as if he remembered his brother was here. "Yes. Unfortunately. I love my brother, but I haven't got a clue how I'm going to handle him for a month."

"Oh. Does he work with you?"

"No." He breathed. "Not at all. He just needed a getaway."

I nodded. "I get that. Did he not want to join us site seeing? He's more than welcome to come along." A nice buffer would be great so I can keep myself in check.

He shook his head. "No. He's currently doing his yoga, meditation, tai chi, I dunno. He's been in L.A. for so long he's started to develop a new lifestyle."

"Got it." I reached up to grab a couple of mugs from the cabinet. "Well, if you guys are free we host a board game night once a month with a few friends if you'd like to join. I know traveling this far away from home for so long you must miss socializing a little." Sure, that's one way to see if he's single.

"Thank you for the offer. I'll let Teddy know, he could use someone else to talk to other than me during this trip." I quickly grabbed the milk from the fridge as he continued. "What kind of board games do you play? Monopoly, Clue, things like that?"

I grin back at him. "I like my friends too much to play monopoly." He smiled at that. "And second," I paused. "You know what, never mind, you're probably going to think I'm a gigantic nerd."

"No. I could never. Tell me." He continued to grin at me as he leaned against the counter across from me. Damn he is tall.

"Fine. Have you heard of Gen Con?"

"I have." He nodded.

"Well, my friends and I go every year and buy new or unique board games. We've come across some interesting ones in the past." I paused after I poured the hot coffee into the mugs. "You think I'm a nerd, don't you?"

"If I called you a nerd that would make me a hypocrite."

"You go to Gen Con?" I stated with disbelief as I handed him his mug.

"Now, look who's calling who a nerd." He joked.

I grin at him, realizing I'm probably standing a little too close. "No, I didn't mean it like that. Do you have a group you go with?" I turned back to stand right back in my spot on the other side and plant myself there.

He shook his head. "No. I've only gone once for work."

"You went to Gen Con for work?" I questioned as I poured the milk in my coffee. "What do you do?"

"It's really not as interesting as you think."

"I beg to differ. If your work required you to go to Gen Con then I need details so I can apply." I joked as I put the milk back in the fridge.

"How about you? What do you do for a living?" He asked as if he was genuinely interested and looked at me like he was ready to absorb any information I told him which only made him even more attractive. Should I be concerned that I'm giving this stranger details about me? If I was really that concerned I wouldn't have let him in my house in the first place. Fuck it, if we're gonna do this, I can't be afraid to put myself out there.

"I'm a Video Content Manager for a small media company. If you want all the gossip on the latest celebrities, and mediocre movie and TV show reviews, we got ya covered." I took a small sip of coffee as he chuckled. "I only handle publishing the videos to about twenty different social media accounts, not the actual written content. One day maybe, but not there yet."

"Twenty social media accounts? Sounds like you have a lot on your plate." He looked over with sincerity as if he knew the feeling of working too much. I can imagine he does, considering he's on an assignment for a month. I don't want to press since his job is his personal business, but I can't help but be even more curious.

My phone went off in my pocket and once I saw the screen I immediately tensed up.

Brock: *Hey Natalie. It's Brock. Let me know if you have any questions about that packet. Also, we'll need to have a discussion on Monday about one* *of your team members. Apparently there was a mix up with the publishing times and someone set the wrong video live. Please set off a block of time after your meeting with the VO talent so we can have a discussion.*

"Son of a bitch." I whispered out.

"Everything alright?" I looked back up at Dean seeing genuine concern on his face.

I shoved my phone back in my pocket. I should've listened to Kayley and blocked his number. I have a feeling I knew which employee he was talking about considering the time of day and she's one of our newest employees. I tried to calm my pounding heart and rage towards my boss, she's still within her first ninety days, of course she's going to make mistakes here and there especially when we have top priority content being pumped through more than usual, but I need more information to fully assess the situation.

"Natalie?" I didn't realize he had gotten closer until I snapped out of my thoughts. The scent of his clean cologne began to ground me.

"Yes. Sorry. I'm fine. Just a work snafu. Nothing that can't wait until Monday." I cleared my throat.

"Are you sure?" He questioned as he analyzed me. I'm probably not hiding my disgust for my boss very well, but I need to put it aside if I'm going to make it through the day.

"Yeah. We should probably start heading out. We have a lot of things to see today."

He pressed his lips into a thin smile as if accepting my transition in conversation. "I thought you said there wasn't much to see around here?" He joked as we made our way out of the kitchen.

I gave him a small grin as I grabbed my purse and keys. "There are a few cool things I have tucked up my sleeve. Have you ever been to an apple orchard?"

"Can't say that I have." He looked down at me with curiosity.

"Have you ever taken an immersive tour to see what it was like during the founding years of America?"

He narrowed his eyes on me as if I was joking. "That's a thing?" He paused. "How immersive?"

I pursed my lips as I thought back. "They have staged cabins, period accurate houses, and talk about history as if they're living in the late 18th and 19th century. Why?"

"Well, if they're good actors, I'm not sure they'll take a liking to me." We both laughed as we walked out the door.

My mouth went agape at the realization. "I totally forgot. Now we have to go, I want to see what they'll say." I locked the door behind me. "I doubt they'll do anything drastic, but if they give you shit I'll be sure to defend you."

"I appreciate it." He grinned back at me. "We can take my rental car if you like?"

"Are you sure? Does your brother need it?"

"No, he said he wants to do some 'inner reflecting' today. Knowing him, that means he's going to be sitting on the couch watching Netflix all day." He opened the passenger car door for me.

"Thank you. You know that can count as self-reflecting, you don't know who you really are until you find out how you react to the season finale of your favorite show."

He raised a brow. "You may have a point."

Before he made his way into the driver's seat he slipped off his jacket, opened the back door, and tossed it into the back seat. "Apologies," He stated as he closed the door behind him, "I wasn't expecting it to be this warm in September."

"Welcome to central Indiana, what's the temperature today? Who knows, good luck." I looked down at the car temp that stated 61 degrees. Yeah, that seemed about right for this time of year. "You might need it later though. Temps can drop out of nowhere, Indy likes to keep us on our toes." I tried not to stare as he shoved his sleeves to his elbows revealing his gorgeous tattoos.

He returned a side smile. "I'll keep that in mind." He handed me a cord to plug in my phone. "For my co-pilot slash tour guide slash DJ."

"DJ?" I questioned. "Oh, you have no idea what you just signed on for."

He buckled his seat belt. "I do have one question before you start. Do you listen to Ell Wyms?"

I scrunched my nose and rocked my head back and forth wondering how to respond. Given how popular she is there's a chance he's a fan and I might offend him.

"Not really, no. I know she's super popular, but I don't really care for her type of music. Especially after her Christmas album last year. It was *everywhere*."

"Brilliant. We're on the same page."

"You don't like her either?"

"Nope. Can't stand her."

"Let me guess, a significant other dragged you to one of her overly expensive concerts?" I tried to ask without sounding too obvious and completely avoided the small knot in my stomach at the thought of some skinny blonde girl dragging him by his hand into a concert.

He gave me a small side eye as he put his hand behind my seat. Seeing him twist himself to see behind us to back the car out caused the butterflies in my stomach to flutter again. I tried to stay completely still as I stared down at my phone sifting through my music.

"No," he continued, "I've never gone to one of her concerts, nor do I ever plan to for personal reasons." Finally, he shifted back into drive and faced forward.

Dammit. Side tracked again.

"Wait. Personal reasons? Do you have *personal* one on one beef with Ell?"

"Something like that." He went on as he ignored the shocked look on my face. "Where to first?"

"I typed in the address, it's ready to go on your dashboard. Now, wait a minute, let's circle back. You have beef with Ell Wyms?" I questioned. "How? Is she a distant ex or something?"

"Oh, dear god, no. Nothing like that." He paused before he went on. "She's wronged a family member of mine. That's really all I can tell you."

My mouth stayed agape. Probably a back stage experience gone wrong with a younger sister, or cousin maybe. "I knew she wasn't a sweetheart behind closed doors. Damn. Well, I'm sorry for your family member whatever they're going through with her. I hope it's nothing too serious."

"Thank you. Don't worry, we're hoping it'll all get resolved soon." He sighed as he gripped the steering wheel.

"I hope it all works out." I didn't want to pry any further since it was a personal topic so I shifted the conversation. "My roommate Kayley, she's obsessed with her fiance, Tanner Brunswick. She talks about him all the time and she's convinced that one day they're going to find each other and fly off to England together."

He raised a brow. "Really? Tanner?"

"Yeah I don't see it either. However, I do admire her enthusiasm."

He gave a half shrug as we came to a stop light. "You never know, he might pop in one day."

"Now you're sounding as delusional as she is." I laughed.

"What's the saying, manifest, attract what you really want, and it'll find you?"

I caught his hazel eyes looking over at me as I replied. "Sure. Something like that."

He cleared his throat. "How about you? Do you have anyone you're manifesting to pop into your life one day?"

I stared back down at my phone as I thought back. I still think it's a rather far-fetched theory, one that I intended to bury, but there's still something about him that seems familiar. If I'm right and that's a slim chance, if it is him… I might freak out a little bit, especially after that very vivid sex dream I had about him last night. Oh no, don't go there, especially now.

"In a sense, I guess I do. But, I don't think I'm trying to attract or manifest him into my life. He's definitely taken I'm sure."

"What makes you say that? Have you seen him with anyone?" He asked with a little curiosity.

"No, but I also haven't seen his full face either. Kind of hard to manifest when you don't know what he fully looks like."

He thought for a moment. "Let me ask you this. How does someone have feelings for someone else when you don't know exactly what they look like?" He asked with no ill intention or judgment in his tone. Just pure curiosity.

"Careful you're poking at the very fabric of a very popular reality dating show." We both laughed before I continued. "I mean, definitely know what he sounds like." I chuckled. "I don't know, I just feel this pull in my heart for him sometimes you know? You don't have to know what someone looks like in order to be attracted to them. You just… feel it."

"That's nicely put." The light turned green as he put his attention back on the road. I tried not to stare at his tattoo's too hard. If he caught me that'd be awkward and I would have to explain myself. Oh don't worry I'm just trying to see if you're the narrator I fantasize about. No big deal.

Then my brain does something bold. "Thank you. Besides, I'd rather find someone by chance rather than try to chase someone popular who has no clue who I am."

"Some people say that's even more unlikely."

I turned my head to face him. "What do you think?"

He glanced back at me trying to hide his grin. "That I am not 'some people.'"

Dean

My girl is phenomenal. Every single problem, worry, anxiety melted away in her glowing presence. The entire day we traveled around the north side of Indianapolis, stopping at shops, restaurants, and activities. One of which was her immersive 19th century theme park. If that's what you want to call it.

Not only did they point me out because of my accent, but Natalie gave it right back as she promised. It was all innocent since there were some children around, but I couldn't help but feel a sense of pride every time.

After all the major landmarks were hit we headed off to dinner. A nice little Italian restaurant that was placed in the middle of an old town square that could be the building blocks to any American small-town rom com.

"So, what did you think?" She asked as the waiter took our plates away. "I know it wasn't much."

"It was fantastic. The art museum was amazing, the 19th century experience was *interesting*, and the apple orchard was informative. I've never seen that many apple trees let alone have the opportunity to pick a few."

"A few? You and your brother are going to have enough apples for you both to take back home."

I shrugged. "Maybe I'll bake them into a few pies or pastries."

"You bake?" She looked at me surprised.

"I cook more than I bake, but if I find a recipe I should be fine."

"I have one you can borrow, it was my grandma's so as long as you can read cursive you'll make the best pie you've ever tasted." She put her elbows on the table and held her chin with the back of her hands.

God, she's gorgeous.

It's taken every ounce of strength I have to keep my hands off of her. Last night was definitely a lapse in judgment. Did I risk everything by climbing through her window last night? Yes. Was it worth it to see her unravel for me? Fuck, yes. Does that make this situation any easier? Unfortunately, no.

"You trust me with a family recipe? I'm honored." I leaned on the table with her.

"Only those who can read cursive are worthy."

"I can, but I may need to have you over just to make sure I'm reading it correctly."

She bit her bottom lip. "Sure. That'd be fun."

After we wrapped up the evening we began walking back to the car. "Can I ask you something?" She stared down at the ground debating whether or not to ask me something.

"Anything."

"Why are you spending Saturday night with a stranger when you could be going out with your brother to a club or something?"

I couldn't help but let out a laugh. "Well. First off, you've never gone with my brother to a club. He's literally a puppy without a leash. I let him go and I don't see him for the rest of the night." She tried to hide her smile as she laughed. "Then someone will either pick him up and take him home or bring him straight to me saying 'he humped my leg please take him and leave.'"

"Oh my god." She continued to laugh as I got lost in her. Her smile, laugh, the way she looks up at me. I wanted to soak up every single second.

"That sounds like Kayley." She giggled. "They might be perfect for each other." I thought back to her comment about her housemate being in love with Tanner, aka my brother. That was a twist I wasn't expecting. A part of me wanted to put them in a room and see what would happen as Natalie and I watched from the sidelines.

"Maybe." I paused before taking another step. "Second. I'm going to be honest, after we met, I wanted to spend some time with you, and thanks to Officer Bradley's help, I thought a tour would be a great way to do it."

"You wanted to spend time with *me*? After we *just* met?" She questioned.

I wanted to say since the moment I found you a year ago, but now was definitely not the right time to dump every secret on her. "Yeah. I thought you were cute and charming, I wanted to get to know you a little more."

Oh okay, we're going bold here.

"Me? Charming and cute?" She began to blush as we continued to walk. "I was wearing a hoodie and you thought I was charming?"

"Of course." I shrugged.

"Says the man who's practically the king of charm over here." She waved her hand over me.

"You think *I'm* charming?" I knew she had feelings for my online persona, but the fact she sees *me* as charming made my heart flutter again. Every time I see her it flutters more and more.

She breathed sharply. "Every single woman was batting their eyelashes at you today, and you have the audacity to question that you're charming?"

I narrowed my brow. "I don't remember anyone batting their eyelashes at me." If they were, I wasn't paying attention to them. My focus was solely on my girl, every movement, every smile, every laugh. All now a core memory, seared into my brain forever.

Yeah, I'm a goner.

"My guy, of all the women that were around us today you could've had your pick of any one of them."

I clenched my jaw to stop myself from pulling her in right here.

My guy?

I've been calling her my girl for so long I never stopped to think what I would do if she called me *hers*. I knew this wasn't an actual *mine* reference, and I'm drastically overthinking it, but the thought of it had me using up that little grip of control I had left.

"I don't want any of them." I let slip out.

"Oh. Really? Is that because you have someone already, or because you have someone in mind back home?"

You. It's always been you. I wanted to say, but instead I took a deep breath and answered honestly. "No. I don't have anyone. Not in a long time." I avoided her eye contact before I let another comment slip and unlocked the car.

I made the mistake of catching her eye again as I opened the door for her. She had me locked in and I can't look away, nor do I really want to.

"If you don't mind me asking. How long exactly is 'a long time'?"

With the way she's looking at me right now she could ask me anything and I'd happily give it up. "I haven't dated in about three years."

She nodded in recognition before she slipped into the passenger seat. "Two years." She gave me a look of reassurance as I helped her close the door.

"Oh I know," I whispered to myself as I rounded the car, "and Aiden will pay for what he did if I ever see him."

I know about every single ex she's had in the past, and I know where they work, where they live, and what kind of car they drive. Just in case I ever see or hear them trying to crawl their way back into her life. None of them deserve to even think about her after what they did.

My hands tightened around the steering wheel as we made our way back to Natalie's house. Of course my girl melted all the stress away as we continued our conversation on baking earlier. *Baking.* Of all things, something that I never had any interest in doing. But now, I'd drop everything to experience it with her.

After I pulled into my driveway I opened the car door for her and took her hand to help her out.

"Thank you." She whispered.

"Of course. Shall I walk you home? Your house seems pretty far, I wouldn't feel right leaving you to walk all that way."

She laughed, "Sure. How gentlemanly of you."

Once we made it to her porch she turned to face me. "Okay." She stated. "I have to ask. Was this considered a date?"

I paused at her bluntness and thought for a moment. "Under traditional circumstances. I would say, no. Only because I didn't ask you properly. Plus, you wouldn't have to question if it was." I paused, realizing she's a lot closer to me than I thought and looking curious. As if to picture what I meant by that. I wanted to say "it's because I wouldn't be able to keep my hands off you". I slowly shoved my hands in my pockets before I acted on that promise.

I grinned down at her now very red face and I don't think as I let my words go. "Natalie?"

"Yes?"

"Would you like to go on a date with me?"

She smiled up at me and I instantly knew the answer. "Yeah. That'd be great."

"Tomorrow too soon?" I blurted out nervously, I dunno what it is about this woman that makes me lose all control, but every part of me wanted to give in.

"Not at all." She paused. "You must really like me if you want to see me so soon."

"You must really like me as well, since you agreed." My eyes flicked from her eyes to her lips.

"Maybe I do."

"Maybe I do too." I whispered back.

Without thinking I brushed a hair away from her face and leaned in until my lips met hers. Our bodies were flushed and relaxed, and I wanted to keep her right here for the rest of the night. I had pictured this moment over and over again, but it was even better than all the dreams, all the late nights I stayed up thinking about how her kiss would taste, about *her*. Her lips were soft, and tasted so sweet as she deepened the kiss. God, I could kiss her all night and never get enough.

She pulled away for a moment and put her forehead to mine.

"Thank you for today. I had a wonderful time." I whispered. If I don't end this now, I'm not too sure I'd be able to stop myself. It's incredibly painful to stop myself from kissing her again.

Slow down, Dean.

"So did I." She took in a sharp breath. "I'll see you tomorrow?"

"Of course. 12:30?"

She gripped my jacket and my thumb brushed against her cheek. "It's a date." I laid a kiss on her forehead before pulling away. To my surprise she caught my arm and pulled me in for one more kiss. I pressed my fingers into her hips as she held my neck down to her. God, she tastes so good. If she keeps doing this there's no way I'm going home tonight. Her lips slightly parted allowing me full access to her.

Fuck.

The last band over my control snaps. Her fingers slipped into my hair and I fucking *whimper*. I never whimper. I knew she'd have me wrapped around her fingers, but my god if she asked me to drop to my knees right now, I would do it in a fucking heartbeat. I pulled her in as close as I could for her to feel what she does to me. I get one last taste of her before I force myself to slow down.

Fuck, I need to gain control of myself, now.

I've thought about this moment more times than I can count. Meeting her, kissing her, tasting her. For a year she's been in the center of my mind… but she needs time to catch up.

She pulled away once again as we both took shortened breaths. "Wow." She muttered.

"Wow, indeed." I whispered as I tried to gain my clarity again.

"I'm sorry. I don't know what came over me."

I moved my hand up to her cheek once again. "You don't need to apologize. Especially when it comes to kissing you." I laid one last small kiss to her red swollen lips before I forcibly took a few steps back. "I'll see you tomorrow, alright?"

She nodded as she licked her bottom lip, tasting me again. The thought has me taking in a few counted breaths so I don't pick her up and carry her inside. "Have a good night, Natalie."

"Good night, Dean." She replied.

I slowly made my way back to the house only turning back once to see her watching me walk away. After I made sure she was inside I leaned against the rental car. I took in a few more long breaths trying to calm my heart and now pulsing dick. I leaned my hands on the roof of the car taking in the night air, hoping it will bring me back down to Earth. At least I didn't come in my pants like I did last night. No other woman has ever made me feel like this. Made me feel this out of control.

I've never stalked anyone, never hunted down their internet scum bucket commentators, never crawled through a window, never used my narrator persona in the bedroom. If what she was saying is true, that she felt a pull towards Dean Craven, *to me*, then I'm feeling it now more than ever.

After a few more breaths I was finally able to calm myself enough to head inside. I quickly grabbed the apples from the car, and I made my way to our porch and paused. The door was slightly open. I took in a sharp breath as I entered to see Teddy standing by the sink looking guilty as fuck.

I slowly shut the door as he turned to me. "Hey. There you are. Fun night?" He grinned as he tried not to break.

"Teddy. Were you watching me through the door?"

"No." He lied. "Of course not."

"You're a decent actor, but you're a terrible liar."

"Am not."

"Look at you. You have almost every tick in the book. Now," I threw my jacket on the chair and set the apples on the table. "Why were you watching me through the door?"

He pointed at the bag. "Why do you have so many apples?"

"Answer the question." I snapped.

"What? I can't be concerned for my brother's whereabouts when he's gone all day?"

"You can, but you don't during the rest of the year. So why do you care now, all of the sudden?"

"You didn't tell her I was here did you?"

I gave him a confused look. "That's why you were spying on me?" I pinched the bridge of my nose. "Teddy. You need to relax, okay-"

"No, I don't need to relax, did you tell her?" He practically shouted.

"Yeah, because I would totally tell our neighbor for a month that my little brother, who's a famous actor named Tanner Brunswick, is staying with me. No, you idiot, I told her my little brother Teddy was here, because she saw us enter the house yesterday after you nearly bit my head off about Ell."

"Just shut up about Ell for two goddamn seconds. Okay? Does she work for the press?"

"For fucks sake. Alright." I grabbed my jacket and his. "We're going for a walk," I threw his jacket at him. "You need some fresh air."

"I don't need fresh air, Dean."

"Did you leave the house today?"

"No."

"You need fresh air. Let's go." I opened the door for him to go first. He thought for a moment before he stormed out the door.

"This will be a relaxing walk." I whispered as I locked the door and Teddy threw his hood up. "For the love of-" I pulled his hood back. "It's 10 o'clock in a quiet suburb, you don't need your hood up. The last thing we need is the cops getting called because someone dressed in all black is sneaking around at night. Then you're really screwed."

"Why are you up my arse tonight?"

"Because you need to get your head out of it. C'mon Teddy, at some point you have to see that your paranoia is starting to affect your daily life. It's never bothered you like this before."

He sighed for a moment and took in a deep breath of the cool night air. "I know. Okay. It's- it's not just that."

"What is it?"

He paused for a moment as he debated on telling me. "I thought about what you said last night. After sitting with it for a while, I'm going to regret saying this, but I realized that you're right. I'm not happy anymore, this relationship is making me lose myself in a lot of ways and only making me feel worse. It got me thinking, if it's like this now, then how is it going to be when we get married? More press, more tours, more anxiety, stress. I don't see this going anywhere good, and I seriously need to consider my options."

"Which are?"

He took in another deep breath. "I have to consider breaking up with her. It's going to be hell, so I have to prepare myself on multiple fronts, but in the end I think it's best for me. I know that seems selfish."

"It's not Teddy, I promise. A relationship should be something you both want. In the end you're partners. You're both choosing to walk through life with one another because you can't picture doing it without the other. If you don't think you're a right fit for each other, then why keep wasting your time forcing it to work when it clearly doesn't."

"I know. There's just that small part of me that thinks it'll change, that one day we'll go back to having movie nights and date nights."

I sighed and debated on telling him it won't. After seeing him freak out earlier I decided to take a breath and go a different route. "Have you tried in the past?"

He scrunched his nose. "Of course I've tried. I tried to surprise her by cleaning the entire house, making up the theater room with blankets, candy, and a movie all ready to go."

"And?"

"She called and said she was 'in the groove' at the studio. I didn't see her for three days after that. I even stopped by to bring her lunch, but the producer stopped me saying she was too busy. Even when I saw her behind the door scrolling on her phone getting her hair done."

I couldn't help but feel sorry for him as the memory flashed through his head. I knew this wasn't going to be easy, and it was going to take time but I still can't help but feel sorry for him. He's trying so hard to catch a spark when he doesn't see the rain.

"I'm sorry, Teddy."

"I don't need your pity."

"No. I'm serious. That sounds awful, I didn't know."

He shrugged. "Yeah. Well. I have a lot to think about over the next few weeks."

"I guess so."

"So. Are you going to tell me about your night, or are we just going to skip over the fact that you made out with our neighbor?"

I rolled my eyes. "That's none of your business."

"No? Are you at least going to tell me her name? If you told her about me, you have to tell me about her." He began to walk backwards to annoy the hell out of me.

"Her name is Natalie, and *I* don't have to tell you shit."

He rolled his eyes. "Fine. I get it, you're not ready." He paused. "That explains why you were on my arse about calling her cute."

"I'll still kick your arse if you say anything like that again."

"Oh. Someone has a crush. When do I get to meet her?"

I raised a brow at him. "Two minutes ago you were paranoid that she was the paparazzi and now you want to meet her?"

He shrugged. "By the way you were ogling her I have a feeling she's going to be around for a while. She'll find out eventually."

I licked my teeth behind my lip. "Alright, fine. You can meet her after you and I go out to lunch in public without a disguise."

"That's not fair."

"I'll give you the sunglasses, but no sweatshirt and no hat. I know you've attached your popularity to Ell, but if you're seriously thinking about breaking it off with her you need to build up your own image again. Not only will that help you get your confidence back, but it will help with your image after everything settles. Deal?"

He thought about it for a moment and reluctantly caved. "Fine. It'll be worth it when I tell her all about your *theater* phase."

"This coming from the man who never grew out of his."

"Mine wasn't all musicals."

"You're just jealous because I'm a better singer than you."

"Yet you didn't make a career out of it?" He argued.

"Because I didn't want to exploit it and have it turn into something I loathe."

"Does she actually know what you do for a living?"

I stayed quiet for a moment too long as he came to his own conclusion.

"Seriously?"

"Again. Not that it's any of your business but I plan on telling her tomorrow."

"Tomorrow? You're seeing her again? Really?" He shook his head as he let out a demonizing chuckle. "Damn, she must be a good kisser for you to ask her out so soon. You know what they say about good kissers-"

I put my hand to his face and in one fluid motion pushed him into a set of bushes in someone's yard.

"Dammit, Dean!" He whisper-shouted as he flailed to get out of the bushes. Once he finally found his way out he caught up to me pulling twigs and leaves out of his hair and jacket.

"What the fuck was that for?"

"For being a prick."

"Consider the message received, ya fucker."

"You know what." I licked my top lip tasting the hint of her left behind. I've suddenly realized that pushing my little brother into a set of bushes wasn't enough payment for that little comment. "How about this? Next week, I'll invite Natalie and her housemate over for dinner so you can meet her."

He narrowed his eyes. "Just like that?"

"Just like that. She's great, and from what I hear about her housemate, I have a feeling you two would get along swimmingly." I wrapped my arm around his shoulder and squeezed as we walked back to the house.

"What's the catch?"

"No catch at all. I just thought it'd be nice for you to make some new friends, especially ones who don't objectify women." I squeezed his shoulder a little tight to make him wince as we walked back up the stairs to the house.

"Brayden is not that bad."

"Really?" I unlocked the door. "Last I heard he's on his fifth wife, sixth child, and hired a sleazy lawyer to make sure his child support payments are zip to none when he makes millions."

"When you put it like that he's-"

"A prick. Yeah. So, while you're at it, you may want to start looking for some better friends." We both walked back inside and shed our jackets. Natalie was right, the temperature definitely plummeted.

"One thing at a time." Teddy stated.

"Has he even contacted you since you left?" I asked as I moved the apples from the table to the counter.

He avoided eye contact for a moment. "Not that I know of."

"How do you not-" I paused. "Has your phone been on airplane mode since we left the airport?"

"No." He snapped. "It's been off." He rubbed the back of his neck.

"Teddy." I gave him a hard look. "What if Mum or Dad was trying to call you?"

"Then she'd call you asking for me. She knows I'm with you, I told her before I left." He took another deep breath. "I just know that if I turn it on, it's going to blow up. I'm just not ready for that yet. Okay?"

I shook my head, realizing it was probably better this way. I'd rather have it off and have him make progress than stare at it all day taking ten steps backwards. "Fine."

"Thank you." He turned to head upstairs while I leaned against the kitchen counter. I turned my head to see there were still a few lights on next door. I quickly made my way upstairs, shut my door and peered through my window.

Her curtains were closed once again, but I can still see the shape of her on the other side pacing and talking on the phone. From her movements it didn't look like a courtesy call either. She looked pissed.

I kept my eyes on her as she paced. What happened between the end of our day and now? She did get a text earlier that made her instantly tense up. Did work message her? What did they say? And who do I need to punish for it?

Natalie

"I want to rip his head off!" I practically shouted to Kayley through Facetime. My face ran hot as the temperature rose in my room from my anger. I cracked the curtains to open my window and get some fresh air in.

"What a dick!" She shouted back.

"This isn't the first time he's done this either, so it's not like the reprimanding he forces us to use actually works. If they actually cared about us they'd realize that we are overloaded and when that happens, *shit happens*." I paused. "But, of course, when I offer up a solution, oh no, no, we can't have them thinking they can slack off. Oh, no, no, no, we shouldn't ask them how they feel about their workload because 'we already know'. Fuck that!" I shouted again.

"Seriously!" Kayley shouted back again, her face looking just as red as mine. "Does he realize that Miranda is the newest member of our team and working twice as hard to learn our systems and steps?" She fumed. "I've said it before and I will say it again until the day I die. *Fuck, Brock*. That man has no idea how to run a company, and will always make a minor mistake look like the end of the fucking world."

"What do they expect us to be fucking automated robots who can pump out a shit ton of content with no mistakes? Especially, when we're being tracked by how long we take on each post every step of the way, how many we put out each hour, and using those numbers to give out warnings." I sat on the bed and blew out one last huff.

"Feel better?"

I let the cool air hit my face. "No. I really don't want to have this meeting on Monday. I already have a full workload, a VO to give a tour to, and now this." I lay my head in my head. "If he pisses me off, I might actually rip his head off."

"You'll make it through. You always do." She paused. "Scream into a pillow portion of our rant?"

I nodded. "Yeah. That sounds good."

We both set our phone down, grabbed a pillow and screamed into it for a good solid minute. I try to let loose of the stress through my muffled screams like Kayley and I have hundreds of times before. By the end of it my chest feels a little lighter, and I pick up the phone to see Kayley fixing her hair.

"Better?" She asked.

"Bearable. You?"

"Same. Now." She took one last deep breath. "Let's move on to better topics." I nodded in agreement. "How'd your tour go with our hot British neighbors?"

I blushed and pressed my lips together. "It was only with one of them but um, great. You know, really," I closed my eyes and thought about the kiss, "really great."

She looked at me wide eyed. "Shut up! Something happened! Tell me! Wait! Wait! Let's add Riley and Blake."

"No, no, you don't have to- oh you're already adding them, okay."

Riley answered first. "Hey guys what's going on? I have Rob and Blake here!" She panned the camera to show all three of them sitting on the couch as they waved.

"Hello!" Rob called out.

"Hi Rob. Hope we're not interrupting?" I moved over to my desk by the window and set my phone in my stand.

"No, not at all. We're scrolling through Netflix watching trailers. We can't decide which show to watch next."

"Rob's being picky again." Blake snacked on her popcorn.

Rob rolled his eyes in response. "I thought about watching Lucifer, but Riley doesn't like cop shows, therefore we need to sift through some other options."

"Oh, that's a good one though!" Kayley shrieked.

"Who's the main actor again?" Riley questioned. Her head tilted as her husband pulled up the preview on screen. She pursed her lips as Rob looked over at her waiting for her to say yes.

"Okay, yeah, we can watch that." She nodded as Blake rolled her eyes and Rob had a look of victory on his face.

"Wait, Rob. You're going to sit there and watch your wife drool over a hot actor?" Kayley questioned.

"Who said she'd be the only one drooling?" He joked.

I couldn't help but laugh as Blake leaned in. "Nat, Kay, can I stay with you guys for the foreseeable future?"

"I wish we could take you in, but we only have two bedrooms." I responded.

"Don't worry, I have no problem taking the couch as long as I don't have to see these two drooling in front of the TV."

Riley rolled her eyes as she turned back to us. "So what's up with you guys?"

"Well, Nat was just going to share how her little tour with our hot British neighbor went." Kayley rocked back and forth as if she couldn't wait to hear about it.

"Oh that's right! How'd it go? Tell us everything!" Riley leaned in ready to hear it as Rob side peeked towards the screen. Making it so not obvious that he was listening in too.

I bit my top lip finally letting my smile loose as the kiss replayed over and over in my mind. "It went great. We hit a lot of the main tourist spots, went to a few shops, and he drove his rental car as I directed him around."

"And?" Rob let slip.

"He was really charming, his accent is so silky, he's about 6'3", hazel eyes, and his arms are covered in tattoos. When I asked about them he said he usually gets a black and white tattoo every place he visits in the artist's style."

"Oh my god, of course he has tattoos. Do you have a picture of him?" Kayley asked.

"No. I looked him up and he doesn't have any social media platforms that I could find."

"That's a red flag." Kayley interrupts. "Who doesn't have social media?"

I gave her a deadpan look. "Not everyone likes to have pictures of themselves plastered all over the internet Kay."

"Whatever, miss four thousand followers."

"Hey, don't bring my Instagram into this." I spat back.

"Whoa, hey, we're getting off topic. What else happened?" Riley's voice elevated as she asked.

I squinted my eyes. "Why did you say that like you know something?"

She averted her eyes. "I don't know what you're talking about."

My mouth went agape. "Were you spying on me?"

"No, no! I wasn't spying on you." She paused. "I just so happened to be on your street on my way home, so I parked far enough away, just to make sure you were, you know, safe."

"You didn't work today!" I replied.

"I was, you know, out shopping, with Rob."

"Rob!"

"And Blake." Rob admitted as his sister hit him in the arm.

"Are you serious! All three of you were watching me?"

Kayley couldn't keep in her laughter, "Oh my god! Wait, what did they do?"

"He kissed her." Rob stated.

"What!?" Kayley gasped.

"Rob!" I shouted.

"Then she pulled him in for another kiss." Riley paused. "That went on, and on. To where I thought for sure you were going to drag that man inside."

"Holy shit! No way!" Kayley gasped again. "Was he a good kisser?"

"Obviously, why would she pull him in for a second if the first one wasn't any good." Blake chimed in. "Not to mention keep him there for a hot minute."

"Okay, okay." I spoke up to stop this madness. "You guys seem to already have this handled so I can go now."

"No, no! Wait. We're sorry, alright. We were just worried about you. He may be hot but he's still a stranger." Riley explained.

"Buzzkill." Kayley whispered. "All of you should be ashamed of yourselves."

"Oh, please if you were here you'd be right there at the window watching them too." Riley spat.

"No I wouldn't. I'd be in the car with you guys just in case they needed the house."

"Okay." I pointed at the screen. "All of you, Life360 privileges are suspended."

Kayley gasped. "How dare you, I didn't do anything!"

"Look," I continued with a stern voice. "I'm starting to like this guy, and with that I need to trust him and he needs to trust me. He can't do that if my friends are watching us make out."

Kayley narrowed her eyes on me. "Wait a minute. You guys are going out again aren't you?"

"As a matter of fact. Yes. We're going out to lunch tomorrow."

"Going out as in…?" Riley questioned as Rob leaned in.

I sighed. "Yes. It's a date." They all erupted in cheers. "Wow, didn't realize my dating life was something you were routing for?"

Kayley collected herself. "So when do we all get to meet him?"

I cleared my throat. "I actually invited him over for board game night after you get back."

"Please tell me you invited the brother?" Kayley pleaded.

"Yes. I invited the brother."

"Is he handsome too?" She questioned.

I shook my head. "To be honest I don't know. I haven't really seen him around much. I caught a quick glimpse of them leaving for a walk but he had his hood up. Then Dean pulled it back as if he was annoyed with him. So, they're definitely brothers, but unfortunately I have no clue what he looks like other than he has dark hair."

Kayley pouted. "Bummer. Hey you know if this works out we'll be sister in laws."

"Whoa, hang on a second. I like him, but I don't hear wedding bells yet. Plus, you haven't even met his brother, for all you know he could be a complete dick?"

"Sounds like your type." Her brother Justin's voice echoed in the background.

"Sounds like you'd be best friends." She spat back.

"I don't associate myself with the people you date because once they leave you they're already dead."

"That better be rhetorical, Justin." Riley stated in a serious tone.

He leaned down to face us. "Always is, Officer." He gave a half assed grin as he left the camera. Out of the corner of my eye I caught Blake's stare lingering at the screen with a small redness to her cheeks.

Interesting.

"Whatever." Kayley rolled her eyes at him. "I'm so excited!"

"Well, don't get too excited, because if it doesn't end up working out, it's going to be an awkward month." I replied.

"Why wouldn't it work out?" Riley questioned.

I sighed. "Look guys, I haven't dated anyone in a long time so I'm not sure how this is going to go. I do like him a lot but I just don't want to get my hopes up." I paused. "Tonight didn't help with every woman staring at him like a piece of meat."

Riley's eyes widened. "Wow, how did he respond to that?"

"I literally had to tell him, he said he 'didn't notice'. From the way he said it and looked, he genuinely meant it."

Kayley's mouth went agape again. If she kept going like this her jaw may actually unhinge itself. "Stop! He did not."

"What?"

"Was he engaging with you the entire time?" She continued. "Like kept talking with you and only you?"

"I mean he gave the waiter his order and paid for everything if that's what you mean?"

"He's so into you." Riley followed up. "Even from the night you guys met, he was *taking you in*."

"Stop, seriously?" Kayley squealed.

"From what Riley described," Rob interjected, "oh yeah, he's into you. With that info mixed with tonight's chemistry my projection, a week max until you're tangling sheets."

Riley nodded. "I'd agree with that." They all began nodding in agreement. "If I didn't know any better from the way he was looking at you I'd say you guys were already doing it."

"Okay, that's enough of that." I waved my hand to change the subject. Suddenly a message from Dean pinged on my phone as if he could sense I was talking about him. I paused my video feed and switched over to messages to read it.

Neighbor Dean: *I had a wonderful time with you today, you're an excellent tour guide and an amazing DJ. Thank you again for showing me* *around, I really appreciate it. We're still on for 12:30 PM tomorrow?*

"Nat? Where did you go?" Kayley questioned.

"Hang on." I replied.

Natalie: *No problem, it was easy, it's like I grew up here, I had a great time with you as well. Yes, if you want to meet earlier let me know!*

Neighbor Dean: *Careful, I might take you up on that offer and you won't be able to get rid of me, my brother is driving me crazy.*

Natalie: *Totally not because you want to see me right?*

"Oh my god, is he texting you right now? He is, isn't he?" Kayley squealed.

Neighbor Dean: *Trust me, even if I was alone, I'd take every chance I get to see you.*

Natalie: *Good night Dean, I'll see you tomorrow!*

I couldn't help but smile and blush at his words. Is this seriously happening right now?

Neighbor Dean: *Sleep well, Natalie.*

I headed back into the Facetime app where my camera turned back on, and my face was beat red.

"I knew it!" Kayley shouted. "What did he say?"

"Nothing, he's just being sweet and thanking me for taking him around today. That's all."

"That's all?" She mocked. "Girl, you have to give me more than that."

"Can we please change the subject?" I pleaded. "Rob, how have you been?"

"Good, you know if you give me a last name I can find out everything we need to know about your neighbor. It's been awhile since I went into a deep dive." He replied. I swear the man is able to find anyone with his research skills. When Riley found out he gathered the same amount of intel about her as she did to him, she practically pounced on the man.

"No. Guys. Seriously, if there's anything he wants to tell me then he'll tell me. Like I said, if he's going to trust me then I need to trust him. So, thank you but I'm okay for now."

"No worries. Hey Kayley, I saw some rumors floating around on a few social platforms that Tanner Brunswick was spotted at Indianapolis Airport." He raised a brow.

"Please, tell me your kidding." Kayley stood straight up. "Knowing my luck he was just there for a layover or something. Since Ell's in Europe for her tour." She snubbed. "Damn. I can't believe I missed my chance to accidentally run into him at the airport."

"Please, like you could get Tanner fucking Brunswick." Justin voiced in the background.

"Shut up, J. Don't you have a little cousin to torture somewhere?" She rolled her eyes as she flipped him the bird.

"What about our neighbor's brother?" I questioned. "You were so excited to meet him."

"Is he Tanner Brunswick?"

"I doubt it. Wait, what color hair does he have?"

"Right now. Blonde."

"Oh. Then no."

"I rest my case."

I rolled my eyes. "He's engaged to someone else Kay, you gotta let him go."

"Rumor has it he didn't get on another flight." Rob added.

"Yeah, but how credible are those sources?" I questioned.

"Not great, but there's still hope." He shrugged.

"Again knowing my luck he'll be gone by the time I get back." Kayley shrugged and sighed like a damsel. "I guess it was never meant to be."

"We already knew that." Justin's voice echoed again.

"Go fuck a paper shredder asshole."

"I take it the trip is a little tense?" I ask as the rest of us stare at her wide eyed.

"Actually it's not bad. Other than sharing a room with my least favorite brother."

"Right back at ya." Justin replied.

She rolled her eyes as she continued. "And, I'm missing out on the most exciting thing to ever happen in the history of living in that household."

"Don't worry, when you get back we'll plan the board game night. Dean seemed to be interested in it."

"Wait, wait." Kayley's eyes went wide. "Did you say his name is Dean?"

"Yeah." I looked at her confused.

"She said his name earlier, Kay." Riley gave her a strange look. "Where have you been?"

"I was imagining our double wedding, okay, so excuse me if I was a little distracted."

"A double what now?" I questioned.

She waved her hand. "No, back to Dean. Didn't *Dean Craven* post on his story that he was at the airport yesterday? What if our neighbor *is* Dean Craven? *The* Dean Craven."

"Do you have to use his first and last name every time?"

"Yes." She stated.

I rolled my eyes. "*He* has an American accent, our neighbor is British."

She gave me a deadpan look. "Aren't English actors known for how well they can pull off an American accent? Craven could be a stage name."

"I don't know, Kay. That seems a little far-fetched." Riley stated.

"Don't worry, she's not entirely insane, I had the same thought as well." I admitted as I thought back for a moment. "There are some striking similarities, but I doubt it. The likelihood that it is him is slim at best."

"Did he tell you what he did for a living?" Kayley asked.

"Well, no not directly. He's here for work, that's all I know, and I highly doubt Dean Craven would travel for a job when he probably has a studio at home."

"Fair point." Kay nodded. "Still. The chances aren't zero, right Rob?"

"Actually, there's about a thirty-five percent chance it's him."

"See- wait thirty-five percent?" Kayley snapped back.

"Yeah. Riley said you're touring a VO around your office on Monday, right? Given that, the day he arrived, his first name being Dean, the accent thing, it's all adding up to be pretty high. Minus the possibility he doesn't do that kind of VO work, knowing he's probably well off from all of his work he's done in the past. Minus taxes and such. It's unlikely he would take this kind of job. It's more like freelance work from what I understand." I nod to confirm. "So put that all together you get about thirty-five percent."

We all blink at him as I muttered, "Thanks Rob."

"That was so hot." Riley raised a brow at him.

"Okay, I'm out." Blake quickly ran away.

"Yeah, same." Kayley scrunched her nose. "If I don't talk to you before Monday, make sure to dress up a little bit, just in case." She winked.

"Good night, Kay." I brushed off her comment before she hung up.

"Hey, Nat. You're joking about the 360 thing right?" Riley pleaded as her protector instincts kicked in.

"Just from the group, not you. I promise." Was I a little upset with her for spying on me, yes. But, there was a part of me that was thankful she was close by. She's the one person I would call to help me in any situation. Flat tire, a drunk at the bar hitting on us, Kayley about to throw hands, she was there.

After we wrapped up our conversation, I went straight to bed. After last night's fever dream and walking around all day I needed to rest. Only, of course, I can't sleep. The percentage Rob threw out seemed a little too high for my liking. Not to mention, bringing up the VO tour. That would make a lot of sense. Plus, he went to Gen Con, for work? Maybe as a guest speaker?

Would I even be mad at him for not telling me if he was Dean Craven? He's spent a lot of time and energy, I'm sure, to keep his identity a secret.

How would I even react to that?

A part of me feels that I wouldn't be angry, because looking at the whole picture I'm a stranger to him. It's not like he would trust any stranger with that kind of information. If he is and doesn't tell me, then would I feel hurt after I found out that he didn't trust me enough to keep his secret?

I began to toss and turn in my bed trying to get comfortable as my thoughts continued.

Not to mention, this isn't his kind of gig. If he was here for our small company, why?

I shouldn't let Kayley's theory get into my head. In a *hypothetical* scenario, if it is him, he'll tell me at the right time when he's comfortable. If not, then I was worried for nothing and I can move on.

However, if they are two different people, and Dean Craven is going to be at the office on Monday, I'm so screwed. Hearing his voice every day would be pleasure filled agony. Knowing he, the man who has been responsible for my orgasms for a while now, would be standing in our booth practically feet away from me would make my job very difficult. Then, go home to go on a date with another man I'm starting to like on an emotional level. Yeah, I'm not sure I'd be able to listen to his work for a while. At least both of their names are Dean?

Goddammit. I turned over again.

"It's just a hypothetical. Calm. Down. You have a date tomorrow. Focus on that." I whispered to myself.

I quieted my thoughts for only a moment when the picture of my neighbor popped into my head and the divine way he kissed me. His soft lips parting and tasting him made my heart race. It was so good the overwhelming feeling of wanting to do it over and over just took over me. Pulling him into another delicious kiss. Feeling how turned on he was made my entire body fill with the need to have him inside me.

Jesus, I need to calm the fuck down.

When I think about it, if Narrator Dean and Neighbor Dean were the same person, that would be… "Fuck."

Dean

"You're working for World Entertainment Media?" My little brother practically stomped down the stairs to meet me in the kitchen.

"Good morning to you too." I sat up from the table to grab another cup of coffee. "Want some toast?"

"No. I don't want fucking toast Dean," he practically shouted. "I want to know why you're working for a sleazy company that's done nothing but shit talk about me."

I've seen my brother get pissed and it usually consists of petty comments and cold shoulders for about a week or until I apologize. Which is rarely the case considering most of the times he's been pissed at me weren't even my fault. However, I will say, this one is on me.

I took in a deep breath before I began. "Look. They're starting a new video series for book reviews, they knew I was a popular narrator and voice over talent, so they hired me." It wasn't a total lie. I'm just leaving the part out where it was all my idea so I could get to my girl's shitty boss.

"How did you even find out?"

"We're in Indiana, it wasn't hard to find the only media company located within this vicinity." He paused as he continued to fume. "Why would you take a job from them? They're known for their shit-posting. Hell, why would you want to tie your reputation to them?"

I could tell him everything right now, would he judge me for it? There's a high chance. Hell, would I *trust him* with that information, hell no. Especially right now while he looks as though he's about to rip my face off.

"I looked into them, Dean," my eyes flashed to him as he continued, "did you know they have their office in Indiana so they can pay their workers a lower salary since the cost of living is way cheaper here? They've had a ton of copyright lawsuits brought against them, they don't give their employees livable wages according to their reviews, and their CEO just bought a yacht while their employees live paycheck to paycheck."

Someone did their homework. I set my mug down before I gripped it too tight. Knowing that my girl is currently working for this pathetic excuse of a company made my blood heat. That wasn't new. I knew that they're nothing but money hungry dumb fucks who don't give a shit about their employees. Granted that's most businesses here in America, but when it comes to her, they're lucky heads aren't rolling. Which was one of my many motivations to get here and see her, and make her see they didn't deserve someone like her. She's worked so hard for them and I want to understand why.

"I know." I gritted out.

"Then why? Do they have something on *you*?" Right now I'm regretting that I didn't convince him to turn on his phone and occupy his time with his messages instead of my business.

"No. Teddy. They don't. Look, you're going to have to trust me on this one, okay?"

He narrowed his eyes on me. "Wait. Are you going undercover or something? To reveal their shitty business practices?"

I blinked at him twice. "You're not allowed to star in any more spy movies." I paused and thought about it for a moment. "Technically, you're not too far off."

Of course it was Natalie's decision alone if she wanted to leave the company. I will support her any way she chooses. However, I will not yield when it comes to bullshit. So, if *Brock* decides to hand me any, I will throw it right back. Especially if he gives my girl any more trouble after what I heard last night from her open window.

Like I said. *Heads. Will. Roll.*

"So you are gathering intel? From the inside?" He pressed. "That's bold. Even for you. You know *she* works there, right?"

My body went still. "Who?"

"Natalie Green. Our neighbor." He put on that little shit grin I knew all too well. "Relax. I know your secret identity is important to you, I've never told anyone and I don't plan to. But, you should probably at least give her a warning before you meet at the office tomorrow."

I smacked my lips. "Do me a favor, Teddy."

"What?"

"Shut the fuck up and stay out of my business."

He tilted his head. "You've been in my business since day one, this is a two way street pal."

"As the eldest, no it most certainly is not. *I* know what I'm doing. *You* do not."

"Oh fuck off, you haven't got a clue. Even if you did, your feelings would get in the way of your judgment. You plan on telling her what you do for a living today, right? Just tell her the truth. It'll be less of a shock for her. You want the relationship to be built on trust."

I scoffed. "Relationship advice? Really?"

He let out a sharp breath as he stared at the ceiling. "I just don't want you to make the same mistakes I did." He gave me a sincere look. "I gave Ell a charming, talented Tanner. Now, when I'm Teddy, I'm invisible to her." He took a deep breath. "So, trust me on this one, if you really like her, just be honest in every aspect."

Great, now I feel guilty for setting him up to have dinner with us and Kayley. "Well, I appreciate your concern. However, you can relax, I was in fact planning on telling her today."

"Good. Now if there's anything I can do to help take down that slimy company, let me know."

I raised my mug. "Will do."

"Hey. What time are you leaving today?"

"I plan to head over early, in about an hour, why?" I pulled out my phone to text her when I paused. "Are you planning on doing something idiotic?"

"No." He raised a brow at me. "How low do you think of me?"

"I don't think you want the answer to that question." I took a sip of my coffee.

"Whatever, I ordered food, so make sure you don't step on it with your Godzilla feet on your way out."

"Teddy. We have a fully stocked fridge for a reason."

"I wanted sushi." He called from the stairs.

"At 10:30 in the morning?"

"I'm on holiday, leave me alone."

"Fucking, Christ." I whispered.

My phone began to ring and I quickly swiped to answer it with a smile on my face.

"Good morning, Natalie."

"Morning. Is this a bad time?"

I shook my head. As if any time would be a bad time when it comes to her. Even if I was recording for the piece of a lifetime, she could still come in just to say hello and I'd welcome her with open arms.

"Not at all."

"Good. I was wondering if you were still interested in meeting a little earlier?"

"What a coincidence, I was about to ask you the same thing."

"Really? How early?"

"Looks like the traffic's light, so a minute tops." I joked.

She laughed, "How about ten minutes?"

"Sounds good, I'll see you then."

"Great, bye."

"Bye." I hung up the phone with a stupid grin on my face that quickly turned sour when I heard Teddy commenting in the background.

"You guys are gross, you haven't even gone on the date yet and it's already mushy."

I glared back at him. "Do you have anything better to do right now?"

"I could be sitting on the couch with my sushi right now but it's delayed." He took out his phone to check.

I pointed at his phone. "You turned your phone back on?"

He held it in his hand as if ready to break it. "Yeah. Then I put it on silent, hid it under my pillow, and took a shower."

"Fair enough." I crossed my arms. "Anything interesting?"

He shook his head as his jaw tensed.

Shit.

"No. Not even a little bit."

"You want to talk about it?" I asked, seeing a look on his face I've become all too familiar with.

"Ell hasn't said a word, or Brayden. It's like they don't even notice I'm gone. We have cameras on the house. She would've gotten a notification when I left." He took in a sharp breath through his nose. "Whatever. It's not like you care anyway."

"Why would I ask if I didn't? I'm here aren't I? I allowed you to come with me on this trip because it sounded like you needed it."

"Because you always know what's best for me right?" He argued.

"I didn't say that."

"I'm the eldest, I know what I'm doing, you do not'." He tried to mock my voice. "I know I'm not fucking perfect, but stop acting like *you*

are."

"Teddy, I know you're upset right now, but don't take it out on me. You know that never ends well." I tried to reason with a warning.

"There you go again, thinking you're all high and mighty, that you can just take me down a peg whenever you want."

"Teddy…"

"No, you know what, save it. I don't need another one of your lectures. You have no idea what it's like out there. To be constantly surrounded but always alone! Being recognized by people who know me as a famous person instead of a human being." He chuckled as his eyes started to water and slowly walked towards me. "To get the messages from people you don't care about while desperately waiting for the ones you do."

"Actually, I do know what that's like."

"Here we go, here comes another lecture, because big bro knows best." He inched closer. I really don't want to fight with my brother, but if I have to restrain him, I will.

"Jesus, Teddy, just fucking listen to me. I know exactly what it's like." I paused. "I may not be surrounded by crowds every day, but don't think for one second that I don't understand what it's like to feel alone. Why do you think I work all the damn time? My best friend is my agent, I'd be alone in this house if you didn't come along, the only messages I get are from my followers looking for a hookup, and I sure as hell don't have a group of friends to have a drink with."

He scoffed. "Yeah, and now you have Natalie, while Ell, the woman I thought I loved, left me on read and sent my call to voicemail earlier. So, you may think you know what I'm going through, but don't think for one second you can compare to it."

"Teddy," I tried to grab his shoulder but he pulled away. "I know you're upset with the world right now, but don't take it out on the one person standing right in front of you who's willing to listen and empathize with you." I stood firm waiting for his next insult or jab. Then a knock on the door broke us out of our heated argument.

"Speaking of Natalie. Have a nice date." He stated sarcastically.

I wiped my hand down my face, trying to cool my rage towards my brother right now. Teddy bolted upstairs as I opened the door to see Natalie dressed in a cute black skirt, tights, boots, and light knit sweater with her hair curled. Immediately all the frustration, anger, all of it was replaced with awe as I saw her. A worried look on her face stopped me in my tracks.

"Is everything okay? I heard you guys all the way from the front yard." She paused. "Also I found this on the steps, I'm assuming it's for Teddy?" She held up the bag of Teddy's food and I'm still left speechless.

"Hey." She spoke so softly I almost broke. She set the bag on the porch and held my arms as I stepped out. "Are *you* okay?"

"Ye-yeah. It's just- Teddy." I couldn't find the right words to say. I wanted to tell her everything, about what he was going through, how I'm trying to help him, but I couldn't get the words out.

"You guys have another argument?"

"Another?" I questioned. "How thin are these walls?" I tried to shift the subject.

She smiled. "They're not, it's just every time I see you two leave there's some tension there." She paused. "Look feel free to tell me if I'm going too far, but if there's anything I can do to help, let me know, okay? I have quite a bit of experience when it comes to family arguments." She paused as she watched me contemplate. "You don't have to tell me things you're not comfortable with, just know that I'm here for you if you need someone to talk to. From what I could hear, it sounded pretty intense."

My girl truly is phenomenal. I shifted my arms to hold her hands. "Thank you, Natalie. You have no idea what that means to me." I kissed the top of her hand and stayed quiet for a moment.

"Do you want to talk about it?" She looked up at me with her light blue eyes ready for anything I might throw at her.

I didn't want to cancel our date, every fiber in being didn't want her to leave. Yet, Teddy's words stick in the back of my brain about how alone he's felt. I haven't been exactly gentle with him over the past few days.

"Here." She pulled my hands to sit on the porch swing with her. "We can either sit here for a minute and listen to birds or we can talk about anything you're comfortable with." She put one leg under the other and faced me as we both sat down.

I shook my head as she continued to hold my hand with her other arm on the back of the swing. I haven't talked to anyone about Teddy, other than to Mum or Dad. They're great listeners, but always jump to the same answer. "Just talk with Teddy, you two will work it out". If only it were that simple sometimes.

"You'd be willing to spend our entire first date listening to the birds or listen to me rant about my little brother?"

She smiled. "While this isn't what I expected, I like to think first dates can be anything you want them to be. That's what makes them so special. It doesn't have to be a fancy dinner or an expensive show, as long as you're spending time with one another and enjoying their company, you can make it as elaborate or as simple as you want. Like, sitting on a porch swing listening to the birds and getting to know one another."

I shifted to fully face her and lean my arm on the back of the swing with hers. I entangled our fingers together as she continued to smile at me.

"I'm not worthy of you." I say softly.

"Why do you say that?"

I don't think as I let the words spill out. I can't keep these secrets from her, Teddy was right, here she is proving as best she can that I can trust her, yet I have given her no reason to trust me. I have to tell her everything, I have to-

The door suddenly swung open to reveal Teddy with no sunglasses, hat, or hood. His eyes go wide as he sees us on the porch. The sun was bright in the sky revealing exactly who he was.

Natalie's eyes went wide for a split second, stole a quick glance at me, then put on a smile. "Hi. I'm Natalie. You must be Teddy, right?"

He stood there shocked, not knowing how to handle this normal introduction.

"Yeah?" He stood as if he was a scared cat being offered food for the first time. I sighed as I pinched my fingers to the bridge of my nose.

Natalie slowly stood as if not to spook him and stuck out her hand. "It's nice to meet you. I've heard great things about you."

He gently shook her hand for a split of a second.

"*Great* things?" He questioned as he gave me a hard stare.

"Dean told me you two were rather close growing up. I envy you both, I grew up as an only child so the closest thing I ever got was our family cat Misty." Watching Natalie calmly approach Teddy like this gave me a sense of relief I didn't know I needed. Watching Teddy on the other hand made me want to slap him awake and remember common human manners.

"Yeah, well, count yourself lucky. Having an older brother is not as great as you think it is."

I gave him a glare as I stood ready to go another round with him, and this time I won't be as fucking polite. Natalie's hand hit my chest encouraging me to wait for a moment. The feeling had me so surprised I stayed still.

"I beg to differ. I've been in countless situations where I wished I had an older brother or sister to talk to. I don't know what it is about older siblings but they seem to give a certain kind of advice that always sticks with you. Is it always the best advice, maybe, maybe not." She shrugged. "Trust me, I have a few friends with older siblings and they all seem to have one thing in common."

"What's that?" Teddy questioned.

"They might call you a little shit, but you're *their* little shit, and will do anything they can to protect you while still calling you a little shit." She laughed, causing the corner of Teddy's mouth to lift.

Again, I'm speechless. Her words were so genuine, kind even. How did she do that so effortlessly? I shared a look with Teddy and I can see the guilt in his eyes.

"Natalie." I lightly placed my hand on her back. "Will you excuse us, for a moment?"

"Of course. I'll be right here." She gave me a quick smile as she sat back on the swing with an understanding look on her face. With a little message of "play nice" in her eyes. I bit my top lip as she crossed her legs.

I couldn't resist as I quickly stepped over to her and gave her a small kiss before I headed back inside.

"Don't go anywhere, I'll be right back." I whispered.

"I won't, I promise. Take your time." She gave me one last smile before I shut the door behind me.

Teddy set his food on the table and began to pace. He looked at me as if he was trying to solve a puzzle.

"She didn't flinch." He whispered as if she could hear him.

I froze. "That's what you're taking away from that conversation?" I scoffed. "Teddy, she's right, all I want to do is help you, relate to you, and protect you even from yourself. I can't do that when you're constantly at my throat. If you want me to listen, then tell me. If you want advice, ask me. Okay?"

He softly nodded.

I took in a deep breath of relief as we finally found some common ground. "Good. I'm sorry I kept trying to shove advice down your throat."

"It's alright. I'm sorry I bit your head off and I wasn't willing to take it. From what Natalie was saying it sounds like it was a big brother instinct." His lip curved into a side smile. "She seems nice."

"She's fucking amazing." I blurt out softly.

"You're scared you're going to fuck it up?" He asked sincerely.

"Extremely." I leaned my head back against the wall. "There's so much I want to tell her, Teddy. She's wonderful, kind, sweet, smart, sophisticated, fucking gorgeous."

"Sure," he sighed. "What in the bloody hell is she doing with a bloke like you?"

I shook my head as I let out a small laugh. "Fuck knows. All I know is, I really don't want to scare her away."

Teddy continued to whisper. "Like I said. Tell her the truth. She seems like an understanding person. I doubt she'll go running to the hills, she doesn't seem like the type of person that would shy away that easily."

"She's not." I agreed. "Are you going to be okay?"

He nodded and took a deep breath. "Actually, yeah I'll be okay. I have my 10 A.M. sushi, and a whole roster of new movies to watch." He patted my shoulder. "Have a good time. If you end up getting frisky, for the love of god do it at her place."

I rolled my eyes as I opened the door once again. There she was unmoved with her eyes closed softly swinging in the sunlight. Every simple thing she does is mesmerizing. She quickly opened her eyes and smiled when she saw me. My heart fluttered against my rib cage.

Teddy followed up behind me on the porch. "It was nice to meet you, Natalie."

"You too. Hey, I was thinking when we come back I can bring over my Switch and we can play some Mario Kart, Smash Bros., or something? If that's cool with you?" She looked over to me. As if she would ever need my permission to do anything. Especially when it comes to spending time and connecting with my family. The fact that she's interested made me even more hopeful that everything was going to be okay.

Teddy looked over at me with surprise then back to her. "You game?"

She shrugged. "I prefer PC gaming, but I have a few classics I hit up every once in a while. I must warn you though I'm ruthless when it comes to Mario Kart."

I raised a brow at her then looked back at my brother. "Uh oh, she's coming for your title Teddy."

"Well, I can't say no to a challenge." He flashed the first genuine smile I've seen since we got here. After one conversation with Teddy she's able to get him to open up, I do it and I'm the bad guy.

I need to learn her ways.

"Sounds like a plan. See you later." She waved as she made her way down the porch.

"Bye!" Teddy leaned over to me and whispered, "Marry her."

"Goodbye, Teddy." I turned back to my girl and watched her lean on the hand rail patiently waiting with a grin on her face. The more I see her, the harder I fall. I didn't think it was even possible to fall further than I already have. There's that tug again as I met her on the stairs and quickly interlaced my fingers with hers.

At this rate I'll never want to part from her again. A pit falls in my stomach at the very thought of leaving her by the end of the month. I knew I wanted to be with Natalie since the moment I found her, but now that Teddy said those two words, the idea made my heart skip. If I thought I was a goner then, I'm good as gone now. And, there's still plenty of time for a fuck up on my part.

Once we got settled in the car, she took a long breath. "Dean. Did my eyes deceive me, or is your brother *Tanner Brunswick?*"

I paused with my seat belt in hand.

Oh shit.

Natalie

"Technically, his name is Theodore Eugene Roberts." Dean paused, looking nervous. "But, some people do call him by his stage name."

"Which is?" I asked calmly.

"Tanner Brunswick." He said it as if I was ready to blow up.

I returned a strange look. "Why are you looking at me like I'm about to freak out?"

"Because that's the usual reaction?" He kept his eyes on me. "Did you know it was him when he opened the door?"

"I had a suspicion since there are look-a-likes out there, but since we've been publishing so much about him lately I've been seeing his face everywhere-" I paused. "Oh my god." I put my face in my hands to hide myself.

"Natalie? Whoa, hey. Talk to me." He took my wrists into his hands. His touch was starting to feel more and more comfortable.

"You're going to absolutely hate me for this." I thought back to all the posts the company has been writing about Tanner's engagement, his past, what kind of food he eats, rating his outfits, even using paparazzi photos.

"Natalie. Look at me." He held my hands in his. I locked in with his hazel eyes and immediately began to relax. "There is nothing in this world that could ever make me hate you. You are the kindest person I've met, hell, you talked my brother down from a seemingly impossible argument we were having earlier without even fully knowing what it was about. You approached him with kind words while putting him in his place. Which is something you'll definitely need to teach me how to do." We both laughed as he went on. "You were willing to spend our entire first date on the porch because you knew I was having a rough morning. There's nothing you have done that would make me hate you."

"Even when I work for a company who judges every single movie your brother stars in, the clothes he wears, and food he eats?" The guilt began to wash over me again.

"I'm his older brother, I do that on a daily basis." He smiled at me as I laughed at his attempt to lighten the mood. "I'm sorry I didn't tell you."

I shook my head. "You don't have to apologize. Coming from someone who works in the media, I don't blame him for wanting to hide away for a while, especially right now." My eyes widened again. "Holy shit! That's why you have beef with Ell! It all makes sense now. Something's going on between them."

He sucked air through his teeth. "Yeah. The details about that I'll leave up to Teddy to tell you. However, I'm sure you can probably guess it's not great since he's here and not in Europe touring with her."

"Yeah, poor Teddy. I know what that feels like. Not the tour thing obviously," I tried to lighten the mood a little more. "But, the rough patches, it's not exactly a party." I caught his jaw clenching before I went on. "Well, I won't pry any further, and I promise I won't tell anyone."

He stared down at our now intertwined fingers that seem to fit together a little too well. "I know. Thank you for being understanding."

"I appreciate you telling me the truth."

He took in another deep breath as if he was about to tell me something else. As if, there was something he *needed* to tell me. I gave him a reassuring look.

"Dean." I whispered as he turned his head to me. "You don't have to tell me all of your deepest darkest secrets on our first date. It's okay. We're still getting to know each other. You don't have to share anything you're not ready to tell me."

He hesitated. "Are you sure?"

"Yes." I laid a kiss to the back of his hand. "Unless it's a significant other you forgot to tell me about. If that's the case I'll steal her for myself and send Riley after you."

That earned me a smile as he lightly shook his head. "Nothing like that."

"Good. So. What do you say we get out of here, have some lunch, and do some first date things?"

"Abso-fucking-lutely." He laid a kiss to the back of my hand before handing me the cable to plug in my phone. "For my beautiful passenger Princess."

A shutter went down my spine. *Beautiful. Princess.* I looked over at him as he started the car and shifted it into gear. Why did my body react to those words? Flashbacks of my fever dream suddenly replayed.

"A beautiful sight, Princess. Your body is beautiful. You are beautiful."

He did have a secret he was ready to tell me. Could Kayley be right? Am I sitting next to *Dean Craven?*

I shove the thought aside as we drove off and reminded myself, if this outlandish theory is true, he will tell me in his own time. He's spent his entire career keeping his identity a secret, he's not going to tell a girl he's only gone on one date with.

Then again *if* it is him, and he's been able to keep his identity hidden for so long, what else is he hiding?

Throughout the entire lunch I tried to keep myself distracted and talked about literally anything other than work or anything closely related to voice acting. Which, in the end, worked out fairly well considering I just found out that his little brother was Tanner fucking Brunswick. That was a bombshell I was not ready for.

I laid my chin in my hand as I leaned on the table, getting lost in his hazel eyes. I could stare into them all day. "So, why did Teddy choose to go by Tanner?"

Dean folded his arms and leaned on the table. His face is gorgeous, one that had women and men kept turning to catch even the smallest sight of him. He blatantly ignored them throughout the entire lunch, so, I did too.

"Mum came up with it, since he started in the business very young she didn't want him to go by his full legal name. The Brunswick portion was Dad's addition. He said it was very 'posh' and 'fit him well'." He gave a half shrug, "I don't remember exactly where it came from."

"Did your parents ever think he would be this popular?" I tried my best to not sound like a journalist doing a documentary on his brother, but I couldn't help but be curious.

He nodded, "I think they knew it was a possibility. They were fully prepared for him to get tired of the acting and move on to something else but," he shrugged, "as it turned out Teddy fell in love with it. He loved the entire world of Hollywood."

"And now?"

"He's having a hard time. He's always loved his job, whenever he got a new project he'd never shut up about it. He used to call me while he was on set, tell me who he's working with, who he got to tackle or make-out with." He chuckled at the memory. "Needless to say I was able to honor *his* NDA more than he could."

I let out a light laugh and thought back to his first comment. "Is he having a hard time because of," I rock my head, "who he's engaged to." With people around us I didn't want them to hear Ell and suddenly perk up like meerkats.

"Yeah." He nodded. "His entire career skyrocketed when they announced their relationship."

"I remember. It was all everyone would talk about."

He nodded in agreement. "He got four movie deals within the first year and a half of their relationship."

"Jesus. That must've been a lot for him."

"It was." He sighed. "And now, after five years they're tying the knot." He took a quick drink of his water, as if he wasn't thrilled about the arrangement. When he talked about it yesterday I knew he wasn't a fan of hers, and he all but confirmed it in the car. Given his disdain right now it seems as though he never did.

"I take it you don't exactly approve?"

"Never have." *Called it.* He shook his head. "Seeing what he's going through right now has only furthered my disapproval."

"And that's why he's here with you on your trip. To mend fences?" Well there went my no work rule.

He nodded. "He needed time to get away and think, so he decided to tag along."

"Wait." I blinked. "You didn't invite him?"

He shook his head. "Nope. I told him I was heading to Indianapolis and he said, 'Great, I'll meet you there.'"

I laughed. "Seriously?"

"Yeah," he smiled. "He's lucky I reserved a place where there was more than one bedroom."

"Oh c'mon you wouldn't share your room with your brother?" I joked.

"For a month, hell no. I'd kick his ass to the couch before I'd ever let him sleep in my room. I can barely handle being in the same house as him, let alone the same room."

I shook my head as I smiled at him. "I feel that way with Kayley sometimes, she has no sense of privacy. She'll just come in unannounced while I'm in the shower and talk about the most random things." He continued to give me his undivided attention as I blushed when he moved his eyes to my lips. "Then when she's gone for a week, I miss her. Is that what it's like to have a sibling?"

"No." He stated bluntly. "Well, not with my brother and I anyway. We can go for months without seeing each other. We call from time to time, but it's been less and less frequent these past few years."

"How come?" He paused for a moment. "I'm sorry." I blinked out of my question. "I don't mean to pry into you and your brother's relationship on a first date."

He reached for my hand, laid a kiss on my knuckles, and started brushing his thumb over the spot. "You can ask me anything. We are on a first date after all, like you said it's where we get to know one another."

"True. I guess on most first dates you talk about your favorite food, work, or the occasional embarrassing story from your childhood." He continued to stroke his thumb over my knuckles as if it was second nature to him.

His eyes softened as he looked up from our hands to my eyes. "A beautiful wise woman once told me that a first date can be anything you would like it to be, as long as you're both enjoying each other's company it can be as extravagant or as simple as you want it to be."

My heart began to flutter once again, this man has me under a spell that I can't seem to break away from, and I don't mind it one bit.

Once we finished off our lunch we took a walk around our town's square, where he handed me a bouquet of lilies as if from thin air. I had no idea where or when he got them, and when I asked he said it was a family secret. One that his father taught him when he was younger. I couldn't help but smile at that. From the way he talked about his parents it seemed like they had a relationship worth looking up to. A part of me was eager to meet them, because they sound like the cutest couple I've ever heard of. Aside from Riley and Rob of course.

Dean had his hand in mine the entire afternoon as we went around looking through antique shops, a local game store, even at a local arcade bar where we stopped for drinks. If his hand wasn't in mine it was at my waist, and if it wasn't at my waist it was at the small of my back. Then landing on the back of my neck as he kissed me and pulled me into a discrete corner of the park. I've never had this need for touch on a first date, but when it came to Dean I needed it like my next breath of air.

He felt so god damn good, so gentle, and mindful until I would give him the green light and kiss him even harder. If we didn't hear a few distant voices we probably would've devoured each other right there behind a tree. Clearly Rob's calculations didn't take into account how this man kisses me, because fuck it's so good. At this rate, I'll have this man in my bed by tomorrow.

We were able to make it back to the car in the garage just before dark. Everything about this date was absolutely perfect. I got to learn about the games he liked, we picked up the most random things we could find at the antique shops, and the entire night there wasn't a single awkward moment. He learned how to make me laugh, he listened to my rants about certain games and books, I even got him to blush at the bar when I put my hand on his thigh.

I could tell it took all of his strength not to take me right there, his eyes were filled with lustful warning. One I really wanted to push to see where it would take me. I found out quickly that it brought me right next up against his car, hands in hair, teeth clicking, tongue fucking, chest heaving, hot and messy make out session. If a car alarm didn't stop us I was fairly certain we would've ended up in the backseat. Not that I mind, but the logical part of my brain is warning me to slow down with this guy. Judging by the way he closed his eyes and pressed his forehead to mine, he was thinking the same thing.

We ended the day with going back to his place and playing Mario Kart with his brother just as we planned. I allowed him to have a few rounds of practice before we started, despite Dean's judgment.

"If you're truly worthy of your title then you shouldn't need to practice." Dean spoke up as he set up the Switch.

"I'm not used to these controllers, I gotta get the feel for it, figure out its quirks." Teddy looked over the controller in his hand.

"You're not test driving a car Teddy, it's a game controller."

"That's exactly what it is."

I tried to keep my laugh in as they innocently argued. While that practice session did help loosen his gaming fingers it didn't help him against the blue shells I kept tossing at him.

Teddy and I sat on the floor, as Dean sat on the couch right behind me watching us try to destroy the other. He had one leg perched on the couch and the other planted to the floor on the other side of me as he leaned into the corner of the couch. While technically being in between his legs it only caused me to lose focus twice.

Teddy was a good sport as I won two out of three, then three out of five. Dean greatly enjoyed watching us play throughout the night. It didn't hit me until after we finished our last round that I had just played Mario Kart with Tanner fucking Brunswick. I had completely forgotten while we were playing and as I listened to the two of them innocently argue for ten minutes. They're just like any normal siblings, and now I don't see Tanner anywhere. Just Dean's little brother Teddy.

"Damn." Teddy wiped the sweat off his brow. "You weren't kidding."

I shrugged. "I had a lot of free time before my friends and I started a book club."

"Well, if my title deserved to go to anyone, I'm certainly glad it went to you." Teddy jokingly bowed.

"Thank you. I appreciate that."

I caught a subtle look he exchanged with Dean. "So. What kind of book club did you and your friends start?"

"Teddy," Dean chimed in, "It's pretty late, maybe you should head to bed."

He shrugged. "I'm still on L.A. time I'm fine."

"You like to read?" I slightly shifted the conversation because I haven't told Dean what kind of books I read yet. It's not that I'm ashamed, I just didn't want to tell my first date's little brother that it's a spicy romance book club.

"I can guarantee you he hasn't read a book in years." Dean continued to stare him down speaking a language that Teddy knows and I clearly don't.

"I read. I'm offended you think I don't. I actually just auditioned for an adaptation of 'The Deal Breaker' and I read the entire book before the audition."

"Really?" I gasped. That's one of the most popular titles in the romance genre right now.

"Really?" Dean questioned in a low tone.

"That's so cool! I didn't know they were turning 'The Deal Breaker' into a movie." We read that one a few months back, of course I listened to Dean Craven's audiobook and we all gave it four point five out five. It really lived up to the hype.

He leaned over and whispered. "You didn't hear it from me, but it's actually a show with the rest of the books from the series."

"You're kidding! I listened to the audiobook and it was fantastic!"

"Really?" Teddy looked over at his brother, who was still giving him a glare. "You like audiobooks too, right Dean?"

"This is probably the last time I'll ask nicely. Please, go to bed."

I looked down at my watch seeing it was almost 11 P.M. already. "Oh, damn, I should actually get going. I have to go into the office tomorrow." I groaned as I stood up. Dean quickly followed, giving his brother one last glare.

"I'll walk you over."

I waved to Teddy. "Have a good night, Teddy! If you get bored I have plenty of books and games for ya to borrow."

He stood and stuffed his hands in his pockets. "I appreciate it. It was nice meeting you."

"You too! I'll see you later." I replied as Dean and I made our way outside to the porch.

"You know. I don't think anyone has connected with Teddy as well as you have tonight." He said in a low whisper as we made our way to the driveway that separated our yards.

"He's a nice guy. Whatever is going on between him and Ell I hope it all works out for the best." He put an arm around my shoulder and kissed the side of my head. God his touch will never get old.

"You and I both. I truly appreciate you offering to spend some time with him. I also really appreciate you taking him down a peg in Mario Kart because that title was really going to his head the last time we played." We both laughed as we approached my porch.

"Glad I could help." I stepped up on the first step that brought me eye level to his lips. "I had a really great time today."

"So did I." His lips met mine for what felt like the hundredth time today. I've quickly come to the conclusion that there is no such thing as kissing this man too much. Any excuse he can find to lay his lips on me I have happily welcomed and I will continue to do so. My mind began to race with thoughts about what it would feel like to have his lips all over me.

No. It's only the first date.

Then my brain went silent as he deepened the kiss and pulled me in closer by wrapping his arms around my back. As he pressed his body into mine I could feel how turned on he was again. For the love of everything I wanted to bring this man inside. I need to know what he feels like, what he looks like.

Fuck it. "Do you want to come inside?" I whispered in a hot heavy breath. So much for waiting. I didn't even know what he was doing here in the first place and I'm inviting him inside to do unspeakable things.

He pressed his forehead to mine and turned in his lips as if he was trying to harbor all control he had left. "You have no idea how much I want to say yes."

I clicked my tongue. "I think I have a pretty good idea." I tried to lighten the rejection.

He let out a soft laugh as he licked his lip. "There's something I need to tell you first."

"Is it about what you're doing here in Indy?" I asked as he lifted his head and his apologetic eyes looked into mine.

"Yes."

Dean

Here I am kissing the most beautiful woman I have ever laid my eyes on, she asked me inside and I said, "you have no idea how much I want to say yes".

I'm a fucking idiot.

I literally crawled through her window to make her fantasy come true and I'm standing here instead of walking inside, *after she invited me in*, because *now* I'm feeling guilty.

My entire body is screaming at me for not telling her about my job sooner.

I must've paused for too long when she replied, "If you legally can't talk about it, I understand. Just tell me one thing."

I gave her a curious look.

"Is it life threatening? Because, I do plan to ask you out on a second date, and I really hope you can make it." Her smile is contagious and lightens the mood within seconds. My girl is amazing at that.

I shook my head. "No. Even if it was, I would do everything in my power to get to that second date."

"Good." She paused and took in a deep breath. "How about this, tomorrow, come over for dinner and you can tell me then. We'll have plenty of time to talk and that'll give you some time to mentally prepare. I know this morning was…"

"A lot?"

"Exactly."

I instantly relaxed. Another thing that's become reactionary whenever I see her. "You continue to blow me away with your understanding. I still don't think I'm deserving of it."

She moved her hands up to my cheeks. "What makes you say that?" I melt under her touch. I take in the feeling as much as I can because I have no idea how she's going to react tomorrow. One of my worst fears could become a reality within a matter of hours.

I just got her, I don't want to lose her, and I will do everything I can to keep her. But… "You may not want to see me again after I tell you."

She shook her head. "After being with you today, I highly doubt that. Whether you're a janitor, a surgeon, or a graffiti artist, I still want to get to know you. Like I said, I plan on asking you out on a second date."

I gave her a half smile as I brushed stray hair from her face. "You are extraordinary."

"I know." She laughed as I kissed her smile and made her blush. I'll never get used to the feeling of having her in my arms. I wanted to savor every moment I had left with her as two people who just found each other.

"I'll see you after work tomorrow?" She whispered against my lips.

I rubbed my nose lightly against hers. "Of course."

We had our final kiss of the night where I barely had enough strength to let her go. Every bone in my body was telling me to never let go, but I had no choice. Once I made sure she was inside, I quickly walked back to the house. There was a little brother I needed to teach a lesson to.

"Teddy!" I called out angrily after I closed the front door behind me. I ran upstairs to find his bedroom door locked.

"Teddy. Open the fucking door."

"Not until you calm the fuck down." He called from the other side.

"Did you at least tell her who you were?"

I paused for a moment as I leaned on the wall. "No."

"What? Why not?"

"Because my little dickhead of a brother bit my head off this morning, and I didn't want to overwhelm her." I yelled back. "You had no right to pull that little stunt you did earlier. *You* do not get to dictate what or when I tell her. "

"I was just trying to help!" He paused. "She deserves to know, Dean."

I leaned back to look for a key to unlock the door. I saw the silver glint on top of the door frame. I let out a short amused breath as I silently grabbed it.

"I know she does." I stuck the key in and lightly turned it. "And she will." I opened the door to find him at the other side of the room, shocked that I unlocked the door. "On my own terms, and after I kick your teeth in."

"Now, wait a minute!" He went to the other side of the bed.

"What the fuck were you thinking?"

He grabbed the side of the bed as if he was ready to throw a sheet at me.

"Look, I wasn't okay, clearly, but you should've told her before you showed up at her office tomorrow. I mean, what are you going to do? Surprise, I'm actually a spicy book narrator, your neighbor, your boyfriend, and your new VO who's infiltrating your shady place of work, nice to see you."

"We went on one date Teddy, we haven't put a label on it."

He looked at me dumbfounded. "That's what you took away from that? Look, I saw the way you were looking at each other. She's going to be around for a while. She's going to find out eventually and it needs to be from *you*." He sighed. "Like I said, I don't want you to make the same mistakes I did."

"I'm not and since when are you so invested in my dating life?"

"Dean, you said it yourself. Your agent is your best friend, and you hardly ever stop working," He put his hand to his chest proudly, "I can't carry your social life and my own."

I made a move towards him as he flinched. "Look, okay, fine, I think she's great, especially for you. I haven't seen you smile like that in a long time." Teddy put his hands up in surrender. "I'm sorry, okay? I was just trying to help."

I took a deep breath as I processed what he was saying. As much as I hate to admit it, he wasn't wrong.

"While I appreciate your concern, please, next time just ask if you can help or wait for me to ask for it. You don't have to try and swoop in with a terrible segway, that probably broke a few NDAs."

"I thought I did an excellent job." He looked offended.

"You're lucky I didn't throw you up the stairs. Also, when were you going to tell me you auditioned for 'The Deal Breaker' series?" I crossed my arms and stood tall at his only exit.

"Now?" He squinted his eyes waiting for my reaction.

"Please tell me you didn't audition for the main character."

"Funny you say that…"

"For fucks sake, okay," I groaned. "Do you know how many scenes are in that one book alone? You haven't had any experience in that area, how the hell are you going to pull off an entire series?"

"The Deal Breaker" was one of the few books that launched my career. The sarcasm, tension, the scenes, all of it flowed together making the perfect mixture for a top rated romance book. Once it went viral, all bets were off. It was only a matter of time before it made its way to the big screen. Though, I didn't foresee my little brother auditioning for it. Especially the main fucking character.

"*If* I get the part I'll have a great mentor. You have experience in this genre." He shrugged as he moved around the bed.

"Not in front of a camera dip-shit." I pinched the bridge of my nose as I took a moment to collect my thoughts. "Why did you audition for a piece like this?"

"I know, I don't normally go for parts in rom coms."

I threw my head back as I closed my eyes. "Wait a minute. Please, tell me you *actually* read the book."

He shrugged. "No. I said I did to connect with Nat and steer you in the right direction to talk to her."

I turned in my lips trying not to give my brother another lecture. "How much of the script did you read?"

He finally relaxed and sat on the edge of his bed. "A few pages. An interaction with the friend, with the female main character, and a confession of his feelings towards the female main character." He thought back. "That's really it. Based on that I figured it was a rom com." He paused. "They did mention something about my experience in action in movies."

I blink twice at him, he really had no clue what he was getting himself into. "Teddy. I want to think about this for a second. What kind of books do I narrate?"

"Mostly female porn."

"Ah, no." I stated sharply. "First of all, romance books are not *porn*. That's a common stereotype of the romance genre. Yes, there are quite a few with sex scenes, some more intense than others. However, that doesn't make it porn. Think of it this way, when you see a couple of sex scenes in a box office film, does that make it porn?"

He scrunched his nose. "No."

"Exactly. Most romance books have a plot, just like your movies. Well, some of your movies." I jabbed as he gave me a "fuck you" look. "Whereas 'porn,'" I continued, "has very little plot and gets straight to *business*. In the romance world, if the scenes outweigh the plot ratio-" I paused. I can't believe I'm having this conversation with my little brother right now. "Back to the point. Try again. What kind of books do I usually narrate?"

He rolled his eyes. "Mostly romance books."

I let the eye roll slide for now. "Good. Now, with my register, I often pick certain sub genres such as Fantasy, Dark-"

"Wait. What does that have to do with 'The Deal Breaker'?" He questioned.

I stared at him for a moment. "You do know I narrated 'The Deal Breaker' right?"

Teddy's eyes went wide. "No!"

"Fucking Christ." This was going to be a very long conversation. I wiped my hand down my face and couldn't help but laugh at my brother's demise.

"This isn't funny Dean!" He stood and began to pace.

"It's a dark mafia romance, Teddy. How the hell did you not know there were very explicit sex scenes in it?"

"I didn't read the packet my agent gave me, okay? I knew it was a book within the romance genre and there were a few funny lines, but I thought that was it!"

I let a few low chuckles slip before he shot a worried look my way.

"Look. I'll tell you what, I'll ask Natalie if she has a copy for you to borrow. Read it, if it's not for you, then tell your agent you're no longer interested. Why did you even audition for it in the first place?"

He went quiet for a moment.

"Ah." I hung my head as I started to piece it together.

"We had a fight because everyone was commenting on the 'chemistry' she had with one of her backup dancers. I tried to talk to her about it, but it turned into a big fight. She said, 'I wouldn't question you like this if you had a romantic scene with a co-star'."

"So you auditioned for what you thought was a 'rom com'. And you thought, what, that kissing a co-star on screen would be a good way to get back at her? Make her see you?"

He nodded. "The script was good though."

"It's a great series. There's a reason why the studio picked it up." I looked down at my brother as he sat back on the edge of his bed. This situation with Ell is really starting to get to him. I promised I'd give him space and time to think things over. However, it's hard to see him struggle like this.

"Just, think about it, if you decide to go through with it, I'll help you. You just have to promise me something."

"What's that?" He turned his attention to me with that look again, one that makes me want to give Ell a piece of my mind.

"Don't do it to get back at Ell. Do it for you, and your career. Okay?" I waited patiently for his response.

He lightly nodded.

"Good. Now that that's settled. Get some rest."

"Yeah." He muttered.

I turned to walk out the door before Teddy said something that halted me in my tracks.

"Hey. Good luck tomorrow, you're gonna need it."

The first thing I do in the morning is look out my window. It's become a part of my routine at this point. Before I even pick up my phone, I lean against the window frame and watch my girl sleep peacefully through the slit of her curtains. When she stirred awake she rubbed her sleepy eyes and turned off her alarm. Six A.M. My girl is up early. Her drive is about twenty minutes to the office, her shift usually starts at nine, but *Brock* sent me an email saying that apparently our tour begins at eight. She better be getting compensated for her extra time. If not, I'll make sure they do.

After the look she gave me last night, it gave me the unsettling feeling that she might have an idea of who I am. My heart raced at the possibility, what is she going to do? Is she going to immediately recognize that it's me? If not, would she try to flirt with me even after she went on a date with… well me? Fucking Christ, am I really getting jealous of myself?

The fuck am I on right now?

I shook the thought out of my mind and started getting ready.

The goal is to be out the door and gone before my girl is even finished getting ready. If she saw Dean Craven walking out of this house, well, I know for a fact we'd be late for work.

I dressed in my usual black pants, black button up with a few open near my neck and rolled up sleeves, a subtle silver chain around my neck, a variety of silver rings, and can't forget the blue contacts. To be honest, I hate these fucking things. Luckily, I brought my newer pair, they fit better, and didn't try to blind me every time I put them in.

When I first started out, I bought cheap ones which was a mistake on my part. I could only wear them for an hour tops while I created content. They burned like fucking acid and made my eyes go bloodshot to where if my parents video-called me they'd ask if I was high.

Once I placed the contacts in, I finished my hair with a wet messy look. I looked at myself in the mirror and Dean Craven was staring back at me. This character I created to protect my identity so I could live a normal life. Reflecting on what Teddy said last night, did I even have a life to protect before this? Is that what I'm doing with Natalie? Will she even want a life with me after this, not just me but Dean Craven too?

I turned to leave the bathroom, grabbed my black face mask and my jacket to head downstairs. I slipped on my jacket to see Teddy already up with a coffee in his hand.

He raised a brow. "Don't you look spiffy!"

"What are you doing up so early?" I shifted to my American accent, if I'm going to be using it all day, better start now.

He tilted his head and raised his brow. "Oh, the American accent too? You're pulling out all the stops."

"I have to, Teddy. Why are you awake?" I didn't mean to be in a sour mood. I had a million thoughts racing in my mind and holding Natalie the way I did last night was all I wanted to do today.

"I just wanted to see you off." He raised his hands in surrender.

"Why?" I looped one strap of my mask around my ear.

"Well, I was going to wish you more luck, but since you're dressed like a wet dream for women with daddy issues, I don't think you'll have a problem." He threw his hands up again as I glared at him. "And to find out what your plan is? That is if you have one?" He questioned with a gossipy look.

"I do have one." I plucked a piece of toast from his plate.

"Mind sharing with the class."

"Nope. Don't burn the house down while I'm gone." Luckily I peered out the window before I stepped outside. Natalie was ready to go and on her way out the door. Dressed in jeans, her company t-shirt, a flowing cardigan, and white converse. It didn't matter what she wore, she looked amazing in everything, and I'm sure it would look even better on the floor.

My thoughts quickly shifted when she locked the door with her phone to her ear as if she was talking to someone. I looked at my phone, it's seven.

Why is she leaving early? Maybe to get coffee or breakfast? Shit.

"She's out there isn't she?" Teddy whispered as if she could hear him. Then I saw her walk over the gravel driveway heading straight towards our house.

"*Fuck.*" I am covered in head to toe Dean Craven and she's about to walk up my front porch expecting to see Dean Roberts. "Cover for me." I whispered to Teddy.

"What? No, just tell her!" He whisper-yelled.

"Now is not the time, Teddy! Fucking cover for me!" I whispered back as I slipped into the downstairs bathroom.

"Shit. Okay? What should I say? You already left?"

"No you idiot! The car is still in the driveway." I immediately regret leaving this to Teddy, but I didn't have a choice. This was not a part of the plan. Then again, nothing on this trip has gone "according to plan".

"Tell her I'm in the shower or something. You're an actor. Improvise."

I shut the door, lock it behind me, and lean against it to listen as she knocked at the front door.

"Hey! Nat! Good morning!" Teddy stated awkwardly and shaky. It took every ounce of control I had to not burst out there and strangle him. How the hell he got cast in all those action movies I'll never understand.

"Morning?" She sounded as though she was questioning his sanity. I was right there with her. "Everything okay?"

"Yeah. Yeah. Ya know, everything's great. Went for a walk this morning so the fresh air got me up and at it."

I pinched the bridge of my nose.

A fucking Emmy nominee? I questioned every god in existence. *Seriously?*

"Got it." She laughed nervously. "Well, I just wanted to stop by before I headed out for work. This is for you and Dean. It's banana bread that you two are *required* to share evenly." I put my forehead to the door. She's so fucking sweet.

"Oh, wow. Thank you so much. That's sweet of you. Smells fantastic."

"Thanks. I couldn't sleep very well last night, so late-night baking it is." I narrowed my brow. I don't remember her waking up. Did I fall asleep before she did?

"I'm sorry about that. Everything alright?" Teddy asked with what sounded like genuine concern.

"Yeah, yeah. I'm fine, it's just work related. Nothing too crazy. Oh. That reminds me. Today, I'm going to have a meeting with my manager and see if we can slow down the coverage on your engagement."

My eyes went wide.

"Really?"

"Yeah. I've been meaning to have this conversation with him about our celebrity coverage for awhile now. It's getting out of hand and I can't just sit by anymore, something needs to change." She paused.

"Wow. I don't know what to say. You'd do that for someone you just met?" Teddy questioned. Of course she would, she's fucking amazing.

"Now, to be fair, I feel like I've known you for a good chunk of my life. Being in the movies I grew up watching and all." She laughed. "Oh. Shit. I gotta go. I'll let you know how it goes. Say hi to Dean for me. I'll see you later!"

"Yeah. See ya, thanks again!" I heard the faint click of the door shut and Teddy being quiet for a moment. "She's gone."

I unlocked the door and slowly walked out.

He set the bread on the table and gripped the back of one of the chairs. He had a serious look in his eye as he stared at the bread.

"You better know what you're doing, Dean. Because if you break her heart. *I'll* kick your arse."

Natalie

I was a little upset with myself that I didn't catch Dean before I left for work. I was hoping to confirm that we were still on for tonight in person, but text I suppose was the next best thing. I texted him right before I took off, and started up my 'House of Mischief' audiobook.

Normally, I don't listen to my audiobooks in the car. Especially Dean's. It got to the point where it was a little too distracting when I needed to focus on driving. However, this morning Kayley called me and asked where I was in the book and that I needed to read the next chapter as soon as I could. It shouldn't be that bad. We just came off a very spicy scene and we're exploring more plot. So, I thought I was safe, until Dean's voice hit me in the face like a truck.

"'Do you love me?' She asked, looking up at me with those green doe eyes."

"Dammit." I whispered to myself, "I'm going to cry aren't I?"

"I wanted to say yes. Everything in my body wanted me, and begged me to say yes. That I love her more than anyone else ever has, more than the moon loves the stars, more than the sand loves the ocean. I wanted to tell her how I've loved her since the moment she walked through my goddamn door.

But I can't. If I do, I'll lose her. She'll be here, but her spark will be gone. I'll lose the very thing I love, this gorgeous, inspiring, intelligent Princess.

My *Princess. If I say yes, that will change her mind. I can't keep her for my own selfish reasons, not when she's finally found something that she knows will make her happy. She deserves better than this, better than* me.

All I've done is lock her away in this dusty mansion, trick her, tease her, scare her, and punish her for trying to leave. A flower who only wanted a little sun, but got plucked and stuck in a vase on a counter because she was pretty.

I'm still the same monster she fears. I'm still the same husband she was forced to marry. She didn't choose me. She didn't want this. She doesn't want me. *I'm still the same fucker who told her to get on her knees and beg, when I should be the one on my knees for her.*

It's too late for that now. She's looking up at me begging for an answer. I can't hold her hostage anymore, she'll lose her spirit if she does. If I say yes, it'll trap her here, if I say no my heart will never heal. I'd rather see her thrive in the sun than see her wilt with me. Even if it turns me cold for the rest of my days, I'll know she's happy living the life she desperately deserves.

I feel a heaviness on my chest. My heart knows what I'm about to say, and it can't take it.

'No.'

She winced as she took a step back as if the word pierced her heart too. She doesn't want me, she doesn't want this, nobody wants this, no one wants to spend their life with me.

'Then the rumors are true. You really don't have a heart.' Her lips quivered as she ran out of the room. My heart sank as I gripped the back of my office chair. It began to crack as I tossed it across the room. Papers floated in the air, and books flew off the shelves as I destroyed my office. I cut my hand on the glass of the frame she gave me with our wedding photo, and I didn't notice until I saw red smears all over my desk.

I found myself on the floor with my bloody hands in my hair, and tears falling down my face as my heart began to ice over... again."

Before I knew it I was already pulling into our parking garage with my mouth agape.

"Holy shit." I whispered, wiping away tears.

"Goddammit. This is why I can't listen to audiobooks in the car." I scolded myself as I grabbed my things and headed out to the office after I checked my makeup and wiped away the last of my tears.

There's a cute little coffee shop that I stop in every morning to grab a cold brew and a bagel. Was it healthy? No. Was it needed, especially this morning, *fuck yes*.

I stayed up way too late tossing and turning again thinking about Kayley's insane theory. A theory that seemed to be piecing itself together and fitting way too well for my liking. That's when I decided to turn my brain off and make some banana bread for Dean and Teddy. There was a little part of me that wondered who I would see at the door this morning. Considering Teddy answered it I wasn't sure if I was relieved or disappointed. He was acting rather strange. I shoved the thought aside.

When Dean comes over I'm sure he'll explain everything.

I made my way upstairs and opened the door at 7:55 A.M. Perfect, on time. This wasn't my usual time, but with Brock wanting to have the tour at eight instead of nine I was obligated to come in early. I'm a little thankful it was earlier, two meetings with Brock and a tour that might take up most of the day, I knew I wasn't going to get much else done today.

I said hello to the video editors that work from eight to four. They all tiredly waved back as I made my way over to the other side of the office.

"Hey Nat!" Charlie, one of the editors, walked up to me. "What are you doing here so early?"

"Hey Charlie! I'm giving a tour to a new VO this morning." I set my stuff down at my desk as he followed.

Everyone's desk was out in the open space. Each area gathered different departments. Mine, of course, held everyone that had to do with publishing content including myself, Miranda, Ben, Megan, and Amy. My team. Another was content quality, video editors, and writers. It's usually pretty vacant, most of the company works from home. So, why do we have a physical space, other than for our tiny ass set? I'm not really sure. It doesn't feel needed since we haven't used the set in over a year anyway.

Then, of course, we can't forget the private offices. They weren't hard to miss since there were only three of them next to our private meeting room. One for Brock, one for the COO, and one for the CEO. *Nathan.*

Off the top of my head, I've only seen him maybe twice. Yet, the man has a full ass office with a desk, computer, TV, couch, and one of the camera's conveniently facing his door just to make sure no one is entering his office. To top it all off, it's one of the biggest office spaces we had. We *could* use it for production equipment storage or even a small VO room.

Since that's not the case, I get to show our new VO our old individual audio booths we have set up in another secluded walled off section of the open layout, next our tiny set.

The booth's age wasn't the problem or the size of the set. It was funneling money towards the things we don't need like, buying multiple audio booths when we don't have enough content for in house VOs or industrial coffee makers, rather than investing in assets that any successful media company should have.

If this VO turned and ran I wouldn't blame them, nor would I stop them.

"That's right." Charlie looked around as he leaned in close. "I heard from Helen in HR that he's really, and I quote, 'nice to look at'. We might need to keep an eye on her to make sure she doesn't break a few protocols."

"Helen is a 68-year-old happily married woman. I don't think we'll have a problem." I reassured him as I pulled out my laptop.

"Or so we think." Charlie gave me a side eye. "Remember the Christmas party? I had to peel her off of Santa's lap."

I tried not to laugh at the memory. "Well, it was your fault for spiking the eggnog. Which was totally cliche by the way."

"Hey, it was a boring ass party, I don't regret a single thing. I also seem to remember you drinking from it after you saw me spike it."

"Fair enough." I laughed. "Look, whoever it is, I'm sure it'll be a one time thing and they'll work from home after they see this mess. That is if they stick around."

Charlie shook his head and whispered. "Actually, I heard he's staying here in person for the entire month."

I whipped my head to him. "Wait… what did you just say?"

"Nat!" Brock's voice sent a chill down my spine. "There you are. Our new VO will be here any minute."

I put on a fake smile and shoved the thought aside. "Morning, Brock." I subtly turned back to Charlie. "Duty calls." What a great start. I'm here a little early and my boss is acting like I'm an hour late. It's going to be a long ass day.

I heard the door to the office open, and I'm suddenly frozen as time began to slow.

A man dressed in all black stood tall as if he owned the place. His familiar black face mask and striking blue eyes made my heart fucking stop as Dean mother-fucking Craven, the man that just broke my heart with his voice in the car this morning, walked towards us. His eyes locked with mine and I think I'm going to pass the fuck out. I could see his eyes soften for a beat as he approached us still as if in slow motion.

Holy fuck.

He looked as if he just walked out of my fantasy and straight into our office. The pictures on his social media don't do him justice. Some of which I totally don't have saved right now. I noticed the small veins and outlines of his knuckles as he shook Brock's hand tightly. The amount of times I've pictured those hands roaming all over my body. Just like he did in my fever dream the other night. Suddenly, the room temperature went up about ten degrees and it's getting harder to breathe.

Holy shit. Holy shit. Holy shit.

"Mr. Craven. Welcome to World Entertainment Media." Brock presented.

"Thank you. Pleasure to be here." There it was. His fucking voice.

I'm. So. Fucking. Screwed.

I caught Charlie behind them mouthing. "What the fuck." I gave him a subtle "yeah, no shit" look.

"This is Natalie Green. Our Video Content Manager, she's currently working with our VO's and will be giving you your tour today. Natalie. Meet Dean Craven. Our newest voice talent."

He locked eyes with me again, and I stayed fucking frozen. Then the smell of his cologne hit me as he approached. A very, very, familiar clean cologne broke me out of the spell and the initial shock of seeing my celebrity crush walk through the door.

There's no fucking way.

"It's nice to meet you, Natalie." He stuck his hand out to shake mine. I lightly grasped his hand, and it all began to fucking click. I thought Kayley was crazy, I thought all my friends were out of their minds, hell even I thought I was losing my mind. But… It's really him, and he's my fucking neighbor.

"Well, I need to head into a meeting." Brock looked at his phone. "Natalie here will show you the ropes and I'll check back in within the hour." He pointed to me. "Take good care of him."

"I have a feeling I'm in good hands." Dean held eye contact with me. Oh you cheeky, little shit.

God, I feel so stupid for not seeing this sooner. Looking back all the signs were there, I just shoved it all aside and called it crazy because it was! Because there's no way in hell fate would align it as perfectly as it did.

I need to get my shit together.

While I may know who's under that mask, hell, kissed those lips under that mask, no one else in the office knows who he is. Knowing him, he wanted to keep it that way. I intend on keeping it a secret, but that's not going to change the fact that we're going to have a long conversation after work today.

I have so many questions. He knew I worked in the media industry, did he have any idea it was the same company? I don't remember telling him the name. He doesn't seem that shocked to see me either.

Then again, maybe he's keeping his cool because it might give away the fact that I know who he is. If people knew that we *know* each other that'd open a whole other can of worms. One that I don't want to deal with, and I'm sure he doesn't either. Was he afraid I'd run because he narrates spicy romance books for a living? Wait... why *is* he here? It's not like we pay well.

I must've stayed quiet for a beat too long as he tried to get my attention. "Shall we get started?"

I shook my head. "Yeah. Of course. Sorry, it's nice to meet you, *Dean.*" I began to smile because laughing at this situation is really the only thing I can do at this moment. "Let's get started."

I did most of the talking as I took him around the office meeting video editors, a few writers, and a couple members of content quality control. All people who usually work eight to four since the nine to five people haven't made their way in yet, thankfully.

If there were any more people in this office to ogle him I'd need to get a broom and tell them to leave the man alone.

The entire time, no matter how many people stared at us, Dean gave me his undivided attention. Just like on our tour of Indy, and our first date. I blushed at the thought. I couldn't help but be attracted to that quality. Especially when he does it so well.

I showed him around the set and then finally the row of the old audio booths in a secluded area of the office. He stayed quiet as he stepped into the booth to check out the equipment.

"I know it's not much, but it's enough for voice overs on five to thirty minute videos." I crossed my arms as I leaned on the doorway. I hung my head debating on breaking my work persona for a moment. "You know, I'm actually a big fan of your work."

He raised a brow at me. "Really?"

"Yeah. I've listened to quite a few audiobooks and I'd have to say you're probably my favorite." I tilted my head. He breathed sharply as I saw his cheeks rise as if he was trying not to smile. "You're very talented." I added.

"I'm flattered. Do you have a favorite?" He asked as his eyes softened again, looking a tad bit red. His contacts must be bothersome.

I sucked air through my teeth. "Well, currently I'm reading 'House of Mischief'. Which made me cry from heartbreak this morning. Thanks for that by the way."

"Chapter twenty?" He asked.

I nodded. "But, I would have to say 'The Deal Breaker' was *fantastic*." I leaned in to whisper. "I hear they're turning it into a series."

His brows went up. "Are they now?" He shook his head with his cheeks still raised as if he continued to smile. "Is that from a reputable source?"

I couldn't help but laugh and lick my teeth. If he was going to be cheeky about this then so was I. "I'd say it's pretty reputable."

He crossed his arms as he leaned back against the wall. "Well, hopefully they get a good actor and don't go for a popular hire like Tanner Brunswick."

"I don't know, I think he'd be a pretty good pick." I smiled.

He laughed. "Well, I hear he's got his hands full, and doesn't have experience with that kind of genre."

"Is that from a reputable source?" I squinted my eyes at him.

He dropped his head as he laughed. "*Very* reputable."

I licked my top lip as I gave him a soft look. I can't be angry at him for keeping this a secret. I understand that keeping his identity hidden is important to him, and I respect him for it. I wouldn't want him to give up something he worked so hard for because we went on one date. However, I still have so many questions that need answers.

"So." I continued, even though I know exactly who this man is, he's still going to be working with me for the next month. That's another thing to think about… nope not right now. I wave my arms around the area with the booths. "What do you think?"

He took in a deep breath as if to remind himself where he was. "This will work. Your equipment is a little outdated, but nothing I can't work with."

I nodded in agreement. "Yeah, unfortunately, this equipment is rather low on the priority list. It's a little dusty, but still works great."

"Like I said. Nothing I can't work with." His cheeks rose again. A part of me misses his hazel eyes and his natural voice. I know it's him under there, but a part of me wants to see *him*.

Whoa. Okay. That's a new feeling. My heart began to flutter again. Yes, I'm attracted to Dean Craven. Very much so. I have for a long time. Yet, I'm also craving to see the man who has made me laugh these past few days, the one who always has his hand nearby to hold. Those eyes are his, but they're not. That voice is his, but it isn't. My feelings began to muddle. I just want to see him, *all* sides of him. This is about to get way more complicated.

I cleared my throat. "That's great. I actually have a couple of scripts for you ready to go. If you wouldn't mind trying out a few lines to test out the equipment. It's been awhile since we've used it and I want to make sure everything is working properly."

"Sure. Anything you need." He reassured me.

My heart fluttered again as I handed him the scripts. "Great. Thank you."

After a few technical difficulties we finally got everything hooked up. I put on my headphones and pressed a button so he could hear me.

"Alright. Let's do a sound check."

"Sure." He took a moment to get comfortable before his voice brushed against my ear. Like it has many, *many*, times before. "Sound check. 1. 2. How did you know it was me?"

I looked towards the entrance to make sure no one was lingering and pressed the button. "Your hands were the initial tip off. Then, your cologne made it all click."

"My hands? Really? Do you stare at my hands often, Natalie?"

I stretched my neck and bit my bottom lip to keep my snarky comments in. It was like I was listening to a book that was tailored for me. Suddenly, the room began to feel warm.

"Natalie." He drew out my name to get my attention. "Are you avoiding my question?" He asked in a seductive tone I know all too well.

I cleared my throat before pressing the button. "Sorry, I didn't quite catch that." I teased.

The sound of his laugh caressed my ears. "Oh look at you pretending not to hear me. Let's try this again. Sound check. 1. 2. 3. Are we really doing a sound check or is this an excuse to hear *your* name on *my* lips?" He paused as I was stunned into silence. "Did that come through or would you like me to say it *over* and *over again?*"

Holy hell this man's voice has me in a fucking choke hold. I took a deep breath to try and collect my thoughts. This is going to be a lot harder than I thought. He, of course, isn't going to make things any easier if he keeps teasing me like that.

I pressed the button. "Dean."

"Yes, *Natalie?*"

Now he's doing it on purpose. "Don't make me come in there."

"I'm more than happy to make you come anywhere you please."

My eyes went wide. I peeled off my headphones and went to open the door to the booth. There he was with that mischievous grin on his face and headphones wrapped around his neck.

"Dean, what are you-?"

He pulled me into the booth with him and shut the door behind me. It was a tight fit with the two of us but Dean had no trouble pulling me close to him.

"Jesus! We're at *work*," I whisper yelled, "you can't just say things like that-"

His lips landed on mine before I could say anything else. His tongue forced entry as the temperature in the booth began to skyrocket, my cheeks were hot as the kiss deepened with his thigh pressed in between my legs. It took what little self control I had left to not grind against him. Suddenly that self-control was gone when he slipped his fingers in my hair. I lightly tugged at the sides of his shirt as my hips began to move on their own.

"I don't give a fuck where we are." He growled into my lips. "Given the fact that you're grinding yourself against my thigh, I have a feeling you don't either." I don't know how or when he did it but the top button of my jeans was open and his fingers are already sinking into me. He kept his lips to mine suppressing my whimpered cry as he hooked his fingers in exploring me as he pressed his thumb against my clit. He suppressed another one of my cries with his lips and released a satisfied groan when he could feel how wet I was.

"Is this why you were staring at my hands, Natalie? Wondering what they felt like inside you?" He whispered.

"Yes." I whispered into his lips.

His grin turned mischievous. "Good. Now, while I'd love to hear you scream my name on those gorgeous lips, I need you to stay quiet as you come for me." He already had me on edge and when he circled my clit and found that special spot with his fingers my body did as he said. His other hand covered my mouth to keep my soft cries muffled as I came around his fingers.

"Such a good girl." He purred with satisfaction. "My god. You look so beautiful coming around my fingers."

"Natalie!" Brock's voice echoed into the room.

Oh fuck!

Here I was still feeling the waves of an orgasm on Dean's fingers and my boss just fucking walked in! Luckily, there was no way to see inside the booth otherwise I'd be in deep, *deep*, shit.

He swiped one more time over my clit that sent a final jolt of pleasure through my body.

Holy fuck this man is going to give me a heart attack.

He kept his lustful eyes on me as he switched hands, putting the one coated with my arousal over my mouth and the other with one finger up to his lips. Telling me to keep quiet while I internally freak out.

He put his mask back on and opened the door enough to where Brock could only see him.

"Ah. Mr. Craven. Has Natalie left you to handle this equipment all by your lonesome?" He sighed. "Apologies. She's supposed to be attached to your hip today."

More like I was attached to his fingers, but sure. I rolled my eyes. Of course he's going to find any excuse to prove that I'm not doing my job properly. Dean's warm hand pressed a little harder on my mouth as if he could feel I was agitated by Brock's insinuation.

"No apologies necessary." He stated in a slightly aggravated tone. "She's allowing me a few moments to get *acquainted* while she uses the restroom."

Yeah. I think to myself. *Getting acquainted with my insides that's for sure.*

"I'm assuming she's allowed to use the facilities at any point in the day," he continued, "or is that on a timely schedule too?"

My eyebrows raised. I wasn't expecting that, and it's taking all of my energy to not react. If my boss finds me in this booth, freshly finger fucked, *my* arousal on *Dean's* fingers on *my* face, with my pants unbuttoned, I'm screwed.

"Oh, uh," Brock stumbled over his words. "O- of course not. I'll let you get back to it."

Dean gave him one last glare before Brock left the area. He shut the door and pulled his mask off. "Does he always call for you like that?" He stated in an irritated tone as he slipped his hand away from my mouth. He brushed his thumb over any wetness he left behind on my lips and cheek and licked it off his thumb.

I nodded as I buttoned my jeans. "Yeah. Unfortunately." I let out a relieved breath before I cleared my throat. "We should get back to work. Before I do something that'll get us both fired." I muttered.

He raised a brow. "If you think what we just did *wouldn't* get us fired, I'm intrigued to know what will."

I paused as I exited the booth. He has a point there. I'm still all hot and bothered and ready for another round but after that incident I shouldn't even entertain the notion. However, it's really hard to do that when he's leaning against the door frame of the audio booth with a sinful grin, lustful eyes, and a bulge in his pants that I instantly regret peaking at because it just made my need *worse.*

After a few takes we finally got a decent sample of the scripts. He read through every line perfectly, and my god I was right. It was going to be a chore for me to control myself while listening to his voice at work. Either I'm going to need to start bringing extra pairs of underwear to work or Dean and I will need to do some sessions *at home*. I squeezed my eyes shut while keeping my thighs firmly pressed together. Remembering every single touch, every single stroke of his fingers inside me. I still can't believe that Dean fucking Craven just finger fucked me in an *audio booth*. A fantasy I didn't think was possible, and didn't know that I had until he was knuckle deep inside me, and I desperately want to do it again.

While I usually find the idea of getting caught in public areas hot, when Brock came in earlier as I was coming *in the audio booth* my heart dropped into my stomach. Reflecting on it now, I wasn't sure if I was more scared of *my boss* finding Dean finger fucking me, or of him seeing Dean's full face.

Obviously keeping his identity a secret is important to him, and the idea of a juicy story makes Brock froth at the mouth. So, I have to help Dean any way I can to make sure he doesn't find out.

I pushed the thoughts aside as I listened to the audio again. Dean's voice was so perfect I almost missed a key factor. These scripts were… ass. They're book reviews, and it didn't sound like the writer even read the book to begin with. Dean sat next to me with his mask on and arms crossed as we listened to what he recorded.

I peeled off my headphones as he gave me an understanding look. "It's garbage." I rubbed my forehead as he raised a brow looking offended. "Not you. You were fantastic." I quickly tried to redeem myself. "It's these scripts." I picked up one of the papers. "They're just…"

"Garbage." He reiterates.

"You agree?" I leaned back in my chair.

"One hundred percent." He flipped through one of the scripts. "I know these are 'opinion' pieces but some of it doesn't make any sense."

"Right? They described the ending to 'The Den at Lion's Gate' as 'predictable' and 'unremarkable'. The book ended with her barely clinging to life. Her love interest's best friend, who wasn't dead like they thought, turned out to be his actual brother, and he was the one who shot her. How can you call that 'predictable'? Lemon Drop Media literally said it had the biggest plot twist of the year. Yet we're calling *that* 'predictable'?"

"Seriously." He agreed. "I remember having to flip through those pages to make sure I was reading it correctly." Dean thought for a moment as he narrowed his brow. "Do you know who wrote these?"

I looked through the names and I didn't recognize a single one. Which was *odd*.

"No." I muttered. I ignored the small alarm ringing in my head. They probably hired some freelancers or something. That wasn't uncommon.

"They must be using freelancers. Which is fine, it just seems like they're getting people who haven't read the books in the first place." I pinched the bridge of my nose. "I'm sorry, Dean."

"For what?" He looked at me confused.

"This." I waved my hand over the scripts. "Unfortunately, this isn't the first time in recent months reviews were written like this. They want the content out so fast our writers barely have enough time to watch the TV show or movie they're reviewing, let alone write and develop opinions about it. If you don't want this attached to your career I wouldn't blame you." I chuckled because what else can I say. It's a shit show here. I'm still questioning why I'm here some days.

"Is this how you sell all your VO's?" His cheek raised behind his mask as if to give me a side smile. God, I wish I could see it right now.

"No. But, between you and me, you're the biggest name on our roster. This is usually where VOs get their start, not in the middle of their established career." I gave him a curious look as he turned to me.

"Are you asking me why I'm here, Natalie?" His eyes looked into my, still a little red.

"Yes." I whispered.

"Natalie?" Brock's voice echoed around the office. I nearly jumped out of my skin when I heard it. I closed my eyes to collect myself.

"Yes, Brock. What's up?" I called back as my boss turned the corner. I can't control what my face does when I see him walking around in his socks and flops. I know this is a casual office space, but the idea of *Brock* changing out his shoes in his office gives me a level of ick I wish never existed.

"Ah, there you are. Hope the tour is going well." He stopped in front of us as Dean gave him a glare that could cut through a diamond. Every instinct wanted me to put my hand on his knee and tell him to turn off the "I'm going to hurt you if you come any closer" look.

"It's going great." Dean's jaw clenched under his mask as he looked through his eyebrow at Brock. "Natalie has been an exceptional tour guide. You should give her a raise."

I turned in my lips trying to keep my reactionary words from spilling out. While I could tell that statement had some serious undertones, Brock laughed it off.

"That's great! How are the scripts? Fantastic, right?"

I exchanged a look with Dean. I gave him a warning look, that he apparently wanted to ignore.

"Have you read any of these books?" He questioned.

Fuck, here we go.

I know these scripts aren't award worthy, but unfortunately there's very little I can do within *that* department. Would I give anything to write book reviews for a living, absolutely. However, I wouldn't get the creative freedom here, nor would I want my writing attached to this company. They have an agenda they want to push and they already don't listen to me about my own department.

I'm already going to be pushing it when I address the tone we use with celebrities. Luckily, I have a curve around that with hard proof and statistics from our platforms. But this? This was a different beast entirely. Brock views this as *his* shiny new project. Therefore, *his* recognition and 'ideas' are the only things he cares about.

"No." He shrugged. "I don't have time for reading these days."

"Hm. That's what I thought." Dean muttered under his breath before he went on. "How about your writers? Did you provide them with a copy of each book to read?"

Brock narrowed his eyes. I knew the answer before it even left his crusty lips.

"No. We tell them the title and request a review within a timely manner."

Dean gave him a judgmental look. "How long did you give," he double checked the paper, "Stephanie, to read and write a review of 'The Den at Lion's Gate'?"

Brock began to shift. I knew Dean couldn't give a shit if Brock was in charge or not, he'd still have a job after this. Brock also knows that Dean is too valuable of an asset to fire, so guess who he's going to blame when things don't go his way… me.

"No more than two days." He shrugged. "I heard it was a hit, so if it's that good, it shouldn't take them long to read it."

Dean closed his eyes for a moment. I could see all the thoughts running through his head, because I was thinking exactly the same thing. Just because it was a hit doesn't mean everyone will like it, let alone read it in *two* days. Not everyone has the same reading pace. This definitely shed the light on how unorganized and how thoughtless the upper management is in this company. If Brock wasn't in front of me. I'd tell Dean to run and it's not even one in the afternoon on his first day.

"This book alone is over 675 pages." Dean responded. "I narrated the audiobook myself and it took me over a week to read it *twice*." The image of him curled up on the couch with a book in his hand made the butterflies in my stomach dance. I would never interrupt someone while they were reading, but my god I'd sit on his lap in a heartbeat if I saw his fingers between those pages.

Stop it. Feral. Jail.

Brock's eyes widened. "675 pages?" He practically shouted. Thanks to him I'm back to reality, the only time I'll ever be thankful for his shrill voice. "Jesus, what do they have to say to take up over 600 pages? Practically the damn Bible."

Dean looked at me with an "is he serious" look. I minorly shrugged as I pressed my lips into a thin smile.

"Mr. Craven. I realize this is your first time working with a media company. As I'm sure *Miss Green* has stated, we're essentially an online newsroom." He went on. "We have deadlines to hit in a fast paced environment. I can't give my writers a week to write a review. The attention span and viral window is very limited."

"I understand that." Dean argued. "However, these are *opinion* pieces on books that came out a couple of years ago. We haven't scratched the surface from books that were published this year to what's being released in the future."

"You're very passionate about this project, and that's awesome. I love that energy." Brock tried to explain as he waved his hands around. "But, we don't have that kind of time. We're still in the early stages of this project. We have plans for it, but for now we have to start small."

I shared another look with Dean. AKA we don't have the budget and we're not going any further until we see a graph that points up. Welcome to World Entertainment Media where they don't care about the content just as long as it gets views and revenue.

Brock turned to me. "Natalie. Have you taken your lunch yet?"

I raised my brows. He's never asked if I had lunch, I guess he really wanted to try and lay it on thick for our guest.

"No." I said suspiciously. "I haven't."

"Great. Before you go, could you send me those copies of the test runs so I can look them over?"

I breathed sharply through my nose and pressed my lips together to keep any unwanted words from slipping again.

"Sure. Will do."

"Thank you. Also don't forget, we have a meeting today at three."

You mean the meeting where I'll defend my newest employee like her job depended on it. Yeah, I promise I won't forget that one.

"Yup." I gritted out.

"Great! Mr. Craven, if you would like to come with me we'd like to take you out to lunch for your first day."

Dean stayed unmoved. Given the look he was giving Brock I would guess he didn't want to go anywhere with him right now. I continued to stare at him confused, because he's never taken a new employee out to lunch for their first day. Ever.

"Actually. I invited Miss Green out to lunch today as a thank you for showing me around. Perhaps another time." My eyes went wide for a moment. Yup. My guess was correct, because we definitely did not discuss that. Hell, I didn't realize it was lunch until Brock came in.

"Oh." Brock looked shocked for a moment. "Of course, yeah, no worries. Here. Take the company card, if you change your mind we'll be at Chuck's down the street." He set the card down in front me. I'm dumbfounded. Brock never gave one of his employees the company card to pay for lunch, nor has he ever offered anyone to join the higher ups at Chuck's.

"Thank you." I narrowed my eyes a bit as I stared at the card. Once he left he wiped a hand down his face as if the man had never seen rejection before.

I swiveled my chair to fully face Dean, leaned back, crossed my leg over the other and my arms across my chest.

His cheeks raised again as his eyes softened. "Would you like to go to lunch?"

I shook my head as I thought for a moment. Still being cheeky. I couldn't help but laugh. "Sure. Let me send this to Brock and we can head out."

"Where would you like to go?" He asked as I opened my laptop.

"Anywhere but Chuck's." I joked as I attached the files and sent it over.

"Agreed." He stood as I closed my laptop and offered his hand to help me stand. I hesitated before I took it. He held it for a moment and brushed his thumb across my knuckles just like he did yesterday. A movement that instantly made me relax.

I still can't believe this is all happening right now. If you would have told me last week that Dean Craven was our new VO I would've been freaked out all over again. I still am a little bit, but it's not because Dean Craven is here in front of me. It's because he's also the man currently staying next door, a man who I've come to *really* like.

Dean

Brock's blood ran from his nose, down his untucked short sleeve button-up, and his back hit the floor after my fist landed straight into his nose. That's what I pictured when he asked me to go to lunch with him in front of my girl. While it's taking all of my restraint to take that motherfucker down a peg, I remind myself who's sitting next to me.

When I walked through the doors this morning, I was so nervous I felt sick. Seeing Natalie's surprised look on her face made my stomach turn, but then she talked to me near the audio booths and I felt an immense sense of relief. I couldn't help myself but pull her in with me after teasing her. I needed my lips on hers, I needed to feel her touch on my skin, her warmth against me. I just couldn't wait. Selfish of me I know, but seeing how quickly she unraveled under my touch, it was worth it.

I know she still has a lot of questions. Ones that I will be more than happy to answer, once we're back home and far away from anyone at the office. Especially *Brock*.

Usually when you look at someone you can get a pretty good guess about their personality. With Brock, I could smell the bullshit from the plane. Telling my girl to continue to work on her lunch hour, while inviting me out right in front of her.

Fuck no.

I can't believe he gets to spend every single weekday with her instead of me. That cockroach doesn't deserve to be in her presence at all. The thought makes me want to scoop her away from this place and bring her back to Chicago with me.

Again, is it selfish? One hundred percent. Is she at that point too? More than likely not. So, stealing her away for lunch every day will have to do. For now.

We were able to sneak off to a little diner down the street to pick up the food we ordered earlier. I haven't had my mask or contacts in for this long and it was really starting to get to me. I thought the newer ones would be better, but I guess it's my eyes not the contacts.

Shit, how am I going to do this for the next month? Now that we know how small this project actually is, with funds tighter than Satan's arsehole, I highly doubt they're going to have me come in every day.

Unless they're having their freelance writers pumping out a couple of scripts every week. Where would they get the money for that if they're spreading it across multiple writers? Unless they're using freelancers they already have. This is their first time making content about books, so if that's the case their writers more than likely are not familiar with the niche. That explains why the reviewer sounded as though they never read the book in the first place. They're giving their writer's assignments they know nothing about.

If that's the case there's a lot more going on than I thought. Thankfully, it's not anything illegal, but it's a shitty practice that will lead to closed doors if they continue like this. If the content's shit, no one will watch or interact with it, therefore no revenue. From the sound of things it's already headed that way and the blame is definitely going in the wrong direction.

"How can you work with someone like that?" I questioned as we walked down the sidewalk with food in hand.

"You know that American accent is really throwing me off." She narrowed her eyes on me.

"Really? It didn't seem to throw you off earlier." She tapped my arm as she laughed and I went on. "I wonder what other accents have that effect." I teased.

"Dean." She laughed as I walked backwards in front of her.

I cleared my throat and imitated each one going down the list.

"Maybe *Russian? No? That one's common in the Mafia genre.*" I thought for a moment and adjusted. "Oh, how about *Italian? I haven't gotten jobs for this one in awhile but it's one of my favorites.*"

She couldn't help but smile and laugh. "Oh my god."

I snapped my fingers. "I got it. How about *Scottish? Ever since that TV show came out that one's been requested a lot.*" She continued to smile as she tried to hide her face at the scene I was making on the sidewalk. "*If this is your favorite love, I'll commit. I'll wear the kilt and the white flowing shirt if that's what it takes. I won't take you to see those rocks though, I'm not losing you to some beefy Scottish lad from the 1700s.*"

Her face was beat red from blushing as she smiled at me.

"So, which one *tickles your fancy?*" I stated in a more posh tone.

She bit her bottom lip as she thought about it. "I think I like… all of them."

I shifted back to my natural accent. "All of them?" I questioned.

"Well, yeah." She lifted her shoulders. "They're all you."

My chest suddenly felt tight as I stopped in my tracks. "What?"

"They're all you." She turned to me. "So of course I'd want to hear every accent you can imitate. You're very talented. However, I will be impartial to your natural one, because that's the one you're most comfortable with and it embodies *you.*"

I suddenly didn't care if we were out in public, I put my free hand on the back of her head and laid a kiss on her forehead. I hated that my mask was in the way, but it happened so fast, so instinctively I didn't even clock it. I was so worried if she would prefer one persona over the other, I should've known that doesn't matter to her, she cares about *me*. She wants to know *me*. *All* of me.

"You don't know how much I appreciate that, Natalie."

She let out a small laugh. "I think I do." She laid a kiss on my cheek as she continued to walk, leaving me behind.

I caught up to her as I raised my brow. I caught up to her as I raised my brow. "You know, the entire time you've been sweet talking to me you've been avoiding my question."

"Which was?" We continued walking.

"How can you work with someone like *that*?" I pointed to the building.

She breathed sharply trying to as she thought for a moment. "I guess I've learned to tune out some of the bullshit over time."

"You'll have to teach me your ways so I can make it through the month without getting a lawsuit on my hands." I stuffed my free hand in my pocket to keep me from reaching for hers. Every muscle in my body wanted me to reach for her again. Since we're in a public space near her office where her coworkers could be nearby I kept myself restrained. I already risked it *twice*.

While I couldn't give a shit if the entire world saw me claim her mouth right here, her job was important to her. And, I'm assuming kissing and getting finger fucked by the new VO is not a part of her job description.

"I don't know. It took years of practice and patience." She smiled up at me.

"Yeah, I'm probably a lost cause." I paused and shook my head. There's that burning question still in the back of my mind. "Okay. I have to ask. What made you stick around all these years? You and I both read those scripts and they were not written by experienced book reviewers."

She nodded as she pressed her lips together. "To be honest. The time sort of slipped away from me. I loved it at first, and back then the content didn't lack the substance it does now. This was before we started cramming writers with insane deadlines and a certain 'tone' to use. Long story short my former manager thought I was good at what I did and recommended me to take over when he left. So, I climbed the ladder and now here we are years later."

She sighed as she reflected. "As time went on I did start to notice they really didn't care about any of my ideas. Or even the writer's ideas for that matter. Opinion pieces turned into the company's narrative, reviews became more 'awe-worthy', or cringy, to get views and comments. That's what happens I guess when you get a peak behind the manager curtain. It's all about numbers, statistics, revenue, and making sure my team doesn't make a single mistake. Which Brock, has a superpower of doing by the way. If a video doesn't do well, *we* didn't publish it at the right time. If there was a misspelling in the video, it's our fault even though it goes through writer's, editors, and content quality first." She hung her head. "I don't know. I guess now I'm just staying for my team and get my experience in before I find someplace else." She let out a deep sigh before she shifted the conversation.

"So, where do you want to sit down and eat? I usually eat in my car to get out a few good f-bombs, or tears depending on the day, before I head back to work."

I stopped in my tracks. Okay, now I'm really pissed. "You go to your car to cry and eat lunch?"

She looked at me like I was crazy. "Yeah. Well, not when I work from home. Haven't you ever had a job where it made you so frustrated you needed to go to your car and spew out a few 'fuck yous'?"

I don't even think back, the image of her crying in her car because she's so frustrated makes my blood boil. Who the fuck do these people think they are to drive someone as amazing as my girl so mad to the point of tears.

My face must've tipped her off to what I was thinking. "Dean? Hey, no need to burn the building down with your eyes, alright? I'm not the only one who does it, I can promise you that."

"Crying in your car because of your workplace should not be a normal or regular occurrence, Natalie." I gave her a serious look. "For anyone."

She shifted the subject again. "There's a park on the other side of the building with a few picnic tables. It's a little after lunch time so it's not as crowded right now, let's head over there."

She took the lead and showed me the way, while she may think this conversation is over it certainly isn't for me.

After having a lovely lunch with my girl we slowly made our way back to the office. With such a "tight budget" I'm curious to know how they can still afford a space like this. Being an online company they do have a very large space and for what? One small set and a few audio booths that haven't been used in years? All of these jobs, from what I understand, could be done from home, why make them come in? Team dynamic? Not likely, the environment of this place was comparable to a really dusty underfunded library. No talking, no smiling, all with the look of exhaustion from trying to meet a deadline.

We walked back into the office and once again everyone was staring in our direction. Almost everyone, not so subtly, straightened up like meerkats looking over the dividers at their desks. You would've thought my arrival was the biggest buzz worthy event to happen in this office in a long time to get this kind of attention.

"We don't get much excitement around here unless there's a breaking news story. Even then it's followed by an 'aw shit' moment." Natalie whispered. "If you need me to get a broom to fight them off I will." She laughed as if she was joking but I wouldn't doubt that if I told her someone was bothering me she'd take care of it in a heartbeat. Just another thing about my girl that makes her so amazing.

She checked in with her team to see if they needed anything or had any questions on our way back to the audio booths.

When Ben asked about a bug he kept running into on one of the social media platforms she automatically had a work around. When Megan asked which video from the priority list should go out first, she looked over the topics and knew exactly which one should go first. She, Megan, and Amy all rolled their eyes when they saw their titles were almost exactly the same just posting to different accounts. My girl is definitely good at what she does, and she's only proving more and more that they don't deserve her. Or any of her employees really. Miranda is apparently the newest of the group, still bright-eyed and excited she gets to work in pop-culture media. An innocence I'm sure Natalie recognizes.

We made our way back to the audio booths where we looked over the scripts again. Highlighting key areas we knew were inaccurate. While I know I'm no fact-checker, I am a reader. If I saw this review on my own time, I'd definitely have questions.

My girl rubbed her forehead looking exhausted. "This is ridiculous." She snapped the highlighter lid shut. "We shouldn't have to fact check our book reviews." She leaned back and tossed the script back to the table.

I thought for a moment. She has her degree in English… but she doesn't know I know that.

"Do you write?" I questioned. I already knew the answer. Of course she writes, that was the job she originally applied for.

"Occasionally." She gave me a weird look. "I only write for myself, except one time in college. I created a blog for one of my classes."

Right, the one for her media class. It was about navigating life on a city campus. It was organized, well written, and actually informative for any new freshman needing information about the campus.

"Why don't *you* write the reviews?"

She narrowed her eyes at me waiting for me to laugh as if I was joking. "You're kidding right?"

I shrugged. "Why not? You said you and your friends have a book club, you're a 'big fan' of my work, your words." She blushed. "Tell me one good reason?"

"Natalie!" Brock's shrill voice echoed on the other side of the wall. *Motherfucker.*

"There's your reason." She took in a deep breath as if to prepare herself for whatever Brock had prepared.

He turned the corner with a tablet in hand writing on it with his finger. I can't help what my face does when I see all the greasy fingerprints on his screen. He's poking at it like a fucking three-year-old leaving prints and shiny streaks all over it. You can really tell how much someone cares for their craft when you see how they maintain their equipment. Let's just say in Brock's case, it makes perfect sense.

"There you are." Once he saw Natalie he put his head back to his tablet. "Are you ready for our meeting?"

Ah yes, the 3 o'clock meeting that Natalie didn't want to have. She didn't have to tell me about it, considering her face said it all when he reminded her earlier. Which totally didn't motivate me to attach a Bluetooth microphone to his belt loop after running into him in the hallway a few minutes ago.

She took in a final breath. "Sure. I'll be there in a sec."

He nodded and pointed to me, he's lucky he's far enough away I can't break it. "Listened to the audio files Natalie sent over. Great work, Mr. Craven. I already sent it over to editing to get the videos together."

What the actual fuck, those were test runs. As in *testing*. Not ready for content. Why the hell would he approve test runs?

Natalie looked at him wide-eyed, having similar thoughts to mine right now. "Are you serious?"

"Yeah. Why?"

"Those were test runs, Brock." She explained. "We found some inaccurate information in the scripts, we need to scrap them and start over."

"Oh." He looked unperturbed. "No worries. We'll cut the inaccuracies out and use it as a teaser."

"Why go through all the trouble of cutting and editing a teaser when we can re-record and have the first episode ready by this Friday?" She questioned. "By the original deadline."

"Plans shifted a bit earlier today. Nathan loved the idea so much he wanted to see results today and published by tomorrow."

Nathan was the man I spoke to on the phone. Shit, did I hype it up too much? Was this my fault?

"Got it." She gritted out before calming herself.

"Great." Brock paid no mind as he walked out with his tablet that was practically screaming for help. "I'll meet you in the meeting room."

Her eyes went dark for a moment as she stayed silent.

Oh shit.

I've gotten to know Natalie very, *very*, well since I found her. I've only seen a similar look on her once, and that was when I saw her having a conversation with Kayley about work that ended with her screaming into a pillow for a solid minute. The meeting hasn't even started yet and it's already pissed her off enough to have this piercing death glare. To be honest I'm thankful that I'm not on the receiving end, but excited to see what she's going to do next.

"Our meeting shouldn't be long, do you need anything?" She asked before quietly assembling her things.

I lightly shook my head and whispered. "Nope. Do you?"

She turned in her lips as if she was about to let her inner thoughts fly. "Job security would be great. Other than that. No. Thank you."

Princess, if only you know how easy it would be. All she needed to do was say the word and I'd have a bag ready and a flight to Chicago booked for us in a matter of minutes.

Given Brock's record, I don't regret attaching the mic to his belt loop so I could hear exactly what he has to say to my girl. However, I do regret walking out to sit next to Ben and watch her argue with her boss through the glass walls of their meeting room, because now it's taking all of my energy to stay put.

"D- Mr. Craven literally just arrived this morning." She argued. "How could you expect him to record an entire episode in *one* sitting, accompanied with a tour, and learn about our procedures?"

I could do it in one sitting, but I don't take offense. I knew where she was coming from. It can be overwhelming especially in an unfamiliar environment with unfamiliar equipment. Plus, with scripts like these there's a high chance we'll need to do a few rereads. We're going to need all the time we can get. While I would love nothing more than to spend every single second with her on this trip, I wouldn't want most of our time to be spent... *here.*

"Look. I understand your frustration, but Nathan needs results." Brock argued.

"Does he really need it on the first day our VO is here?" She crossed her arms.

"Yes. He wanted to make sure he's a good investment."

"Have you seen his portfolio? Of course he's a good investment." She replied. I couldn't help but grin at her comment as I blankly stared at the scripts I brought with me to pretend to read.

"I don't see the issue here. If he's as great as you say, then why not use the test runs to push out a teaser or two?"

"Like we said earlier, the reviews he read are inaccurate." She paused. "Just tell me this, did they go through a fact checker before you sent them to me?"

He lifted his shoulder. "No. They're opinion pieces. They don't need fact checkers."

She pinched the bridge of her nose. "Yes they do. Especially these, we're starting up a new profile with these book reviews. If we want to gain a following there needs to be trust and accurate information." She paused. "If *I* don't catch these, then content quality will. Either way, it's wasting time. Time we could use to edit, re-record, and have an episode ready by Friday. *The original deadline.*"

"I agree that we need to start on a stable foundation. But, Nathan needs something up by tomorrow, *period.*"

"It takes at least seventy-two hours to get an accurate reading on account and post statistics. If he wants results by tomorrow it's impossible."

Brock sighed. "Fine. Have Mr. My Chemical Romance out there read a few lines that are usable and I'll have one of our freelancers put together something quick."

I scrunched my nose and narrowed my brow at the nickname. That was uncalled for. It's more creative than the nicknames I have for him. Well, we can't have that.

"It can be used as our promo," Brock went on, "it won't take up too much time, and it'll make Nathan happy. Good?"

"Better." She replied.

"Great. Now let's move on to Miranda." Miranda? I knew she was new, is this a reflection on her first ninety-days or something? I remember hearing a little bit about it the other night through her window, but I didn't have much context.

"Okay." She stated hesitantly.

"As you know she put out one of the top priority posts earlier than it was supposed to." He stated.

"The 'Tanner and Ell's History Together' video." She nodded.

"Exactly." Brock stated. "She switched it. It was supposed to be 'Ell's Engagement Ring' video, not the one about their history."

I adjusted my earphones, did I hear that right? Is he seriously upset over switching up posts about the same people?

"Brock. They were both top priorities. The subject matter was the same. Tanner, Ell, engagement. Yes, Tanner and Ell's history was a longer video, but if you wanted it out at a specific time on Saturday, why wasn't there a note on the file?" She paused and flipped around her laptop. "There was no time indicator on this file. Since the history video was a longer post with more content she probably thought it needed to go out sooner rather than later."

No wonder she looked so frustrated after our tour. After she screamed into her pillow I debated on knocking on her door to see if she was okay, but when she started talking about me I couldn't pull myself away. While screaming into a pillow can be effective it's not as satisfying as, say, a bat to his headlights.

"It is *your* job as a manager to *manage* the content schedule." Brock snapped with a disgusting and unwarranted snarl. "*You* should have known this was a longer post therefore put a specific time indicator on the file."

Yup, I'm finding his address.

"This was on Saturday. On weekends I am available for my team if they need me. They have my personal number to call or text me when something comes up, but I am not online on my days off. If this was a *major* post that *needed* a time indicator I would've clocked it before the weekend. Seeing how this was a top priority and not an *ultimate* priority, a label that only comes from *you* or Nathan himself,

I would say that a post with the same priority level going out an hour later is not that big of a violation. She is within her first ninety days. This is her first mistake. If she didn't make *any* mistakes I would be concerned. How else will she, or anyone in this company, grow if we are not allowed to make mistakes?" She paused as she waited for his response.

The look in her eye as she stood her ground, presented the evidence that it was in fact *his* fuck up, all the while looking him dead in the eye. She's in control, calm as she can be, and ready to strike it right back.

That's my girl. Fucking gorgeous.

I caught Ben out of the corner of my eye giving Miranda a reassuring look while the poor girl was on the verge of tears. Over one fucking post with the same topic. This entire situation just reminded me to whoop Teddy upside the head for good measure when I get home.

"Mistakes are unprofessional and could cost us everything." Brock spat.

"Making mistakes and learning from them are the building blocks of *experience*." She replied. "If you have never made a single mistake in your career, then I question all of the *experience* you have on your resume."

I raised my brows and froze as I watched Brock's face turn from pale to pink within seconds.

"Natalie. If this was a post with exclusive footage that we are required, by contract, not to release yet, I would have no choice but to let her go. I can't trust her."

She scoffed as she shook her head. Fucker is missing the whole goddamn point.

"Yet. It wasn't." She responded. "And I know for a fact that she wouldn't touch an exclusive content file."

"You can't guarantee that." He scoffed.

She held back a frustrated grin as she looked through her brow at him. I remained frozen, I will do everything in my power to make sure she never looks at me like that. Because holy fuck my girl is ready to do some damage.

Get'em Princess.

"Yes I can. Because, those files are handed to me *directly* from *you* and *I* take care of them. A rule that *I* put into place with *your* approval to make sure *this* never happens to exclusive content. Remember? A few months back it was a concern while we were hiring so I offered the solution and you took it." She paused. "Back to the main point here." She cleared her throat as she flipped around her laptop to start typing. "I think you need to thank Miranda for her *mistake*, if you still want to call it that, because," She flipped around the computer again, "The Tanner and Ell history post went viral. Our first post, over thirty minutes long, hit 1.2 million views and climbing. Would that have happened if it was posted at its original time? Probably not. Considering we haven't had a single Tanner and Ell post go viral in that spot on the schedule yet. It's amazing how much one hour can affect a post's visibility."

And Brock's face... back to pale. I leaned back in my chair and tried to control my pride for her.

"I suggest we make that one of our permanent time slots for this profile. Don't ya think?" She held her eye contact.

Currently shitting his pants Brock cleared his throat. "Sure. I'll talk with Nathan." He gritted out. "Anything else you'd like to share?"

"Actually yes. While that post about Tanner and Ell did go viral, with help from the time shift, we lost a little over two thousand followers because of it. Our narrative about celebrities needs to change or we're going to keep losing loyal followers." She crossed her arms again.

"We didn't get the following we have today by beating around the bush."

"I realize that, but we're going viral for the wrong reasons here. Celebrities are human beings, how would you feel if someone took pictures and made videos about you and your relationship with your wife? Posting it all over the internet and exposing your private life for everyone to see?"

He lifted his shoulders. "Flattered and surprised they want to take pictures of my wife."

Am I recording this? I looked down at my phone to check. Oh look at that I am. Brilliant, I'll save that just in case.

"What would you have us write then, Natalie? I'm not sending writers to red carpets to talk about the meaning behind their work. It doesn't get the clicks we need."

"Have you tried? It's better than showing paparazzi photos of a couple just trying to enjoy a night out. Or reporting on what they eat in a day, how they 'allegedly' lost weight, or who ran over a rabbit on their drive home labeling them a 'rabbit killer.'"

"That wasn't Tanner or Ell."

"No, it was Ingrid Grant who got canceled for two years because of it."

"And it paid for your salary, I don't see the problem here." He looked at his phone. "I have another meeting to head into, talk to Miranda, send me screenshots proving that she acknowledges her mistake, and have Fall Out Boy out there read those lines."

Now he's just being a dick. Next on the to-do list, make a copy of the recording and send it to his wife. Brock was already on the phone and diving into his office when I saw my girl put her forehead in her hand looking drained of her energy and spark. Seeing her like that only raises my need to plant my knuckles into Brock's face.

Without thinking, I stood tall and made my way over to Brock's office. Before I made it anywhere near close, Natalie was already next to me.

"Mr. Craven. We have work to do. I'd like to get it done before five. Audio booth, two minutes, I'll be right back."

I blinked twice, looked at the meeting room and right back to where she's standing.

How'd she do that?

I could feel the stares piercing through me around the room. Given the same look I saw earlier is currently pinned on me, I didn't give a shit about anyone around us right now. All I can do is wonder how I fucked up within point two seconds to make her pin me down with a stare I never wanted to be on the receiving end of.

Natalie

The minute I saw that Bluetooth microphone attached to Brock I knew exactly who was responsible. When he walked out into the open seating area it all but confirmed it. I continued the meeting as per usual, but my frustration with Dean did make me a tad bit bolder than normal. Now, I'm not sure if I should thank him or yell at him for managing to break a few HR guidelines on his first day.

I sprinted over to Dean as soon as I saw him head towards Brock's office. Since he heard everything I'm sure he wanted to have a small chat. If I didn't catch him, not only would he get fired but I would be an accomplice since I saw the mic and didn't say anything.

I ordered Dean to head back to the audio booth area while I checked in with Miranda. I'm done being pushed to my limit today.

Poor thing was almost in tears as I sat her down in the meeting room and had a sincere conversation with her.

"When I first started I did the same thing."

"Really?" She choked.

"Oh yeah, a few times actually. So has Ben, Amy, and Megan. Even Brock." I chuckled. "You know how a lot of our content is very similar across multiple accounts? To the point where it's literally the same content just with a different aesthetic?" She nodded. "I had the hardest time making sure videos were published to the right profile.

When you're under pressure to get as much content out as possible, things slip right by." I paused. "Miranda, I promise you're not in trouble, okay? Mistakes happen, we're human. Especially when we start a new job. You're still getting used to how things run, and that's okay. Just remember to keep a close eye on the schedule. If something pops up and you're unsure, you can always call me or text me."

She nodded. "Thank you. I hope it didn't cause the post to flop."

I raised a brow and held back my grin. "It didn't. It got 1.2 million views."

"What?" Her eyes widened.

"Yeah. It went viral. We're making it a permanent spot for future content."

She leaned back in the chair. "Wow, that's awesome. I guess it was meant to be, huh?"

"I guess so." I took in a deep breath as I stood to go face a certain voice actor who needed a lesson on boundaries. "Just remember, keep an eye on the schedule, if there's any indicators you don't recognize on the files, reach out alright?"

"Will do. Thank you again, I appreciate it."

I pressed my lips into a thin smile. I knew she was nervous, but when it comes to my team, I don't want them to be afraid to come to me if they have questions. I was terrified to go up to a manager or Brock when I first started, and I hated that feeling. I chuckled in my head at that thought. Now he won't leave me alone. Amazing how things have changed.

"No worries. I'll send a recap message of our meeting your way. Just make sure to reply acknowledging you received it and that we talked things over." I hated this part. Brock and his trust issues required every single manager to make a copy of the acknowledgment after "incidents" like this and file it away. He says it's for HR purposes. However, he actually collects it as receipts to back him up in cases where he wants to fire someone or needs to let someone go due to budget cuts. His level of what he classifies as "incidents" is expanding by the day. Which is only even more concerning. I hate that I fuel it, but if I don't *I'm* the suspicious one.

"Sounds good. Thank you!" She skipped back over to her desk next to Ben and got back to work. He's been a great help with training her when I get pulled to other projects. Like the one currently sitting at the table in the audio booth room looking like a kid who just got suspended.

I am pleased that he followed my direction… the thought sent a small shiver through my body.

Oh, that's new.

That can wait, he's still in trouble and I need a minute to cool-down before I say something I don't mean. I didn't waste time as I picked up the scripts and highlighted the first few lines.

"I need you to read these lines, preferably before the end of the day." I cleared my throat as I handed him the scripts.

"How was your meeting?" He questioned as he stood and analyzed me.

"I think you already know how it went." I crossed my arms. "Read the lines please, and then we'll talk when we get home."

Once five o'clock hit everyone darted out of the office. Dean rubbed his eyes as he got out of the booth. I finished listening to the files and sent them off to editing. Brock of course headed out early, but not before interrupting Dean to tell him it was a pleasure seeing him today. Dean didn't return the sentiment, making him uncomfortable and swiftly taking off as he reminded me to lock up.

We were silent the entire time we packed and walked out of the office. I thought I could use this time and the drive to cool off but it was very difficult as Dean stayed within a few feet from me like a towering bodyguard.

When we finally got home I was exhausted, to be honest I wasn't sure if I had the energy to talk to him tonight. Then I saw him get out of his car and followed me up to the porch and remembered exactly what he did.

Yup, I'm ready now.

I opened the door and threw my backpack on the couch as Dean stepped inside and laid his backpack on the floor next to the couch. I really need a drink, but that'll have to wait, I need to be sober for this.

He closed the door behind him. "Ready to talk?" His British accent made me pause as he peeled off his mask.

"To Dean Craven who attached a microphone to Brock's hip or my neighbor Dean Roberts who I went on a date with?" I questioned.

He nodded as he followed me into the kitchen. "I'm sorry I didn't tell you."

I shook my head. "You don't have to be sorry about that, I understand why you didn't tell me. You've kept your identity a secret for a long time. I know you wouldn't tell a random stranger because it means a lot to you and you wouldn't put something like that at risk. Thinking you can listen to a private conversation with my boss is what I don't understand." I hung my head as I leaned on the counter. "Why'd you do it?" I wanted to give him the chance to come clean.

His tired eyes turned mischievous. "Do what?"

I stood tall and crossed my arms. "You know exactly what you did."

"I've done many things." He replied as he grinned back at me. I have missed seeing his smile all day, and the one time I get to see it is when we're getting ready to have an argument. The sight of him makes me want to drop it entirely.

No. Stay focused.

I licked my teeth. "This is not a joke."

"Never said it was."

I stepped right up to him, pinning him to the counter so he had nowhere to go. "A Bluetooth microphone Dean? Are you fucking serious?"

He blinked down at me as his jaw clenched, realizing how close I was to him.

"Deadly." He used a tone I'm all too familiar with. My thighs tensed at the sound. With that lustful look in his eye I bet he did that on purpose. I shouldn't have told him I was a fan of his, now he's going to use that to his advantage.

Fucking fantastic.

"Don't do that." I gritted out.

"Do what, Princess?" His eyes pinned to me, keeping me in place.

"Stop it. Dean, we're not finished with this conversation." I'm suddenly starting to realize that pinning him into the counter was not the best idea. I could feel the heat radiating off of him as he leaned close to my ear.

"I agree. Your boss really has some nerve to talk to you like that. Why do you let him?" He leaned back as he waited for me to answer.

"This isn't about what he said-"

"You're right, it's about the way he treats you and everyone else in that office." He cut me off.

"I can't believe this." I scoffed. "Who do you think you are? You're here for one day and you're eavesdropping on a conversation with my *boss*. Thinking you know what's best for us?"

He scoffed. "You can't believe someone cares about you so much to keep one ear in on a conversation, to make sure *you're* okay? Ready to jump in and support you any way *you* see fit?" I froze as his tired eyes stared right into mine. "That's who *I* am. I can't turn a blind eye when I know someone is disrespecting you. I know you can hold your own, believe me, I heard every word you said in there. But, if you're telling me to just turn the other way, I can't do that."

Of fucking course he did it with the best intentions. How the hell am I supposed to be mad at him when he's supporting me in every situation?

"Look. I appreciate your intentions, but I don't need your help, I'm perfectly capable of handling these situations on my own." I turned away from him to add some distance.

"I know you are, but that doesn't mean you have to do it alone." He straightened as he stood his ground.

I turned back to him. "Supporting me and crossing a line are two different things, Dean." I reminded him and myself. "It was uncalled for."

He held his stare as he licked his top lip and stepped closer and closer until he had *me* pinned to the opposite counter.

"If it'll make you feel any better, think of it this way. I'm here under contract. A contract, thanks to your boss not reading every single line, I can break any time I want and record in the office wherever I am comfortable." He lifted his shoulders. "I just so happened to be connected to a microphone owned by my current employer that somehow got stuck to his belt loop. Very unprofessional. If anyone is crossing the line here it's your pathetic excuse of a boss, and it was one thousand percent called for after hearing the things he said."

He held both sides of my head with his thumbs on my cheeks.

"Listen to me." His natural voice filled the thick air around us. "When it comes to you, I will do anything to make sure no one hurts you or disrespects you. Even if that means you get pissed at me for it later," he continued as he brushed my cheek with his thumb, "because you are the kindest, strongest, most beautiful person I've ever met. If you want to handle a situation on your own I will respect it, but I will always be right behind you."

"Dean…" All my words slipped away from me. "I- I don't know what to say."

He let out a short deep breath as if to realize his error. "I apologize for not clearing my actions with you first. If *Brock* wasn't a slimy prick, I wouldn't have gone into protective mode. Which can be… unpredictable. Especially with you."

"I appreciate your honesty. " I shook my head. "But, this is my workplace, there are boundaries."

"*Our* workplace."

"That doesn't make it better." I chuckled as I let out a stressful breath. "If anything, that just makes this more complicated."

He leaned close enough to where his nose brushed against mine. "Workplace or not, I will not have some low level man think he can talk to you like that, make you cry in your car, and cause you day to day stress. You deserve more than that." He paused as he kissed my forehead.

"We've only known each other for a few days and gone on one date. For all you know, it very well could be what I deserve."

He brushed his thumb against my cheek again as his eyes softened. "It's not. I heard what you said in there. I saw the way you calmed my brother down. Hell, you brought over banana bread this morning just because. Shitty people do shitty things and deserve shitty karma. You, Princess, are not one of them." He laid another kiss on my forehead as I leaned into his embrace. His clean cologne filled my senses as his warm body pressed against mine. I took in an exhausted breath as he put his hand behind my head.

"This just got way more complicated didn't it?" I muffled into his chest.

"Technically, you and I did have a date *before* we started working together. However, I can see dating your favorite narrator, coworker, and neighbor all at the same time can get a little *complicated*."

"Before we discuss that, take your contacts out."

He narrowed his brow as he gave a confused look. "Why? You prefer your hazel eyed neighbor over your blue eyed bad boy celebrity crush?”

I pressed my lips together to keep my smile from appearing. *“Minor celebrity.”* I jabbed.

“Ouch.” He clutched his chest as he smiled down at me.

I inspected his eyes again. They looked dry and itchy, but he stayed unmoved as if he didn't care.

“Your poor eyes look like they've suffered enough for today.” I brushed the side of his cheek. I'm still stunned that this man is the same person who's had a choke hold on me for years, and he's looking at *me* as if I'm the only person in the world. Saying things to me no one ever has. I didn't miss those keywords, there's just so much I haven't processed the weight hasn't hit me yet. Or maybe, it's because deep down I feel the same way.

After he took out his contacts and placed a few drops in his eyes I pulled out everything I needed to make dinner.

“What are you doing?” He asked.

I gave him a strange look. “Making dinner?”

“Absolutely not.” He stated outright as he entered the kitchen.

“Excuse me?” I glared at him.

“Here. Sit down.” He pointed to the bar chair on the other side of the counter. “I'll cook, you ask me questions. After today, it's the least I can do.”

“You're offering to cook me dinner?” I asked as he guided me to the bar chair.

“I told you, I like to cook. Baking is where I struggle. And, technically I'm not offering, it's non-negotiable.” He winked.

“Right. So…” I paused. “I don't even know where to begin.”

“Well, let me ask you this. How long have you been following my work?” He began to familiarize himself around the kitchen.

I pressed my lips into a thin smile, debating whether or not I should tell him the whole truth. To be honest I wasn't sure if I wanted to say. It's not that I'm embarrassed, I just don't know how he's going to react when I've practically stalked him for a few years now. I took a deep breath. "A while."

He caught my eye through his brow looking intrigued. "How long's awhile?"

I sucked air through my teeth. "About three-ish years now."

He looked a little surprised. "Really? Three years?"

"Yeah. Look, if that makes you uncomfortable, I understand. However, if you're going to judge me for it then we're wasting our time."

He gave me a serious look as he walked over to the counter to face me. "Natalie. Why would I judge you for reading a genre you love? Especially when *I'm* the one reading them to you."

My heart began to flutter again. "Fair point." I muttered as he went back to the stove.

He paused and turned to me again. "So, what do you think, now that you know who's behind the mask."

"I thought *I* got to ask the questions here." I smiled as he raised his hands in surrender.

"Apologies. Just curious."

I thought for a moment. "If you're asking me if you were everything I thought Dean Craven would be, no." He nodded as he hung his head. "You're more."

I saw the slightest peak of his smile as he turned to walk around the counter, hooked his hand behind my neck and brought me to his lips. It felt as though he had been waiting all day to touch him again. Pressing his lips harder against mine as if he couldn't get enough just like he did in the booth.

"Dean," I pulled away for a moment as he began kissing my cheeks. I couldn't help but smile and laugh, "Dean, the stove."

"Dinner can wait." His mischievous grin made me smile harder.

"Are you really going to serve me overcooked chicken after telling me you like to cook?" I joked.

"Oh god, no. We can't have that." He smiled as he laid one last kiss to my forehead before heading back into the kitchen.

I put my elbow on the counter and propped my head up with my palm as I watched him. "What made you want to become a voice artist?"

"Oh. We're getting into serious questions now?" He grinned. "To be honest, there wasn't a specific thing that got me into the industry. Teddy was a young actor and I was a teenager who loved being in theater and musicals but never wanted the same glamour. I got gigs here and there and then I found audiobooks. The rest is history really."

"Musicals?" I perked up. "You were in musicals as a teenager?"

"I was. Nothing fancy, I just… I don't know, I enjoyed using my voice. Experimenting with different accents, testing my pitch limits, it was all just *easy* and I loved it."

"So wait a minute, not only can you mimic some of the sexiest accents in the world, but you can sing too?" I put my hand over my mouth to hide my expressions. Holy shit, I need to thank his parents for creating this talented human being.

"I can. I don't do it very often anymore. I love to sing, but I never wanted to profit off of it. If I did I was afraid I'd end up, well, in a similar situation Teddy's in right now."

I connected the dots. "Loathing something you used to love."

"Exactly." He switched over to start making the sauce.

I thought for a moment. "So, where does Dean Craven fit into all of this?"

"Craven just started out as an alias. Again, I saw what Teddy was going through with all the fame and stardom and I quickly realized I didn't want any part of it. The red carpets, the cameras following you everywhere, the anxiety and the stress. So, I put on a mask, bought blue contacts, used an American accent when I did interviews, and leaned heavily in the 'bad boy' aesthetic. Thus, Dean Craven was born."

"So he's a front to protect your identity?"

Dean paused for a moment, thinking of his answer. "He's a way of protecting my life outside of work. Which to be honest as of late has been taking over more than I would like. To be honest for a while I wasn't sure if I had a personal life to protect anymore."

"I get that. My work life is blending so much into my personal life I'm not sure which is which anymore." I took a deep breath as I moved on to the next question. "So, who else knows about you?"

He thought back. "Teddy, my parents," he turned to face me. "And now you."

My eyes widened. "Four people? That's it?"

I swallowed hard. This man entrusted his biggest secret, one that only his family knows about, to me after a few days and one date? I'm a good secret keeper but this is one hell of a secret to give to someone who's practically a stranger.

"Yup. That's it." He replied as he sent a smile my way.

"Why did you tell me?"

"Technically, I didn't. You figured it out." He kept his eye on the stove.

"Okay, true," he got me there, "but you were going to tell me what you did after work today anyway, right?"

"Yes." He stated confidently.

"Were you going to tell me the truth?"

"Of course."

"Did you already know that you were working with the company *I* work for?"

He lifted his head. "You never told me your company name but,

I... had a feeling. Look," he hung his head again, "after our date yesterday, finding out about Teddy... I didn't want to throw another truth bomb on you. And, to be honest, I wasn't sure how you would react given my career choice."

I grinned at him. "How did you think I would react?"

He chuckled. "Most women wouldn't take lightly to the thought of their partner reading romance books for a living and having what's basically a thirst trap page for people to *look* at."

I smiled. "You mean to thirst over?"

"As one of my followers you tell me." He grinned my way before turning off the stove and finished putting dinner together.

I blushed as I rolled my eyes. "Well, first of all, as you pointed out I listen to you read those books on a weekly basis, why would I judge you when I enjoy them? Secondly, you don't have to worry about your page. I have public accounts too. They're not thirst trap worthy by any means, but I get it." I stood up and walked over to the kitchen.

He dressed the plates and turned to face me. "I don't know, I looked you up after our first date, you might have some thirsty stalkers out there too."

I narrowed my eyes on him as I leaned against the counter. "Sounds like something one of my thirsty stalkers would say?"

"What if I was?" He crossed his arms, playing along with this game of banter. He shifted his gaze up and down my body as he approached me slowly.

"Then you're lucky." My thighs shifted together. The thought of him being the one to stalk me made my body temperature rise. Looking at my photos, learning about me, wishing he could touch me. He placed both hands on either side of me on the counter keeping me there. I looked right up into his hazel eyes as I went on.

"Stalkers only get the privilege to look, not touch. So, they can look all day if they want to, and one day they'll be looking at the one person I approve of touching me."

He lifted his eyebrow as the corner of his mouth turned into a grin. "Who might that be?" He whispered.

"The one man who's been craving to touch me again since I walked out of that booth. If he plays cards right." I teased. Without warning he lifted me up to sit on the counter and pressed himself between my legs. The sudden movement took my breath away. He sunk his fingers into my hips to keep me there before brushing my hair away from my face and slipping his hand to the side of my neck.

He whispered in a low growl against my lips as I smiled, "Sweetheart, you have no idea."

Dean

I know exactly what I'm having for dinner tonight.

Holy fuck.

My girl continued to surprise me. Not only does she support my career, but she wants to show the world that I'm the only one who can touch her? Am I dead? Is this the afterlife, because every moment with her feels and tastes like heaven.

If she came to me and asked to do a couple's shoot for my page or hers, I wouldn't hesitate. The chance to show everyone that she's the only one who gets to feel me, taste me, show her off to the world, and vice versa, I'm fucking here for it.

I deepened the kiss as she wrapped her arms and legs around me. God, I'm so hard I can't think straight. If I wasn't careful I'd take her on this counter right here. She's right, I've been craving this the moment she left the booth, and the second she teased me the band around my control snapped. Considering she's got me locked in place and kissing me like I'm about to go to war. I'd say she's feeling the same way.

How did I get so lucky? She slowly threaded her fingers through my hair at the back of my head making my breath hitch. She lightly put my bottom lip between her teeth and let it go.

Fucking Christ.

"Careful, Princess." I growled. "Keep it up and I won't be able to stop myself."

"Who said anything about stopping?" She whispered.

My breaths were still heavy as I whispered back. "Are you sure? Once we do this, that's it, you're *mine*."

I say that as if she wasn't already. I was certain after the first time I saw her, and I would do everything in my power to make sure it happened. Her entire body shuttered under me.

"Normally, I wait until the third date to do anything physical or put on labels. However, considering you've already made me come more times than I can count with your voice alone for years now, I'd say this is a very special circumstance." She brushed her nose against mine. "I only feel bad because I haven't returned the favor. You've only known me for a few days."

My jaw clenched as the realization hit me like a truck. I have known her, she's the whole reason I'm here. She deserves to know *everything*. But, I'm so close, she's right here, ready to say yes, ready to be mine.

"Dean?" She searched my face trying to decipher what I was thinking. "Are you okay?"

Shit.

I must've been quiet for too long. I can't let her say yes without telling her the truth. I just can't. "What if I told you, I've known you for a lot longer than a few days?" There it is. No going back now.

"What do you mean?" She kept her arms wrapped around me as she stroked the back of my head. Making me feel safe and soothed.

I squeezed my eyes shut. I'm right back where I was last night. A moment that could make or break everything. I brought her close as I wrapped my arms around her torso. She kept her arms in place holding me tight. The small strokes continued along the back of my head, making me bury my face into her neck.

I don't want to lose her, I can't, I'm here now, I'm kissing her, I'm making her dinner… I don't want to let go… not now, not when I'm so fucking close.

This is what I get for not telling her sooner. I can't believe this is happening *again*. I only have myself to blame. My fingers press into her back to take in this feeling, being in her arms like this felt as natural as breathing.

She chuckled for a moment. "It was the comment I left wasn't it?"

I lifted my head from her neck to meet her eye. "What?"

"I left you a comment on one of your posts a year ago, thanks to a bottle of wine. You liked it, and let me guess, you checked out my profile because you were curious?" She didn't move as I stayed frozen in place, waiting for her to go on.

I blinked. "Yes."

"So you weren't lying when you were saying you might be one of the 'thirsty stalkers' on my profile?" She looked into my eyes trying to search for more information.

I swallowed hard. "Yes."

Her eyes went wide for a moment. "You've never tried to reach out?"

I breathed sharply as I closed my eyes and shook my head. She remained unmoved, still wrapped around me, still keeping me close. "I've stared at that empty text box more times than I can remember."

"Oh," she whispered as she began to put the pieces together. "Then you decided to see me in person?"

"Yes."

She breathed sharply and licked her lips as everything fell into place. "You didn't come here solely for the VO gig did you?"

I felt her body tense under me.

Fuck.

No, no, no. Suddenly it became harder to breathe. "Natalie. Please."

"It isn't a coincidence that you're my neighbor. Is it?"

My voice cracked, "Please, stop." I peeled myself away to step back.

It's happening and it's all my fault.

She hopped off the counter. "You found my address, flew here, and got a job where I work?"

My heart began to beat against my ribs as I looked down at her. My chest was still tight as the air in the room became thin. I felt my eyes begin to water as she approached me. Every muscle tense, throat tight, oxygen not making its way into my lungs fast enough.

"Natalie…"

"Why?" She choked, looking up at me wanting all the answers.

I took in a shaky breath. "Because from the moment I saw you, I wanted to be *yours*. You are the most beautiful woman I've ever laid my eyes on, inside and out."

I slowly reached up to cup her face. I half expected her to slap my hands away but she didn't.

"When I found out you loved the books *I* narrated, I only fell harder. From the first moment I saw you… you were *my girl*. When I saw how hard you were working and how your boss was treating you I got on the next flight I could because I needed to make sure you were taking care of yourself. You always take care of everyone and I admire you for it, so much, but I couldn't stand back and watch you give and give while no one gave in return." I wiped away a tear that fell down her cheek. "While you've known me for years as your 'book boyfriends'," she let out a small breathed chuckle. "I've known you as the woman I don't deserve, but desperately want to spend the rest of my days proving myself to be worthy of."

I pressed my lips into a smile as my voice shook. "So, you can kick me out, scream at me, call me names, call Officer Bradley, whatever you want to do. Just know that no matter how far away you try to send me I will *always* look out for you, and I'll *never* stop protecting you." I paused and took in what air I could as I prepared myself for what she was about to say.

She put her hands on mine as I wiped away more tears. The fear in her eyes was long gone and replaced with a look of… admiration.

She quickly moved her hands to the back of my neck and pulled me down to her. She met my lips with hers like a fucking magnet.

"Here's what I want." She whispered against my lips and continued to brush away the tears from my cheeks. "I want you to take me upstairs, and make me believe what you just said, and fuck me like you meant every single fucking word."

Without hesitation I threw her over my shoulder before she even tried to turn to the stairs. I dropped her on the bed and crawled over her, the shock on her face quickly turned to lust as I pressed my body to hers. Her heart rate was going a mile a minute as I firmly held the back of her neck to slam her lips to mine.

God, I can't get enough of her.

She tugged at my shirt as if to pull me even closer, then she tugged as I helped her slip it off. She gripped harder as her nails dug into my skin. I've been waiting for so long to feel her hands on me like this. I wanted her to mark me, I wanted her to *claim* me just as I was about to claim her. I slipped off her shirt next and my god she's beautiful, I shifted my lips to her neck and sucked and bit as if my life deepened on devouring every last bit of her.

My breath hitched as she pushed me down to the mattress and straddled me. At that moment, everything stopped… my heart, time, the hum of the world.

She's a goddess as she sat straight up. Her messy hair, her curves, every single part of her glowed as the light from the window illuminated her. I brushed my fingers over her hips as her greedy worshiper and I suddenly lost myself.

I'm hers, that's it, that's who I am, hers and only hers forever.

I wrapped my arms around her as I sat up and pulled at the back of her bra so hard the hooks bent, ripped, and snapped open. I'll buy her as many as she wants, but right now, I'm tearing everything off. Every single piece of clothing that gets in my way will be ripped. She told me to make her believe it and fuck her like I mean it, like I meant every single word I said, and that's exactly what I'm going to do.

Her breaths were heavy as I kissed and bit her neck while I filled my hands with her. She grasped the back of my neck as if to keep me there and hang on for dear life. My cock is pressed so hard against my zipper I hissed as I threw her back to the mattress. I hovered over her and took one of her nipples into my mouth making her back arch and moan. Jesus, she's going to make me burst if she moans like that again.

I tugged at the waistband of her jeans and pulled as hard as I could. Another snap, another rip, as both her jeans and underwear tear away. She gave me a cute frustrated look. I returned a lustful smile and licked my top lip as I looked through my brow at her. She can yell at me later. I tilted my head, God I could look at her like this all day if I could. I hooked my arms around her thighs and pulled her to me at the foot of the bed.

I knelt down in position to worship her and whispered. "You get so wet and needy when you think about me. Don't you, *Princess*?"

Her eyes widened, "It *was* you…"

I cut her off as I licked and sucked on all of her sensitive areas. Ones I've already tasted and memorized. It's even better than I remembered. I locked her in place squeezing her thighs around my head as she moaned and cried. This time I'll let her hands roam, she'll need to hang onto me for dear life before I'm done with her. Who am I kidding, I'll never, ever be done with her. Every time she sits down tomorrow I want her to be reminded of me, every lick, every suck, every thrust.

Every. Single. One.

She threaded her fingers in my hair and held on tight, keeping me right where she wanted. *Fuck,* she's already almost to the edge and I can fucking feel it. I'm right there with her as my cock continued to pulse with need.

Not yet.

"Dean…" She whispered.

Hearing my name on her lips only made me lick her slower. I continued the pace as her back arched again, pulling the tension closer, closer, until she shattered around my tongue. I gripped her thighs tighter as I let a growl slip, sounding hungry and needy for more. Her legs began to shake, but I kept her right where I wanted her as she let out another cry. I gave her one last lick making her thighs tremble around my head. Another satisfied smile spread across my face as I licked my lips tasting her. Her breath hitched as I laid my lips to her inner thigh. I wanted to leave these little memories on her as a reminder of exactly where I've been.

She shifted under me riding her high and let out a short breath as I pressed my bare chest to hers. This skin to skin contact sent a charge through my body keeping me right where I needed to be. Before I could react she already had her hands on the waistband of my jeans and ripped it open at the button breaking the zipper. She gave me a smirk as she continued to breath heavily, and licked *my* lips curving her tongue as if to tell me to get closer.

I could barely get the words out as I placed my hand to her throat and put my thumb to her bottom lip making her mouth open wider.

"This mouth is going to get you in trouble."

I slipped my other hand down and shoved two fingers inside her making her melt under me. "Dean… please…"

"Please, what?"

"Please fuck me like you mean it… please!" I pressed my thumb over her clit as she let out another small cry. "Fuck, Dean…" she whimpered.

"I love hearing my name on your lips." I placed myself at her entrance and I'm already falling apart around her. "Now," I sunk my fingers into the back of her hair and lightly tugged as I whispered into her mouth, "I know you're on birth control, because I know my girl better than anyone."

"I want to feel you inside me…" She whispered. "All of you…"

I couldn't help but smile down at her. "Is that what you want, *Princess*? You want me to fuck you *raw*? You want to feel every inch of me inside that beautiful cunt of yours."

"*Yes, please…*" She pleaded, her glassy eyes filled with lust.

"*Good.*" I rasped, "because I want you to feel every single movement I make." I thrust in halfway, and allowed her a single moment to adjust to me. "How *raw* you make *me* feel." I thrust myself all the way in. "What the thought of *you* does to *me.*"

A twinge of pain and pleasure spread across her face. We both caught a breath as I pulled her body flush to mine. She's so tight it almost puts me over the edge, "Fuck… you're taking me so well Princess."

She wrapped her legs around my waist to keep me right where I am. She's got me locked in place as I slowly and steadily find a rhythm. Her hands wandered down to my lower back and dug her nails into my back. I hissed at the pain but I welcomed every single mark she wanted to leave on my skin.

She stopped. "Did I hurt you?" She looked up at me with concern.

"No." I smiled at her, "I want you to leave your beautiful signature for me to admire long after."

"As long as you return the favor." She whispered against my mouth. *God this woman.*

I thrust all the way to the base again, feeling every single part of her as she clenched and cried. "After tonight, you won't need marks to be reminded who you belong to."

She pressed her forehead to mine. "It's not to remind *me*." She tightened her legs around me to send me deeper if it was even possible.

I threaded my fingers into her hair again to expose her neck to me. Her breath hitched from the movement. I already saw a few small marks I left earlier.

I licked the marks and found a perfect spot right under her ear. "Where have you been all my life, Princess?" I whispered against her skin.

"Right under your nose, *Heartthrob*." I thrust hard at the mention of this new nickname she's given me.

Heartthrob.

She really is perfect. I sucked hard on her neck and shifted my hand to the other side of her neck to keep her there. If she wants a few marks, I'll give them to her. She turned her head to give me better access and took my thumb in between her teeth. I thrust with an even pace as I continued to lick and bite while she dug her nails in my back so deep it burned.

I began to feel her rise and rise again, but I kept my pace the same and landed my hand back to her throat.

"Come for me, *Natalie*."

I gave her a few more hard thrusts as she unraveled around my cock, "Oh God... Dean!" She cried out, the feeling got me so close to edge it's fucking painful. If I move I will surely follow. I kept myself in as deep as I could while her legs trembled and chest heaving against mine. Our sweat, tears, and saliva all over one another creating a beautiful mess.

Two more thrusts and she's shattering again as I follow right behind her. I saw stars behind my eyelids as an ethereal feeling filled my body. I buried my face into her neck again, the smell of us, sex, and sweat, filled every sense in my body. And it's fucking otherworldly. Our breathing synchronized, as I stayed unmoved. Her hands were in my hair again giving me another soothing feeling.

I put my arms under her with one hand at the back of her head, and the other around the middle of her back. There's no going back, this woman is *mine*. All of her, every piece of her, every drop of her is *mine*.

I didn't stop kissing her, and she didn't stop kissing me for what felt like minutes. I could kiss this woman all over forever, even if it meant abandoning everything. My cock pulsed again inside of her as she pulled me to her swollen lips. I kept my hand on the back of her head and pressed her lips harder to mine. I'm inside of her the entire time but yet I'm *still* not close enough.

She sucked on my tongue and took my bottom lip in between her teeth and pulled. I moved my hand from the back of her head to her neck as she let it loose

"What did I say, *Princess*," I wiped my thumb across her wet bottom lip. "That mouth is going to get you in trouble."

"This coming from the man with the filthiest mouth in the world." She whispered to my lips.

"A mouth you've come on a few times now." I leaned down to her ear, using a tone I can only describe as hoarse and from the bottom of my gut. "And we've only scratched the surface." Her body shifted as small goosebumps began to appear. "You told me to fuck you like I mean it. I will *always* fuck you like I mean it. Whether it's with my cock, tongue, fingers, or toy, every single time I will devour every inch of you until the day I'm no longer breathing."

I slid down her body again slowly, taking one of her nipples into my mouth as I sucked hard. Her grip on my hair tightened. "God, this can't be real."

"I can assure you Princess," I laid a kiss on her ribs, "this is all," another on her stomach, "very," another inside her thigh, "*real*." I gave her a few hard licks against her clit making her even more wet for me. "This tongue." In one swift motion I flipped her to her stomach and pulled her to the edge of her bed.

I pressed my body to her back feeling her thick arse against my now very hard cock. I slid my fingers up to the front of her throat to bring her head back and look up at me. "These fingers." Her beautiful eyes looked back into mine with a carnal stare.

I thrust my cock back in with a little more ease as she shuttered under me. "This cock." I brought her whole body close to me and slid my fingers down stomach straight down and lightly stroked her clit. Another delicious moan slipped from her lips.

"All of me." I breathed, "*I* am *very* real. And *I* am all *yours.*"

Natalie

I found myself wrapped around Dean's warm body tangled in my sheets. My cheek to his chest, his right arm supporting my head with his left on my back, and our legs intertwined together. I stayed still listening to his heartbeat, slow, even, and calming, almost lulling me back to sleep.

From what I remembered, I practically passed out after what was… our fourth go around. I still can't believe he's here *for me*. It still feels like some fantasy dream come true. He found out where I worked, he found out where I lived. The first thing to do, when we're not in bed together, is find out where he found all of this information so I can make sure it's not as easy to access. I really should be creeped out by this, I should be terrified, I should call Riley, but I don't. Being here, in his arms, is… honestly… the safest I've ever felt. What does that say about me? Am I delusional? Do I really feel this *unseen*? *Unnoticed*? Then there's all those things he said.

"Because from the moment I saw you, I wanted to be yours. You are the most beautiful woman I've ever laid my eyes on, inside and out."

"From the first moment I saw you… you were my girl.*"*

"I couldn't stand back and watch you give and give while no one gave in return."

"I've known you as the woman I don't deserve, but desperately want to spend the rest of my days proving myself to be worthy of."

My eyes began to water at the memory. Never in my life has anyone ever cared about me this much. So much to where he dropped everything to find me and make sure I was taking care of myself. If only he knew he's been taking care of me for a long time.

I listen to audiobooks and read because I often need a place to escape. It doesn't matter if it's a fantasy realm or a mafia boss's basement. It takes me to a place where I don't have to worry about a breaking news story that involves a celebrity's dog or the next big divorce. Where all of my problems dwindle down to zero. Where I'm living the story through the main character, where I can feel seen by *someone*.

He's provided me with that escape for years, and he has no idea how many times he's helped me with some of the most difficult days of my life. He drowns out those little voices that make me think, *why am I here, what am I doing.* It's gotten easier since Kayley moved in, but nothing could save me from those destructive thoughts like he could.

Now that he's *here*, sleeping in *my* bed, it's like he's taken me to a safe place that I never want to leave. With him all my problems are non-existent, all my anxiety has been taken away, all my constant thoughts are calm. I don't know how he does it, or what it is about him that has me feeling like myself again, but I know I don't want him to leave.

"I am very real. And I am all yours."

I couldn't hold in my tears.

He wants to be mine, *he wants to take care of* me... *he wants...*

I feel him shift next to me but I don't leave his chest, hoping he didn't just come to some insane realization that I'm not the person he thought I was.

I may portray this strong and happy person who works too much, but deep down my heart aches all the time. The negative voices are always there to tell me I shouldn't eat because I already had lunch and 'what do I need dinner for', telling me to keep working and I don't need water right now I only have one more thing to do.

"Natalie? Hey, hey. What is it?" Dean whispered with a rasp to his voice from waking up. He held my face and looked me over with a worried look. "Are you alright?"

I nodded. "Yes. I'm fine…" I look back into his hazel eyes filled with concern. He wiped away one of my tears and I turned to kiss his palm. "I just have a lot of thoughts in my head right now."

His look didn't shift. "Tell me."

I paused for a moment, debating whether or not I should share this part of myself with him. I shifted my gaze to the clock on my computer that displayed 8:45 A.M.

"Shit! We're late!"

Before I could throw off the covers to get ready Dean tightened his arms around me and pressed his lips to mine. I didn't pull away because kissing him is so addicting he might as well be a drug, and because I would give anything to stay here in this bed all day with him instead of going to work. His tongue licked my mouth and suddenly I have no job to go to, I have no bills to pay, and I have no reason to leave… except I have to.

"Dean." I whispered against his lips. "We need to go to work."

"Who said we *have* to?" He whispered back.

"My bills."

"I'll pay them." He whispered against my lips. "We can just stay right here. All day."

I couldn't help but chuckle. "Tempting. But, the last thing I need is for Brock to have another reason to give me shit." I gave him one last deep kiss before slipping out of the bed to get dressed.

He propped himself up on his side with his elbow and watched me get ready for work. Then when I exited the bathroom he was gone. I narrowed my brow, what the hell?

I ran downstairs to find him holding a bag with a cream cheese bagel, an apple, and a to-go coffee mug with coffee already in it. I gave him a confused look when I was ready to head out the door. He was still shirtless with pants that had a broken zipper. I rubbed my lips together trying to hide my grin at the memory of literally ripping his pants off.

"Why aren't you dressed?" I grabbed my phone that I found out was at five percent because I forgot to charge it last night.

"Because *someone* broke the zipper on my jeans." He looked down at me with hungry eyes. "So, I'll need to stop by home before I head off to work."

I smirked up at him. "Only because *someone* literally ripped off my bra *and* underwear last night."

"And I don't regret it." He returned a mischievous grin before I gave him one more kiss.

"I don't either." I whispered against his lips.

He took a deep breath as he stared down at my lips, my eyes, and back to my lips. "Are you sure we have to go to work today?"

"Unfortunately yes, there's still a lot of work we have to do." He handed me the bag and the coffee.

"It's not as much as I would've liked to make for you this morning but I know you're on a time crunch." He brushed a stray hair from my face as he took in every angle.

"You didn't have to make me anything, honestly the sight of you shirtless in my kitchen is enough to get me through the day." I teased.

He raised a brow. "While I'm happy I can fulfill your *hunger*, but you still need some food. And there is no way, I'm letting my girl leave this house without breakfast."

My girl.

God, could this man get any hotter. Seriously, do we need to work today? I took the bag and mug from his hands and gave him an appreciated look. "Thank you." He did something so simple yet it's already made my entire day.

He gave me another smile and kissed my forehead. "I'll meet you there. If Brock gives you any shit this morning, let me know."

I sucked air through my teeth already dreading the thought of Brock ruining my perfect morning. "Don't worry, I can handle Brock. It's *you* I worry about. You're the one on a contract." I grabbed the backpack I threw to the couch last night.

"If he lets me go, he'll be in deep shit. His boss is foaming at the mouth for this project, so if I'm gone, so is his project." He threw on his jacket over his shirtless torso. I'm so behind this morning I don't even question why he didn't grab his shirt.

"I wish I had your confidence." I swung open the door as he followed.

"You do. You're amazing at your job. I know it, you know it, and Brock knows it. He can't function without you. So, like I said, if he pisses you off and you don't want to deal with him, let me know."

I locked the door behind us as I thought for a moment. He stood tall and gave me a serious look, as if he was far from joking. Ready to do anything if I said the word. A wave of protectiveness hit me like a truck. I forgot, this man literally found my address, got on the plane, and booked the house next door just to make sure I was okay. How could I not see that he also came with book boyfriend levels of protection and possessiveness. I wasn't sure if I should be relieved, terrified, or turned on. Maybe a mixture of all three?

"I appreciate it, but I can handle him." We walked down the stairs of my porch. "This isn't the first time I've been late and I have a feeling after last night it won't be the last." He opened my car door with a wink and let me slip inside before laying one last kiss on my lips.

"Drive safe. I'll see you there." He peeled himself away as if he didn't he would climb on top of me in the car. An image that has me shifting in my seat, and blushing as I exit my neighborhood.

When I got to work I pulled down my mirror to try and fix myself as if I didn't just roll out of bed. My eyes went wide as I saw a small trail of hickies speckled down my neck.

How the fuck did I not see these this morning?

I pulled on my t-shirt collar and checked my chest. "Shit." I quickly pressed the shirt to my chest that was currently covered in hickies and bite marks. While I love giving and receiving little marks during sex, I was about to walk into my place of work, late, and Dean was going to trail in behind me not long after.

"Everyone will know. No, I'm overthinking this." I say to myself. "No one is going to connect the dots." I took a deep breath to calm myself. If anyone asks, I burned my neck with my curling iron 1, 2, 3… 4 times, I still have some curls left. Sure… we'll go with that.

I put the bagel that Dean made me in between my teeth and ran into the building, at 9:05 A.M. which was a new record for me. I don't even think about the traffic violations I made on the way over or the fact I might have to get my car towed because I'm dangerously low on gas.

Luckily, Brock was in a meeting all morning so he didn't even notice. Once I finished setting everything up I thought I was in the clear until Dean came walking through the door looking devilishly handsome in a Henley with the first couple of buttons unbuttoned that revealed a small hickey. His cheeks slightly raised behind his mask as if he was grinning. He definitely did that on purpose.

As I looked a little closer I could see the faint scratch marks from my nails at the top of his shoulder that lead to his back. I haven't seen his back yet, but I have a feeling with that little sneak peak it's more than likely covered.

"I want you to leave your beautiful signature for me to admire long

after."

The memory replayed in my mind as he stopped at my desk. "Good morning, Natalie."

I held up the to-go mug he handed me this morning. "Good morning, Mr. Craven."

This situation has me fucking giddy. I woke up next to *him* this morning, a man who is ready to worship me at any moment. And I cannot wait to worship him when we get home tonight.

Just when I didn't think this day could get ruined I heard Brock's shrill call.

"Natalie!"

Dean remained unmoved as Brock approached my desk, looking him up and down as if he didn't get his permission first. The glare made Brock still for a moment.

"Morning, Mr. Craven. I trust Natalie has everything set up for you?"

"She does." He stated shortly even though he hasn't been back there to check. His sleeves were halfway up his arms revealing his gorgeous tattoo sleeves. When he crossed his arms his muscles flexed and made Brock a little pale and pause before he said anything else.

I shifted my gaze to Dean with a stand-down look. He didn't budge. Because of course not.

"Everything is set up in the audio booth." I tried to reassure him.

With my phone's dying breath I connected it to the printer while I rushed in and printed off the scripts Brock emailed me last night. Which gave me the time to set up the booth and finish right before Dean walked in.

"Great," Brock cleared his throat before turning to me. "Can you stop by my office before you guys get started?"

"Sure." I nodded as I watched Dean like a hawk out of the corner of my eye to make sure he didn't attach another mic. If I found out he bugged his office somehow we're really going to have a talk.

"If you want to go over the new scripts they're in the booth ready for you. I'll meet you there in a few minutes." Dean shifted his eyes from Brock's office back to me. As if to ask me if he could come with me.

"I'll be fine." I whispered to him before I followed Brock to his office. I turned back to catch Dean in a muscle twitch and a neck stretch at my desk. He caught my eye again as if he was being pinned to my desk against his will. I gave him a reassuring look before Brock closed the door behind me. While I appreciated Dean's concerns and his good intentions, I can handle this. And, so far today, he's respecting that. Which to be honest I'm proud of him for because given the look on his face it was very difficult for him to do.

I was brought back to reality as Brock let out a deep sigh and rubbed his tired eyes as if he'd been up for hours.

"So," he began as he made his way over to his chair. "Tell me. How was your first day working with Mr. Craven?"

You mean besides the mind blowing sex and hickies he left all over me?

"Pretty good. He was able to get the scripts done within a couple of takes and he's very… professional."

Sure we'll go with that.

"That's great to hear." He leaned over his desk and started twirling his pen. My heart sinks.

Fuck.

Every time he hovers and twirls that fucking pen something big is happening, it could be anything from a shift in leadership to deleting one of our profiles due to low interaction and views. I hate that I know that, but either way it's going to involve a lot of work we're not equipped or lead to a shitty fucking day.

He paused as he squinted at my neck.

For the love of every God in existence don't say anything, don't say anything, please...

"Are you okay?" He pointed to his neck as if to refer to mine.

Well, fuck.

I covered one side of my neck with my hand. "Oh, yeah. I'm fine. Just a few curling iron burns."

He nodded as if it was the last thing he wanted to continue talking about. I cleared my throat and tried to move on. "So, what did you want to talk to me about?" I tried to move my hair nonchalantly to cover my neck.

"Right, I had a meeting with Nathan this morning. He loved the trailer we put together, and he wants three videos by Friday for this new channel." He paused waiting for my response.

I thought for a moment. "With the rate Mr. Craven was reading yesterday, that shouldn't be too much of an issue on *our* end. The editors might get a tight window but we could have the audio by tomorrow at the earliest-"

"That's not all." He continued to twirl his pen. "I haven't had a chance to tell the rest of the managers yet, but we had to let go of a good chunk of our freelance writers today."

Hiring and letting go freelancers wasn't new, but something didn't sit right when he said that. "How many?"

He shook his head. "Over half."

There it is.

"Jesus." I whispered. "Okay, so how is this going to affect our content flow? How low are we talking?"

He gave me a strange look. "It won't."

"What do you mean it won't?" No writers, no scripts and articles, no video content. Then it clicked. "You're giving our very few full-time writers and our left over freelancers *more* work? They're already working at maximum capacity."

"We have no choice. This was a necessary decision to make. If we want our profiles to keep making money then we can't slow down on content."

"They're going to be overworked, Brock. If they're overworked, that can lead to burnout, which turns into simple mistakes, making us spend more time and money fixing them." I blurted out.

That was meant to be a thought in my head but somehow it slipped through my lips and the look my boss gave me in return was the same frustrated look I saw yesterday.

"Remember your position, Natalie. If there was something I could do I would." I almost scoffed at that statement as he continued. "My hands are tied with this one."

If that were true then it's with a loose knot. He has all the power to think for a moment and give our advice to Nathan, but no, all he does is rollover and scratch the CEO's ass for approval.

This has a million alarms ringing in my head. He has no idea how this will affect our chain of video production and publication. Hell, if they even think about raising the hourly post count, *again*, we're all going to be so busy we won't have time to create decent content anymore. Which of course leads to more mistakes, higher chances of them slipping through the cracks, views going down, and charts going into the red.

I rubbed my forehead trying to calm all the racing thoughts going around and around the race track of my brain.

How the fuck does he not see this.

"But," he tried to sound chipper. "I did have the scripts run through content quality so we shouldn't have any errors for the ones Mr. Twenty One Pilots will be reading today."

I licked my teeth behind my lip. "I don't think Mr. Craven would appreciate your 2014 angsty boy band nicknames for him."

He lifted his shoulder. "Then he should stop dressing like one."

Said the man who wears flops around the office. I let out an unamused chuckle as something snapped in my heart. "Let me rephrase that. *I* don't appreciate it. He's very talented and very respected in his field therefore *we* should also treat him with the same respect. We're *very* lucky to have him here working with us. So, I will only say this once," I kept my eye on Brock making him feel pinned to his chair. "From this moment forward please only refer to him as Mr. Craven."

Or I will cut off the pitiful excuse of your manhood and feed them to the turkey vultures on the street.

He raised his eyebrows and studied me for a moment as he slowly nodded. "Noted."

"Great, I'll get those audios to you by tomorrow EOD." I pressed my lips into a thin smile as if I just didn't almost threaten my boss because of a nickname he was giving to *my* Heartthrob.

Oh. Son of a bitch... I get it now.

"Perfect. Thank you." He watched me closely. "As you get each one just send it over as soon as you can. The earlier we can get started the better." He stood to open his office door. He paused for a moment and turned to me. "Before I let you go, has *Mr. Craven* mentioned anything about me?"

I raised a brow. *What is this middle school?*

Of course he has, but there was no way in hell I would tell him that.

"Not to me." I lied. "Why?"

He shook his head as if to shake the thought away. "Nothing, I just got the impression that he's a little…" He struggled to find the right word.

"What?" I crossed my arms. Oh, I couldn't wait to hear this.

"Angry? Maybe a little frustrated? He seems to like being around you, which is great. Do anything and everything you can to keep him happy."

I dug deep to keep my smile from appearing because last night I definitely kept him *happy*.

"But," He went on, "Nathan will be stopping in next week to meet him. I just want to make sure we're on good terms."

Oh boy. If Dean hated Brock, he's going to loath Nathan.

"I can ask him what he thinks about working here so far." A very floppy attempt to throw Brock off the trail.

He chuckled as he opened the door. "Great. Well, that's all I have for ya for now. And, hey, get a new curling iron; those burns can leave nasty scars."

I breathed sharply and nodded. "Will do."

I quickly exited his office and went straight to the back room with the audio booths. Dean was sitting at one of the tables reading over a script before his now blue eyes softened when he saw me enter the space. A look I don't think I'll ever get tired of seeing.

"How was your meeting?" He asked as I set my stuff down next to him and plopped into the chair. "That bad huh?"

"You have no idea." I blurted out as I rubbed my forehead.

He turned back to the script. "I would if you would let me listen in."

I lightly shook my head as I chuckled at his statement. "We're cutting our freelance writers in half." I whispered.

He set the script down and leaned back in his chair. "That's not good. That'll affect your content output. How bad is that going to impact you and your team?"

"Brock said it's not going to affect our output. If anything we're still full speed ahead." I paused and shook my head. "It's going to double, if not triple, the amount of work for the poor writers we have left. They're already at capacity, so if they're giving them *more* work they're going to rush and make more simple mistakes."

"Which leads to everyone else wasting time and the company money to fix those mistakes that could have been avoided from the beginning." He added.

I pointed my hand at him. "See. You've only been working here for two days and you see the problem. Brock has been here for ten plus years and he might as well be a hockey ref with blackout glasses."

Dean chuckled at that reference. "You like hockey?"

I shrugged. "I've been to a few games… with my book club." I added.

"Let me guess." He narrowed his eyes on me. "'Pucking Perfect'?"

"'Naughty and Ice'", I shook my head to get back on topic, "but that's not the point."

He raised his hands in surrender with what I could tell a playful smile under that mask. "Did he mention any more cuts?"

I shook my head. "No. Thankfully. But, it's a slippery slope. All the departments are at or over capacity. If anyone piles up a list of mistakes they'll have no problem letting them go one at a time. One less salary means more money for them." I tried to keep my voice to low whisper so no one else could overhear. The last thing I wanted was to spread panic around the office. Everyone knows we're not doing great so the mere mention of a layoff or firing would send people spiraling. Not to mention have Brock find out that I'm telling our newest VO talent temporary confidential company information.

"Are you worried?" He gave me a concerned look.

I nodded. "For my team. Yeah. They're great at what they do, Ben was able to buy his first new car, Megan and her husband just bought a house, and Miranda is fresh out of college with loans to pay off, Amy is getting married next year, and Kayley is well, let's just say *window shopping* for something new. It'd tear me apart to have that conversation."

His cheeks lifted as he hung his head. "You have such a big heart, Natalie. But, I didn't ask if you were worried about your coworkers if that situation ever arrived." He reached for my hand and held it tight under the table. "So I'll ask again. Are *you* worried?"

I didn't want to lie, this is the largest cut the company has made in a long time. If my department is gone I doubt they'd keep me around, and I wouldn't know what to do with myself if they did. I've been here for so long I've forgotten what I wanted to do with my life.

Honestly, this is all I know how to do. I've been tailored for this unique position and I doubt there's any others like it out there. If anything I'm worried that I may not know what I truly want to do. After being here for so long, I think I've forgotten that part of myself. I squeezed his hand and that was all the confirmation he needed.

Dean

My girl has had a long day.

I could see her internal battery drain as she got pulled into meeting after meeting to a sudden celebrity death that had her and her team working non-stop. Every once in a while she'd check in and listen to my clips. I savored each moment I had with her, and it took all of my energy to restrain myself from pulling her back into that audio booth and hiding her from the world and its problems.

I couldn't help but feel a sense of pride watching her shoulders loosen as she listened to my voice. As if it was my secret superpower to take her away from this place if only for a couple of minutes. It didn't matter if it was about something mundane or a review she didn't really align with, every single time without fail she would close her eyes and listen to it intently. Luckily, she didn't have to focus on the content too hard. Even after it's checked with content quality I gave it once over to make sure. So all she had to do was listen, make sure it's up to standard, and send it to Brock.

That man is reaching higher and higher on my shitlist. He asked me once again if I would have lunch or dinner with him after work. Both of which I declined because I would rather sit bare arse on hot coals than have a private lunch with *him* and other suited up former frat boy dickwads. I'm not here for that. The only reason I'm still working here is sitting right in front of me. He doesn't realize how lucky he is in that regard, because if it wasn't for her, he would've been long gone by now.

I leaned against the frame of the audio booth watching my girl listen to the final script.

She slowly slipped off the headphones and rubbed her eyes giving me a small thankful grin. "That sounded perfect. I can't believe you pulled off three scripts today."

I shrugged as I sat in the seat next to her. "It wasn't too bad. The goal was for you to have one less thing on your plate."

Her tired eyes looked over me. "You finished these scripts so that *I* don't have as much work?"

"Yes." I stated confidently.

She tried to cover her smile. God, she's so cute. "If we weren't in the office, I'd climb you like a tree right now."

"Really?" I raised my brows and leaned back in my chair, hoping she'd take a seat right here on my lap. "Who says you can't?" She bit her top lip looking tempted.

"Natalie!" Brock's voice echoed throughout the office. Right on fucking cue.

I let out a dissatisfied groan straight from my gut. *"Motherfucker."*

She laid her hand on my knee under the table and lightly squeezed. "Stand down, Dean."

I whipped my head to her. "Did you just give me a command?"

"Stop going into attack mode every time he's in the room and I wouldn't have to." She whispered.

"When he gives you and your team sizable raises I'll consider it." I groaned out.

"Dean, I need you to promise me, no matter what he says you won't say a word." Her serious look made me straighten for a moment. "Please?"

This was important. She knew something. I searched her eyes for answers before I got an idea. She doesn't want me to say a single word. Fine. I'll occupy myself in the meantime.

"You want me to stay silent, Princess?"

She nodded.

"Okay," I removed my mask, "I'll stay quiet. Let's see if you can."

"Wait-" she whispered as I dipped under the desk. "Dean. What ar-"

I shushed her as I glided my hands up her legs, gripped her tattooed thighs under her skirt, and pulled her close.

"Shit…" I heard her try to whisper. Luckily, these desks were large with enough coverage to hide my frame so Brock won't know I'm down here unless my girl can't control herself.

She knew that staying silent in these situations was difficult for me, so I'll give her a little taste of what it feels like.

Brock's footsteps got closer before I slid her underwear aside and pressed my tongue inside of her. I shifted her left leg on top of my shoulder to gain better access as she muffled a small pleasured moan into, I assume, her hand.

"There you are." Brock's voice echoed in the room as she stiffened around me. This will be fun. "Where's Mr. Craven?"

"Um-" She muttered before a semi-long pause. I slid my tongue up slowly, trying to get her to speak again. "Restroom. He went to the restroom."

"Oh. Got it. How's everything going with the scripts?"

Of course he doesn't ask how she's doing, if her workload is too much, or why she hasn't left yet because it's after five. I put my focus back to my task before I lose control of myself. She was soaking wet for me as I swiped my tongue over her clit, over and over.

"Great." She breathed as she tried her best to control herself. "I'm sending you the final clips."

"Oh, wow. Fantastic." He paused. "Did you happen to ask him about what we talked about earlier?"

I slowed my pace and sucked on her clit which earned me a small jolt. She didn't ask me anything. "Oh- uh, no. Not yet. He's been swamped, I've been swamped, we've all been swamped."

I grinned against her, she's rambling, cute.

"Huh, no worries, just curious. Let me know when you do alright?"

"Sure." She answered with a shaky breath. "Was there anything else?"

He snapped as if he remembered. "Yes, I wanted to let you know we have about five more videos coming through the pipeline about Alan Jenkins death tonight. So, I'll need you to stay for another couple hours and keep an eye on your messages tonight. We'll also need to move to every other hour publish times for the rest of the week on our celeb news accounts." He paused. "Nothing but Jenkins or Tanner and Ell engagement, unless it was approved by Nathan or myself. Did you happen to talk to Amy about a schedule shift to nights for the next week?"

Are you fucking kidding me?

That's why she wanted me to stay silent. He's asking her to work overtime, after the day she's had? She knew this was going to happen and she knew I wasn't going to like it. I quietly maneuvered my hand to sink two fingers into her. Her thigh tensed up on my shoulder as she tried to control her breathing.

"Yes." She breathed. "Yes," she cleared her throat, "she's fine with it. Ben has also offered to be on call in case the load gets to be too much."

"She can handle it," Brock stated, "but good to know."

I glided my tongue over her clit in a slow motion as I hooked my fingers, knowing exactly where I needed to be.

"You can tell Mr. Craven he's free to go for the evening and let him know the offer is still up for Chuck's tonight."

Fuck no. I thought to myself as I began to feel her rise.

If he thinks for one second he can offer me dinner while my girl and her team work their arses off on overtime?

I'll say it again. *Fuck. No.*

"Will do." She quickly stated.

"Great, I'll see you tomorrow, keep your phone on."

Natalie sunk her fingers into my hair, let out a relieved breath, and leaned back in her chair once he left the room. I gave her one last lick leaving her still wet and needy for more.

"Dean, what the fuck was that?" Her breaths labored.

"That's how it feels, Princess. The need to explode, to make him pay for everything he does to you…" She stayed silent as I brushed my thumb against her clit making her tense. "…but can't." I put my lips to her thigh. "You knew he was going to ask you to stay over, didn't you?"

Her heel dug into my back as she tensed. "I did. Just like I knew you would get upset and you wouldn't be able to stay quiet."

"You're right." I rose, making her chair roll back and put myself between her legs. "I would've told him to go eat dog shit."

"Dean, you need to understand that things like this happen with every big celebrity death. We're an online media company of course we're going to be working overtime to push content."

I placed my elbows on her arm rests and wiped my hand down my face. "I realize that, but your team is already overworked as it is. With Ted- *Tanner's* engagement, our project, and now this?" I paused. "Please tell me they at least give you overtime pay."

She stayed silent for a moment.

My eyes widened. "Are you serious?" My tone came out a little harsher than I meant as I stood.

"Does taking off the same amount of hours you worked over off the next day count?" She gritted her teeth as she fixed her skirt.

"Fucking Christ, Natalie."

"Dean. I don't need you to tell me, okay, I realize it's a shitty compensation system but they won't budge on that policy so I've made my peace with it."

I placed my hands on my hips and shook my head. "They're literally taking advantage of you and this entire office. How can you be at peace with that?"

She took in a tired sigh. "You know what, I don't have the energy to fight you on this. This is just the way they operate. I know it's not the best company in the world but it's also not the worst. I get to work from home most of the time, they match my 401k at five percent, and I'm getting the experience I need to move on *when I'm ready*." She began to stand to collect her things. "Go home, Dean. I'll see you tomorrow."

"Natalie."

"Go home, please." Her voice raised a bit before putting it back down to a whisper. "I have enough shit to do without you telling me things I already know, okay? Go. Home. I'll talk to you later."

"Natalie." I called again. She turned her back to me and walked out of the room.

"Fuck." I wiped my hand down my face and realized she left her bag on the chair next to hers. After taking a few seconds to cool down I grabbed our things, put my mask back on, and headed toward her desk. She wasn't there, but Ben looked up from his desk as I approached.

"What's up, Mr. Craven?" He asked with tired eyes and a polite tone.

"Please, call me Dean. Natalie left her bag in the audio room. Wanted to make sure she got it." I stated shortly.

"Gotcha. I'll let her know." He replied.

"Thanks." I stuffed my hands in my pockets. "Don't work too hard, alright?"

He chuckled. "Thanks." He rubbed his eyes. "So, how do you like working here so far?"

I spotted Natalie out of the corner of my eye talking with one of the other managers. "It's been great, actually. You have a fantastic boss."

"Yeah, she's awesome." He leaned on his desk. "Brock definitely takes time to get used to," He whispered. "But, Natalie makes it look easy."

"She's great at her job." I replied. "Just wish she was a little more appreciated."

"We got her covered on that front." Ben continued as he leaned over and whispered. "Trust me. We hear it too. Between us, Brock is a complete dickwad. I don't know how she handles with his bullshit every day." Miranda, Megan, and Amy all gave slight nods of agreement. A little bit of worry lifted off my shoulders knowing that Natalie's team was also looking out for her.

I took out my phone. "How long do you think everyone is sticking around tonight?"

He blew out some air. "Probably for another couple hours minimum. Why?"

"Perfect. Would you mind doing me a favor?"

He looked at me curiously. "Sure?"

I typed out a message on my phone and showed it to him. His eyes widened after he read it and looked back up at me. "Are you sure?"

"Positive."

About forty-five minutes pass and I'm waiting at the front door of the office building downstairs. Two cars showed up with ten boxes of pizza in their back seats. I use the key fob on Natalie's keys I slipped from her bag to let the delivery guys inside.

I can't pay them for their overtime or send them home to see their families, but I can at least make sure they have some fuel to get through the next couple hours.

"Got an order here for World Entertainment Media?" One of the delivery drivers approached.

I waved my hand. "Office space is on the second floor, gentlemen." I texted Ben telling him they arrived and to open the doors for the delivery men. He waved from the top of the stairs leading the guys to the office.

"You sure you don't want to join us?" He called down.

I shook my head. "I'm alright. You guys have a lot of work to do and I'll just get in the way. Have a good night."

"Dean." He called and paused as I turned back. "Thank you. From all of us. We owe you one."

"Don't mention it. Just don't say it was me, alright?"

He nodded before leading the guys into the office. As I made my way to the car park, I felt my phone go off and answered.

"Holy shit you're alive." Teddy joked on the other end.

"So are you." I relaxed and shifted back to my natural tone. "When I stopped by this morning you were dead asleep with empty crisps bags surrounding you on the couch. I'm surprised your body didn't go into shock. What do you want?" I pulled my bag from my car.

He scoffed. "Right to it huh?"

"Yes. That's how conversations go, Teddy. Or did you forget how to communicate since you've been hiding in that house for four days?" I set my phone on speaker as I peeled out my contacts. God, these fuckers aren't getting any easier to deal with.

"Ha. Ha. Very funny. How'd everything go with Nat? I'm assuming well, since you didn't come home last night. Bow chicka wow wow." He started mocking me.

"You done?" I peeled off my mask and slipped on a jacket before locking up my car and headed straight for Natalie's.

"Nope." He sounded giddy. "At least tell me about her reaction to finding out you're *the* Dean Craven."

I sighed as I slid into her driver's seat and adjusted it to my height. "She was shocked but she took it well."

He kept quiet as if waiting for more. "That's it?"

"What were you expecting? A detailed novel?" I questioned as I drove off to the station next door. I noticed Natalie's tank meter this morning was almost at empty and made a mental note to fill it before she left today. How this car was able to get here this morning was beyond me.

"No, but a little detail would be nice, I need a good story to tell at your wedding." He joked.

"Teddy." I snapped as I pulled up to a pump.

"Oh relax, I'm messing with you. What's got your knickers in a twist?"

I shut the door and began to fill up her car. Honestly, I'm surprised I made it to the pump, this thing had to be running on fumes. "Her boss is a piece of shit."

"What happened?"

I set the pump to automatically fill the tank before getting back in the car. "Alan Jenkins died so now she's working over time."

"Yeah, I saw that on the news earlier. Shame really. He was a nice guy. Wait. How does that relate to her boss exactly?"

I gripped the steering wheel remembering the look of defeat on her face. She already knows this company is shit I didn't have to remind her of that by giving her a lecture.

"Apparently, their staff don't get overtime pay. They compensate them by 'making up hours'. If you work over two hours you can take those two hours off the next work day."

"That's shitty. And a great way to keep that overtime pay in the pockets of higher ups while taking advantage of the little guy's time."

"Yeah. Not to mention they cut some of their freelance staff today." To be honest I felt a bit of relief getting this off my chest. "Right now, Natalie's more worried about her team than herself."

"Yikes. I'm not surprised she thought of her team first though, Nat's a caring person."

I heard the pump click and removed it to put the cap back on. "She is. She does everything she can for her team, but she forgets about herself." I slipped back into the driver's seat to head back to the car park.

"Well, that's what you're there for. As her friend, lover, boyfriend whatever you want to call yourself. Be there for her when she needs it most." He paused. "Just like she did for you on Sunday."

"Right." I agreed. This wasn't new information. That's why I went to fill her tank, made sure she, and her team, ate dinner, and left the flowers I bought her this morning on her driver's seat with her keys and adjusted everything back to where it's supposed to be.

I will never stop doing everything I possibly can to take care of her. Even if it's as simple as filling up her car, or making her breakfast just to make her smile. Anything I can do to make her life a little bit easier every single day.

After talking with Teddy a little while longer and making sure Natalie was on her way to her car. I took off towards Chuck's to see a certain someone.

I told Teddy to meet me there and be discreet. Thankfully he dressed casual, no hoodie, and took my advice by popping in the brand new set of colored contacts I brought. We sat in a corner booth as I watched Brock laugh at the bar with a few people I didn't recognize. They definitely weren't from the office.

"How the fuck do you see in these?" Teddy blinked rapidly.

"It's easier to see when you don't blink every fucking second." I whispered.

He rubbed his eye for the millionth time. "You don't have to bite my head off dickhead."

"Don't you wear colored contacts in movies all the time?"

He pressed his palm to his eye. "Yes but they're not cheap. Not to mention they're tailored to *my* eyes, not yours."

I let out a dissatisfied groan. "They're not *cheap*. If they bother you that much, take them out. We're here to keep an eye on Brock. We can't do that if you're fucking blind."

"Right." He sighed and blinked one last time before taking a swig of his beer. "So, what do we know about him so far?"

"Other than he's a gigantic prick who likes kissing corporate arse. Nothing too exciting. He's got a wife, two kids, and a dog named Lucky." I handed him my phone with all of Brock's basic public info.

"Wow. Does he have the picket fence in a nice neighborhood too?" He scrolled through the info.

"Yeah. They have the daisies out front to prove it. Him and his wife Debbie were high school sweethearts, been married for thirty years, and given the way he talks about her I have a feeling it's not as perfect as the family portrait displays." Brock took out his phone and started typing away.

"Hm. Do you think he's ever cheated on his wife?" Teddy tried to think.

I shook my head and pursed my lips. "Doubtful, back in the day maybe, but he's too much of a workaholic to maintain another relationship."

"Who said it was a relationship? He may be a one night and done kind of guy, he's an arsehole right?"

I raised my brow and gave him a doubtful look. "The man switches from his sneakers to sandals at the office, and leaves his socks on. I highly doubt he's getting his own wife to sleep with him let alone someone else."

Teddy scrunched his nose. "I didn't need to know *that*."

"How do you think the people in the office feel about seeing it?" I took another small drink of my beer as I watched Brock continue to type. "Apparently, he's missed every basketball game for his eldest, and every tennis match for his youngest. Textbook corporate dad from the 90s."

"How do you know that?" Teddy gave me a weird look.

"Debbie's Facebook is public, and very *detailed*. I'll leave it at that. The only pictures with Brock in them are family vacation photos taken once a year. Even then I can spot his work laptop in the background."

"Hm." He glanced back to see him still typing. "A workaholic indeed. Who do you think he's texting right now?"

I licked my teeth under my lip. "If I had to guess, probably the only person in the entire company that has a heart of gold who will do anything to make sure her team isn't overworked."

Teddy's eyes widened. "You think he's messaging Natalie right now?"

"Either her, another manager, or the CEO Nathan Richards." I paused. "Who's a fucking delight by the way."

Teddy blew out some air with wide eyes. "Yeah, I read about him when I found out you were working for them. Apparently he got into the media business because he wanted to bring a 'new side to pop culture'. The man doesn't own a single social media account yet his entire company runs off of social media content."

"He's in it for the money. He doesn't give a shit about the content or how it works. All they want is results and green arrows that point up." I sighed, unfortunately he leaves all that to Natalie, Ben, and everyone else in that office.

"Brock's the middle man between Nathan and Natalie." I continued. "He has *some* experience in the area and, come to find out, Nathan only hired him because they were frat brothers. His *experience* came from his days at uni which is a bit of a stretch considering he barely graduated. Probably with some favors from Nathan I'm sure. So far, from what I've seen, his day to day is making sure the CEO stays happy by any means necessary. Even if that means firing people so they can continue to line their pockets when their company is losing money."

"Welcome to corporate America." Teddy lightly rubbed his eye. "Got any other dirt on him?"

"Caught him bad mouthing his wife, he recently got a $10,000 bonus, and his salary is now up to $175,000 a year."

Teddy practically choked on his beer. "Jesus, who are you right now? How'd you get this information?"

I lifted my shoulder. "I accidentally got connected to a Bluetooth microphone that just so happened to be attached to his belt loop for the good part of the day."

Teddy blinked. "I don't know whether to be impressed or terrified." He paused as he thought for a moment. "Fucking hell, $175,000 a year? That's pretty high for his position don't ya think?"

"Exactly. I'm not sure what he's doing to get that kind of money, but I have a feeling there's a lot more going on behind the scenes that Natalie isn't aware of. If it's something illegal or dangerous, I don't want her anywhere near it."

He let out a concerned sigh. "Do you really think a midsize Midwestern media company could be doing something illegal or dangerous? All because, what, her boss is a prick and the CEO is walking rubbish? You do realize that's most of corporate America right?"

I gave him a deadpanned look. "Yes. And how many stories have you seen about a corruption case that usually involves a CEO of a business in corporate America?"

He pursed his lips. "Fair point. Even if they are, how are you going to find evidence? You're not a detective."

I caught a picture of Brock looking at another woman's chest. "If I was able to get this much information in two days, I'll bet something else will pop up by the end of the week. Once I find it, I know a policewoman I can hand it over to."

"You know a policewoman? Here?" He whispered. "Do I even want to know how you know a *police officer* in a town where you literally know no one except for Natalie?"

"She's one of Natalie's friends. She's good at her job, and on her way up to detective, so I'm sure she's already got some information on them." I took one last sip of my beer and watched Brock wobble over to a table in the corner and pull out his laptop.

"Is he…?" Teddy looked back with a strange look.

"Working?" I nodded. "I think so."

"Hasn't he been drinking?"

"Yeah. He's had at least five beers since we sat down, and I'm pretty sure he's been here since he left the office."

Teddy turned back to me. "You mentioned how Natalie and her team get pinned on the littlest things right?"

"Yeah."

"What if *he's* the one making the mistakes? Or worse, making it look like they're the ones making the mistakes in order to get people fired."

Intriguing point, one that makes a little too much sense for my liking, but I'll take it as a theory. Suddenly, Brock headed over to the restrooms leaving his laptop open and my brain immediately told me to do something stupid.

"Follow him." I stated as I slipped from the booth.

"What? Why?" He quickly followed me.

"Keep Brock in there as long as you can. Do what you have to, just don't make a scene." I whispered.

"Seriously? I get piss duty and while you get to do some 'Under-cover: NYC' shit? You know I was the lead in that movie, I have experience in this area." Teddy continued to argue with me as we approached the table.

"You have experience with typing random keys on a keyboard, a display screen, and CGI, go." I pushed Teddy towards the restrooms with a disgusted look on his face.

I made it over to his table and pulled out my phone. The bar was relatively busy so it wasn't hard to take discrete pictures of his screen as I flipped through the tabs with the bottom of my shirt around my finger. This keyboard has a certain shine to it that made me want to bathe in bleach.

I opened his email tab and froze.

I read his most recent email three times to make sure I read it right. Of all the things I would've expected from someone like Brock this was a whole new level of shit. Since I didn't hear any distress calls from Teddy, I searched through his messages. I saw Natalie's name towards the top. The most recent time was five minutes ago.

Don't click on it... don't do it.

I clicked on the conversation with Nathan. Nothing but calls, and messages to call the other. Great way to cover his fucking tracks. A ping went off and it was a message from Natalie to Brock.

Natalie Green: *Thank you for bringing this to my attention. I will have the schedule rearranged here in a few minutes. We're currently pretty overloaded with videos and it got caught up in the mix. Apologies.*

Was he blowing up on her *again*? I couldn't help myself, I had to see what he was saying to her and if it's about another small error that wasn't a big deal, I was going to lose my shit. I scrolled to the message before.

Brock: *The Alan Jenkins Autopsy and Alan Jenkins Cause of Death are supposed to be two posts apart.*

When I looked back on the sheet, Miranda had been the one to schedule them one after another??

We had this conversation just yesterday Miranda needs to be held accountable

We can't have another video mix up

If it happens again we need to have a serious talk about how you manage your team. This can't keep happening - no more excuses

"You've gotta be fucking kidding me."

All I see is red as I quickly stood and before I could get anywhere I ran into Teddy who was already on his way out.

"Aw fuck. I know that look." He guided me away from the door. "We're leaving before you do something stupid or reveal your identity."

"Get out of my way Teddy." I gritted out.

"No." He stood firm. "If Natalie finds out you tracked down her boss and beat the man while he was drunk, she'd be more than just pissed. We're leaving. *Now.* He's not worth it."

Teddy gripped my shoulder as he guided me back. Once we passed by Brock's still empty table, I bumped into it and tipped over his lukewarm beer on his laptop.

Once we made it outside Teddy gave me a look like Dad used to give us when we were in trouble. "Seriously? You're such a child."

"He's lucky that's all I did after what I found."

"What did you find? Something useful I hope. That restroom was abysmal." I stayed silent as we made our way to the car. "Hello? Earth to Dean? Care to share with the class? I just listened to Brock piss for the last five minutes for you, at least give me something."

"They're downsizing. Majorly. They didn't cut half their writers, they cut almost all of them." I spat.

"Wait, what? If they don't have any writers, how are they getting articles?" Teddy put his arms on the roof of the car.

I wiped my hand down my face. "They're sampling articles from their competitors and filling in the rest with AI. No wonder that script sounded off. When I clocked it they must've used one of the few writers they have left to write a new script."

"Jesus. Isn't that copyright infringement? They can get sued for that." We both slipped into the car. "Not to mention highly unethical."

"It is and, apparently, they already are. According to the emails with HR they're doing what they can to sweep it all under the rug. But, that isn't the worst of it." I handed my phone to Teddy to show him the pictures I took.

"Dear god, there's more?" He winced.

"They're trying to find new ways to replace their employees with automated systems. Apparently there's a new scheduling and quality control system they're looking into. According to that email, he's going to try and push an impossible quota for employees to hit every week."

"So when they don't hit it, that'll give him a 'justified' reason for letting them go one by one." He zoomed in on the photo trying to get a better look.

"Exactly." I shifted the car into drive. "They've been keeping their managers so busy they don't have the time to take a closer look at what's going on."

"Why go through all this trouble?" He asked. "Why go one by one, instead of one or two massive layoffs?"

I lifted my shoulders. "Probably not to cause an alarm and risk someone snooping around."

"Jesus. What are you going to tell Nat?" He set my phone down.

What was I going to tell her? Hey, sorry to be the one to tell you this but your company is stealing articles. Also they're going to fire you and everyone you care about at the company to replace you with an automated system. She's already pissed at me for giving Brock a glare every time he steps foot into her peripheral vision. I know she's trying to keep me out of trouble and the only reason I'm complying the best I can is because Brock's immediate response is to blame Natalie for it.

"I need to find out more before I tell her anything." I replied as we headed back to the house. "And I'm trusting *you* to keep this to yourself."

He looked offended. "Hey. I can keep my mouth shut."

"Like you did about 'The Deal Breaker' audition?"

He scoffed. "Okay that was different, I was trying to help you come clean."

"You broke your NDA in front of someone who works for the media. Your lucky Natalie is a fucking saint and would never throw you under the bus like that." I sighed. "Just please, keep it to yourself for now."

"Fine. For the record, I knew she wasn't going to say anything."

"Sure you did." I pulled into the driveway and noticed all the lights next door were dark except the one in my girl's room. I clenched my jaw, it's 10 o'clock she better not still be working.

I hate the thought of her getting taken advantage of. Their overtime policy is nothing but proof that they take advantage of all their employees. Hoping the employee will either forget the amount of overtime hours, or get too busy to notice at all. In this case, Natalie has so much to do she doesn't even think about her makeup hours.

My phone suddenly pinged and I can't help my grin when I see it's from my girl.

My Girl: *Do I need to start hiding my keys from you?*

Dean: *I'll still find them if you do.*

My Girl: *I don't know I have some pretty good hiding places*

Dean: *Like I said last night, I know my girl better than anyone, if you have a hiding spot I will find it, I will fill up your car if you need it, bring you flowers when you least expect it, and making sure you eat when you're working late*

My Girl: I knew that was you!!

Dean: *Have a good night Princess*

Dean: *If I find out you're still working, I will come over, bind you to that bed, and lock you in your room where I can guarantee the last thing you'll be thinking about is work*

The bubbles appear and disappear. I smiled as I got out of the car and leaned against the siding facing her window. I wish I could see her flustered face right now.

"Don't wait up Teddy." I called out.

He returned a disgusted look. "Figured as much, Romeo. Use protection. Last thing the world needs is a mini version of you." He shut the door as I brushed off his comment.

My Girl: *Good luck, the door's locked*

Dean: *Why would I use the front door when I have perfect access to your window?*

I looked up at the window and crossed my arms as I leaned against our house. She drew her curtains and opened her window to find me. She tried to hide the peaks of her smile, and I'm suddenly captivated. She looked down at me with her hair up in a messy clip, the shirt I left this morning, headphones around her neck, and no bra. She put her chin in her hand as she grinned down at me.

"And here I half expected you to be halfway up the trellis by now." She called down.

I took in a deep breath to try and control myself, seeing her in my shirt set something off in me that I have little control over. "Are you still working?"

She stayed silent for a moment. "No."

"You're lying, Princess." I walked forward. "Do I need to come up there and handcuff you to that headboard to make you stop? Or are you going to close your laptop and get some rest like a good girl?"

She bit her top lip. "Doesn't the prince usually come to *rescue* the

Princess from her tower?"

"I am no prince." I walked over to the trellis. "I'm the monster who's keeping you all to himself." I paused as I tested the sturdiness. "I'm sorry about earlier."

"For which part? Eating me out under my desk in front of my boss?"

The memory flashed through my mind as I chuckled. "No, I will *never* apologize for that." I paused for a moment. "I'm sorry about what I said earlier. It wasn't my intention to add more stress on you like that. I hate seeing you get taken advantage of when you already have a lot on your plate. I shouldn't have taken out my frustration with them on you. I am truly sorry, Natalie."

"Thank you. I know. I'm sorry too." She replied. "On days like this it's easy to forget how shitty they are. You get so caught up in the work and it just flies past you." She shrugged. "That's probably why I've been there for so long. Seems like every day is a long day." She smiled down at me. "The gas tank and flowers were a nice touch by the way."

I smiled back up at her. "I'll do it every single day. Anything to make my girl's day a little easier."

She chuckled. "Well. You don't have to fill my gas tank every day."

"True, but I still have a few tricks up my sleeve."

"Really? Care to share?" She leaned on the edge of the window.

"That depends. Are you going to open the door to let me in?"

She raised a brow as she stayed unmoved. "Are you going to steal my keys again?"

"Probably." I stated confidently.

"Then I don't know." She let out a fake exasperated sigh. "I think I might just lock up and work all night instead."

She bit her lip as she watched me start to climb the trellis up to her window. I'm up there in seconds using the same technique I used the first time. "Over my dead body." I sat on her windowsill before stepping into her room.

"I can't believe you actually climbed that. *Twice.*"

She backed herself into the wall allowing me to pin her there as she breathed heavily. I leaned close to her ear, "I will do anything for my girl. Even if that means tying you to that bed or using me to keep yourself busy. Anything to make sure you're not overworking yourself."

"Anything?" She whispered as her eyebrow raised.

"Yes." I stated confidently. "Anything you want, Princess."

"I want you on your knees, Dean Roberts." She whispered into my mouth. I took a couple steps back and did as she asked. One knee after the other hit the floor and I leaned back on my heels as she circled me. I felt her hand slid across my shoulders. "How's your back?"

I swiftly slipped off my jacket and shirt then turned to show her the beautiful little hickies and nail marks she left on me. She traced the outlines of the small marks. "Your signature is all over it."

"Does it hurt?"

"No. Not at all." I whispered as she shifted her hand to my throat and lifted my chin to look at her. The back of my head rested on her lower stomach. "I fucking adore it." The mixture of her scent and mine from my shirt almost made me pull her down to the floor with me.

"Good, because I'm nowhere near being done with you." She whispered against my ear.

Jesus fucking Christ. I clench my fists and take long breaths to control myself.

I licked my teeth as I narrowed my eye on her as she stepped to stand gorgeously tall in front of me.

"How many of my audiobooks have you listened to?"

"Almost all of them." She shrugged.

I raised my brow. "If I didn't know any better Princess, I'd say you were obsessed with me." I teased.

She grinned as she took my chin in her fingers, forcing me to keep my eyes to hers. As if I would even think about averting my eyes from her.

"And how many of my pictures did you jerk off to, *Heartthrob?*" The question left me speechless. She got me there. "That's what I thought. Stand up for me."

I slowly did as she asked and rose to my feet, shirtless, and towering over her.

"There's one more thing I need you to do." She traced her fingers down the tattoos on my arms.

Fuck, I don't think I can stay still much longer. "What's that, Princess?"

She gripped my belt and pulled me to her. "I need your back to my bed, right now."

I instantly wrapped my arms around her and took her with me. She said my back needed to be put to the bed, she didn't say anything about not taking her with me. She laughed and squealed against my lips as we kicked our clothes off.

She pulled off her shorts, revealing she had on no underwear and straddled me making my cock pulse and now soaked with precum.

She leaned down to my ear, "Now be a good boy and keep your hands up here." She repeated my movements from the other night pinning my wrists above me. "You move, I stop, and we start all over again. Do you understand, Heartthrob?" She purred.

"Fucking, hell." I bit out. *"Yes."*

My chest heaved as she rubbed her thumb across my lips. I gripped the headboard for dear life as she left warm kisses, and licked all the way down my body. It's taking every ounce of control I have to keep my hands where they are.

How the fuck did she do this?

I threw my head back into the pillows with short breaths. God, she hasn't even touched my cock yet, and I already can't control myself. Next thing I knew she had her hand around me and spreading my precum around the tip. I sucked in a breath as I tried to remain still. She looked up at me with a joyful look in her eyes. She knew exactly what she was doing and she's loving every second of it.

All my thoughts are lost when she puts her lips around me, slowly licking up and down. "Fucking hell… Natalie." I tried to channel every ounce of control I had left, I wanted to put my hands on her *now*. She slowly explored every inch of me, and every swipe of her tongue had me begging for more.

My grip tightened on her headboard and I began to sweat when her lips held tighter while she slowly took every inch of me down her throat.

"Nat… Christ…"

I was never a holy man by any means, but the feeling of her mouth on my cock was as close to heaven as I could imagine. She licked and sucked, making me see stars and lights behind my eyelids.

I could feel the tension building and building higher already. God dammit, I can't come now, not when she just fucking started. I should know better, I lose all sense of control when it comes to this woman. She has me in her choke hold and I fucking live for it.

Just when I thought I had it under control, she wrapped her hand around me and began to move along with her swirling tongue and… I break, she doesn't stop as I come in her mouth and down her throat, more stars, more light, and entire sensory overload. I felt like my heart was about to beat out of my chest as if I just went for a run, and gripped the headboard so tight I thought for sure I was going to rip it from the bolts. Then I saw the most beautiful sight. She crawled back up to me, wiping the corner of her mouth with her thumb after having swallowed every last drop.

I put my hands in her hair and rose up to claim her mouth again. God, she smells and tastes like me… like… *mine*. I don't feel how sore my fingers are from white knuckling her headboard like my fucking life was on the line.

She's straddling me again and her wetness pressing against my cock has my body already pleading to go again. To fuck her to tears as she screams my name over and over again until the sun rises.

Natalie

Usually when a big celebrity death occurs while you work in the media industry you have two reactions. A sympathetic, if they were a decent human, "Aw, damn" shortly followed by "*Aw, damn* this is going to be a long month".

This week alone has been filled with countless hours, multiple shift switches, and multiple content scheduling checks with lots of 'coffee breaks' with my narrator in between.

Dean has been constantly attached to my hip this week, but never to the point of getting in my way during my normal work hours. My water is never empty, he takes me to get lunch every day at noon on the dot, and if I'm not ready he'll loom over our desks until we wrap up our last task.

I should get frustrated with it, but to be honest, it's a little freeing. It's one less thing to remind myself and it makes me stop to realize that I need food and a break in order to function for the rest of the day. Plus, it seemed as though I wasn't the only one benefiting from it. The minute he approaches Ben knows it's time to finish up his task and take lunch which has the rest of the team following. Usually on week's like this we don't stop until we realize it's three o'clock and we forgot to take lunch. Not that Brock minded it at all. He couldn't care less as long as the work gets done.

After a few conversations with Dean, and making sure he didn't have any Bluetooth devices on him when I went into meetings, he's… *behaved.* I use that term lightly given he still looks like he's about to rip Brock apart every time he enters the room. I let the glare slide not only because it helps keep Brock from barging in whenever he feels like it but I've been feeling the same way lately.

The way he bit my head off the other night for another tiny mistake that could've been fixed in two seconds was appalling. When I told Dean about it, pissed was an understatement. I begged him to not barge into his office the next day. If he did then it would be a clear sign that Dean and I are together and that I'm telling him things that I technically shouldn't. However, I'm not exactly holding him back from scaring him off while we're busy.

Thanks to a little slip from Helen, I found out about how he let go of almost *all* of the writers, not half. So after lying to me and talking to me like I'm human garbage, he's lucky I'm not letting Dean have at him in the middle of this fucking office. He's lucky *I'm* not calling him out in front of the entire office.

I took a deep breath and got back to the matter at hand. I started looking over our metrics over the past month *again* while Dean was in the audio booth recording another script.

The amount of content we've pushed out over this week was insane. While Alan Jenkins death took over as ultimate priority, we were still pushing Tanner and Ell engagement content.

I rubbed my forehead and took a deep breath. We're spamming the shit out of our profiles and it's not doing us any favors. While our engagement is still high, and bringing in a good chunk of cash from monetization, it's not good engagement. Our poor moderator looked like he hadn't slept in days, filtering all the comments that are calling us out for it.

With titles like "What Alan Jenkins Would Eat In A Day" and "Alan Jenkins Autopsy Will Shock You" I'm nowhere near surprised. The more I look at these titles the more sick I feel about posting them.

It's not illegal to shit post on the internet, but it still feels like throwing plastic into a bonfire. It's not going to kill you but the fumes are fucking fowl and it literally contributes nothing to benefit the fire.

We're still losing followers at a slow constant rate. Slow enough that Brock doesn't seem to care and I'm sure Nathan hasn't noticed. All Brock's going to see from these metrics is that it's going up and it's bringing in money. That "we need to keep up this pace if we want our engagement to keep rising" which is honestly the worst idea. We go through the same shitty cycle every time multiple big news stories hit at once. Spike in views, spike in profit, Brock runs on a content high, then it plummets until the next big story or movie release. Which can take anywhere from a week to months.

That being said, once our content quota goes up it hardly ever comes back down. So, when we don't meet that quota, *we're* the problem. Brock has yet to see that it's impossible to hit a quota when there's no content to hit it with.

My team is already feeling the burnout after this week, and frankly so am I. The stress of missing a misspelling or posting the correct content to the correct profile even though it's the same story just with a different title and aesthetic is overwhelming. I've been where they are, I know this process better than anyone, and I know we can't keep this pace up with five people and over twenty profiles.

I made myself close my laptop and took a second to collect my thoughts. This isn't new. I have these same thoughts every single time we have an overload of content. Ever since Dean arrived I've been questioning myself more and more as to why.

Why are they not listening? Why are they lying? What else are they hiding from us? Why is it the more I speak up, the quieter it gets? Jesus fucking Christ how did we end up here?

I took in another breath and made my eyes stop themselves from watering. I can't break down, not right now, my team is right outside, Brock could walk in any minute, and he *will not* see me break.

Thank god it was Friday, I was so ready to spend this weekend with a very hot neighbor and sexy narrator.

Has Dean stayed with me every single night this week? Oh yeah, and it's been incredible. He made me breakfast every morning, showered with me before bed, and stood guard over my laptop after five. With the exceptions of emergencies from either Ben, Megan, Amy, or Miranda.

Since Kayley is coming home on Sunday we have two nights left with the house to ourselves and I wanted to get as much private time with him as I could before she's back within ear shot. I've never been talkative or loud during sex, but this man had me doing things with my mouth I swear are borderline illegal or cause for a noise complaint.

He said he had no problem kicking Teddy out for a few hours if we wanted to use his place. He may not have an issue with it, since he sees him as an annoying little brother, but I do. I'm not going to kick Teddy out of the house while he's going through a tough time. I'm definitely not going to kick Kay out after she gets home from a week's vacation all for some amazing sex. So, I told him we'll have to get creative and his brow raise indicated he was definitely intrigued.

Dean opened the door to the audio booth after finishing his last script. "There's my girl."

I side eyed him. "Someone's going to hear you."

He lowered his tone as he leaned to my ear. "Let them listen." He pulled down his mask and laid his lips to the side of my cheek. "You'll always be my girl. I don't care who hears it."

My heart began to flutter which has been a normal occurrence every time I see this man. I couldn't help but smile as he brushed his nose to mine. I could feel his warmth across my skin making me crave his touch.

"While I do love the sound of that. We're still working under the same roof, and *you* need to be on your best behavior so we don't get fired."

He licked his top lip before putting his mask back on. "I don't think I'm the one you need to keep reminding."

I suddenly became aware of how tight I was clenching my thighs together as flashes of us in the booth this morning filled my head. My cheeks instantly flushed.

He sat in the chair next to me as I opened my laptop, forcing myself back to reality. "Everything go okay with this last read?"

Dean hung his head for a moment. "It was, alright."

"Alright?" I questioned.

There was a look in his eye as if he wanted to tell me something. "Have you noticed that some of these scripts are…"

"Getting worse?" I tried to fill in the blank.

He nodded side to side. "Yeah."

I pressed my lips together as I nodded. "I'm not surprised, we only have a handful of writers left, they've got their hands full." I rubbed my forehead. "I knew this was going to happen. They're so swamped and rushed to meet deadlines that the quality of the scripts are declining. I should reach out to Jackie and see what's going on. If they're this swamped we need to help them somehow."

"Right." He shifted in his chair and leaned forward putting his elbows on his knees. "Have you considered talking to Brock about taking over this project fully?"

"Taking over as in, writing the scripts?"

He shrugged. "You have the experience. You're great at it. It'd take a load off the department."

"Dean, we talked about this."

A couple of days ago he brought up our conversation about writing scripts again. I thought that alluding Brock as the reason why I'm not a script writer would be the end of it. Clearly not.

I told him, again, that I only write for myself, especially after hearing about some of the horror stories that came from the writing department. I wanted to steer clear of that pile of bullshit. Even the opinion pieces are skewed in a more "company favorable" direction. I didn't want to put myself through that, not when I love writing.

I showed him a few book and movie reviews I wrote in the past along with a few story ideas. After every review was finished I'd print it, put it in the binder, and forget about it until the next book, movie, or TV show and he loved it. Despite some unpopular opinions about certain book titles that I defended with my whole chest. Leaving him both delightfully frustrated and smiling from ear to ear.

When he brought it up recently though something shifted. I wasn't quite sure why but I knew it couldn't just be because these scripts aren't the best.

"I know. And I support you not wanting to write *here*."

I gave him a weird look. "Are you telling me I should quit my job to become a writer?"

"Is that what you want?"

I thought about it for a moment. Even if I wanted to write full time, that's not exactly a stable career. "I can't do that."

"Why not?"

"Because it's fantasy, Dean. I can't just say 'bye', write a bestseller and host a raving blog about books, movies, and pop culture overnight. It doesn't work like that, I have bills to pay, I need a stable income." I surprised myself when I said those words. Is that what I want?

"What if I helped?"

"What do you mean by *help*?" I narrowed my brow at him. He paused for a moment, his jaw tensing as I searched his face for answers.

"Dean, what is going on? What are you not telling me?"

"Natalie!" Dean gave a disgruntled sigh as Brock entered the room. "We have a company meeting in about ten minutes. I need all the managers in the meeting room in the next five. Mr. Craven, you're welcome to join us."

"Sure. We'll wrap up here and head that way." I gave him a fake sense of enthusiasm.

"Perfect. See you both there." Brock tapped the door frame as I looked back to Dean. Still glaring at the doorway.

I nudged his arm. "Stop mean mugging the door, it hasn't done anything to you."

"On the contrary, it hasn't kept Brock out of this room *yet*. If I didn't know any better I'd say he had a third sense to find the perfect time to interrupt us. Though I highly doubt it, considering he doesn't have any senses." He stood tall as he stretched his back.

I gave him a deadpanned look. "Dean."

"I'm not kidding." He stated in a serious tone.

"I know and we can vent and rave about it later. But, right now, I need you to be on your best behavior." I began to gather my things from the table.

"Only if he is too." He whispered.

I gave him one last pleading look as we made our way out into the open area. Dean and I trailed in as the final two to enter the meeting room. Everyone around the room shifted looks our way, mainly at Dean. I was used to it by this point, and Dean couldn't give less of a shit. If anyone else looked at me on the other hand he would stare right back waiting for them to turn their eyes away. I get it, a 6' 3" man with tattoos, a face mask, dark clothes, and a glare can make anyone cower. Me on the other hand, I have to try very hard to keep my hands to myself and keep a safe distance.

I was suddenly smacked back into reality as Brock began the

meeting. I really hope this meeting is quick, I have a laundry list of things to do today. It's launch day for our newest profile with Dean's videos. Usually on launch days like this Brock sends me the file, I look it over, upload it, create the description, tags, schedule it, everything. Yet, this time, not a single peep.

"Alright, managers, thank you all for joining me before the company meeting starts. I wanted to give a special thank you to Mr. Craven," he gestured towards Dean, "He's done a wonderful job with our newest project, and we're very excited to have 'The Book Nook' launch today."

Okay, so we're still on schedule. Why the hell hasn't he looped me in? He pulled up the profile on the big screen showing the first video scheduled and a few others already uploaded in drafts.

My eyes were glued to the screen. He already scheduled it? Tags, description, thumbnail, everything. Did he get impatient, did he think I was too busy? Why wouldn't he communicate this with me? He's already lied to me, what else is he not telling me?

"If you guys haven't seen the video yet in passing I highly recommend you go check it out," Brock went on, "Mr. Craven did a wonderful job with those scripts."

"All thanks to Natalie." Dean interrupted. I whipped my head to him. "She's guided me through the entire process and helped me settle in here. So *all* the thanks should go to her."

I pressed a thin smile as everyone nodded, acknowledged, and agreed. I couldn't help but feel a little embarrassed when the spotlight moved to me but I appreciated the recognition. Especially since it looked as though it annoyed Brock to all hell. The distraction from my thoughts only lasted for thirty seconds before my boss dropped another bombshell on us.

"Since productivity has been high for these past couple of weeks, we have decided to require everyone, who lives locally, to start working in-office again." He paused as everyone looked at each other wide-eyed. "It'll help us collaborate and communicate more effectively. I'll be sending all of you an email with some of the finer details."

"That's bullshit." Greg, our manager of Moderation, spoke up. "You know that we can do these jobs effectively from home and that productivity has only gone up because two high profile stories are happening at the same time."

Dean and I raised our brows. I wasn't expecting that. He was definitely saying what we were all thinking, but Greg? Of all the managers to speak up, he's the chillest, most nonchalant, man in this office and he's *pissed*.

He stood up from the table. "You're only doing this to micro-manage us."

"Greg-" Brock tried to get a word in.

Greg threw up his hands. "No. I'm sick of it, we're all sick of your bullshit, you have no accountability, no morals, and no respect for any of us. Find someone else's neck to breathe on."

After Greg stormed out we all looked back to Brock looking shocked as he tried to find the right words to say. Dean and I exchanged a "holy shit that just happened" look.

The room was dead silent until the chime of a video call from Nathan to start the company meeting bounced across the room.

Brock cleared his throat. "Helen, if you would please escort Greg out of the building."

She nodded still with wide eyes and left the meeting room. Brock went on in a hushed tone. "Everyone, if you please join in at your desk with a set of headphones and set your mic to mute. Thank you."

We didn't need to be told twice as we all quickly and silently exited the meeting room.

Dean

"Well that meeting was a waste of time." Natalie pulled off her headphones and closed her laptop.

I shrugged. "Well you can't compare it to the one we had earlier, no meeting in history could reach that level of satisfaction."

"Fair enough." She crossed her arms. "I still can't believe Greg, of all the managers, was the first to snap. Go with the flow, chill, 'what up bro', Greg."

"You know what they say, the quiet ones hold the most secrets." I paused as she continued to stare off. Something has her brain in a loop.

"Yeah. But, that was so out of character for him. Something else was going on that made him tip over the edge like that." Her leg began to bounce as she thought. I rolled my chair over and put my hand on her thigh to calm her.

"What's on your mind, Princess?" She placed her hand on mine and began brushing her thumb over my knuckles.

"There's something they're not telling us. Profile launches are something I help take care of. Brock sends me the file, I write the description, tags, look over the video to make sure there are no errors, upload it, schedule it." She stared down at our hands as she twirled her fingers around mine. "For this launch, he didn't send me anything.

No files, no schedule times, reminders, *nothing*. Yet, there they were plain as day, set and ready to schedule."

My brain immediately went to the email I found on Brock's laptop. If he didn't send her anything like normal, he must've used the launch to test the automated systems they were looking into. The worst part. It worked.

"I don't know what to think. First, eliminating almost all of our writers, then forcing us into the office because of 'productivity', and now he handled this launch on his own? Something's not right." She sighed. "I might just be paranoid, I have been busy this week so maybe he thought I didn't have the time."

God, I have all the answers she's looking for but how do I say it? She knows I want her to leave this place, if I tell her everything would she believe me?

"Sorry, I didn't mean to dump all this on you." She shook her head.

"Natalie." I lifted her chin so her eyes could meet mine. "You don't need to apologize. I asked you to tell me what was on your mind and you did. I may talk for a living but I also have great listening skills." She laughed as I returned my hand to hers. "You can tell me anything. I'll always be here to listen." I unlooped one side of my mask and laid a kiss to the back of her hand.

Once five o'clock rolled around I stood next to Natalie at her desk and talked with her team while everyone packed up. What everyone was doing for the weekend, and the drama that unfolded earlier. Apparently after Greg stormed out he grabbed his bag, a box that already had all of his desk supplies, and was escorted out by Helen. Since she's 5' 3" and in her late sixties she had hard time keeping up with Greg according to Ben.

"Mr. Craven." I stretched my neck at the shrill sound of Brock's voice. "Could I see you for a moment before you leave?"

Everyone looked back and forth at each other as my girl looked right at me with a "what did you do" look. While I'm not surprised that was her immediate thought, I'm still a little offended she didn't give me a little credit. I've been a gentleman all day. Which was pretty easy considering I only saw the dickhead once today. While I would rather swallow wood chips than be alone with this fucker for five minutes I knew Natalie has been urging me to play nice so they don't suspect anything between us. While she hated her job she wasn't ready to leave it yet. So, I'll comply until the millisecond she changes her mind. Whatever my girl wants, my girl gets.

I nod. "Sure."

"What did you do?" Natalie whispered.

I tilted my head. "Nothing. I promise. He probably wants to talk about the launch." I paused as she gave me a worried look. "Don't worry Princess, I'll play nice. I'd offer you a Bluetooth mic but, according to one of the managers here, that's violating a few HR rules." I teased.

She licked her teeth behind her lip and tried not to smile. "You cheeky little shit." She muttered.

"I'm *your* 'cheeky little shit.'" I whispered before I took a few steps back to head towards his office.

It was a little larger than a man of his job description needed. He stood at his standing desk still with his socks exposed and slip-on sandals. I understand wanting to be comfortable at work, but this is just unhygienic. The man was 5'11" at best, so he had to turn his head up to make eye contact when I entered. Which with me wasn't often.

"Have a seat, Mr. Craven." He didn't look away from his brand new laptop. I doubt he got any heat for damaging company equipment but it made me feel better knowing he had to start from scratch on another laptop.

"I think I'll stand, thank you." I crossed my arms.

He looked at the door I left open and back at me. He knew I wasn't moving. After a moment of silence he walked over, shut the door and went back to his desk. Men like Brock are easy to figure out. He acts all top dog until someone bigger, smarter, or above his pay grade comes around. Then he does whatever he can to get on their good side, whether that's being the CEO's minion or putting down someone else to make him look tough in front of them. This man is the scum of the Earth and I'll make him remember that if he uses this meeting to piss me off.

"First, I want to apologize for Greg's *outburst* earlier today, he was under a lot of stress and I think the news of the change may have triggered him to lash out." He tried to explain. "That's not how we run our business here I can assure you."

If I didn't have this mask on right now Natalie would be digging her elbow into my side to fix my face.

"Outburst"? "Lash out"?

Given everything I've witnessed since day one I think it was justified and Greg knew exactly what he was saying. The man used his entire chest, you couldn't convince me that he just *happened* to "lash out". The man already had his box packed for Christ's sake.

"Second, I feel as though we may have gotten off on the wrong foot. If there is anything I have done to offend you I apologize."

Really? You don't say?

"Lastly…"

Dear god, there's more?

"Nathan has requested that you join us for lunch here in the office next Friday."

"No, thank you." I let out nonchalantly.

"I'm afraid it's not up for debate. Nathan has some things he wants to go over with you." He stood firm on this one.

"Only if Natalie joins us." I quickly replied. "She's involved in this project as much as I am. Anything he needs to say, she should hear too."

He bit his bottom lip in defeat. "Okay, if that makes you *comfortable*, then she can join us." I analyze him for a moment. He has an idea, but not the full picture, slimy prick.

"You and Natalie have really hit it off this week," he began to push. "I'm glad she's making you feel *welcome* here." He rounded his desk and leaned on it. "She's a nice girl, good at her job, and definitely has certain *assets* that are finally proving useful this past week." He stated in an annoyed tone.

Now I'm seeing fucking red. I took a step forward and grabbed the collar of his shirt. "You wanna run that by me again?"

His face immediately went pale as he tried to keep a brave face. He knew exactly what he just said.

"Suddenly can't remember? Here's what I heard. It sounded like you were insinuating something highly inappropriate about one of your most esteemed employees." I'm fucking seething as this pathetic excuse of a man began to crumble in front of me. "If I *ever* hear you talk about her that way again, I promise you, I will make sure it hurts, and that you never work in this industry again."

"Is- is that a threat?" He snubbed.

"With all the shit you've pulled I will have no problem keeping my promise." I paused. "The only reason my fist isn't in your face right now is *because* of Natalie. So If I were you I'd show her the respect she deserves. Do we understand each other?"

He quickly nodded.

I tapped my hand to his face to make him flinch. "Good talk. See you on Monday." I released his collar making him stumble back into his desk. I opened the door to leave and saw my girl waiting for me at her desk biting her thumb nail nervously. She immediately stood as I approached her.

"What happened?" She began to question. "What did he say?"

"Nothing important." I stated nonchalantly. "Ready to go?"

She narrowed her eyes on me. "If it wasn't important, why not tell me?"

I tilted my head as I looked down at her. "It was about Greg's quote 'outburst', nothing we don't already know."

I opened the door for her to leave the office. "Ah. Let me guess, 'I can assure you that's not how we do business' speech?"

Brock caught my eye as he locked his office. I gave him a hard stare as he fumbled with his keys. "Word for word."

When we got back home I made a stop next door to grab a few things for this weekend. My girl was adamant about using what time she had left with the house and I intend on spending every second I can to fulfill her every need and desire.

As I zipped up my bag I heard footsteps near my doorway. "Wow, already spending the weekend together, huh?"

I turned to see Teddy leaning against the doorway. "What do you want?"

He lifted his shoulders. "Nothing. Just seems a little quick don't ya think?"

"Nope. She has the house to herself for another day and we're going to take advantage of it."

He scrunched his nose. "Fucking animals, you lot. Remind me to not sit anywhere in that house."

I rolled my eyes. "That reminds me. You, me, Natalie, and Kayley. Dinner, Sunday night."

He rubbed the back of his neck. "Yeah about that…"

"You can't back out of this one." I grabbed my backpack and pushed past him. While my initial plan was to have him meet Kayley as payback, it's now turned into an attempt for him to make better friends. Natalie and I talked about meeting her friends officially next week, and with Teddy's situation we decided to start including him slowly.

"What if she's some crazy fan who knows everything about me and ends up throwing herself at me?" He followed me down the stairs.

I couldn't help but chuckle. While yes, Kayley was one of his fans, I highly doubt she would throw herself on him. I shook my head. "She's not going to throw herself at you. That I can promise."

"You don't know that." He spat back. "I appreciate you trying to find me some new friends but it's not necessary. I'm doing just fine."

I set down my bag at the table. "You have made progress. I'm not denying that. But, the only people you've interacted with this week are Natalie and myself." He scoffed. "When was the last time Brayden or Ell reached out to you?"

He stayed quiet for a moment. "Ell's on tour. She's busy."

While I don't see that as a legitimate excuse for her behavior I let it slide for now. "And Brayden?" I pressed.

He shook his head with a look of defeat. "What time?"

"Five o'clock. Don't worry we're having it here." I picked up my bag. "I promise, making your own friends is a good step forward."

"Yeah. Until she starts stalking me and spreading the news of my whereabouts." He scoffed again.

I sighed. "Teddy. There's a reason why we're having you meet Kayley first. While yes, she knows who Tanner Brunswick is, she's not going to spread around that information. Natalie trusts her therefore I do too."

"Have you met her?"

"Not yet."

"Then you can't promise that."

"Teddy, relax. Everything will be fine, not everyone is a crazy fan."

"I'm sorry Dean, but you're very trusting of a woman you just met a week ago. She's shown that she's a good person, I've seen it, I get that. But, do you really know everything about her and her friends?"

I paused for a moment. I mean, technically I do. I took another moment to ponder what I'm about to say. "Okay. What if I told you that Natalie's actually a fan of mine?"

He shrugged. "She's a reader in a book club, I'm sure she's heard of you."

I raised a brow as I tried not to grin. "She's been following my career for three years. Now that she knows who I am, not once has she ever tried to expose me. If anything, she's done everything she can to make sure my identity is kept a secret. I trust her. I trust her judgment. If she trusts her housemate, then I trust them too."

He squinted at me. "You're telling me you're dating one of your fans?"

I closed my eyes and pinched the bridge of my nose. "Do you trust me, or not?"

He analyzed me for a moment. "Questionable. But, for the most part, yeah."

"I'll take it." I threw my backpack over my shoulder. "What are your plans for the next couple of days?"

He shrugged. "Not sure. Run, maybe start reading 'The Deal Breaker.'"

"Now, Natalie is letting you borrow her copy, so be careful with it." I reiterated.

"Yeah, yeah, if I break the spine you'll break mine, I remember." He picked up the book from the table. "Why are there so many tabs in it?"

I licked my teeth behind my lip, and nodded. "You'll find out. And don't dog ear her pages. If I find out you're not using a bookmark I'll kick your teeth in."

He set the book down and threw his hands up. "Alright, Jesus, am I allowed to touch the damn thing?"

"Only after you wash your hands."

"Seriously?" He looked at me as if I was the crazy one. She took care of her books, and she was kind enough to lend one to my little brother, so naturally he'll pay if he does anything to it.

"Seriously." I reiterated. "Have fun. Don't burn the house down."

"Yeah, yeah. Give Natalie my condolences for having to put up with your arse for two days."

"Jokes on you, she loves my arse." I closed the door as Teddy sounded out a notable gag.

Once I made my way over to my girl's house I opened the door and called out for her. "Natalie?" Something about opening the door to her home and calling for her felt satisfying.

I heard her rustling in the kitchen. Her head popped up from behind the counter. "There you are. One second."

"You know it's dangerous to leave the door unlocked." I turned the deadbolt over. "An intruder could come in at any second."

"Are you an intruder?" She replied.

"I could be." I smirked.

She popped up from retrieving a bowl from her bottom cabinets. She brushed her hair from her face and leaned against the counter, wearing nothing but an apron that covered her chest and cinched at her waist. "Well then. This is an awkward situation, mister intruder."

My jaw is on the fucking floor. I have no words. All thoughts, all problems… gone. All I knew was I needed to have her right here, *right now*.

"Princess," I made my way into the kitchen and wiped my hand down my face to find out she is in fact completely naked under that apron.

"Heartthrob." She replied as she turned to me, putting her hand on her hip and licking a spoon that I'm quickly becoming jealous of. "You've been supportive this week, so this is for *you* to devour."

I licked my top lip as I looked down at her. Whatever she's making can wait. I quickly lifted her and set her on the counter and brought her lips to mine. She was already addicting, now she tastes like forbidden candy that I can't stop consuming.

I gripped her thighs as she wrapped her legs around my waist. I untied her apron, revealing her gorgeous body and slowly kissed, licked and sucked all the way down her neck, chest, and torso. Then I spread her legs wider to reveal herself to me. Already, she's practically dripping with arousal onto the counter. I put her thighs to my shoulders as I began to kiss and suck on her inner thighs, leaving more of those little marks she adored along the way. Once I felt I teased her long enough I licked her from top to bottom as her thighs squeezed around my head. She let out a moan that had my cock so hard it was almost painful.

I unzipped my jeans to relieve the pressure, and my god I wanted to be inside her. Feeling her wet cunt around my cock as I fucked her on the counter.

"Fuck… Dean…" She moaned out and that was it. That was all it took for me to lose all sense of my control. I needed to be inside her, I needed it right now.

I gave her one last lick before I stood tall, brushed off her wetness from my lips with my thumb, and licked it off. I slid my hand to the back of her neck and laced my fingers into her hair. Her breath hitched as I brushed her clit with the tip of my cock before sliding all the way inside of her.

"Fuck." I almost came right there as she wrapped her legs around my waist with one hand gripping the counter and the other at my back to keep me right there.

"Is this what you wanted, Princess?" I whispered as I kept a controlled thrust. "For me to fuck you to tears on the counter?"

"Yes." She whimpered out.

Fuck.

I peeled off my shirt and lifted her off the counter to flip her around. She pressed her chest to the counter as I reinserted my cock. I threw my head back at the sensation and dug my fingers into the stretch marks on her hips. I wrapped my arms around her body and brought her back to my chest as she raised her arm to reach around my neck.

"Don't worry, my love, whatever my girl wants, she will get. *Tenfold.*"

Natalie

I woke up to the sound of a door opening and shutting downstairs. Realizing Dean was still wrapped around me my heart rate began to rise.

Someone's in the house.

Another shuffle from downstairs made me raise my head and send an emergency text to Riley. Dean must've woken the same time I did because he immediately and quietly slipped out of the bed.

He slipped on his sweat pants as I put my shorts and t-shirt on. "Stay here." He whispered.

"Fuck no. I'm not letting you go down there by yourself." I whisper-yelled back. I pulled my bat and my old metal twirling baton from underneath my bed. I gave him the bat as he gave me a strange look.

I shrugged. "I don't like guns." I held up my baton. "Trust me. This thing can do damage if you swing hard enough. I had enough bruises from practice as a kid to prove it."

"I'm going to need more context later." He shook his head. "If you're not going to stay here, stay behind me."

I nodded as he opened my bedroom door. The shuffling got louder as we made our way down the stairs. It's coming from Kayley's room. Dean put his finger to his lips for me to stay quiet. I nodded as he went ahead. In a flash I saw someone come up behind him and with all my strength I swung the baton behind his knees taking the man to the floor.

"Ah! For fuck's sake Nat it's me!" He yelped.

I squinted realizing who it was. "Justin?"

Dean picked him up by the throat and pinned him to the wall. "Dean! Stop!"

"What the fuck is going on?" Kayley ran out.

"Kayley?" I looked over at her with wide eyes.

Justin hit Dean's elbows getting him out of the lock, but not before Dean threw him to the floor.

She looked over at Dean with an impressed look. "Neighbor Dean?"

"Yes." I nodded.

"Beat his ass!" She called.

I narrowed my brow at her as he picked up Justin by his jacket. "Dean! Stop! That's-"

Suddenly the front door flew open as Riley and Rob came running through the door. "Drop him! Put your hands where I can see them!" She yelled out pointing a taser in Dean's direction.

"Whoa! Whoa!" I stepped in front of her. "Stop! Everyone just stop!"

Riley tilted her head. "Is that your twirling baton?"

I gave her a look before I turned to Dean who currently has his sole focus on Justin. Who let him have the control for the time being with a playful look in his eye. As if he was eager and waiting for Dean to strike again.

"Dean! Drop him!" I shouted.

"No. Keep going, he deserves it after the car ride he put me through." Kayley interrupted.

I rolled my eyes. "Don't listen to her. That's Justin, Kayley's brother."

They exchanged hard looks as he roughly released him and made his way over to my side.

"You're lucky Natalie cares about you so much." Justin spat.

"Otherwise your brains would be on the wall."

Kayley blew a raspberry. "Please! That man had your ass on the floor before you could get another word out."

"Hey, I'm sleep deprived." He shot back.

Dean towered behind me with his hand on my hip to keep me close. I took in a deep breath of relief. "Are you okay?" He whispered.

I nodded. "Yeah. Just filled with adrenaline is all." I gave him a thin smile as he kissed the top of my head.

Riley tucked her taser away. "Mind telling me what happened here?"

"Dean and I heard someone downstairs. Since it's Friday night and thinking Kay wasn't going to be home until Sunday," I looked over at my roommate with a questionable stare. "I thought it was an intruder. I didn't realize it was Justin until he was on his back. Dean had no idea who he was so naturally he jumped into action."

Justin rubbed the back of his knees. "I'll give you points for aim, Nat. But, damn."

I looked up to Dean and raised the baton. "Told ya." He let out a small breath with a chuckle. I turned to Justin and shrugged. "Sorry. You should've called us, or at least announced yourselves." I scolded.

Kayley shrugged. "I didn't want to wake you, or… *disturb* you."

I rolled my eyes. "Why are you home so early?"

She shrugged. "Family vacay ended early."

"What happened?" I questioned.

She waved her hand. "Some family business related bullshit that J refuses to explain." Justin rolled his eyes as he began walking toward the door. Looking completely over this conversation.

"Because it doesn't concern you. Least of all anyone else." He muttered.

Riley stuck her hand out before Justin could leave. "Anything you need to tell me before you leave, Justin?"

He stood tall and confident as Riley gave him her very serious and suspicious look. A sudden chill went down my spine.

"Nope." He turned back to glare at Dean. "You, however," He pointed at him. "Lay your hands on me again, I won't be as lenient." Dean didn't flinch at the comment.

Kayley rolled her eyes. "For fuck's sake. He beat your ass, just accept it."

"Okay, okay." Riley raised her hands. "Go on. Get out of here until this turns into a real disturbance. Give your father my best." She practically pushed Justin out the door before shutting it.

Rob chimed in. "While I'm glad this wasn't a true break-in, I hope this changed your mind about getting a security system? With that trellis by your window you're lucky no one's tried to climb through your window."

Dean looked down at me and turned back. "That's what I told her." I lightly nudged him in the torso.

"Yeah, after tonight that's shot up on my to-do list."

"So, we're all good here?" Riley gave a hard stare at Dean then to me.

"Yes. We're fine." I tried to reassure her. Dean turned back, looking me over again and breathing a sigh of relief himself.

I suddenly realized I'm literally bra-less in a t-shirt while Dean stood tall in only his sweatpants that didn't leave much to the imagination. What a way to meet my friends for the first time.

Riley tried to hide her smile at his reaction of looking me over. "Okay. We'll get out of your hair. Have a good night." She winked at me before they shut the door behind them. Once I locked the door I turned my attention to Kayley who was still leaning against the doorway trying to keep her words in.

I turned to Dean. "Could you give us a minute?"

He looked at me, the door, to Kayley and back at me. As if he was still on edge and worried about someone else coming through that door. I gave him a reassuring look before he reluctantly nodded and kissed my forehead.

"I'll be upstairs. Call if you need me."

I nodded back and watched as he went upstairs. I waited for the door to shut and I turned back to Kayley.

"Ho…ly… fuck. He's gorgeous!" She tried to whisper.

"Okay. In your room, now." I pointed and pushed her in before I shut the door behind us.

She threw herself onto her bed. "My god! Thank every being in existence he has a brother!"

I turned my lips in.

Shit.

I had initially promised her an introduction, but that was before I knew said brother was Tanner fucking Brunswick. A celebrity crush she's had since we were teenagers. Who is currently engaged and about to go through a difficult break-up with a famous pop-star.

I took a deep breath. That's tomorrow's problem when Dean's not here and after I get some sleep. Right now, I need to focus on what the hell just happened.

"Okay, let's circle back here. Why did you come back early?"

She scoffed. "Seriously? I told you family business bullshit."

I leaned against her door so she couldn't escape. "Seriously, Kay. Is everything okay?" I knew very little about what her family did for a living. Every time it came up she either ignored it or brushed it off. Just like what she's doing now.

"Yeah. Why wouldn't it be?" She gave me a weird look.

"You're here two days early from a 'family vacay' that ended because of 'family business' in the middle of the night. Not to mention Justin seemed a little on edge before he left."

Her face went flat. "You mean after he got his ass beat by your 6'3" ripped British boyfriend? Highlight of my month by the way. I think anyone would be on edge after taking a beating from him."

"You know what I mean." I sat on the bed next to her. "The 'it doesn't concern you' bit he muttered before he left."

She rolled her eyes as she stood to get one of her suitcases. "He was just being an asshole." She threw the suitcase on the bed and flipped the top open to reveal a pile of clothes.

"I don't know what's going on," she continued, "but to be honest I could care less. Anything to get me out of that dusty Airbnb." She quickly began unloading the clothes into a laundry basket. "Don't worry, I have all the time in the world to tell you about it. Go back upstairs and suck that man off. He deserves it after the way he protected you tonight. I promise I'll have my 'booty tapping' headphones on, after I dust them off."

"Kayley."

"What? Did you already do that earlier?"

I choked on my words as she waved her hand and went on before I could get a word out.

"I know we weren't 'real intruders' but he snapped into action. Not to mention looked *fine as hell* whilst doing it. I saw those little nail marks and hickies. I need *every single detail*."

I couldn't help but let out a small laugh. "Sure, only if you tell me about what happened during your trip."

She narrowed her eyes on me and grinned. "Touche."

"Goodnight, Kayley." I reached for the door handle to leave.

"Given what's waiting for you upstairs I don't need to tell you to have a *good* night." She shook her hips and licked her teeth as she mocked.

"You are absolutely feral." I laughed.

"So are you apparently." She continued to smile. I couldn't help but smile back. I didn't realize how much I've missed her this week. With everything going on it's nice to hear her quips again.

I rolled my eyes at her statement. "Good to have you home, get some sleep."

Once I made my way back upstairs I found Dean sitting on the edge of the bed rubbing his hands together waiting for me. Once he saw me he straightened his back.

"Everything okay?" He asked.

I closed my door behind me, put my baton back under my bed, and crawled in. "I'm surprised you're not asleep by now."

My cheek met his chest as he wrapped both arms around me and held me close. "Knowing you're downstairs after what happened tonight, absolutely not."

I took a deep breath through my nose trying to calm my thoughts. I know it was just Kay and Justin, but what if it was someone breaking in? The thought made me bury myself further into his chest. This is where I feel safe, right here, in this bed in his arms. He gripped me tighter. I know the thought scared him too, but the way he immediately went after Justin, he didn't care who it was. All he knew was someone was in the house and was right next to me.

"If there's any future break-ins at least we know we make a good team." I tried to joke the fear away.

His chin rested on top of my head as he slowly brushed his thumb on my shoulder. He adjusted to where his lips were in my hair. "I'd like to see them try. I will never let anything bad happen to you. *I promise.*"

My heart quickened. Yes, he's become a safe space for me, yes, I care about him a lot, our chemistry is fantastic, he'd do anything for me, and I'd do anything for him… but do I *really* know everything about him?

I brushed his cheek, brought him to look straight down at me, and let the words pour straight from my heart.

"Promise me you won't break my heart Dean Roberts."

His pupils grew as he looked at me with a yearning I've never seen before. He turned to kiss my palm and laid his cheek against it as I rubbed my thumb across it.

"I promise." He whispered.

He leaned down to press his lips to mine. Within a few seconds it turned from warm and gentle to hot and needy. His hand slipped to the back of my neck to keep me there as his tongue brushed against mine.

God, he tastes so goddamn good.

Tonight was a bit of a thrill for both of us. It made me realize that if someone really came in and took him away from me I don't think I could survive it. I really hope this man keeps his promise, because I'm starting to think I'm falling so deep it'll be impossible for me to recover.

I woke up the next morning to the smell of coffee being brewed downstairs. At this point this was our usual routine, coffee, breakfast, then straight to work. I peeled out of bed and stretched, feeling sore after our few rounds last night.

The excitement and thrill definitely got me worked up, making me want to fulfill every moment I could with him. Not to mention seeing him throw Justin down like a football was fucking hot. So of course I had to reward him for protecting me, and he *definitely* rewarded me for being "such a brave girl tonight". A chill went down my spine hearing his voice in my ear all over again.

Once I got downstairs, I was greeted to my usual sight. Only this time his shirt was on. I get it, Kayley is home now, and I love her, but damn I am going to miss my shirtless breakfasts.

I assumed Kayley wasn't out of her room yet since her door was shut, no surprise there. If anything she'll wake up at noon or one in the afternoon at the smell of lunch.

Once Dean saw me in the kitchen a smile spread across his face. I smiled back up at him and laid a kiss to his lips. It's slowly become a natural movement with that same spark that occurred every single time without fail. All of my second thoughts from last night began to fade as I looked up into his hazel eyes.

We have time, we have a connection, everything will be fine.

"Good morning, Princess. How'd you sleep?"

"Soundly, knowing you were there." I whispered.

"I'll always be there to protect you." He said it so smoothly it sounded like one of his lines he's read in the past. While any man can recite book boyfriend lines, it's rare they can actually back it up with action that doesn't involve sex. Last night, and every big and small thing he's done for me, proved that he meant every single word.

I rested my arms on his shoulders as he held my waist. "I'm sorry our weekend alone took a sharp turn."

"That's alright. It doesn't change any of my plans for you." He paused. "Well, only a little."

I raised a brow. "How's that?"

"Let me put it this way." He whispered. "Have you gotten to chapter eighteen in 'House of Mischief'?"

"Yeah, I'm almost finished with the book…" My eyes widened. "Oh. *Oh.* Are we recreating book scenes now?"

He looked down at my lips and back to my eyes. "Anytime, any place. Like I said, whatever my girl wants, she will get. *Tenfold.*"

Holy shit.

Red flags be damned, stalking me for a year, he just wanted to get to know me. Crawling through my window to give me the best orgasms of my life, he can crawl through my window any time.

What the fuck is wrong with me.

My heart fluttered against my chest at the idea of him fulfilling another fantasy of mine. Holding me after, just like he did last night, and making us breakfast the next morning. Then it hit me. I don't

want to be without this, without him. There it was, the confirmation
I needed. Yup, I'm falling in love with this man.

Dean

After last night, it took everything I had to not ask her to move with me to Chicago. If I wasn't here, and that wasn't her housemate and her brother… I can't even think it has me so worked up. Which is how Justin ended up in a choke hold on the wall and tossed to the floor. I will say, I am proud of my girl for knocking him down to the floor in the first place. I questioned what she called "protection" when she pulled out that baton, but it proved useful in the moment.

Since I had a feeling she's not ready to make a big move just yet, she needed a security system. It was easy for me to climb up to her window, watch her through her thin curtains, not to mention her doors and windows are a little older, therefore easy to break. The entire situation now has me feeling uneasy. The more I think about it, the more worried I get.

How easily can I convince her to get a security system that I have access to?

"Dean?" Her voice broke me out of my thoughts.

"Yeah?" I blinked twice before rubbing my eyes.

She gave me a worried look. "Are you okay?"

"Yeah," I nodded and lied, not wanting her to worry. "I'm alright. Apologies. My mind was… somewhere else."

"Is it about last night?" I stayed silent for a beat. "If it makes you feel any better. I have a doorbell camera and a few other security related things in my shopping cart. I'll talk with Kayley when she gets up."

I perked up. "May I have a look?"

"Sure." She nodded and handed me her phone. "Last night scared me too, and since I refuse to have a gun in the house, and my poor baton can only take so much." I smiled at her comment. "I figured this will at least get me a head start if there was ever an actual break-in."

To my surprise it was the same company I used for my security system. I looked over what she had in her cart and it was a good start. My fingers took over as I used my login, added a few things, upgraded the package, and paid for it.

I handed her phone back. "It'll be here on Wednesday."

She narrowed her brow and opened her phone. "Wait- what?"

"Your new security system. It'll be here on Wednesday." I took one last sip of my coffee and began to pick up the dishes. "It's the same company I use. I already had an account, so I ordered it for you."

Her eyes widened when she saw the price. "Jesus Christ, Dean! This is way too much to spend on a security system."

"When it comes to *your* safety there's no such thing." I leaned against the counter.

"Dean," She pinched the bridge of her nose. "Thank you, but I can't accept this, why do you think I chose the basic set? I can't afford something like this."

"You don't have to. You wanted a security system, I bought you the best one they offer. Whatever my girl wants, she will get *tenfold*. Remember? That doesn't just apply to sex, Princess."

She blinked at me not knowing what to say or do before wiping her hand down her face. "I can't believe this is happening right now. This sounds like something I would read in one of my books."

I grinned over at her as I threw a towel over my shoulder and I started doing the dishes. "Get used to it, Princess."

I paused and turned the water off as I heard some muffled voices coming from outside. I turned to Natalie who had her ear turned to the door. She looked back at me with a confused look on her face.

"I'm assuming you don't have many shouting altercations in your neighborhood?" I asked.

"No." She paused for a moment. "I think that's Kayley?" She quickly stood as I threw the towel to counter and followed her out the door.

We both stepped onto the porch to a sight I never thought I'd see. Kayley standing in the middle of the road shouting towards my rental car. Which is currently parked with Teddy, in a face mask, standing behind the driver's door shouting back at her.

"Just answer the damn question! Why the fuck are you following me asshole?" Kayley shouted.

"For the tenth time I'm not following you! I'm just trying to get home, you lunatic!" Teddy shouted back.

I exchanged a look with my girl as I crossed my arms. "Well. There goes our Sunday dinner plans."

"We don't know that yet," she tried to sound reassuring, "maybe we can still salvage this."

"Says the man in a mask who's been eye fucking and following me since the gym!" Kayley pointed her keys at him. "Did Justin send you to spy on me?"

"Who the fuck is Justin?" Teddy lifted his shoulders looking genuinely confused. "Look lady, clearly you've lost your marbles just let me pass!"

"A man who follows *me* home says *I've* lost *my* marbles? Oh that's rich! If it weren't for men like you who like prey on gullible pretty blonde women, maybe we wouldn't feel the need to protect ourselves!" She continued. "I may be blonde and pretty but I'm not fucking gullible."

I continued to watch the scene play out while Teddy scrambled to find the right words to say. I knew their first interaction would be entertaining but I didn't expect *this*.

"Yeah, never mind, I don't think we can salvage this." Natalie sighed. "I need to reign her in before she brings out her taser." I lightly grabbed her wrist before she could go anywhere.

"Not yet. Let's see where this goes."

She narrowed her eyes on me. "You are enjoying this way too much."

I shrugged. "He's on a humbling journey, let him get his arse handed to him for a minute. He thinks everyone sees him as hot shit, but he needs a small reminder that he's human like everyone else." I paused as she continued to give an unapproving look. "I promise once the taser pops out, or neighbors start to get nosy, I'll help you reign her in."

"Aren't you a ray of fucking sunshine!" Teddy shouted. "Look lady, I have no interest in you whatsoever! Please! For the love of god, get out of my way before I run you over!"

"Are you threatening me? Who the fuck do you think you are? You know what. Say it again! Say. It. Again motherfucker! I have had a shitty week and a life full of trauma ready to unleash on your ass!"

"Now that makes perfect fucking sense! No wonder you're so fucking crazy, anyone who's willing to step in front of a car the way you did is clearly *desperate* for attention."

"Big talk for a man hiding behind a car door and a mask. Why? All this fighting giving you a hard on? Or are you scared to say that misogynistic bullshit straight to my face?"

"I'm keeping this mask on so I don't contract any lunacy that's dripping off of you!" He spat back.

"Really? Then stop looking at me like you want to lick it off asshole! Now, get out of my neighborhood or I'm calling the cops!"

"Let them come! You're the one holding me fucking hostage in the middle of the road!"

She scoffed. "You know what! Fuck this!" She pulled out her taser and made it pop.

"Whoa! Whoa! What the fuck are you on? Stay away from me!"

"There it is." Natalie and I ran out to the street. "Kay! Stop! Put that thing away!"

She looked at her confused. "Are you siding with this asshole?" She popped the taser towards Teddy as he jumped back with his hands up.

"Dean what the fuck?" Teddy spat. "You know this lunatic?"

"Call me a lunatic again! I fucking dare you!" She took one step forward before Natalie grabbed her wrist, pulled her away, and pushed her towards the house. Clearly she's done this a few times.

"That's it. Everyone in the house. Now!" Natalie ordered. I raised my brow as I checked out my girl. God, damn that was hot.

"That's Kayley?" Teddy whined as I'm immediately brought back to reality. "Are you fucking kidding me?"

"Put the car in the driveway, Teddy. We'll talk inside."

Once everyone was inside I shut the door behind me as I watched Kayley and Teddy glare at each other. Natalie stood in front of them with her arms crossed holding the taser out of Kayley's reach.

"Someone wanna tell me why this asshole is in our living room right now?" Kayley pointed to Teddy.

"Believe me I don't want to be here either, Sunshine." He mocked her before I whacked him upside the head.

"Ah! For fuck's sake Dean, what was that for? I was the one minding my own fucking business before *she* jumped in front of *my* car like a *lunatic*." Teddy explained.

"Wait." Kayley's eyes darted between me and Teddy before landing back to Natalie. "Is he-"

Natalie pressed her lips together. "Kayley. Dean's little brother, Teddy. Teddy. My roommate, Kayley."

Kayley pointed to Teddy. "You were going to set me up with *this* asshole?"

"Set up?" Teddy and I say in unison.

Natalie took in a breath and looked over at me. "That was before I… *got to know him.*" She raised her brow trying to insinuate without revealing Teddy's true identity.

"Before you knew about his little gawking at blonde women in the gym fetish?" Kayley spat back.

I looked over at Teddy with a frustrated look. I knew he was probably feeling a little cooped up in that house by himself, but seriously?

"Start talking." I stated.

He rolled his eyes. "That's not what I was doing. I went to a nearby gym so I could get out of the house and think. After about an hour I noticed that little Miss Sunshine over here was staring at me."

Kayley scoffed. "Oh please! You're confusing your fantasy with reality. I looked at you once because you looked familiar. Next thing *I* knew you were eye fucking me and following me home."

"And you say *I'm* the one confusing fantasy with reality. If anything you were the one eye fucking *me* while I was lifting weights."

"Get off your high horse jackass I would never!"

"Okay. Okay. No one's *eye fucking* anyone." Natalie sighed. "I can't believe I had to say that out loud." I couldn't help but chuckle and shake my head. We knew exactly what was happening here and neither of them had a clue.

"Clearly you're not including yourself or Dean in that statement after last night." Kayley muttered back nonchalantly. Natalie tapped her arm and pinned her with a glare as she surrendered.

"Is she always this vulgar?" Teddy looked over at me.

"Hey." Kayley snapped. "If you're going to talk shit about me, say it to my face asshole. That is if you have the balls to say it without hiding behind that fucking face mask."

"Why? Can't wait to see my handsome face, Sunshine?" He teased.

"Call me Sunshine again and I'll make you choke on your own dick."

"I'd like to see you try, *Sunshine.*" Teddy mocked.

Kayley tried to lunge at Teddy before Natalie grabbed her.

"Alright." I stood in between the two. "That's enough. As entertaining as this is, it ends now. Clearly this was all a misunderstanding." I tried taking a page out of Natalie's book.

"Agreed." Natalie let go of Kayley after she calmed herself. "Let's take a day. Cool off, and we'll reconvene on Sunday."

"You're out of your goddamn mind if you think I'm going to have dinner with that prick." Kayley spat at her.

"Holy shit, something we agree on. Seriously, Nat, that's a terrible idea." Teddy spat as I whacked him again, a little harder this time. "Fucking Christ, Dean! Stop hitting me!"

"Stop being a prick." I stated.

"I cannot believe I'm siding with *you* over my best friend right now." Kayley scoffed.

"Feeling's mutual, Sunshine."

She tilted her head at him with a frustrated look. If he kept pushing her like that I was half tempted to let her have at him.

"You want to choke on your own dick?" She spat.

"I'll leave the choking to you," Teddy spat back "with that mouth I bet that's your specialty." I rolled my eyes and went into the kitchen.

Natalie gave me a strange look as they kept fighting. "What are you doing?"

"Making popcorn. They're not backing down any time soon, might as well watch them wear each other out." I put a bag in the microwave.

Kayley laughed. "Don't get it twisted asshole. I don't choke, I make *men* choke. Either come up with better comebacks or get out of my sight."

Natalie sighed and nodded with defeat as she sat on one of the stools at the counter. She set the taser on the counter after pulling out the battery, a move she seemed familiar with. Just in case Kayley would try to dive for it again, I'm sure.

Teddy crossed his arms, having no idea that Natalie and I moved to the kitchen. "This coming from the woman who hasn't taken her eyes off me since I walked into this house."

"Only because I'm still trying to find out where you get all of your fuck's and audacity."

"In that case you can find them right here," He pulled out a middle finger from his pocket. "And, here." He pulled out the other.

"Interesting. I thought you were keeping them behind your mask with the rest of your basic human decency. That is if you have any since you refuse to take it off and face me like a real man."

"Nah. I think I'll keep it on just to piss you off."

Kayley scoffed. "Wow, you're cute if you think wearing a mask pisses me off. I'm a dark romance girly jackass, I don't care if you're covered from head to toe. But, if you're going to be a colossal douche I expect you to say that shit without hiding like a fucking coward. If you really mean it then say it with your whole fucking chest."

I poured the popcorn in the bowl and put it between us.

"Do you think we should stop this?" Natalie whispered.

"Why?" I chuckled.

"I don't know your brother that well, but if I know Kayley she's not going to go easy on him." She popped a few pieces of popcorn in her mouth.

Teddy stood tall in front of her. "Must be exhausting to be this fucking petty."

"Please. I grew up with four brothers, I can go all fucking night asshole. Why? What's wrong *Teddy Bear*? You getting sweepy?" She mocked even as she looked up at him from her 5' 7" to his 6' 2". "If you're exhausted now, your stamina must be shit. I feel for every person unfortunate enough to sleep with you. That is if you've slept with anyone in the first place."

I shrugged. "He'll be fine. If anything it'll give him a sense of normalcy again."

"Normalcy?" Natalie questioned.

"Yeah," I began. "She doesn't know who he is, so she's treating him like any other little brother of her friend's boyfriend. Plus, you never know, this might turn into a friendship down the line."

"I don't know." She took in a long breath. "I've seen her use this tactic in both a serious and flirty way."

Kayley blew air from her mouth at something Teddy said. "Please, you look like a man who thinks the g-spot is a myth."

I scrunched my nose and shook my head. "Yeah, I doubt it'll get to a 'flirty' point. Besides he's still with Ell as far as I know."

"Who he plans on breaking up with soon." She whispered with a little insinuation. "What will happen after the breakup? Kay will poke at him, sense he's off, and when she finds out what happened she's out to kill whoever hurt her sparring partner."

"Has that happened before?" I gave her a questionable look.

She rocked her head back and forth as she thought. "Once. But from their interactions alone you can't tell me that this isn't a classic enemies to lovers set up."

I shook my head. "I doubt Kayley would be interested in someone like *Teddy*." I grabbed a handful of popcorn. "She's been laying into him since she met him. *Literally*."

"You don't know her like I do. You just see Teddy as your annoying little brother. Kayley sees him as a man that gives her a challenge, and who's currently checking her out."

Kayley snapped her fingers. "Eyes up here asshole! Next time I catch you staring at my rack I'm going to start charging you."

"See." Natalie pressed a thin smile. "I guarantee you if we're ever out together and Teddy catches another man staring at her he'll snap."

"You guarantee it?" I smiled at her.

She nodded confidently. "Not just because I think he's attracted to her, but because it seems like it's a family gene."

"A family gene?"

She nodded confidently. "How would you feel if you saw another man checking me out?"

I licked my top lip as I pulled her stool closer to me. "I will destroy any man who tries to touch you."

My girl blushed as I kissed the side of her neck. "My point exactly."

Natalie

"This is complete and utter bullshit." Kayley complained in the car on the way to work. "If I wanted to work in the office I would've been driving to said office months ago. This is completely unnecessary and driven by corporate greed to keep us under their thumb because heaven forbid you actually trust your employees."

"You said the same thing on Monday, and yesterday." I took a drink from the coffee Dean made me this morning. Since Teddy's been alone a lot and our initial attempt for him to make a friend backfired, we decided to go back and forth between houses. Thankfully, if I needed anything it's literally steps away.

"And, I'll keep saying it until Brock realizes we don't need to be in an office when our entire business is *online*." She let out a sigh of frustration.

A notification from my phone appeared on the dash. It's from the security company stating that our cameras will be delivered and their team to install it is stopping by today.

Kayley smiled. "I still can't believe your man bought us a top of the line security system when there wasn't even a break in to begin with."

"You weren't on the other end of that experience." I argued. "I literally thought someone broke in ready to kill us. It made me realize we're drastically under prepared."

"Give your baton a little credit, it was able to take Justin out just fine." She laughed. "He still has bruises on the backs of his knees."

"I still feel bad about that. I hope he accepted my apology."

She waved her hand. "Oh relax. He's fine. If anything he was impressed and happy you knew where to aim."

I sighed as we pulled into the parking garage. "Does he still hate Dean?"

She shrugged. "Don't know. Haven't talked to J in a few days. But, considering he can hold a grudge for long periods of time, I'd say yes." She looked back to her phone. "I wouldn't worry about it though it's not like they cross paths every day."

"True." I muttered as I stepped out of the car to grab my things.

"Where's Dean this morning? Did he talk his way out of work this morning? Lucky bastard." She shut the door a little hard as she complained.

After Dean and I were able to pull the two apart from arguing, he escorted his brother home while I explained everything about Dean to Kay with his permission.

"I knew it! I knew it! I knew it! I fucking knew it!" She shouted in victory.

"No." I replied as I locked my car. "He's doing a half day today. He'll come in later after he makes sure the security system gets installed properly."

Kayley stopped at the door to exit the stairwell. "*Dean* is installing our security system?"

"No. The package he ordered comes with a team to install it for you. He's just there to make sure no one destroys the house or fucks up any wiring." I reassured her.

She shook her head and laughed. "Have you learned anything from our book club?"

"What are you talking about?"

"Hello. Stalker romances usually involve access to some kind of security system. They do that to make sure their partner has everything they need. And to make sure no one fucks with them." She sighed. "God, you lucky bitch. I bet he steals your keys to leave you presents in your car too."

I stayed silent as I turned my lips in.

"No." She gave me a dumbfounded look. "For fuck's sake what did he leave you?"

"Flowers."

"Okay, a little basic but I'll take it."

"And a full tank of gas."

"Stop it."

"After he ordered pizza for everyone who was working late."

"Ugh!" She threw herself into the door to open it. "God! Of course he did while he's tall, tatted, and handsome, just to rub it all in! And from those hickeys and moans I heard from upstairs he's great at sex with a massive schlong as the cherry on top." She threw her hands up. "You know what. If he is a stalker fuck it. I'll wave hello every time I leave the house. 'Have fun breaking my roommates back tonight.'" I couldn't help but laugh as she continued. "Why can't I find someone like that?"

"You and Teddy seemed to have some *chemistry*." I poked as I opened the door to the building.

"Absolutely the fuck not!" She stated with her whole chest. "I'll suck my own dick before I ever think about dating *him*."

I stood in line with her at the coffee shop. "And what about Tanner Brunswick? Are you still holding on to your fantasy that he'll find you and sweep you off your feet?"

Since Teddy still refuses to reveal his identity to her and she's so focused on fighting with him, she doesn't even notice. So, I'll let the reveal come naturally. Until then, I'm not telling her anything. She might get mad at me for it, but it's not my secret to tell.

"Of course. I'll never give up on Tanner. He'd never treat me like that." She paid for her coffee.

How does Dean do this? Not just with Teddy's identity but with his own too? Hearing people talk about Dean Craven or Tanner Brunswick must drive him bonkers. I'm trying so hard to keep a straight face, right now. He makes it look so easy.

Once Kay got her coffee, we made our way upstairs to our section of the building. This is the first morning without Dean here, and to be honest, I hate this job now more than I ever have. Brock is up my ass and every single issue we run into today is triggering.

As the minutes ticked by I got more and more overstimulated with the combination of pings and the increasing amount of keyboard clacks that have now tripled since the in-office mandate.

What the fuck is wrong with me this morning? Have I finally gotten to a breaking point?

Then everything started to quiet down when I felt a familiar hand on my shoulder. The smell of clean cologne filled my nose as he leaned against my desk. Twelve o'clock, right on time for lunch.

I slowly turned to him and sighed tiredly. "Hi."

He raised a brow. "Nice to see you too." He eyed my laptop then back to me. "Long morning?"

I rubbed my forehead. Had it really been a long morning or was it a normal day with sudden awareness of how shitty my day to day had become.

Oh god, is this what Dean sees?

"It's been… fine. Give me two minutes and I'll be ready to head out."

There was a whole list of things I still needed to do. Before I could get back to it, Dean lightly closed my laptop. The veins in his forearm and the back of his hand were defined as his silver rings shined under the fluorescent lights. My thighs shift at the memory of those fingers wrapped around my throat last night, gripping my hips, and the number of times I've come around those very fingers.

"I promise whatever it is can wait. You are more important than anything on this screen." He whispered.

"I know, I know." I rolled my eyes as I gathered my things.

"You'll pay for that eye roll later, Princess." He whispered as he helped me organize a few things.

I tried to hide my smile from him. It was the same statement every time I tried to bargain for a couple more minutes. He's right, I know he's right. This morning without him has pushed me back into a few old habits. Once I thought about it a bit more, I haven't stood up since this morning, I haven't opened my water yet. I've downed three cups of coffee thanks to Kayley refilling my mug when she refills hers. My back is stiff, my eyes ache, I'm on the verge of a migraine, and if I hear another ping on my computer or Brock's voice *again* I'm going to blow up on someone.

Wait a minute.

Today, no one famous has died, divorced, or derailed, our output is still pretty high, we have one new movie to cover, no new platform glitches, *holy shit.*

This is a normal fucking day? How the hell have I handled this for years?

"What's on your mind?" He asked as he held my bag for me.

Oh, nothing, just having an existential crisis about my career all because you've made me realize I've been neglecting myself basic needs and now I can't unsee it thanks to your heart of fucking gold.

"Nothing too crazy." I shrugged. "Ready?"

"Hey, Nat, Dean." Ben's voice made me turn to face him. He had a nervous look in his eye while Dean was still analyzing me as if he could read my mind. He definitely wanted to talk about whatever had me in a trance earlier.

"What's up, Ben? Everything okay?" I asked with a concerned look. I know my team's usual flows and moods. This wasn't a normal look for him, and with the way his eyes are darting around the room, it looked like he found something he wasn't supposed to find.

"Yeah, do you mind if I join you for lunch? I forgot mine today."

Dean and I exchange a confused look. "Sure. Yeah. Are you ready to go?"

He nodded before throwing his entire backpack on his shoulder. Once the three of us got in my car Dean leaned his ear to Ben in the backseat.

"Where to?" He asked.

"Some place where our coworkers won't find us, preferably." Ben responded.

Dean and I twisted to face him.

"Jesus, Ben. What's going on?" I gave him a concerned look. "Why do I feel like you're about to share classified documents from the government or something?"

"Not exactly." He sighed. "Let's go back to that Irish bar near your neighborhood."

"Lenny's?" I asked. "We haven't been there since-"

"Since you got promoted." He finished. Before I could think too deeply about how the dynamics have changed between myself and my coworkers he dug into his backpack. "Since we only have an hour I'll tell you guys the basics on the way there."

He pulled out an older laptop and opened it. I squinted my eyes. "Is that-"

Dean shifted his gaze between the rear view mirror and the road as he drove us out of the parking garage.

"Brock's old laptop. Yup." Ben didn't look up from the screen. "You know how Brock goes to Chuck's every night after work but is always online doing work related shit?" I nodded. "Well, one night last week, man must've gotten so sloshed that he spilled his beer all over his laptop."

Dean went still. "What kind of person brings their work laptop to a busy bar?"

Ben scoffed. "If you couldn't tell by now, he's a workaholic and pretty sure borderline alcoholic. That combination can make you do some stupid shit."

"So why do *you* have his laptop?" I asked in a worried manager-tone.

He made eye contact with me. "Relax, boss. Brock gave it to me because of my background." He slightly turned to Dean to explain. "I used to work at a small tech repair shop while I was in college. I used to fix water or beer damage like this all the time." He paused. "So, *Brock the Cock* came to me, asked if I could fix it. After looking it over I determined it was a dud. When I found out he pitched it, I fished it out during one of my tech dumpster dives. From looking it over the first time I knew there were parts that were still usable and in my house, we recycle our tech. So, one thing led to another and somehow I got it to turn on again."

Dean gripped the steering wheel.

"Why do I feel like I shouldn't be hearing this?" I put my hand to my forehead.

"The same reason we stopped going out to Lenny's." He stayed silent for a moment. "So, for all you know, I found this laptop in the dumpster. Which is entirely factual. It just so happens to be my boss's boss's laptop."

The air suddenly got heavy. I kept my eyes on the road and changed the subject before I had another existential crisis. "So, why are we going to Lenny's with Brock's old laptop?"

He sighed. "Because there's something I need to show you, and I can't risk anyone else seeing it."

"So why am *I* tagging along?" Dean asked in a low tone.

He closed the laptop. "For one, while you seem like a decent guy who's helped Nat over the past couple of weeks you've got at least three inches of height and probably a good thirty to fifty pounds on me. I don't think I could get rid of you even if I wanted to. And two, it concerns both of you."

"As in?" I asked.

"It's better if I show you."

Once we made our way into the bar, Dean surveyed the area to make sure there weren't any coworkers around. Luckily no one goes this far out with only an hour lunch.

We got situated in our booth as Ben took out the laptop again. "So," he began. "God, I don't even know where to start."

While Dean was leaning his back to the booth he still seemed stiff. He twirled the paper straw between his fingers as he kept his eye on Ben ready to hear every single word he was about to say.

"Okay." He took a deep breath. "Let's just rip the band-aid off." He flipped around the computer and showed multiple pictures of Dean without his mask on, in front of the house, in the car, and *oh shit*.

"Dean." I muttered. "Is that-"

"Yeah." He whispered back in an angry tone.

A picture of him and Teddy on a walk, Dean and I in the car, going out to dinner, Dean on a run. There's a shit ton of photos with timestamps over the past week, one of which was us standing on the front porch of my house kissing.

Shit. Shit. Shit.

"If Brock has these he knows *everything*. Your identity, Teddy's, *us*." A chill went down my spine. I've never felt more exposed. Dean may have been stalking me online but *this*, this was different. Someone was following us, following *him* with an agenda. Whether Brock hired someone or did it himself it still felt… unnerving.

Ben sighed. "You think he had Dean followed to try and get the next *big* story?" An exclusive celebrity exposure would send our numbers through the roof. Is that why they were so adamant about this project? Use him where they could and toss him to the streets when they were done. I rubbed my forehead trying to think.

"It's a possibility." I whispered.

"It's his insurance policy." Dean muttered.

I look over at him confused. "Why would he need an 'insurance policy'? You haven't done anything heinous to start extorting you."

He stayed silent for a moment. "He's going to use this to make sure I don't step out of line. He stumbled on a gold mine with Teddy and I have a feeling he's going to use this to his full advantage."

I gave him a hard look. "Why would *you* step out of line?"

He squeezed his eyes shut as if reflecting on something he did. "Remember when he called me into his office?"

"Yeah." I stated hesitantly.

"He said something about you. I snapped, and I may have told him that if he ever says anything like that again I will make sure he never works in this industry again."

"Fuck, Dean." I put my face in my hands. "What did he say?"

He shook his head. "Reflecting back I should've caught it. He said you 'have certain *assets* that are finally proving useful'. Since he has photos of us, I'm assuming he had his suspicions and had me followed so he could have leverage if I ever came at him again."

Ben let out a deep breath. "I knew Brock was spineless but this is way over the top."

My migraine began to grow as I squeezed my eyes and rubbed my temples. I appreciate the fact that he stood up for me, even when I wasn't in the room, but this is another instance where he's taking action before thinking about the consequences. Granted, I don't think any of us thought that Brock would have the time or the energy to go this far.

I ignored Dean as he waited for my reaction. "Since these are photos that have been taken as early as two days ago, I'm assuming that this is in WEM's online drive?"

"From the looks of it." Ben responded. "I tried to look for the same file from my computer, to see if he was dumb enough to have it public for the entire company to see." He shrugged. "But I couldn't find it."

"So it's under his account? Are you able to wipe it from this laptop?" I asked with a twinge of hope.

"I tried that this morning, but the folder needs a password to confirm before you delete it. Brock's an idiot but he knows how to cover his ass."

"Shit." I looked over to Dean who had his fist clenched as if he was ready to land it straight into Brock's face. Not if I get there first.

"I'm not going to let him expose you or Teddy because you stood up for me. I promise, I'm going to do everything I possibly can to make sure that doesn't happen. I'll break into his office if I have to."

"You'll get fired for that." Dean replied softly.

"I don't care." I shook my head. "I don't care if he fires me, I don't care if he puts me on a blacklist for other employers. You stood up for me, you've always been by my side, you don't deserve this, and *he* is not going to get away with it. Like you said, shitty people who do shitty things deserve shitty karma. And I will happily be delivering that shitty karma with a bobby pin, Rob on the phone, and possibly Kayley and I taking a baseball bat to his car."

His eyes looked over me with a loving look. "You're taking a page out of my book, Princess. It might get you arrested?"

I shrugged. "If it means your identity and Teddy's are safe, it's worth it. I can always call Riley. No one, and I mean, *no one* extorts my Heartthrob or his family." His eyes were still soft as he brushed my hair behind my ear and held the side of my cheek.

"Natalie..." he whispered.

I kissed his palm and put his hand in mine as he tried to find the right words to say. "We'll figure it out. I promise, I'm not going to let him win."

"You two are disgustingly adorable." Ben began. "But you may want to upgrade your baseball bat to sledgehammer, and invite me when you do, because there's more."

I looked at him with disbelief. "He's already having Dean followed to use his identity and brother for extortion, what else could he possibly be doing?"

"Replacing all of us with AI." Ben stated sharply. "And, by using any means necessary to get rid of us quietly without a huge layoff that would set off any alarms."

"What?" I froze. Suddenly and all at once everything around me went silent.

Dean

Natalie scrolled through the emails that Ben was talking about. The same ones that I took pictures of and have on my phone this very instant.

I should've told her sooner.

The look on her face made my heart ache. She's scared, angry, and confused. The job she tirelessly worked for years for is all of the sudden kicking them to the curb all so they can save a few salaries worth to put back into their pockets.

"I can't believe this." She muttered.

I could tell she was already having a pretty rough morning. When I walked in she was so focused on her tasks I was surprised she even saw me. The fact that she worked so hard for this pathetic company made my stomach turn. It's not right. None of it is.

"That's why those first few scripts didn't sound right. They were written by AI and poorly arranged clips from other articles." She paused. "Why didn't I see this? I should've taken a closer look. No wonder I didn't recognize any of the writer's names, they didn't fucking exist."

She leaned back into the booth looking as though she wanted to shrink and hide. I put my hand on her thigh and she lightly put her hand on top of mine. She's ready to go to war for me, she was ready to lose her job for me before she found out about being replaced.

At that moment I almost let those three little words slip. Because it's true, I love this woman. I have for a long time. She loves my career as much as I do, she's willing to do anything to make sure my identity stays hidden, she's just as obsessed with me as I am of her.

She's perfect, she's extraordinary, my girl, my Princess, my love, she's everything. Right now, she needs me more than ever.

"This isn't your fault." I whispered to her as she continued to stare at the screen. "Natalie. Look at me." She turned to face me. "You have a million jobs on your plate, and not one of them should be making sure your company isn't using AI to write their articles. No respectable company should be replacing raw human talent with AI. *Ever.*" I looked into her sorrowful eyes. *"This isn't your fault."* I repeated. "They made their bed, and we're going to make sure they lie in it." She nodded and straightened as she took a deep breath.

"You're right. We will." She stared at the screen reading the emails again as she collected her thoughts. A focused look that I saw from earlier spread across her face. She's strategizing with what she knows.

That's my girl.

"What should we do?" Ben asked, looking just as pissed.

She took a moment to think. "I say we sit on this."

"What?" He looked at her surprised.

She shrugged. "If they're going to play dirty then so are we. If they try to use these photos against Dean, then we'll leak these emails to our competitor. Since Brock took a few of their articles I'm sure they'd be more than happy to send their lawyer over to have a conversation."

I couldn't help but grin under my mask. Damn, I'm proud of her.

Ben nodded in agreement. "Sounds like a plan. Just let me know what I need to do, boss."

"Back up what you can from this laptop. Anything of use, we need to have multiple copies just in case."

Ben slid over two flash drives. "Already did. I got it on an external hard drive at home, and I have plenty of flash drives. I may have included screenshots of Brock talking like shit in our group chats over the past year. Just a little cherry on top."

Ben seemed just as motivated to expose Brock and the company, as if he was waiting for a moment like this. Seeing what Natalie has gone through as a manager I can't imagine what her employees must go through on a busy day if she's not around.

She pursed her lips and nodded as we grabbed the drives. "I should've known you already created backups."

He shrugged his shoulders. "What can I say? I watch a lot of spy movies. Speaking of…" he turned to me and I cut him off before he could say anything else.

"Trust me, Teddy will give you anything you want if you help keep these pictures from seeing the light of day."

He shrugged. "I just wanted you to tell him I said 'thank you.'" I tilted my head.

Thank him for what? He's a little shit what could he possibly want to thank him for?

Ben continued. "Watching his movies motivated me to fulfill a goal of mine. I've always thought stunt choreography was so cool. When I saw his movies I thought, 'how awesome would it be to be able to do that'. So, I went to the gym, took a few classes and haven't looked back. Now, I'm just waiting to rack up enough money to move to L.A. and become one myself."

While most of Teddy's stunts were done by stunt doubles he did do a few on his own against our Mum's judgment. Hearing that someone looked up to him and achieved a lifelong goal because of him reminded me of how much influence he really had.

"After this I'll introduce you two, I think he'd like to hear about it from you." I nodded. "Just know, he can be a little shit."

Natalie elbowed me in the side. "You're just saying that because he's your brother."

"Yeah. And?"

Ben laughed. "What else can I do?"

She gave me a warning look before turning back to Ben. "If you could, keep an eye out for any videos that may come through about Tanner Brunswick's current traveling or location and Dean Craven. I highly doubt he has the balls to sneak an article in about you without us flagging it but he might try."

She held her forehead in her hand. I know my girl well enough to know when she's pushing herself to her limit. From what I could tell she's well past that point and she still has half a day to get through.

Not if I can help it.

"C'mon. I'll take you home." I stated softly.

"Wha-"

"Our food just got wrapped up, I'll drop you off at home, and I'll take Ben back to the office."

She shook her head with a confused look. "I'm fine, I don't need to go home." A work message pinged on her phone that almost made her throw it across the room. Ben and I both gave her a concerned look.

"Uh, Nat." Ben began. "If you're ready to kill your phone after a work message ping, I don't want to know what will happen if you see Brock."

She smacked her lips. "I'm fine. I've suppressed my anger for this man for years. I think I can handle a couple more days. If I need to, I'll beat a pile of pillows with my bat. Or maybe his car." She turned to the waiter who handed us our packed food. She gave a calm smile, thanked him, and turned back to us.

"Natalie. You're on the verge of a migraine, you haven't been drinking your water, and this is the first time you've been away from your desk all morning." I stated, giving her a stern look. I don't want to force her to go home, but I will if that means she'll get to feeling better.

"How do you know?"

I held up her water bottle that was still full.

"I'll go wait in the car." Ben grabbed his box of food and walked outside.

"I don't need to go home. *I'm fine.*" She gritted out.

"You're lying, Princess." I whispered in a low tone. "You just found out the company you've worked so hard for is lying to you, your inbox is full of messages, and your lower back is aching from sitting for three hours straight."

She blew out some air. "That's a normal day for me, Heartthrob."

"This is not *normal.*" I quickly responded. "The company you're working for shouldn't be lying to you, making you cry in your car, or working you so hard you're in physical and mental pain."

"I know," she snapped. "Alright, I fucking know it's not normal. I know the company I work for should care about their employees but it doesn't always work like that, Dean."

"It should."

"You don't think I know that? You think I haven't tried?" She scoffed. "You think I didn't try to get my employees more than a three percent raise? You think I didn't work my ass off and watch as my male coworkers got eight percent raises while I got four percent? *You think* I didn't try to set boundaries? You know what happened when I tried? They threatened to demote me, Dean. They thought I wasn't a 'team player' and that maybe I would be 'better suited down a level'. All for trying to set simple fucking boundaries. How dare I try to do what's right for me. How dare I try to make sure my team is getting the compensation they deserve, and how fucking dare I even attempt to talk about overtime pay. That's what they think. 'The audacity of this woman.'" She paused and couldn't help but laugh. "I've tried looking for other jobs." She lifted her shoulders. "I guess no one needs my skill set, if they do I'm too *expensive*. Apparently what I do is so easy, why hire a professional when a machine can do it. Right?"

She sniffed as she wiped her eyes.

"Now that that's out of the way." She shifted out of the booth. "Let's get back before Brock gets even more suspicious."

"Natalie." I grabbed my box of food as she walked away. Once we got to the car I set my food on the roof and stood in front of her driver's side door.

"Dean-"

"I *know* you've tried. I know you are an amazing boss, and an amazing person because I've seen it. I watch you try every single day, I watch you work so hard for a company that doesn't deserve you. Any of you." I pointed over to Ben. "And it kills me. That's one of the reasons why I got on that plane in the first place. To remind you and show you that you are worth more than this company could ever pay you. That you shouldn't have to work yourself into pain for a company who doesn't give two shits about you." I peeled off my mask and put both hands on her cheeks. "*I* care about you, Kayley cares about you, hell Ben and your team care about you. We want you to be happy, to do what you love without sacrificing yourself. My love, you deserve all the happiness in the world and I will do everything I possibly can to make sure you have it. If that means you need to stay here for the paycheck then I will be right by your side whenever you need me. If that means you decide you want to storm out and say fuck you to Brock I'll pin him down to make sure he listens." I brushed her hair away from her face. "Whatever you decide to do, I will support you. Remember, I know you can take care of yourself, but you don't have to do it alone. Okay?" Her eyes began to water as she nodded. "Now. Take the rest of the day, do what you need to do, I'll handle Brock, and I'll bring home some Chinese food tonight."

She smiled up at me, laid a light kiss to my lips, and pressed her forehead to mine. "I think you need to stop reading so many romance books. You're getting way too good at this."

I smiled down at her. "It's not the romance books, Princess. It just comes naturally when I'm with you."

She lifted her head to look at me as she sighed. "You win this time, Heartthrob." She sniffed. "You're lucky my head is pounding otherwise I'd continue to argue." She looped my mask back around my ear, covering my face once again.

"I know." I opened the passenger door for her and handed her her water bottle as she gave me a look. "Drink it."

"I don't know if I should be happy for you both, or terrified at the power couple you two make." Ben spoke up as I lightly shut her door before turning to him. "Don't worry, I'm not going to say anything. While I'm not surprised by the way she's looked at you over the past couple of weeks, I am happy she found someone." He paused. "How'd you do that, by the way?"

"Do what?" I questioned.

"Get her to go home when she was very adamant about going back to work."

I crossed my arms and gave him a curious look. "Why do you ask?"

He pursed his lips and shook his head. "Just curious."

I narrowed my gaze on him while I headed back to the driver's side. "Does Miranda do the same thing?"

He avoided eye contact. "I didn't say anything about Miranda. Wh-why would you assume that?"

"It's hard not to when you're looking at her for most of your work day." I paused as he continued to avoid eye contact.

"Promise me you won't tell, Nat?" He pleaded.

I laughed. "Don't worry, I won't." He took in a deep breath before I continued. "She already knows." I slipped into the driver's side as

Ben quickly entered the back seat.

"Wait- wait- did you tell her?" He pointed to my girl.

She looked up from her phone with a confused look. "Tell me about what?"

I turned on the car without looking back. "Miranda."

"Oh. Yeah. Ben, just ask her out already." She shifted to face him.

"How long have you known?" Ben's voice raised a pitch.

She blew out some air. "I've known since the moment you laid your eyes on her." She paused. "You've got some charm Ben but you're not exactly subtle."

I couldn't help but chuckle at her comment as we drove over to her house.

"Is it really that obvious?" He asked.

"Yes." My girl and I state in unison.

"Dammit." He leaned his head back.

"Relax, from the way she returns those looks I'm sure she feels the same way." Natalie explained.

"She's been looking at me?" He questioned excitedly as I pulled up to the house.

Natalie turned and gave him a dumbfounded look. "Seriously?" She turned back to me. "Is he serious?"

I laughed. "I'll talk to him. Let me walk you up." Before I could unbuckle my belt she stopped me.

"Don't worry about it, you're cutting it close on time to get Ben back to the office." She already opened the door before I could argue. She leaned over, pulled my mask down, kissed me, pulled it back up. "Be careful driving back. Don't forget to grab Kayley, she'll throw a fit if you leave without her."

"Will do. I'll see you tonight. I texted you the pin to your door lock, and your panel. It'll beep for a few seconds, but once you put the pin in it'll stop. FYI, Princess, if you're working on your personal computer, I will know." I held my phone in my hand.

The package I bought her came with outdoor cameras, one for each side of the house, and two indoor cameras. One that's able to capture the kitchen and living room, and one facing their backdoor. Luckily, one of the security company's free gifts was a really nice webcam you can access from the app.

After seeing the kind of focus and overstimulated state she was in any guilt I had for attaching that camera to her computer quickly left the building.

She narrowed her eyes on me as she analyzed what I just said. I figured she'd try to fight me on it and force me to show her where the camera was. Instead she smiled at me. "I didn't know this package came with a full time security guard."

I laughed as I looked back into my girl's sparkling yet exhausted eyes. "It's included in the protective boyfriend package."

"Good to know. Thank you for setting that up for me." She gives a grateful look with her pink cheeks and light blue eyes.

I've told her multiple times that she doesn't have to thank me for taking care of her, but she still says it while looking up at me with grateful eyes and a smile on her face. I've given up on that battle after seeing her smiles and began simply responding with...

"Anything for you, Princess."

Natalie

I threw myself onto the bed right after I took some migraine meds and chugged some water like I haven't drank in days. Jesus, how did I go this far without seeing how destructive I've become with myself. Dean's right. This job is draining the life out of me. My mental health, my physical health, my social life, my free time, everything has all been revolving around this job. A job that I won't have soon, a job that doesn't care about me or the work I've literally abused myself for, a job that's going after *Dean*.

My building rage was suddenly halted when I heard my doorbell ring. I raised a brow and looked at the time.

It's 1:30 who's ringing my doorbell?

I checked the security app and tapped on the doorbell camera. An account I'm sure Dean has access to, and is probably looking at his phone at the same time. To my surprise and relief it's Teddy. I swung my legs off the bed when I got a ping on my phone.

Dean: *Don't answer the door.*

I rolled my eyes.

Natalie: *I appreciate your concern, bodyguard, but it's just Teddy*
Dean: *Exactly.*
Natalie: *What if he's in trouble or needs my help with something??*
Dean: *Then definitely don't open the door.*
Natalie: *Don't make me revoke your security system privileges on your*

first day Heartthrob

Dean: *You're cute*

Natalie: *I'm serious. I will change this password... you're lucky I like it when I know you're watching me, otherwise I would've been the one surveying the install this morning*

I ignored another ping when I opened the front door and greeted Teddy. His face looked a little pale with his mask over his face.

"Hey, Teddy. Everything okay?" I asked with a worried look.

He looked around. "Is the lunatic or your boyfriend around?"

I chuckled. "No, but I do need some fresh air, wanna take a walk?" I asked as I grabbed my keys and shut the door behind me. While I'm sure Dean will want to know what's wrong with his brother, spying on us through the doorbell camera wasn't the way to do it.

He shoved his hands in his pockets. "Why are you home? I saw Dean drop you off earlier and leave."

I took a deep breath. "Short version. It's been a long ass day. How about you? You doing okay?"

He stayed silent for a moment. I haven't known Teddy long, but he and Dean share a very similar bothersome look. Something's going on that he's been keeping inside.

"Ell and I had an argument this morning."

My eyes widened. "She finally answered?"

He nodded. "On Facetime. It was the first time I had gotten to see her, let alone talk to her in a while. One thing led to another and I just had enough. I broke up with her."

I stopped in my tracks.

Holy shit.

The words must've been sprawled across my face because he nodded and went on.

"Yeah. Surprised me too. I've had the idea in my mind for a while and I thought I'd need more time to prepare myself, but I guess my heart was ready before my mind was."

I quickened my pace to catch up with him. "Wait- what happened? What were you guys arguing about? How'd she take it?" He raised his brow at me. "Sorry, my inner journalist is showing, *are you okay?*"

"I'm-" he paused as he thought. "I'm relieved. Sad. Upset. A little angry maybe." He sighed and hung his head as he watched the sidewalk move under his feet as he took each step. "I'm sorry, I didn't want to drop this news on you, I just-" he paused again trying to hold back his emotions. "I just realized I don't have any close friends to talk to about this."

"Aw. Teddy." I put my hand to his arm to get him to face me. "You don't have to apologize for anything. I'm always here if you need someone to talk to. Okay?"

His eyes began to turn red and now I can see his swollen eyelids as if he had been crying for hours. My heart broke for him, I'm all too familiar with this feeling. A broken heart can take months, if not years to heal, and even then there are days when you think it'll never heal. Until someone comes into your life, and not only helps you forget about those long days, but also loves you ten times more than anyone ever could.

I instinctively gave him a hug and he quickly followed by wrapping his arms around me and squeezing me tight. Tears and sniffs swiftly followed as he broke down right here on the sidewalk. He thinks he's on this journey alone, but I know that Dean has always, and will continue, to be there for his little brother in more ways than he could think of. He's not just Dean's little brother, he's become a close friend of mine over these past couple of weeks. Now that he's come to me for help, I will do everything I can to help him get through this.

I was able to get Teddy back to our house as he filled me in on everything that happened during an impromptu Facetime call this morning. We sat in the living room and snacked on some dehydrated apple chips that Teddy made on a whim a few days ago, using the apples that Dean brought home after our tour. They were really good, and Teddy seemed really proud of himself which was a nice moment of calm in between our talks about *her*.

I understood why Dean didn't like her after everything he's told me, but hearing it all from Teddy. I wanted to rip her heart out. Which is a whole new level for me, most of the time I'm pretty understanding, but this bitch I have no remorse for.

According to Teddy when he called her this morning, she didn't answer the first time. When he called her again, she answered with an annoyed tone. After weeks of not talking or seeing one another that broke Teddy's heart. He wanted to talk to her, see her, ask her how the tour was, but what he got in return was short answers and annoyed sighs as if he was bothering her. She didn't bother to ask how he was doing, what he was up to, or even where he was.

"It was like I was a stranger, like a fan pestering her or something." He tapped one of the chips on the plate. "Then someone came into her dressing room. Whoever it was she clearly had eyes for. She looked up and down with that lustful look in her eye, the same way she looked at me when we first got together." He leaned back into the couch.

"There were cheating rumors in the past that I approached her about. But," he paused. "She would always turn it around. Saying that I was attacking her, and that I was just jealous." He continued as I listened intently. "When I called her out for it she said I was being 'dramatic'. Her exact words were, 'are you practicing for a new role as a dramatic and jealous boyfriend because you nailed it.'" He took a deep breath. "That's when I said, 'I'm done. I can't keep doing this with you. I loved you, but it's clear that you've never loved me. This relationship is over, I'm done'. She rolled her eyes and said, 'No you're not. Your career can survive without me.'"

"What did you say to that?" I spoke softly as I stayed curled up in my chair.

"I said, 'I'm not doing this for my career. I'm doing this for *me*. If my career dies with this relationship, then so be it. I'll be out of the house before you're done with your tour. Goodbye Ell.'" He blew out some air. "Before I hung up I heard Brayden's voice. He was the one who entered the dressing room earlier. The one she was looking at."

"Did you hear what he said?" I asked.

"He said, 'Damn, what a whiny bitch.'"

I closed my eyes and it took everything I had not to hop a plane with Riley and Kay so we could beat *Brayden* with bats. I took a deep breath to collect my thoughts. Teddy chuckled at me. "What?"

"It's true what they say. Couples who spend a lot of time together do start to look alike. That's the same 'I'm going to kill someone' face that Dean has." He took a drink of his water.

I couldn't help but smile and laugh at myself. "Yeah, his habits are starting to rub off on me." I paused. "I'm sorry you had to go through that, Teddy. Is there anything I can do to help?"

He shook his head. "Not right now. Thank you for listening to me bitch and cry."

"First of all, talking about breaking up with someone in a long term relationship is far from bitching, okay? Second, I'm always here if you need someone not blood related to talk to. Last but most certainly not least, I will be joining Dean's mission in finding you new friends, because Brayden is an absolute dickhead and you should stay as far away from him as possible. Red flags can appear in friendships too and that man has at least twenty from what you've told me." I took a drink of my water as he laughed.

"Thank you." He whispered.

"Of course. Now, what's the game plan?"

He shrugged. "Game plan?"

"Yeah. House, car, moving, signing up phone numbers for spam callers, spray painting Brayden's car, all that fun stuff."

He gave me a concerned look. "He has a motorcycle."

"Oh. Even better." I shifted in my chair with a giddy evil look.

"Remind me not to take you to L.A. to help with the move."

"Oh no I'll be there." I nodded. "If I happen to see his motorcycle approach the house I'll just so happen to kick it over and accidentally stab the tires with the box of knives that I'll be carrying." I tilted my head as I pressed a thin innocent smile.

"You're terrifying."

"Only to people who hurt my friends."

He smiled and nodded. "To be honest I'm not quite there yet. The story probably won't go public until I move out and the paparazzi see the moving trucks at the house. Ell won't stop the Europe Tour for anything, so I'll have at least till the end of the month to figure it all out. But, right now, I just feel like breathing for a bit. Maybe process for a day, embrace the calm before the storm."

I nodded in agreement. "I get that. Just be sure to call me when you're ready to go to a rage room."

"Will do." He laughed. "Just promise you won't bring the lunatic with you. I don't want to be in the vicinity when she's in a smashing-things-with-a-golf-club mood."

I laughed at the image of Kayley chasing Teddy down the halls with a golf club in hand. "I promise."

"Good. Now, since we're friends I'm going to return the favor. Tell me. What happened at work today?" Teddy continued as he sat straight up on the couch ready to listen.

I let out a long breath. "Where do you want me to start, replacing their employees with AI, stealing from other articles, or forcing people to quit due to impossible standards they know we can't meet?" I didn't include the bit about Dean and his identity because I wanted to wait until he got home so we could tell him together.

He blew out some air. "Yikes. Yeah. That's a lot."

I narrowed my eyes on him. He didn't seem as shocked as I thought he'd be. "You don't seem too surprised."

He shrugged as he ate some more apple chips. "It's a shitty company from what I hear, so I'm not surprised they would do something like this. When Dean showed me those emails I was pissed for you."

I went still in my chair. "What did you just say?"

He suddenly froze as his face went pale again. "Dean told you, that's how you found out right?"

"No." I whispered with a shaky breath as my anger began to rise.

His eyes went wide as he wiped his hand down his face. "Oh. *Shit.*"

"Teddy. I need you to tell me everything you know, *right now.*"

He shook his head and pursed his bottom lip. "There's nothing really to tell…"

I stood and crossed my arms pinning him with a stare. "Don't lie to me. You just said Dean showed you the emails. Who's emails did he show you?"

He swallowed hard. "Before I tell you, he did this because he cares about you, okay, he knew there had to be something fishy going on so…"

"What did he do?" I kept my eye contact on Teddy as he tried to look away.

He sighed as he caved. "We followed Brock to Chuck's one night, he left his laptop open when he left for a minute, and Dean did some digging."

"Oh my god." I whispered in a shaky breath as I started to pace. "He knew, *you* knew what was going on before I did?" I scoffed. "And let me guess, the beer that was spilled on his laptop, that was Dean too?"

He squeezed his eyes shut. "Yeah." He put his hands up. "Not my idea, I promise. But, Natalie," He stood up from the couch to face me.

"You have to understand, he did it because he was worried about you, he hates seeing you sacrifice yourself every day for these scumbags. He wanted to tell you but didn't know how."

"Instead he kept it from me. Why? For him to say 'I told you so'?"

He shook his head. "No, no, of course not. He wanted to help you."

"If he wanted to help me, he would've told me."

A sudden knock at the door made us both freeze. It wasn't Dean or Kayley, they would've walked in already. Riley's in Indy. Rob's working. Teddy and I shared a concerned look. He held out his hand saying to stay back as he put his mask on.

I checked the doorbell camera, but it was black. "What the fuck, Teddy wait-"

Before he could peer through the side window the door suddenly flung open sending Teddy straight back to the floor. I yelped as two burly men knocked through the door and made their way into the house.

I quickly ran over to Teddy who got the wind knocked out of him. "Teddy! Are you-" One of the men pulled on my hair and pulled me back. I screamed out as I swung my arm and my fist landed right on his nose, I must've swung a lot harder than I thought because now his face is gushing blood.

"Ah! You bitch!" He yelled out as he dropped me.

"Natalie! Run!" Teddy tried to yell out before the other guy wrapped tape around his mouth.

My eyes widened as the one with the bleeding nose quickly grabbed me before I could make a move towards the security panel to call for help. He wrapped his arms around me, keeping my arms to the side and lifting me in the air. "Let me go you motherfucker!" I kicked just right into his kneecap making him wince, once he loosened his grip I broke free and bolted for the panel.

The other man quickly caught me before I could make it. I screamed out before he put a towel to my face with a strong chemical smell.

No, no, no, stay awake Natalie, fight it, fight it!

I tried to break free but my muscles kept getting weaker and weaker as everything faded to black.

Dean

The more I stared at my phone, the more I think I'll stare a hole right through it. I haven't heard from Natalie or Teddy in hours. After what she said earlier I decided to let her be and stay out of the security app. Whatever Teddy wanted to talk about he seemed pretty shaken up over it and Natalie is the best person to go to in that situation. Given the circumstances I'm assuming it has to do with Ell, and if it is I'll see if Mum is up for a little concert trip with me.

I put my phone in my back pocket and took a breath. Whatever it is, I'm sure I'll hear about it later, there's no use in me hovering over my phone. Still, I can't help but feel a little unease in my gut. Surely one of them should've texted or called me by now.

Kayley flung open the audio booth door and nearly gave me a heart attack. "Jesus fucking Christ, do you knock?"

"Nope." She stated with a pop. "Have you heard from Nat?"

I shook my head. "No."

She groaned. "God dammit."

"Why?"

"Nathan is here already and he wants to see you and Natalie in like two minutes."

I shook my head with a frustrated look. "Of fucking course he does. She has a migraine and took the rest of the day off, can't he wait till tomorrow or Friday like he planned?"

"Apparently not."

"Kayley!" Brock's sharp tone made her groan and slowly close her eyes as if she was counting down her anger. "What are you doing back here?"

"I needed a pickup, didn't know that was a crime." She lied as if she'd covered her tracks multiple times.

He shook his head, looking done with her attitude. "Ben needs your help with another post."

"What's wrong with it?" She asked with a disgusted undertone as she faced him.

"It's some kind of schedule glitch."

She discreetly rolled her eyes and mouthed 'good luck'. Brock's the one who needs good luck, he's stuck here alone with me and after what I just heard I'm not playing nice.

"Mr. Craven, please, pause what you're doing and follow me."

I set the headphones down and followed him out of the secluded audio booth area right to Nathan's, larger than it should be, office. Seriously, what's the point? The walls held each follower count achievement award for every account, fake plants with a layer of dust on them, and a muted corporate color palette from the early 2000's that could make anyone feel depressed. Brock shut the door behind me and sat in one of the chairs off to the side.

"Ah, Mr. Craven. It's a pleasure to meet you in person." He stood, buttoned his tan suit jacket, and stuck his hand out for me to shake. I looked at it and crossed my arms. He cleared his throat before putting his hand back in his pocket. "Not the hand shaking type?"

"No." I stated. I am just not with greedy men who think they're above everyone else.

"I see. Well, have a seat. I'd like to talk to you about a few things."

"I prefer to stand." Brock snuck a look my way as Nathan licked his teeth behind his lip and clapped his hands together once.

"You know what. Great idea." He took a few steps back. "Sitting is the new smoking after all." He continued to smile as he began to pace.

What the fuck his he so chipper about?

There's a reason why they moved the meeting to today. I explicitly told Brock I wanted Natalie here in this meeting with me, yet here we are, on the same day Natalie went home early. How convenient.

"Let's get down to brass tax." He stated nonchalantly as he paced around his office. "You have been doing a fantastic job with our scripts. So good, in fact, 'Book Nook' has skyrocketed into our top five accounts. After only a week. How incredible is that?"

"I may be the voice-over in those videos but all the thanks should go to your employees. They're the ones who make the videos, they're the ones who write the scripts, and they're the ones who make sure they get posted on time." I tried to keep the frustration out of my voice but I can't fucking help it. Nathan's face looks so damn punchable it makes me sick.

He held up one finger and shook it at me. "Ah yes, I've heard you've gotten rather close with one of our managers here, Natalie right?" He looked over at Brock as he nodded to confirm.

This fucker.

"She's amazing at her job." I stated as I kept my eye on Nathan.

"From the looks of it." He held eye contact with me as he flipped the monitor around to reveal a picture of us kissing on her porch. "She's amazing at a few other things too, just look at that tongue action."

I quickly stepped forward and grabbed the edges of his jacket to get into his smug fucking face. He put his hand up to stop Brock from standing. As if that little fucker could do anything to stop me from killing this man.

"Now, *Mr. Roberts*, I suggest you let me go, before your identity is revealed to the world and Natalie's chances to find a new job in this industry are slim to none." He pressed a button on his keyboard revealing a draft of a story with the headline, 'A Spicy Narrator Caught Sleeping With a Content Manager To Keep His Identity a Secret'.

My eyes are glued to the screen, if that story goes live, Natalie's career is ruined. I know how much her career means to her, how much she wants to leave this place and do something she actually loves doing.

She wouldn't be able to do any of that. I can't let my actions hinder her future. The fact that this fucker is willing to fire her and ruin her career just for the hell of it makes my blood burn under my skin. I can't risk it, *I* can't risk *her* career. I slowly let go of his jacket and took a couple of steps back.

"Good. Now that we understand each other, let's move on." He adjusted his jacket. "You are going to be taking on more scripts for a few other accounts. I want you *here* every single work day for the foreseeable future. If you don't, this," he points to the screen, "will go live. If you tell the authorities about what we just discussed, I will find out, and it won't be pretty for you."

My fists are clenched so hard they're white. I don't care if he reveals my identity at this point, I couldn't give less of a shit about that right now. But, Natalie, I can't let them expose her. A workplace relationship would hinder any chance she would have at making a name for herself. The fact that they would use her like this... I remembered to breathe and tried to think logically before my fists could take control.

"We have a contract. You break that my lawyers will have a field day with you."

"Like I said. You talk, the story goes live within seconds. You have no leg to stand on here, Mr. Roberts. Besides, that contract is so riddled with loopholes on your part *my* lawyers will have a field day with *you*."

They found a pressure point, and they're going to use it every chance they get. If that's what it takes to protect Natalie, then so be it. We still have our edge, I can play nice until then.

"I live in Chicago."

"Then I suggest you move here. Welcome to the Hoosier state, Mr. Roberts. I'm sure you have a permanent place of residence in mind." He gave me a wink as he opened his office door as an invitation to leave his office.

I quickly turned to leave before I paused next to him. "You will pay for this."

"Oh, so broody. Relax, do as I say, and your secret is safe with me."

I scoffed. "Why should I trust anything you say?"

"Because you can't afford not to. Also you should bring your brother in for an interview, we'd love to have a chat with him. Wouldn't want to get his location leaked now would we?" He whispered. "Now," he raised his voice. "Keep up the good work, glad to have you aboard full-time."

I quickly made my way to the back hallway and burst into the men's room, my fist landed straight into the metal towel dispenser that hung on the wall. I punched it again, and again, I didn't feel the sting or the blood dripping from my knuckles as I stopped and leaned on the sinks.

I cursed myself again and again. How could I have let this happen? If I had been more careful, if I hadn't stuck my nose where it didn't belong, if I didn't make that fucking call she wouldn't be in this position. I didn't hear the door open as Ben looked over at me in horror. My breaths were still quick as he slowly approached.

"Dean?" His eyes went wide after he saw the towel dispenser barley hanging on the wall with dents and blood all over it. "Jesus, what the hell happened in there?"

I shook my head. "Do you still have the laptop?"

"Of course." He nodded.

"Good." My fingers shook and stung as I typed out a message on my phone just in case for some ungodly reason he has the bathroom bugged. I doubt it but right now I can't be too safe.

We're going to need it. Keep it safe. See if you can find out who sent him those photos.

He nodded and whipped around to see the door bust open as Kayley walked in without a care in the world.

"Kayley what the fuck? This is the men's room. Right?" Ben asked as he looked around.

She rolled her eyes. "Relax, Benny, everybody shits, it's not like it's a shower room." She lifted her head to me. "You ready- holy shit." She looked down at my bruised and bloodied knuckles. "Who did you hit? And why didn't you invite me?"

I checked my phone, it's five o'clock and still no messages from my girl or Teddy. "No one. *Yet.*" I turned to leave.

"Damn. Then what happened? Natalie is going to freak out when we get home."

"Keep quiet until we get to the car." I whispered before I turned back to Ben. "Keep your phone on."

"Will do." Ben nodded as we all left. Once Kayley and I finally made it to the parking garage we slipped into Natalie's car. I checked the security app and the camera feed was offline. Shit. Did she turn it off?

Kayley took in deep breaths as she buckled. "Jesus, you walk fast. What the hell is going on?"

"You want the long version or the short version?" Once we got to the road I picked up the speed.

"A version where you slow the fuck down."

I tried to call Natalie again, and this time straight to voicemail.

Something's not right. "Dammit!"

"Dean what the actual fuck, you're scaring me and I don't scare easily." Kayley's eyes were glued to the road as she held onto the passenger handle for dear life.

"Nathan knows who I am and knows that Natalie and I are in a relationship. He had me followed and got pictures of Natalie and I together."

"He had you followed?"

"Yes. He also has a lengthy story written up exposing our 'workplace relationship' that could put her future in jeopardy. He said if he found out that I told the authorities or didn't cooperate he would publish it."

"That fucker, I knew he was a piece of shit but this one takes the whole god damn cake." She breathed. "So, what's the plan?"

"We have leverage. We know that they've been stealing other articles and filling in the blanks with AI, not to mention they're going to push out as many employees as they can without raising alarm bells. They've been hit with multiple copyright suits and have been sweeping them under the rug for years like dust bunnies. Ben has Brock's old laptop, earlier today, we were able to find out that he's keeping all of the photos in a private folder we can't delete without a pass code."

Kayley thought for a moment. "If Nathan has a story written up then they have copies on copies. We have to fry the entire server. Not to mention confiscate every single external hard drive, computer, and thumb drive in the fucking building."

"I have a feeling he wouldn't leave it on any kind of external drive in the office where someone could grab it either on accident or on purpose." I sighed. "If they do it's in their offices, which have cameras right outside to see who's entering and exiting."

"So, we cut the power to the building, take a baseball bat to every piece of tech in their office."

"What's with you and Natalie and baseball bats." I interrupted.

"I'm not done. We sweep up all the pieces with a shop-vac and blend them, all the while Ben mass deletes every single file in existence on the WEM drive, and then I'll get into the drafts and mass delete every WIP." She paused. "Then we get Brock so wasted he passes out, put him in his office, and when the police come to arrest him for extortion he'll be so miserable he'll cave at the first loud noise."

I look at her with a confused look. "How-"

"Don't ask."

"Who-"

"Don't. Ask."

"Kayley, if we delete everything we won't have any evidence to pin against them."

"Good point. That usually works when you want to make someone, or something, disappear." She shook her head. "We'll think of something. I'll make some calls." I'm about to interrupt her again when she puts her hand up. "Discreetly, I promise, this isn't my first rodeo."

I raised a brow. "Does Natalie know about this side of you?"

"No. Have you heard from her by the way? She's not answering my calls either."

"Why do you think I'm speeding and violating a few traffic laws?"

She shrugged. "Fair enough. I'm tracking her on Life360 and it says her phone is at our place? I wonder why she's not answering."

"Teddy came by to talk to her about something so she probably had her phone on silent."

"I swear to God if your dumbass brother did something to her I will cut both of your nuts off, blend them, and force it down your throats."

I scrunch my nose at her comment. "That was graphic. You know they're friends right?"

"Like hell they are!" She crossed her arms. "Slimy prick. Have you tried calling *him*?"

"Unfortunately he hasn't answered either. Look I know you hate his guts-"

"I hate his very existence." She interrupted.

"Whatever, he's been going through a lot these past few weeks, so whatever is going on right now, please put it aside for two minutes until all of this blows over?"

"Oh fresh tea, spill."

I sighed. "Let's just say, my brother is about to go through a very public break-up and he needed some time away to think things over. He joined my trip, and now his identity and location is also at risk of being leaked by Nathan and Brock."

"Public break-up? Is he famous or something?"

We finally pulled up to the house, I turned off the car and ignored Kayley when I saw her front door frame was chipped as if it was busted open.

"Natalie!" I quickly ran up to the porch and rushed through the door with my heart beating so fast it could explode. "Natalie!"

I suddenly went still when I saw Teddy tied to a chair passed out with two big brutes behind him. One with what looked like a bruised nose and dried blood on his face. In front of him was the last woman I thought I'd see today.

She turned around, flipping her long blonde manicured hair dressed in a sweatsuit with a face full of makeup.

"There you are Deano!" Her giddy smile made my stomach turn.

"Ell." I frantically looked around the room. My breathing quickened as I quickly realized Natalie wasn't here. If I didn't need information from Ell I'd crush her windpipe so she could never speak again.

"Where is she?"

She looked at me with playful confusion. "Whoever do you mean?"

I took a few steps forward and got right in her face. She held up a hand to her men who were about to approach.

"Don't give me that bullshit." I growled. "Where. Is. Natalie."

"Ah yes, your most recent muse."

Without thinking I quickly grabbed her throat and started to squeeze.

"I'll ask again. *Where's my girl?*" I heard a small click and metal pressed against my head.

Ell smiled and let out a choked laugh as I let her go. "I can't believe, Dean thirst trap Roberts, finally has a girlfriend." She coughed as she rubbed her neck. "You two will have a very interesting story to tell your kids one day. 'Daddy, how'd you meet Mommy'?" She mocked in a childlike voice. "'Simple, I just stalked her, cornered her at her job, and viola she was mine!'" She paused seeing the confused look on my face. "Please, Deano, you should know by now that I keep an eye on people in my inner circle. I like to know things, ya know, just in case they decide to choke me out." She rubbed her neck.

"Dean, I can't find Natalie anywhere!" Kayley ran in through the front door. "Oh, shit." She looked at me with a gun pointed to my head, Ell, then to Teddy who currently doesn't have a mask on. "*Oh, shit.*" She muttered.

Ell rolled her eyes. "Would one of you knuckleheads lock that goddamn door? If it still shuts. Fucking animals." She looked Kayley up and down disgusted as the man who was guarding Teddy now stood in front of the door so no one could leave. "Who the fuck are you?"

Kayley crossed her arms. "The girl who's going to rip out your fugly extensions if you don't tell us where Natalie is… and let Teddy go."

Ell laughed. "Not happening. But, to make things more fun and to make sure Deano doesn't go ballistic again. Ron if you please?"

The one standing at the front door went into Kayley's room and carried Natalie out with tape over her mouth, barely conscious. He set her up on a chair next to Teddy and tied her to it.

I went to move but the other guy pressed the barrel of the gun harder against my skull. "I'll break your fingers for touching her."

"Oh." Ell fanned herself. "Book boyfriend mode activated."

Kayley scrunched her nose at her. "Okay. Someone please explain to me what the fuck is going on?"

Ell sighed. "I think this will be better when the whole party is involved." She reached into her bag and retrieved some smelling salts and put it under Teddy's and Natalie's nose after ripping off their tape. They both took in a quick breath as they came to. Natalie coughed as Teddy groaned. They both tried to move but to no avail. Ell brushed her fingers through Teddy's hair as he flinched and tried to move his head away from her.

"Get your claws off my brother." I shouted.

Natalie's head began to rise and squinted over at me. "Dean?"

I let out the air from my lungs with relief.

"Dean!" She squirmed as she saw the gun to my head. I let out a relieved breath seeing her awake in front of me.

I tried to keep the worry off my face, but the tear that rolled down the side of my face instantly gave me away. "Hi, Princess."

Dean

"Ugh. You guys make me sick." Ell gagged as she rolled her eyes.

"Are you okay?" I ignored her and focused on my girl. A small bruise looked to be forming on her arm and a small cut on her cheek made my anger rise up again.

"I'm fine." She groaned as she shifted her gaze to the man holding the gun to my head. "You might want to ask him though, such a soft nose for such a big guy."

I chuckled. I'm not surprised my girl put up a fight. She didn't think twice when she thought Justin was an intruder, so I have no doubt she fought like hell. The guy must've taken my chuckle a little too personal as he kicked the back of leg making me drop to my knees.

Natalie and Teddy struggled again to get out of their bonds.

"Touch him like that again I'll rearrange your face motherfucker!" Natalie growled.

"Oh! Damn Deano she's feisty! I like her already!"

"Ell just stop!" Teddy spoke up. "You have me okay, just let the others go."

"We're not leaving you with *her*." Kayley spoke up as she tried to take a step forward before the other guy pulled out a gun and pointed it straight to her back.

"God dammit, Sunshine you can't shut the fuck up for two goddamn seconds." Teddy gritted out as he struggled to get free.

"Excuse me for trying to save your ass!" Kayley kept her hands up.

Teddy rolled his eyes. "And you're doing an excellent job of that!"

Ell looked between Kayley and Teddy. "Oh, excellent, I can use a cheating angle too. This day just keeps getting better and better. I was originally gonna go with murder suicide or drug overdoses but that," she kisses her fingers. "chef's kiss."

Everyone went silent.

"Oh. That got your attention! But, before we get to the messy part, let's stir the pot with some last minute deathbed secrets." She lifted her shoulders. "I love some good drama. The question is where do I start? Oh. Deano." She leaned on Natalie's chair. "When were you going to tell precious Natalie here that you were the man behind the project that was used to make her obsolete?"

Her eyes went wide. "What?"

She pointed her head to Natalie. "Tell her, Deano. You were the one to call Nathan and pitch this grand idea to start a brand new bookish account. Then, how you'd be more than willing to narrate it yourself *in person.*"

"Is that true?" She whispered.

Ell began to pace as everyone listened. "Of course it's true. He was obsessed with you. He would hunt down anyone who dared to disrespect you online. Making people lose their jobs, their relationships, their dignity. Some of them I'd say they deserved it, but damn, he was ruthless. Then he became so desperate to see you in person." She sucked air through her teeth. "But, sadly, your boss used that account as an experiment for some new AI tech making you *useless.* So, if you think about it, it's all Dean's fault you're in this little pickle."

"Dean?" My girl's pleading voice made my heart ache.

"It's not what you think." I muttered.

"If it quacks like a duck, and waddles like one, it's a duck Dean."

"Fuck you, Ell." I spat.

She scoffed. "You bore. I was expecting something a little more creative." Natalie's eyes filled with tears as she turned her head, refusing to look at me. It took everything I had not to choke Ell out again. "Oh careful Dean, you might blow a blood vessel."

She went over to Teddy and lightly brushed her fingertips across his shoulders. "Don't you just love a little bit of drama, honey. By the way, how does it feel," She straddled my brother's lap. "Knowing that your brother is more concerned about saving his precious Natalie, than his own little brother."

Kayley's lip twitched as her stare turned downright vengeful.

"I won't let you get in my head. Dean's done nothing but help me. He knows I can take care of myself and that I won't let you get away with this." Teddy stated in a low tone.

"I can assure you I will, sweetie. I can already see the headlines. 'Ell Wyms Grief Stricken After Her Fiance Dies From an Overdose' and," She turned to me. "'Famous Narrator Identity Revealed in a Shocking Stalker Case'. I already have Brock on speed dial for that one, have for awhile now. And you're right, he really is a slimy prick. I kinda like it though. Makes this more fun."

"God you are a snake." Teddy groaned.

"It's called keeping my reputation intact, baby. How did you think my image remained spic and span all these years. I've worked too hard to get it and I'm not going to let you or *anyone* ruin it." She dragged her finger down my brother's face. I shifted as the guy pushed the gun a little harder against my skull.

"I can't have you running around spreading 'rumors' about me." She continued. "I was surprised you had the balls to break up with me, and then I realized, if you're confident now, you'd be confident enough to start talking shit. I've worked very hard to build my sweet innocent image. I'm not going to let a boy tarnish it. Plus, I think a grieving album would be great character development. So," she lifted her shoulders, "Two birds." She turned to Natalie. "You know, you and I would've been great friends Natalie. It's a shame you were here to see this."

"Fuck you, Ell." She spat.

"Oh Deano, she really is perfect for you." She squeezed Teddy's cheeks as he struggled. "Aren't they perfect for each other?"

Kayley took a few steps forward before the guy behind her grabbed her hair and pulled her to his chest.

"Kayley!" Natalie shouted.

"Get your hands off her!" Teddy called out.

Ell giggled as the man sniffed her hair while holding the gun to her head and laughed. Kayley winced as he pulled harder.

"Motherfucker!" She yelped. The more she struggled, the more his grip tightened on her.

The man with the gun on me pressed harder into my skull conveying the message that if I move he'll shoot.

"You're going to regret that." Teddy snarled.

"Oh, Teddy, Teddy, Teddy. Her? Really?" Ell rolled her eyes as she finally got off my brother's lap.

"Brayden?" Teddy returned the tone. "Really? You want drama? How many people have you slept with since we've been together?"

"Look at you, nosy." She teased. "Fine, fine, you caught me, Brayden and I have been fuck buddies for years now. But, that's only because I wanted some raw fucks, ya know, no feelings, no attachment, none of that 'look into my eyes' boring shit." Teddy slowly closed his eyes as if she stepped on the broken pieces of his already broken heart.

"God, you really are a basic bitch." Kayley spat. "You know," she breathed heavily. "From the start I knew you had no fucking soul. I almost feel sorry for you."

"Hm." She walked over to Kayley. "Out of the two of us, who's a multi-millionaire pop-star? Oh that's right, *me*. If anything I feel sorry for *you*, because you can never live up to me. No matter how hard you try, Teddy will always and forever be mine. Soon, mine to mourn."

Her phone rang in her pocket as a timer went off. "Ope, that's my cue." She gave Teddy a kiss on the cheek as he winced. "I'd love to stay and chat, but I have a plane to catch. Ron, Don, you know the plan." She walked towards the door as she put her sunglasses on. "Oh, and uh, have fun with it. It was nice knowing you all. Don't worry, Teddy, I'll give you an extravagant funeral and write sad songs so the world will remember you."

"Go to hell." Teddy spat.

"Aw, I'll miss you too." She blew a kiss and walked out the door more than likely to meet her driver.

"Any last words, pretty boy?" The man with the gun to my head stated.

"Yeah, actually." I looked up at Natalie who looked as though she was almost done getting her ties loose. "You know there's a wireless camera in the corner of the living room right?" Once he looked up I knocked his hand with the gun aside making him lose his grip and drop it.

Once I was up I landed a punch to his jaw, chin, and cheek. Out of the corner of my eye the other guy pointed his gun in our direction. Before he could shoot Kayley dug her nails into his skin making him shout out in pain. Once his grip loosened she pulled out her taser and landed it right on his balls. He shook and screamed out as he dropped to the floor.

I took a punch straight to the gut and face before getting pushed into the wall.

"Dean!" Natalie shouted.

Kayley quickly helped her and Teddy get free before the other guy slowly stood up and went after Teddy.

I took kick after kick until Natalie jumped onto his back, wrapping her arm around his neck to choke him. He rammed her back into the opposite wall. "I told you!" She grunted. "You touch him again, I'll give you more bruises to match, motherfucker!" She squeezed harder making his face turn red.

I tried to catch my breath and get to my feet as Teddy tackled the guy that held Kayley hostage. He punched and punched at his face making him a bloody mess. He then caught Teddy's fist and twisted it, almost breaking his wrist.

Suddenly, he was thrown to the ground and before the guy could get up Kayley kicked him down again. He quickly grabbed her foot, making her hit the floor hard. Once Teddy was up he quickly swung his foot into the guy's face knocking him out cold. "Like I said." He huffed. "You'd regret that."

"Oh please." Kayley rolled her eyes. "I did most of the work."

"You know a simple 'thank you' would suffice. Oh, sorry, forgot that word isn't in your vocabulary." Teddy spat trying to shake the pain from his wrist.

Natalie then got thrown to the floor making her yell out.

"Natalie!" I put her behind me as I grabbed a shard of glass slicing his fingers that were coming straight for me. He stepped back and screamed out as he held his dangling bleeding fingers.

"Keep your hands off my girl." I gritted out.

He dove at me again with an adrenaline fused rage. I was ready for him, then suddenly a shot fired with a silencer from behind that went straight through his skull.

"What-"

Justin stood in the doorway looking bored with a few other men strolling in behind him. I continued to stand in front of Natalie as she gripped my arm and buried her face into my back.

I turned and wrapped my arms around her, burying her into my chest. I held her head as she held onto my shirt for dear life. "I got you." I let out a breath of relief. "You're okay." Everything hurt, but I didn't care as long as I had her right here. *Safe.*

Kayley put her hand on her hip as Teddy stared at the scene. "Took you long enough. Did you stop for fast food along the way?"

He gave her a deadpanned look as the men rummaged around the house with cleaning supplies. "I was on the plane from New York. I could only go so fast Kay." He paused and pointed his finger to her neck. "Which one did that to you?" She pointed at the man on the floor. He scrunched his nose as he looked down at the unconscious brute. "Is he still alive?"

Kayley crossed her arms. "Yeah, you're welcome for your entertainment for the next week."

"Appreciate it." He leaned down to inspect him. "You take him down by yourself?"

"I'm offended. Just because I'm out of practice doesn't mean I don't have muscle memory." Kayley caved after her brother gave her a look. She rolled her eyes as she pointed to Teddy. "It was a joint effort."

Justin nodded with approval. "Nicely done." He turned his attention back to the man on the floor with an evil look in his eye. "We're going to have fun with you. Also here's your phone," He handed Kayley's phone back to her. "Remember any footage you caught of-"

"Us or anything incriminating us, cut it out, and run it by dad first, Jesus J, I got it." She quickly took her phone from his hand. "You act like this is my first time."

"Kayley what the fuck?" Natalie questioned.

"Surprise." She let out an awkward laugh. "Welcome to the family business."

"Please tell me it's crime scene cleanup related." Natalie begged.

She rocked her head back and forth. "You could say that."

"Lockwood Security at your service." Justin followed up.

"As in *our* security system Lockwood Security?" Natalie muttered. "Kay, I thought you said it was a *small* business."

"It was… at one point. Why do you think I never let J put in a security system? My family already spies on me enough."

Justin waved at the cameras. "Your video files before they cut the connection are already secure, Dad made sure of it. Also, he needs to talk to you." He turned to Kayley.

"About what?" She spat.

"Just call him. It's the least you can do after this mess."

"You know what," Natalie stepped away from me. "I need a minute."

"Put your clothes in trash bags." Justin called out. "We'll clean down here, and then upstairs once everyone is finished."

"I can't believe this is happening right now." She whispered as she climbed the stairs.

"Nat-" I tried to follow.

"Don't." She snapped as I froze in place. "Don't follow me. Please. I need a minute."

"Natalie, I'm not going to leave you alone after what just happened."

"Dean, please not right now." I followed her to her room and shut the door behind us.

I grabbed her wrist before she could make it to the bathroom. She struggled for a minute before she gave in my embrace and started crying. She gripped my shirt on my chest as I held her tight.

"I'm so sorry." I whispered. "Natalie, look at me." I put her cheeks in my palms as she looked up at me with watery eyes.

"Is it true? Did you call Nathan and pitch the idea to him?"

I stayed silent for a moment. She pushed on my chest making me take a step back. "What else are you not telling me? What else are you *hiding* from me?"

"Nothing." I breathed as I shook my head. "I'm not hiding anything from you."

Tears began to fall down her cheek. "You just lied to me. You knew what Brock was up to, and you didn't tell me."

My heart sank to my stomach, no, no, no. "I was going to tell you but-"

"When?" She shouted. "Before or after I got let go, before or after Ben showed up with Brock's laptop?"

The air became thin again as I watched more tears fall down her red cheeks.

"Natalie, please, I was going to tell you I just didn't know how, then all of the sudden Ben came in with his laptop and it didn't matter anymore. The only thing that mattered was making sure you had the support you needed."

"Oh my god, Dean, I can take care of myself! I don't need you to be stalking through my security system, I don't need you to tell off my bosses, for fuck's sake I just needed you to be honest with me, I needed you to listen to me!" She paused as I tried to breathe. "Instead you're hiding things from me, and having this 'ready, fire, aim' mentality with *my* job, *my* life. For Christ's sake this can't keep happening, I can't keep forgiving you for not telling me something and calling it protection. I thought I could trust you to tell me the truth, to be transparent with me, I guess I was wrong."

My eyes began to fill with water as the air was still and silent.

"I'm going to take a shower, please go home. I think we need to take a step back for a while."

In that moment my worst nightmare was coming true, as my heart broke into a thousand pieces. I hung my head as I nodded and tears rolled down my cheeks. "Remember what I said, Natalie. No matter how far away you try to send me I will *always* look out for you." I let out a short breath as tears fell down my sore face. "I'll *never* stop protecting you."

Natalie

I t's been over a week since Ell took us hostage and since I told Dean that I needed some space. He's still arriving at work, he's still living next door, and he's still keeping his distance. Instead of reporting to me, he's been going straight to Brock or Nathan, which to be honest, was a surprise. He still looked irritated every time he left their offices, but the fact he's tolerating them at all was something I did not expect.

He's still hiding things from me.

I almost started crying all over again when I saw that broken-hearted look on his face in my mind.

"He lied to me." I told Kayley as we sat in the sushi restaurant down the street from work.

"Wrong." She argued. "He didn't tell you."

"Like you did about your little 'family business'." I argued back. "Either way. That's still not telling me the truth."

She waved her hands over the table. "And you still forgave *me* for it."

I narrowed my eyes on her. "Yeah, because if I don't you'll hunt me down and store me on an island somewhere."

She rolled her eyes. "We don't have an island. We have real estate, there's a big difference." She picked at her sushi with her chopsticks.

I blew out some air. "I can't believe you're in the mob." I whispered.

"Ah. Correction." She held up her utensils. "I am a family member, not a 'business' member. We went over this."

"Yeah, and I argue, again, that goes against every book we've ever read."

"Those are fictional, Nat. Like I said, my family does things… a little differently."

"Which you refuse to tell me."

"Because if I did, you wouldn't believe me. I'm already on thin ice with J as it is, and if I reveal anymore Dad will need to get involved."

I shrugged. "I've met your Dad, he doesn't seem like the… type."

"Trust me, that bubbly personality can turn dark real quick. The last thing I need is your hunky Heartthrob getting pissed because you inherently joined the business after I told you too much."

I leaned back in the booth. The tears streaming down his face pulled at my heartstrings again.

Noting the look on my face Kayley put down her chopsticks and leaned in close. "Nat. C'mon. I know you miss him."

I cleared my throat to change the subject. "Are we still on track for tomorrow? Were you able to include the footage from our cameras and your phone?"

She stayed silent for a moment completely ignoring my attempt to steer the conversation. "Nat, I'm serious. He hasn't been the same, hell you haven't been the same since that night. I know that kind of 'action' can stir up a lot of emotions."

I looked at her through my brows. "I know you and Teddy had your ears to the wall. You two have been getting rather close lately, wanna talk about that?"

She shook her head as she rolled her eyes. "There's nothing going on with me and that prick, he's an asshole and the definition of 'never meet your celebrity crush'. Don't change the subject." She paused. "You love him."

"No, I don't." The words left a bitter taste in my mouth as they slipped out.

She scoffed. "And you're lying. To me and yourself." She pointed her chopsticks at me again. "Don't think I didn't see you attacking that guy for him. Nearly choked him out because he 'touched your man'." She tried to lighten the mood by using a swoony voice. "I'm really proud of you for that by the way. Where did you learn how to do that?"

"*That* was adrenaline." I argued.

"He protected you that night too. Slicing that guy's fingers almost clean off. Actually, now that I think about it, you two would make a great team with J. Well, *you* would. Dean, however, might take more convincing."

"Absolutely not."

"Because…" she drew out. "You love him and you don't want to see him get injured like that again?"

"Kay."

"C'mon, just admit it. You love him, and he clearly loves you. Why are you torturing yourselves with this third act break-up nonsense?" She leaned on the table. "The video is ready and we're going to be marching into that office with the biggest fuck you of the decade. Dean is going to be there. He's just as involved as you are. No more of this Ben said Dean said high school bullshit. You two need to straighten out your issues before tomorrow, we can't afford to be distracted."

"You don't get it Kay, he hid the fact that he hurt anyone who was ever mean to me online, that he created the project that's being used to get rid of us, and followed my boss around to get incriminating intel." I paused. "If he hid all that from me, there's definitely more."

She stayed silent for a moment. "You'll never know if you keep ignoring him."

I shook my head. "I'm not ready to face him yet."

"Why? Is it because you're afraid of finding out you were right? Or that you're wrong?" She looked me dead in the eye. "Nat, I know you feel betrayed right now, but you can't let that stop you from finding out the truth. If you don't at least talk to him you're going to regret it when he's gone in a week."

I hung my head, as much as I wanted to argue I knew she was right. But, "I'm just not ready. So, can we please move on?"

She threw her hands up in defeat. "Fine."

I cleared my throat and my mind. "Do we have an update on the photographer they hired?"

"Yeah. And you're not going to believe who it is."

"Who?"

"Chad Byte. Apparently he's a private photographer for a certain psychotic pop-star."

"Ell?"

"Bingo. Apparently, Ell's team and WEM are a lot closer than we thought."

I lifted my shoulders. "Snake and a snake's den are a perfect fit."

She laughed. "Fair enough."

"Is he still-?"

She shook her head. "Oh hell no, once J found out, he and Riley teamed up and got him arrested."

"Are you sure Riley doesn't know about your 'family business'?" I narrowed my eyes on her.

"Not *mine*," she corrected again, "my father's and if she does she doesn't talk about it. If anything she has a 'don't tell me what I don't need to know' policy when it comes to J."

"Why do you think that is? Riley has always been a rule follower, there's no way she would just turn her head the other way from your families 'activities'."

Kay tilted her head back and forth. "If I had to guess, there's a mutual favor involved somewhere."

"Any clue on what it is?" I tried to ask while keeping my voice down.

"Honestly. I'm on the same page with Riley in that aspect. The less I know, the better." She took a drink of her water. "She knows what she's doing and she can certainly protect herself."

I nodded in agreement, it's probably best to not go down that rabbit hole. If she didn't loop us in it's for safety reasons and given Justin's job choice, it's best to stay away from that with a ten foot pole.

"Fair enough." I agreed.

She looked me up and down.

"I know that look." I pointed at her.

"What look?"

"You're not done with our previous conversation."

She lifted her shoulders. "I don't know what you're talking about. However, since you brought it up, just tell me. Do you love him?"

I sighed as I licked my teeth as my annoyance began to surface, she really wasn't going to let this go and I'm so done with her pestering.

"Fine. You win. Yes. And that's what's fucking sad, Kay. I opened my heart to him, I fought for him, I almost *killed* for him." I whispered. "He still hid things from me, he still lied to me, and I should've known better."

Tears began to fill my eyes again and began rolling before I could stop them. "I made him promise, I said 'promise me you won't break my heart, Dean Roberts' and that's exactly what he did." I quickly grabbed my purse and stepped out of the booth. "I'll see you back at the office."

"Natalie, I'm sorry." She called out. "Nat!"

Dean

I quickly sat up from my table and headed towards the door of the sushi restaurant.

"Slow down lover boy. Let her cool down." Kayley called out unmoved. I stopped in my tracks and turned to face her. She pointed her head towards the booth. "Have a seat."

"Why? Are you gonna force a confession out of me too?" I bit back.

"Relax. I just want to talk." I looked to the door and back at her. "She's fine, the office is five minutes away on foot. J and my brother Hayden have eyes on her. Two minutes. I promise you can go back to following her afterwards."

I pressed my lips together and slowly slipped into the booth. The air still smelled like her and her warmth still lingered. My muscles relaxed for the first time in a week before Kayley began.

"You really have it bad don't you?" She smiled as she drank from her water.

I looked off to the side. "Are you going to mock and scold me, or do you want to have an actual conversation?"

She leaned on the table. "I'm not here to scold you or mock you, I'm sure you're doing enough of that to yourself for the both of us." I pressed my hands to the table to leave before she stopped me. "I'm not done."

"I am."

"You're a smart and passionate man, Dean. I know you know you fucked up." I slowly sat back down as she continued. "I also know you care very deeply for her, and that *this* was all some kind of twisted timeline where your secrets came out before you had the right moment to tell her." She paused, crossing her arms on the table. "Now, I'm trying my best to help her see that, but you need to do a little more than stalking around during our lunches."

I narrowed my brow. "How long did you know I was here?"

"Oh please." She waved her hand. "I've been clocking you since this morning. I see all, Dean. Don't forget that." She held up a finger. "Which brings me to my next point. Tomorrow, we're still green lit on our little mission. You will distract Brock and Nathan while Ben pulls what he can from Brock's computer. Nat changes all the passwords to the social accounts. Ben will hand over the computer and passwords to Riley and tell them you're being extorted for your services 'as we speak'. They arrest them for extortion and multiple cases of copyright infringement that Riley already has her hands on secretly thanks to yours truly." She wiggled her fingers under her chin.

"What about any physical copies Brock or Nathan could have at home?"

"J's got a team for that." She cleared her throat. "That's all you need to know. Have you decided how you're going to distract Tweedle Demon and Tweedle Dumbass?"

I had a few ideas, it's been difficult to keep their attention when they've been hovering around Natalie for the past week. I know they're doing it on fucking purpose when I'm nearby. Knowing that if I do or say anything they'll make sure that story goes live. I wiped my hand down my face over my mask as I tried to calm my frustration.

My luck turned yesterday when Brock asked if I was 'gifted musically' when I asked what the fuck that meant he took a couple steps back. Him and Nathan may have the high ground for now, but

I can still make the little shit jump out of his skin.

Turns out one of their accounts is music related, hard rock specifically, and their host for their live streams is out sick. So they asked me to fill in since 'I fit the vibe'. Brock quickly ran out of the room after he saw my reaction to that statement and agreed to host it here. If I can get them in the studio and watch the live event to 'make sure I follow the rules' then that'll be the perfect opportunity for Nat.

"Yup."

"Mind sharing your master plan?"

"Nope."

"C'mon I showed you mine, show me yours." She spat.

"No. It will keep them occupied and that's all you need to know." I groaned.

"Seriously?"

"Yes." I stated.

"Fine." She pouted. "Does Nat know? Oh wait, my bad, you'd actually need to speak to one another for that to happen."

I hung my head. "She's not ready to talk to me."

"She wasn't ready for you to fall into her life," She pointed her hands at me. "Yet here you sit. You love her right?"

"Of course I do." I said without hesitation.

"Then do something about it, for fuck's sake."

"Great pep talk. Is that all?" I groaned.

"No." She stated with a straight face. "How'd you find Natalie's trolls online?"

I lifted my shoulders. "Why didn't you tell her about the family business?"

"I have my reasons."

"I have my resources. Anything else?"

"Did you have any idea, they would use your idea as an experiment for AI scheduling and editing systems?"

"Of course not." I gave her an obvious look.

She narrowed her eyes. "Why did you pitch it?"

I stayed silent and thought about what I was about to say. "When I found Natalie, everything shifted. The entire world shifted. She's passionate, caring, funny, gorgeous, I wanted to give her the world." I paused as I slid my fingers up the glass of water she left behind and brushed my thumb over the lip imprint at the top of the glass.

"I thought that if her company created an account that catered to books, ones that she loved, I thought not only would that be the perfect way to meet her but it would give her a chance to finally do something even remotely related to what she cared about." The water droplets fell down the glass over her thumb print distorting the lines.

"I wanted her to see that she deserved more, I wanted to give her a chance to see that you don't have to be stuck in a place where they don't give two shits about you. I want to see her thrive, I want to see her be happy, and help her light shine even brighter." I let out a long breath. "I guess I pressed a little too hard."

Kayley hung her head as she took in my words. "Well, fuck. That definitely didn't go according to plan."

I looked through my eyebrows at her. "You don't say."

"Now, just say *that* to her, exactly how you told me. I expect you two to at least have some kind of contact before tomorrow. I'd prefer to do this with as little damage to body parts as possible, it's messy, and a snag is definitely not an option."

I rolled my eyes as I stood. Before I took another step I paused and turned back. "Did you press her to express her feelings for me because you knew I would hear it and somehow get motivated to talk to her?"

She took a drink of her water without looking at me. "It worked didn't it."

I stayed silent as I made my way out of the restaurant and heard

Kayley mutter. "That's what I thought."

Every single day since I left Natalie's house I've been watching her closely. Just because she needed time away to think, that doesn't mean I'm going to let her out of my sight. She changed the password to the security system the minute I left. It was cute how she thought changing it from GreenHouse1996 to GreenHouse1995 would classify as a new password.

I stared down at her tired face on my phone while she worked on her computer in her room, when she should be here in my arms resting. She's slowly been slipping away from the good habits I've integrated into her daily routine.

She skips breakfast by avoiding the food I leave her on her desk every morning and gives it to Ben. She doesn't stand or get up from her desk unless she has to. Like for a loosely wired fire alarm that makes us evacuate every other day. She's also been drinking way more coffee than water. Conveniently, a couple days ago, the coffee maker went missing from the office and their soda orders to refill the vending machines have halted, which made her start drinking water a little more frequently. Then of course sending Kayley cash to take my girl out to lunch every day. Doesn't matter where as long as it gets her away from the office for the full hour.

Just to name a few.

Tonight, she cried into her pillow again, and all I wanted to do was bust down the front door and take out whoever or whatever it was that made her cry. Only this time, it was me. I made her cry, I made her feel this way. My punishment? Watching her heart break, when I promised I wouldn't, knowing there isn't a thing I can do to help her feel better.

I'm sitting on the foot of my bed with my elbows on my knees. Watching and waiting for her to fall asleep. Some nights it takes a few minutes, sometimes a few hours.

I kept my eyes on my girl as I heard a small creak in the hallway. I stayed unmoved as Teddy leaned against the doorway.

"How long have you been torturing yourself?" He spoke softly.

"Since the moment I left her house." I stated in a low, quiet tone. "What do you want?"

He cleared his throat. "Justin's team finished fixing the walls and putting together the furniture at Natalie's place. I don't know how they did it but it's immaculate."

After the fight broke out Justin, who I still don't like, was able to fix and clean everything as if nothing happened. I'll give it to him on that one, but the look in his eye when he found out one of the guard's was still alive was down right evil. I hate the fact that he just walks into Natalie's house like he owns the place. After finding out what he does I wouldn't be surprised if his family owned the whole fucking neighborhood. He said we don't owe him a favor, but I wouldn't doubt he would use this against Teddy and I at some point.

"Knowing Ell Wyms won't be producing music after this is payment enough. We'll take care of it. *With pleasure.*" His words.

However, that's far from my main concern right now.

"Okay." I said bluntly.

I already knew they finished. I watched every move each of those men made to make sure they didn't do anything they're not supposed to or hide anything per Justin's request. I don't care if the fucker is Kayley's brother, I'd throw his arse to floor again in a heartbeat if he did.

"Justin also said that he's been sending Ell updates on the guard's behalf and intercepted communications with WEM, so she doesn't suspect a thing. If everything goes according to plan tomorrow, Justin will let his connection know over in France, and she'll get arrested before her next show begins."

Of course he has a connection. "Good." I continued to stare straight through my window into Natalie's room as she slowly began to fall asleep.

"Dean. When are you going to talk to me?"

"When you learn to keep your mouth shut." I snapped.

"For the tenth time, I thought *you* told her. That's very specific information, how was I supposed to know that she found out through her employee?"

"I don't want to have this conversation again, Teddy." I continued to avoid his stare.

"Okay. Fine. How about the one where you're working your arse off in order to keep Natalie and I safe?"

I wiped my hand down my face before I stood to face him. "Are you and Kayley talking in private now?" He stayed silent as I scoffed. "Figures. You both have the same inability to keep things to yourselves, you're fucking made for each other."

"Don't-"

I raised my brows. "Don't what? Talk about her like that?" He stayed silent for a moment avoiding eye contact as I let a low chuckle escape. "That sounds awfully familiar."

"You don't know what you're talking about. She's vile and you're changing the subject."

"So are you." I nudged past him and made my way downstairs. "If you think she's so vile, why call her 'Sunshine'?"

"Because it pisses her off, can we get back to the main point here? You've been keeping us in the dark about what you discuss with those cockroaches."

I sighed as I filled my glass with water as he went on.

"Why aren't you telling us anything? What else are they holding over your head?"

I finished off my water and put the glass in the sink. "Are we done here?"

Teddy stepped in front of the stairs. "Far from it. Is it true what Ell said?"

"Which part?" I groaned.

"Any of it. The stalking, beating people who were mean to Natalie online, the project?"

I pressed my lips together. "Teddy, for the last time. I don't want to talk about this right now."

"Then when? Huh? I've kept my mouth shut for a week Dean, and I feel like I don't know who you are anymore." He let out a breath. "You were *stalking* her? For a year? Why didn't you just reach out to her, like a normal fucking person?"

"Are *you* judging *me* right now?" I got up in his face. "*Your* ex-fiance just tried to have us killed. You didn't have to join this trip, you didn't have to stick your nose where it didn't belong, if you hadn't tagged along *none of this* would've happened."

"Then I'm sorry." He let out a sharp breath. "I'm sorry that I've been such a burden for you. I'm sorry that I needed my brother during a difficult time in my life, and I'm sorry that I hoped we could be brothers again. I can see now that's beyond the point of redemption. But, I wasn't the one who kept secrets from her. *You did.*" He paused. "The minute Justin gives me the all clear I'm flying back to L.A., I wouldn't want to cause you any more trouble."

He quickly went up the stairs and slammed his bedroom door shut. Leaving me at the bottom of the stairs with my chest heaving and aching.

Natalie

I woke up with the feeling of my comforter being pulled to cover my shoulder. As I stirred I felt a familiar hand brush through my hair. Someone is in my room and it wasn't threatening, I didn't feel scared, if anything all I felt was comfort. The smell of clean cologne filled my senses and made my heart flutter as he backed away.

"Dean." I whispered.

No response.

I turned my head to see him standing near the window with a hoodie and sweats. The moonlight from the window highlighted parts of his gorgeous face, one still filled with small bruises and a healing cut on his cheek. He looked exhausted and drained, physically and mentally.

I took a deep breath and put aside all my thoughts, just for now.

I lifted the comforter. "Get in."

He lifted his head. "What?"

"It's late, and we have a long day tomorrow. Get in, before I change my mind."

He stayed silent as he made his way over to the bed, kicking off his shoes, and crawled in next to me. His warmth quickly filled the space as we adjusted. I put my arm under his head and laid the comforter on top of him as he wrapped his arm around my back. He buried his face into my neck and took in a long and relieved breath.

God, I've missed his presence. His touch, his smell, everything. Our legs intertwined as I pulled down his hood and began massaging my fingers through his hair. I could feel his wet cheeks on my chest as I held him tight. I could almost feel the cracks from his heart in his tense muscles. Ones that slowly loosened as I guided my fingers through his hair. He kept rubbing his thumb back and forth on my back making me fall back asleep within minutes.

I woke up the next morning to find Dean still in bed with me now pressed against my back. Without thinking I took his hand, intertwined his fingers with mine, and brought it straight to my chest. He used that same arm to pull me closer and hold me tighter. This doesn't change the fact that he wasn't completely honest with me, and my body currently doesn't get the memo. All it knows is that Dean is here with his dick pressed against my ass, and when he's here, he's *mine*. Mine to hold, mine to kiss, mine to love.

My chest tightened.

No. No. Stop it.

I knew this was a bad idea, yet I remained still. I rubbed my thumb over his hand. I don't want him to leave, I don't want reality to set in, I just want to be here, silently, with him. I'm terrified of what might happen today, I was so scared of losing him once, I don't know if I can do it again, if things go south...

As if he read my thoughts he laid a kiss to the back of my head.

"I've got you." He whispered.

How fucked up can I be if the one man who can comfort me is the same one who broke my trust. Tears began to fall again as I turned and buried my face into his chest. He held the back of my head with his arm around my waist keeping me right where I've been wanting to be.

Somehow I fell asleep again, and woke up to my alarm. I turned and to my disappointment, an empty bed.

Once I was ready for work I met Kay downstairs. "Morning."

She sipped her coffee with a stupid grin on her face. "Morning."

I paused. "What?"

"Nothing." Her voice raised an octave. "Sleep well?"

I gave her a side eye. "Fine."

"Hmm." She raised her eyebrows as she raised her cup to her lips. "I bet you did."

I turned my head to her as she raised her hands for a truce. "Hey, I told you to talk to him, not sleep with him."

"Kay what the hell? How did you-"

"I stopped by your room to see if you were up and I saw a very cute couple looking at peace while they rested then quietly retreated back down here. That's all I promise." She paused, trying not to sound giddy. "So? Did you guys make up? Make-up sex is otherworldly."

"No. And definitely not." I shoved my work laptop into my bag.

"Aw, damn. I was hoping to get some juicy details this morning." She snapped as she remembered. "Speaking of. Don't forget, Spice Shelf meeting next week."

My eyes widened. "Already? Shit."

"Don't get too excited." She looked offended as we walked out the door.

"No, it's not that, I haven't had time to finish 'House of Mischief'."

"Really? I figured Queen of the audiobooks would've been the first one to finish it."

I glared at her as we got to her car. "I would've if it weren't for, I don't know, almost getting killed by the most popular pop star in America right now. Or the fact that the company I work for would rather extort its employees than give them decent raises."

She lifted her shoulders. "That and, you know, getting railed by the narrator every night. I can see how that can get a little *distracting*."

I gave her a deadpanned stare. "Please, stop. I'd like to keep Dean out of my head as much as possible today."

She blew out some air. "Yeah, that's definitely not happening." She paused before she put her hand on the roof of her car. "Hey. Are you ready for today?"

"I have the one chance in a lifetime to take down a company who's done nothing but abuse its employees. Yeah, I've been ready."

She shook her head. "No. I'm serious. Are you sure you don't want me to help Ben while you help Dean?"

"Kay." I looked into her eyes over the car. "I promise, I'm fine. You recorded Ell, edited the video, and recruited J into helping us. I can handle the social media accounts. Besides, Dean doesn't need my help."

It's the truth, he doesn't. But, I couldn't help but remember that night. The way that man attacked him, rage filling his face as he charged towards him with nothing but blood lust in his eyes. I doubt that Brock or Nathan would try such a thing, but if they're going to be put in a tight corner like that, who knows what could happen. I squeezed my eyes shut before my head started to spin.

"He'll be fine. Okay?"

Before I could get into her car I caught Dean out of the corner of my eye leaving the porch with mask on, hair wet, and sleeves of his black button up rolled up to his elbows revealing his tattoos. He caught my stare when he opened his car door and stood there with his hands on top of the car staring right back at me. I went to open my door and heard a small click of Kayley locking the car.

"Kayley." I gave her a warning look. "Unlock this car."

She looked at her keys. "Oh no, my fob isn't working." She lifted her shoulders. "Must be on the fritz. Looks like you're riding him to work."

"What?"

"You're riding with him to work."

"That's not what you said."

"Ride him, ride with him, whatever, just go. It'll give you two a chance to talk before shit hits the fan." Before I could argue my soon to be kicked out roommate waved at Dean. "Morning! She's riding you to work- I mean riding with you to work."

"Seriously?"

"Ope, would you look at that my door is still unlocked thank goodness." She slipped into the driver's side. "Talk to him."

I slowly turned to find him leaning against the passenger side of his car with his hands in his pockets. God dammit he looks good, as if he had gotten his first full night of sleep in the past week.

"I hear you need a ride?" He said in a low tone as I approached.

"Apparently." I sighed.

He opened the door for me, made sure I was in, and lightly shut it behind me. Once he slipped into the driver's seat his damn cologne glided over to me. My thigh muscles tightened as if to recognize the smell and welcome him home. His hand gripped the steering wheel, revealing the veins in his muscles as if he was fighting to keep his hands where they should be. My concentration broke as he handed me the aux cord. Something so simple and out of habit for the both of us.

I held the cord in my hand and thought for a moment before I let my hand fall into my lap.

"Dean."

"Yes, Princess."

My heart tugged at the sound of my nickname. "Why'd you come through my window last night?"

He stayed silent as he pulled out of the driveway. I saw his face mask move as his jaw clenched, thinking of the right words to say.

"Door was locked. Why'd you invite me into bed?" He kept his eyes on the road.

I shook my head and stared out the window. "Because I missed you." I admitted. "I felt like shit, and I needed the one person who could make me feel better at that moment."

His hand gripped the wheel. "Exactly." We stayed silent for another moment before Dean broke it again. "I'm sorry, Natalie."

I took in a deep breath trying not to burst into tears again. "I know you are. But, that doesn't mean I can automatically trust you again."

"You trusted me last night. You trusted me when those men attacked us, to put up your security system."

"That was different."

"How?"

I stayed silent as he continued. "You keep telling yourself you don't know me, but you do."

"You kept the truth from me Dean, how can I trust you when you don't tell me the whole truth?" I began. "I- I understood keeping your job a secret because you've hidden your identity for a reason. I understood keeping Teddy's location a secret because of his situation, I understood you stalking me for a year because I've done the same thing to you for three. Maybe not to the same extent, but I didn't feel threatened by it. If anything it felt nice to be seen which sounds fucked up, and something I should probably talk to a therapist about. But, making people pay for being mean to me, making an entire project at my work that will lead to hundreds of people losing their jobs, trying to convince me to quit when I have no backup plan. I'm sorry but I can't sit by and let you insert yourself and make decisions in *my* career, *my* life, without my permission or at least communicating it with me first."

Dean took a deep breath. "And *I* can't sit by and watch you get taken advantage of, watch people say hurtful things to you, watch you suffer at the hands of people like *Brock* and *Nathan*." He paused. "You deserve the world, Natalie. You can hate me all you want, but

I'm not going to stop until you hold it in the palm of your hand. I will do everything in my power to help you make that happen and take down *anyone* who stands your way."

Another heavy silence weighed on us as we made our way to work, pulled into the garage, and parked. His words hit me like a truck and I'm not sure my heart can take anymore of this.

Before I reached for the handle he locked the car.

My heart rate began to rise. "Dean. Let me out."

"Not until we go over a few things." He turned to me with his now serious blue eyes. In that moment, I realized that this isn't just Dean, my neighbor who I've fallen in love with, but the narrator who has helped me through some of the darkest times in my life. Now, he's here again without fail, ready to walk through every single step of one of the most important days of my life. I'm about to lose my job, with no backup plan, and…

Shit.

Everyone *will* be out of a job if I go through with this. Now my heart was racing for a different reason.

"Natalie?" Dean looked over at me as if trying to read my mind.

His voice brought me back to reason. They have pictures exposing his identity and holding it over his head as we speak, they had us followed, and they're going to replace us with cheap AI. I took a deep breath as I remembered we're being thrown overboard without life jackets either way. We might as well hold on tight and take them down with us to make sure they don't drown anyone else.

"Fine." I cleared my throat. "What do you want to go over?"

His eyes flitted over me, knowing that I'm deflecting. He looked around the garage to make sure we were alone. "Let's go over the plan."

I relaxed a little as I rolled my eyes. "You distract Brock and Nathan, Ben and I will pull what we can from Brock's computer, I change the passwords, Ben takes it to Riley, and everyone gets arrested."

"And…"

"And what?" I narrowed my eyes on him as he looked back at me. "You're really going to make me go through each step?"

He held his stare on me. "We can't go into this unprepared, Natalie."

"We both know the plan. You're just trying to keep me in this car."

He let out a small chuckle. "If I wanted to keep you in the car I would've tied you up and threw you in the trunk." He used a tone that I'm all too familiar with.

I rolled my eyes. "Cute, but that's not going to work on me."

"Your thighs are indicating otherwise." He paused as I unclenched my thighs. Curse my body for always giving away my deep and depraved thoughts. "Still mad at me?" He purred.

"Yes." I bit back. "Extremely."

He reached into my bag behind my seat and took out the extra pair of underwear I've been bringing to work.

"Then I guess you won't need these." He held them in front of me. I went to reach for them but he quickly retracted and wrapped it around his hand. I know he has a smug smile right now under that mask.

"Hand them over."

He lifted one of his shoulders. "Why? If you're mad at me, you shouldn't need them, right? Admit the thought of me tying you up, throwing you in the trunk, and taking you where no one can hear you scream turns you on and I'll consider it." His eyes turned lustful. "Don't forget, Princess, I know my girl better than anyone, so I'll know if you're lying."

Well fuck.

When I snapped at Kayley's comment this morning I knew it came from a place deep down where my sexual frustration was beginning to reside. The need for him to press me to the mattress and fuck me to tears this morning was a lot higher than it should have been.

Not wanting to give him any satisfaction I stayed silent. Just because my body was pulling to him like a magnet doesn't mean he's forgiven. However, the thought of him fucking me on the hood of this car out in the middle of nowhere had my body heat rising so fast I'm surprised I'm not sweating.

"I'm not admitting shit. Now, please, let me out." I muttered.

I could practically see a smile forming under his mask. "Since you asked so politely, sure. After you tell me the final and most important step."

I put the back of my head to the seat with a frustrated laugh slipping. "Fine. Help Ben get the info to Riley, and wait outside with the police. Good?"

"Yes. Was that so hard?" His voice was low and satisfied as he unlocked the doors.

"Not as hard as your dick was against my ass this morning." I pulled on the door handle.

"Says the woman who brings spare underwear to work because of *my* voice." He called back as I shut the door in his face.

I retrieved my bag as he stood tall in the garage. I don't know what bratty confidence took over my mouth as I shut the back door and rounded the car.

"When this is over, I'm finding a new favorite spicy narrator to read to me and obsess over." Before I could make it to the stairwell he grabbed my arm, pulled me close, and pinned me with my back to the driver's side door.

"I don't care if you read or listen to other books, in fact I encourage it. But, know this Princess, if you even think about touching yourself to another person's voice I will remind you who you belong to. You come on my face, my fingers, my cock, my toys, and my tongue. Mad or not, *you are mine*. Don't forget that."

His eyes were serious as he looked down at me. My body betrayed me again, feeling the cool car against my back and the warmth of his body against my chest. I pushed his buttons and this was the consequence, was I truthful about finding a new narrator to listen to, no. I was just pissed, and now here I am trying to not to be aroused by his tone. I can't let my body take over my brain, so I said the first thing I could think of to remind myself of what he did.

"*You* broke your promise. *You* had your chance. *You* broke my heart." I whispered. "Don't forget *that.*"

He kept his eyes on me as I ripped myself from his grip and went straight to the stairwell without looking back and tears falling down my face.

Dean

It's almost five, I've been waiting all fucking day for this. Seeing Natalie this morning gave me a little more hope that things are going to work out. Then after what she said in that garage, that hope got beat to hell.

"You broke my heart."

The pain shot through my chest again at that moment. The same pain from the night of the attack. I lightly rubbed my eyes while trying to keep my contacts in place. I'm not going to stop fighting for her.

After being this close I don't think I could ever stop. Every single part of her is etched into my memory, her marks still on my skin, her taste still on my tongue, and this week without her has been physically and mentally painful.

It was my fault. I should've told her everything and been truthful from the start. I'll admit that until the day I die. But, there isn't much I can do about the past now, all I can do is do everything I can to prove to her that she *can* trust me, that she has *always* trusted me. That she is the only person that I trust with *all* of me. That I love her with my entire being, and a life without her simply isn't worth living.

I knew the pull we had was still there for her too when she opened up her bed to me last night. The moment she touched my skin I melted to her. Everything weighing on my shoulders suddenly felt lighter, and everything for a moment seemed right with the world.

I didn't want to leave this morning. I needed to get ready for today, and I knew she did too. I laid a kiss to her forehead and winced at the pain of taking that step back. A promise that this isn't over.

Teddy was still in his room as I was about to leave the house this morning. I regret yelling at him and he was right. None of this was his fault, he didn't tell Ell to try and kill us, he didn't keep all those secrets from Natalie. I stood outside his door debating on knocking to see if he was ready to talk to me. Once I did, there was no answer.

"Teddy."

Still no answer. I hung my head, taking the hint.

"I'm heading out." I paused for a moment, trying to find the right words to say. "Listen, I shouldn't have yelled at you like that. You're not an inconvenience. I'm actually really glad you came with me, and I'm so proud of how far you've come. You took a stand, and I'm sure it wasn't easy. Especially when you have a dickhead of an older brother who didn't listen when he should have. You also helped me in ways I didn't know I needed. I realize I'm not 'brother of the decade', but I'd really like to try, Teddy. So, thank you, and I'm sorry. For everything." I checked the time, realizing it was time for me to leave. "If you still want to leave I understand, but if not we can talk when I get back. I'll see you later."

The memory quickly faded as one of the employees called out, "Striking." The lights from the set illuminated the dusty, clearly budgeted, set. I get working with what you have, but with a company who's willing to pay over $100,000 to *one* of their higher-ups clearly could do better.

Kayley looked over another employee's shoulder at the computer hooked up to the camera for the live stream. Once Nathan entered she was out of the set and on her way over to hover near his office, making sure no one entered to wipe his computer or publish those pictures.

Brock swiftly followed behind him meaning his office was now free and ready for Ben and Natalie to make their move. I took a deep breath as I sat on the stool in the middle of the set with a dark gray backdrop that looks as though it was used for school pictures.

Brock shooed the rest of the employees out as he took over the computer to run the stream.

She'll be okay. I think to myself. *As long as I keep them here, she'll be okay.*

Nathan locked the door to the set behind him, locking himself and Brock in here with *me*.

I still have no idea what I'm doing for this thing. I've done streams before on my own account, but not for an account dedicated to music. Do I know enough to get me by, sure, but that doesn't make me an expert like their previous host.

"We're all set." Brock leaned back in his chair.

"Fantastic." Nathan boasted.

I rolled my eyes. Shifting to my American accent while I'm here has become second nature at this point. "Either of you ass-clowns mind telling me what I'm doing during this stream? If you're making me strip that's gonna cost extra."

Nathan chuckled. "Such a smart mouth for someone being held by the short and curlies."

I licked my teeth behind my lip trying to keep my words in. It doesn't work. "That's definitely gonna be an up-charge."

He slowly walked up to me as he threaded his fingers through his short blonde hair. He invaded my space as he whispered. "You seem to have forgotten your current situation. One text, and Natalie's career will be tarnished, *forever*."

He paused as my anger began to build. I looked past him out the window to see Natalie and Ben conversing at their desks, about ready to make their move.

"Suddenly, nothing to say?" He leaned to my ear as I tried to lean away. "Remember. We own your ass. So, shut up, play your part, and everyone goes home with their career intact." He stood tall and slapped a hand on my shoulder. "Good talk."

I stretched out my neck and tried to suppress the overwhelming urge to rip his god-damn arm out of his socket. Nathan sat at the table with the computer as Brock adjusted the camera.

"First, we'll start off by just interacting with the comment section." He opened his laptop where I could watch the stream and read the comments. "Then we'll move on to trivia." He handed me a set of index cards with questions and answers. "And if anyone donates money, they'll be able to put in a song request." My eyes widened as he brought up a mic stand.

"What?"

Brock looked at me as if I was dumb. "Song requests. There's a list for them to choose from, all rock-ish, for you to sing to them."

I quickly stood and threw the cards on the side table. "This was not a part of the deal, nor is it in my contract."

"Oh, Mr. Roberts, I think we threw out our contracts when we found out you poked holes in it. Like a desperate cheerleader trying to trap a quarterback." Nathan paused as he leaned on the table. "Plus, I've seen the resume you tried so desperately to bury. You're a pretty good singer, so good I'm surprised you're not in a band yourself." He narrowed his brow. "Why would you let a talent like that go to waste only to read books?"

"That's none of your god-damn business." I spat.

I only ever sang in projects I took on for fun, or ones I felt a connection with because that's where it becomes some of my best work. I never wanted my talents to be forced, to turn into something I hated. Yet here I am.

Nathan shrugged. "Actually. It is." He paused. "If anything I'm giving you an opportunity of a lifetime here. You know how many people in the industry follow this account? Huh? You could get discovered, travel the world, have thousands of women scream your name as they cream themselves in the front row."

I stiffened. "No."

Nathan smiled. "No?" He shrugged as he shared a look with Brock before he turned to his phone. "Then I guess Natalie doesn't mean as much to you as I thought."

I looked out the window again to see Natalie and Ben. The only ones left in the office after Kayley sent out an email secretly telling everyone to go home. Natalie brushed her hair away from her face before checking her phone. She caught my eye and froze with a twinge of worry on her face. My heart began to ache as she looked at me for answers.

"What did you do?" I shot Brock with a death glare that made him lean back.

Nathan lifted his shoulder. "We might need her in here for some assistance if you're misbehaving. Just imagine the look her pretty face would make if she found out her career was over, *because of you.* Unless, you've changed your mind."

I shut my eyes, still seeing her face on the other side of my eyelids. She means more to me than anything this universe could ever give me. She's my girl, *my world.* I would do anything for her, and if that means doing the one thing I told myself I would never do with my full face on display, then so be it.

"Where's the song list?"

Nathan revealed his triumphant grin. "Good choice."

Natalie

"If you keep pacing like that you're going to create a line in the carpet." Ben stayed glued to Brock's screen.

I suddenly paused and wrapped my hands around my arms. "Sorry." Brock's message earlier about "staying on standby for the live" had me so anxious Ben had to follow behind me into Brock's office to make sure I stayed on track. They're using me as fuel to keep Dean obedient, I know it. The way he looked at me then back at them all but confirmed it.

I pulled up the stream on my phone because I couldn't take it anymore. While I could hear Dean's muffled American accent through these paper thin walls, I couldn't make out everything from here. Plus, this is the last account that needed a new password so I can lock them out the minute they're done.

I stared down at Dean's masked face on my screen. He's definitely putting on a performance.

"How's he doing?" Ben asked as he continued to type.

"Fine so far. He's keeping Brock and Nathan entertained and that's all we need." I paused. "How's the *hacking* going?"

"It's not hacking when you leave your computer open." He chuckled. "He's such a dumb ass, he'll create a pass code for a folder but doesn't use a password to lock his computer. Not even a pin. Seriously." I couldn't help but chuckle and nod in agreement as he continued to type and click. Then he suddenly stopped. "Huh."

"What?" I stood straight.

"Has Brock been holding anything over *you*?" He looked over at me with suspicion.

I narrowed my brow. "No. He has no clue that I know about the pictures or anything really. Why?" I rounded the desk to see what he was looking at. He scrolled through draft after draft of stories about Dean and I. Talking about scandalous workplace relationships, stalking a co-worker, Dean sleeping with me to keep his identity a secret, and me using Dean to get to Tanner Brunswick for a career boost.

"He didn't use these against you?" Ben questioned.

"No." I let out in a fuming tone. I knew Ell had her connections to Brock to keep her in a positive light and to keep control of her relationship's narrative. But this…

Then it hit me as I reflected on the look Dean gave me earlier. I froze there in pure anger.

"But, I do know one thing, he didn't write those stories to use them against *me*. They're not just using these pictures as blackmail, they're creating a whole goddamn story with them to boost their views. He knows I'm important to Dean, if Brock threatened him with these he'd do anything to make sure they don't go public." I admitted as I looked down at my phone. "Hosting a live stream for starters."

"Fuck, that's dirty." *Click.* "On to the drive it goes. Sounds like he really cares about you. Singing on a live stream in front of thousands of people, you couldn't pay me enough-"

"Wait. Wait." I cut him off. "Singing? No. We stopped the performances a long time ago when we kept getting dinged for copyright."

"Didn't Brock tell you?" Ben muttered as I put my hands on my hips. "He got an 'approved' list of songs they could use for the streams.

Whether that's true or not I have no clue. They clearly don't care about copyright dings as much as they used to."

"If anything it's a list of songs they haven't performed yet or gotten the copyright notice for." I took a closer look at the stream background as Dean continued to flawlessly answer some questions in the comments.

"Shit." I muttered as I noticed a mic stand on the left side of the set.

"What's wrong?" Ben questioned. "Is he a terrible singer?"

"Quite the opposite actually." I've heard him a few times in the shower, but I haven't heard him perform in a professional setting before.

Dean does have a beautiful voice, but I know that was a boundary for him. He didn't want to use his singing voice for work, he didn't want it to be exploited, or turn into something he hated. It was just for him. Yet, at any moment they're going to force him to perform in front of thousands of people and…

My eyes went wide. *Fuck.* "If they're going to make him sing, he has to take off his mask."

Ben's eyes widened with mine. "Shit." He muttered. "He's risking his identity being exposed."

He's being forced into a corner because of me, because of his feelings for me. The fact that he was willing to do that to protect me made my chest tight. I can't let them get away with this. They've done so much already it's sickening.

I held my stomach as my heart sank. "Please tell me you have everything."

"Just the folder, that's all that's left." He pulled out a flash drive, stuck in the port as a program popped up.

I gave him a confused look. "Justin?"

He shrugged. "50 Justin. 50 Me." Two clicks later he had the file open and started copying everything to the drive.

Kayley popped her head in. "How we lookin'?" She questioned.

"One more minute and we're done." Ben replied.

"Fantastic." She looked down at her phone. "Riley will be downstairs in fifteen."

I whipped my head to her. "Fifteen *minutes*? Dean doesn't have that kind of time."

She looked at me like I was crazy. "What are you talking about? The stream is for another hour at least. Plus, he's doing great."

"Is there any way she can get here faster?"

She narrowed her eyes on me. "There was a nasty accident this morning and the cleanup took longer than expected, but she's still within her time frame. Look, as long as he keeps the stream live we'll have Tweedle Demon and Tweedle Dumbass arrested before they know what hit them."

I stared back down at the screen as a donation popped in with a "host choice song request". *Fuck.* I quickly shared the live to Riley as Dean got set up for the song.

"Shit, shit, shit." I set my phone down as I shifted through Brock's desk for an extra pair of keys.

Kayley still looked at us confused. "Okay. Mind telling me why you're rummaging through Brock's landfill of a desk?"

"Dean's being forced to sing on stream, Kay. You know what that means?" I finally found some spares and desperately looked for the one labeled "set".

"That he'll start a new career?" She shrugged.

"Got it." Ben pulled out the drive and quickly packed up. "Everything's uploaded."

I stood tall. "It risks his identity being exposed. I can't let him risk that for *me*."

"Fuck me." She groaned.

We all froze as we heard the strums of a guitar playing Seether's version of 'Careless Whisper'. I looked down at the stream to see he hadn't pulled his mask off yet.

"Slight change of plans." I began. "Kayley, go with Ben. I already sent the stream to Riley. I'll be able to lock them out and stop the stream from here, hopefully Dean will keep their attention enough they won't notice until the police get here."

"Are you sure that's going to work?" She questioned.

"It has to." They both took off as I stopped the stream from my laptop, changed the password, requested to logout of all devices, and ran back towards the window. I stayed out of Nathan and Brock's view but just enough to catch Dean's eye again. I watched Brock's computer and my phone anxiously as the stream ended right before Dean peeled off his mask and began to sing.

"I feel so unsure. As I take your hand and lead you to the dance floor."

I took long, relieved breaths as his eyes closed to feel the music and the words flow from his lips to the mic.

"I'm never gonna dance again. These guilty feet have got no rhythm. Though it's easy to pretend. I know you're not a fool. I should've known better than to cheat a friend."

He sang as if he hadn't sung like this in ages, with his full heart, and full chest he watched me with sorrowful eyes. As if he was singing to me and me alone.

"And waste the chance that I've been given. So I'm never going to dance again." His eyes lock with mine. *"The way I danced with you."*

The notes from the guitar filled the air as it traveled through the paper thin walls. Tears began to fill my eyes as I watched and listened to his voice. He doesn't know that the stream is down, but he still took off his mask, he still sang his heart out, all to protect us. To protect me.

In about thirty seconds it'll prompt them to sign in again officially tipping them off that something is wrong.

Dean's voice went gruff and full of heart as he went into the next verse.

"Tonight the music seems so loud. I wish that we could lose this crowd. Maybe it's better this way. We hurt each other with the things we want to say."

More tears fell as he continued. I can't let him keep going like this. I jumped over to the door and slipped the key into the lock.

"We could have been so good together. We could have lived this dance forever."

The key fucking snaps. "No. No." I go back up to the window to catch his eye again.

"But now, who's gonna dance with me? Please stay!"

The verse hit me with every single emotion he's been keeping inside. The love that he's shown me, the happiness he's shared with me, the pure heartbreak and agony I saw in his eyes the night of the attack, and the night he thought he scared me away.

I stared down at the door and channeled all of my energy and all of my strength. I turned my back to it as I took a deep breath and braced the sides of the door frame. I lifted my foot and swung it back as hard as I could. Luckily this door wasn't the sturdiest and it went down easy, scaring the shit out of Nathan and Brock. Dean's eyes were wide with a surprise then a proud look spread across his face as he turned off the music.

"Natalie! Jesus! What the hell is wrong with you?" Brock shouted. "You could've tapped the window, you didn't have to break down the goddamn door!"

I put my hands on my hips as I caught my breath. "Oh, I'm sorry, I thought we could do whatever the fuck we wanted considering your making Dean Craven, known for his secret identity, take off his mask to expose him to thousands of strangers on the internet."

Nathan quickly got in my face. "You just kissed both of your careers goodbye. I'm calling the police before you damage any more property."

I quickly swiped his phone from his hand, banged it on the edge of the table, shattering it, and tossed it out of the set. "No need. They're on their way already. And Brock. I'd step away from that phone and computer if I were you. Unless you want Dean to release all of his pent up anger straight into your face."

"*Please*, reach for it." Dean stood tall proudly as he gripped the mic stand ready to swing it if he had to. Brock put his hands up as he stepped back and stared him down.

Nathan scoffed. "I should've known. Let me guess. He told you about the articles? Should've known Mr. My Chemical Romance over here couldn't keep his mouth shut."

I crossed my arms. "Actually he didn't, and if you call him that again your face will match your phone screen. I have had a shitty fucking week, *don't test me*." I caught a small smirk on Dean's face as I went on.

"Considering he was ready to reveal his identity to the entire world, I'm assuming you hung me over his head to get him to do whatever you wanted, including keeping him quiet. Here's the problem with your plan though. You focused all of your energy on Dean because let's face it you're scared of him. When really you should've been scared of *me*."

"Please. You?" Brock scoffed. "What could *you* possibly do?" Dean inched closer making him hit his back into the wall.

"I'm not going to let you keep bullying and harassing your employees just so you can make a little extra cash."

"You think you're the first person to barge in thinking you can change things?" Nathan scoffed as he leaned in disgustingly close. "Guess what *sweetheart*, whatever you and *Dean* are planning, it's not going to work."

Dean's eyes were burning as I tried to give him an "I got this" look.

"I think it is." I stood my ground as I went on "You know... the original plan was to set up an exchange. The photos for this." I held up the flash drive. "A video of Ell Wyms holding people hostage and a full confession that she was going to kill her fiance to keep her image safe. We figured you'd be foaming at the mouth for this kind of thing. But..." I shrugged as I put the flash drive in my pocket. "Then we figured, why dangle the fruit? Let's go for a cleaner route. And..." I looked around the room. "Look how that turned out. *You* wanted to play dirty, so we're playing fucking dirty. Of all the celebrities for you guys to have connections with, Ell was the last person I expected. It amazes me how little work you actually put into this thing. Ell did most of it, sending *her* photographer, giving *you* photos. Must've stung when she didn't include you in her little homicide plans."

"Please." Nathan scoffed. "You're bluffing. You have no proof."

"Don't worry. You'll see the proof plastered all over our rival media sites in about two minutes. That is if you're not in handcuffs by then."

"Once our lawyers get involved *you'll* be the one handcuffs." Brock scoffed.

"*And you.*" I turned to Brock and began to walk over. Dean softly and slowly stepped back to stand in the doorway to make sure Nathan didn't make a break for it.

I pointed to him still up against the wall with his hands up.

"Your actions and verbal threats made this office an unbearable workplace. Then, lone behold, I found out you were going to replace us with an AI scheduling system, AI editing systems, and stealing other media outlet's stories while filling in the rest with, you guessed it, A fucking I." My voice wavered. "All so you can get more *money*, you greedy fucks."

Brock stuttered. "H-How did you-"

"Not important." I stated.

Nathan laughed. "Please. Anything you think you and your boy toy have on us won't see the light of fucking day."

"You're *still* not seeing the point? You were going to force people, good people, out of their jobs. How do you fucking live with yourselves? Through all the gas lighting and manipulation? Throwing people to the street so *you* can make more money."

"It's called business, *sweetheart*. Get fucking used to it, you think we're the only ones looking for cheaper alternatives? Please, good luck trying to find a job without getting on your knees first." Nathan boosted before Dean kicked the back of his knees making him hit the floor. He yanked on his hair making Nathan look at him.

"Say that again." He leaned down as he let out a low growl. *"I fucking dare you."*

"Also," I went on as I brushed away Nathan's comment. "According to my sources. You ass-clowns gave all those poor writers you let go *an hour* to sign an NDA, and if they didn't, you weren't going to give them their severance. Pretty sure that's not exactly legal either is it? Not to mention a shit ton of witnesses and screenshotted proof." I turned back to Brock. "Because, I know you love a good paper trail."

I could practically see all the color from their faces leave in an instant. "I guess I should've led with that, huh?"

"What do you want?" Nathan gritted out.

I tilted my head. "It's too late to ask me what I want, Nathan. It's all already in the hands of the police, who should be here any minute. Now, I just want to see you all fall on your asses. Because if we're going to lose our jobs to AI and shitty business practices, *you will too.*"

Brock suddenly took me by surprise as he pushed me down, forced his hands around my neck, and began to squeeze.

"I am not going to jail today! Not because of *you!*"

Dean swiftly wrapped his arms into a lock around his neck, peeled him off of me, and threw him off to the side before leaning down to check on me. He lightly put his hands on my cheeks.

He inspected my neck as I continued to cough and tried to take in the air I could. Suddenly his eyes went dark as he saw the marks already beginning to form around my throat.

His jaw tensed as his eyes began to burn again. "Stay here, and turn your head. You're not going to want to see this."

He laid a kiss to my forehead, and made his way over to kneel down in front of Brock.

"Oh Brock, I told you I would make it hurt if you ever *talked* about her like that again. Not only did you ignore my warning, you took it a step further, *you put your hands on my girl.*" He growled. "The last man who did that lost his fingers before a bullet went through his skull."

Brock's body shook with fear as he held his eye and begged for mercy. "Pl- please- Don't kill me. I- I can give you money, please! I don't want to go to jail! Just let me go home to my family! Please!"

"Your family?" Dean chuckled. "You should've thought about them a long time ago. This morning your wife got all the info she needed to leave you stranded. Now, you did most of the work, but one little text with photos of you checking out other women and a clip of your voice badmouthing her, was all the proof she needed." Tears began to roll down Brock's face as Dean tilted his head.

"Awe, don't worry, I'm not going to kill you… but I will make you beg me to."

He grabbed two of Brock's fingers and pulled back as hard as he could. The sound of the cracking bones made me wince as Brock yelled out in pain.

Out of the corner or my eye I saw Nathan trip and fall as he tried to flee with fear in his eyes. I peeled myself off the floor to go after him into the office area. Before I could catch him Kayley out of nowhere tackled him to the floor.

"Get off of me! This suit is worth more than your salary!"

"Weird flex but okay." Kayley spat. "I'll be sure to rip the shit out of it."

He was able to twist himself out of her grip and throw her to the ground. He kicked her hard in the gut as Teddy came out of nowhere swinging a computer monitor like a baseball bat straight to Nathan's face.

"Holy shit!" I muttered.

He tossed the monitor aside as he stood over Nathan's unconscious body. "On behalf of every person you've exploited for money, *fuck you.*" He reached down to offer a hand to Kayley. "Looks like I'm saving your arse again, Sunshine."

She smacked his hand away. "Whatever, ass-hat." She groaned as she held her stomach. "I had it under control."

He rolled his eyes. "Sure seemed that way as he kicked you in the stomach." He looked her up and down. "Are you sure you're okay?"

"Awe. Look at you trying to be all caring and shit. Fuck off, I'm fine." She held her stomach as she winced.

"I'm not. Just testing to see if you had a concussion, you lunatic."

Dean came up next to me as they continued to bicker. I couldn't help but chuckle before turning to him.

He lightly outlined the marks on my neck before moving up to my face. "Are you alright?"

"I'm okay." I nodded. "I'm sorry. I'm sorry for-"

"Princess, you have nothing to be sorry for." He brushed a few hairs from my face.

I buried myself into his chest as he put his hand behind my head and cheek to my hair. My heart began to calm as his warm hold made me relax and allowed me to slow my breathing.

"You two are so cute I could vomit." Kayley announced as she held her stomach.

"Are you sure that's not from the kick to your gut?" Teddy chimed in as he handed a bottle of water to Kayley. She reluctantly grabbed it, twisted off the lid, and flicked it hitting him in the side of his face.

"Lunatic."

"Prick." She snubbed as she took a drink of the water. "Why are you here, again?"

We both turned to them, giving Teddy a strange look.

He shrugged. "What? You think you're going to have all the fun of taking down an entire bloody media company without me?"

"Yes." Kayley said bluntly.

He ignored her and looked over at Dean. I gave him a reassuring look and walked over to check on Kayley.

"I heard what you said this morning." Teddy began.

Dean took in a breath. "I meant it. I shouldn't have gone off on you like that. All you needed was your big brother and I spat in your face."

Teddy hung his head as he nodded. "I know you didn't mean it. When Ell held us captive all I could think about was how I let you down. If I hadn't broken up with her that morning none of it would've happened, I wouldn't have put everyone in danger."

"Teddy, listen to me." He held his shoulder. "There's no way in hell you could've predicted her actions. That was all her. *None of that* was your fault. Even when you knew it had the potential to destroy your career, you still did what you thought was best and I'm so proud of you. "

"Speaking of." Kayley interrupted their moment as she waved her phone. "That video we sent to Lemon Drop Media went viral. Oh, and her arrest video is trending too. Ha! Who's the lovable pop-star now, bitch!"

Finally, the police came rushing through the door with Riley heading straight for us and the FBI right behind her. She went over her usual checks making sure everyone wasn't hurt or needed an ambulance. She fussed over Kayley the most since she got kicked in the gut pretty hard but she insisted she was fine and to focus on the two that were passed out on the floor. After one look at my neck Riley didn't even question why all of Brock's fingers were broken.

"We have teams over at Brock and Nathan's homes." Riley put her hands on her hips. "Apparently, this isn't the first time Nathan has been investigated. Last time they weren't able to turn up anything. More than likely any time he caught wind of the search warrants and cleared everything out before they got there. This time however, from what they've found so far, he wasn't as prepared."

"Why do you say that?" I crossed my arms with Dean right by my side and arm wrapped around my waist.

She eyed us both. "Let's just say there was evidence *everywhere* which is uncharacteristically sloppy of him." She sighed as she pulled us aside. "Listen. I don't need to know every single detail about what happened here, but I know Justin was involved. You two need to be careful, I love Kayley and her family, but don't be racking up favors with them."

She sounded as though she spoke from experience. "Riley, what's going on with you and Justin?" The question just slipped out as her eyes bolted around. She stayed silent as if she wished she could tell me everything.

"We'll talk about it later." She looked over my shoulder and saw a group of cops surrounding Teddy talking and asking him questions. "Hey! Ladies, you can drool over him later, get back to work! Jesus."

Once we were cleared to head home we stepped outside and saw a crowd of local news stations setting up and getting ready to report about World Entertainment Media's downfall. When we got to the parking garage, Kayley left to go check in with her brother, and Teddy rode in the back seat with us.

"So, does this mean you're going to be sticking around for a few more days?" I asked Teddy.

He sighed. "Unfortunately, no. The police are gonna have a few questions for me and probably already in the process of getting a search warrant for the house. I'm hopping on a plane tonight."

Dean looked in the mirror. "Do you want me to come with you?"

He grinned as he looked out the window. "Nah, I'll be fine. Mum and Dad said they're flying in to help. Even after I told them it wasn't necessary."

Dean tilted his head. "You know Mum."

"Yeah, apparently Dad had to put her on house arrest because she was threatening to fly over and 'strangle Ell with her own hair extensions'." Teddy explained.

I couldn't help but smile. "I can't wait to meet your Mom."

Dean chuckled at that comment. He looked back at Teddy. "Are you sure you don't want me to come with you?"

He looked between the two of us and shook his head. "I'm sure. I think you have some unfinished business here to take care of first." He paused as we got out of the car in Dean's driveway. "Just please wait until I leave, I really don't need to hear *that*. I'm already scarred as it is." Dean gave him a glare that made his little brother quickly run to the house with a grin on his face.

"Prick." Dean muttered.

I walked over to the driver's side as he leaned against the car. I tapped his shoe with mine as he put his hands in his pockets. A chill breeze whipped through the air as he looked down at me with tired eyes.

"So what now, Heartthrob?"

He took a deep breath, taking in the cool fresh air. "Tell me what happened in there."

I lifted my shoulders. "Besides me busting through the door and Brock having the balls to try and choke me out."

Dean's jaw clenched as he tried to hold in his reaction as he looked over my bruises. "Natalie."

I paused for a moment to collect my thoughts.

"Ben and I saw the articles they made about us. Some about you, some about me, some about us together." I closed my eyes for a moment trying to collect myself again. "I put it together, they dangled our careers in front of you to make you do whatever they wanted. To make you stay quiet, record more scripts, host a stream, even reveal your identity to the world." I paused before looking back up at him. "Dean, I saw you take off your mask, I watched you sing. Why? Why did you risk the most important things in the world to you?"

He looked down at me confused. "Because they're not the most important things in the world to me anymore. *You* are. And I would do it again if I had to."

I sniffed as he kissed my forehead and brought me close. "You know I stopped the stream right before you took off your mask."

He looked down at me with a bit of surprise. "You did?"

"Of course I did. Dean, I finally understand where you were coming from. Watching you get used like that it… it tore me apart. It made me want to kick down the door and beat the shit out of anyone who made you do it."

He chuckled softly as he brushed my cheek with his thumb. "Careful, Princess. I've heard that's not exactly the best way to approach that situation."

I chuckled and nodded as he continued to take me in. "Dean, I'm so sorry. For everything." Tears began to fall again as Dean immediately began to wipe away the tears. "For thinking I couldn't trust you anymore, for pushing you away like that."

He shook his head. "I should've told you. I just-" He paused, "I wasn't exactly sure how."

I pressed my lips together. "Looking at the situation now, how could you tell someone you care about that they're about to lose everything they worked so hard for. I shouldn't have reacted the way that I did. It was a minor detail among the whole picture."

"You had every right to react that way, Natalie." He paused. "Given my record, I get it."

"To be fair, I figured it out before you had the chance to tell me those things." I shook my head. "All you've tried to do, from the moment you arrived, was show me that I am worth more than this company could ever pay me. Your words." I smiled up at him as he smiled back.

"Remember what else I told you?" The corner of his lip raised as he whispered.

"That no matter how far I send you, you'll always protect me?"

"And?"

I tilted my head trying to remember.

He put his forehead to mine. "That you deserve all the happiness in the world and I will do everything I possibly can to make sure you have it. *No matter what.*"

Tears filled my cheeks as I fell back into his hold, his arms wrapping around me so tight no one could pull me away even if they tried. His hand moved into my hair as he pressed his lips to the top of my head. The sensation flowed through us as if to lock us together.

"Please tell me you're not leaving anytime soon." I whispered.

"Awe, Princess." He sniffed. "I'm not going anywhere."

We stayed there for a moment before I broke the silence. "If I find out you're keeping any more secrets from me intentionally I will hurt you." I muffled into his chest.

He couldn't help but chuckle. "I promise. No more secrets."

"Even if you kill someone. I need to know so I can help you hide the body."

He let another chuckle as he put his cheek to my head. "Noted.

As long as you promise to tell me when you improvise so I can be prepared."

"When it comes to protecting you, the only man that I love in this world, no promises." I muffled again.

"Hey now," He found my chin and brought up my face to look me in the eye. "It's only fair."

I put my chin to his chest as I looked up at him. "Oh, so it's okay when you say it?" He gave me a pleading look that I couldn't deny. "Fine."

"Thank you." He paused as he brushed the hair out of my face from the cool breeze that whisked by us again. "And, Princess."

"Yes, Heartthrob?"

He smiled down at me as he brushed his thumb against my cheek. "I love you too."

Dean

Six months later…

"You know the consequences of your actions, Daphne. I yell out into the woods. You can run all damn night until morning, but you will get tired, you will slow down, and I will catch you. A small snap of twig a few trees over makes me turn my ear. *There you are.*" I paused the recording and listened back to it. I winced at the clip, definitely could put a little more gruff and growl into it.

I lifted my head from the script and caught sight of my girl on the other side of the door of my studio. I gave her a smile reassuring her that I was finished recording for now.

She loved to watch me work, and I loved seeing her thighs shift when she hears it.

She opened the door to the spare bedroom where I turned the closet into a fully functioning audio booth, with the rest of the room filled with backdrops and gear to make my online content. A few of which recently included Natalie. She hasn't shown her face but she loved showing off her body. One photo I have her bra unhooked with her back to the camera, my masked face over her shoulder, and my hand clawing at her back, simply captured, "Mine".

Then another, a personal favorite, I'm kneeling in front of her as she pulls on the back of my hair. As if to force me to look up into her eyes full of lust and trust. Of course that led to us staying in the bedroom for hours.

As she walked in with wet hair, one of my old t-shirts, and the shortest shorts known to man, all I could think about was how I wanted to devour her right here.

She stood in front of me as I stayed seated in my booth.

I wrapped my arms around her waist and pulled her close. "You smell amazing." I let a low growl slip. "Did you take a shower without me?"

"I had to after packing for the past few hours."

"My love, you don't need to pack for me." I insisted "I can hire movers for that."

"I know. I just needed a distraction."

"If that's the case why didn't you come in sooner?" I lifted her onto my lap.

She gasped at the sudden movement then let out a small giggle. "Because I knew you needed to get some work done, and because we're moving in less than a month and you're nowhere near organized."

I looked up at her a little offended. "I'm organized."

"You have your t-shirts hanging in between your winter jackets, and don't even get me started on your bathroom."

"What's wrong with my bathroom?"

"Who puts their clean towels under the sink?"

"British people with tiny bathrooms." I couldn't help but laugh. "Tell you what, when we get to the new house, I promise all towels will go straight to the linen closet." She gave me a thin smile. "What's on your mind, Princess? Why do you need a distraction?"

I knew why, but I wanted her to tell me in her own words so I could fully understand what she's feeling right now. I know she's stressed with writing her first book, moving, starting up a pop-culture media site with her old team, it's a lot of uncertainty for her. All I can do is support her in every way I can, and listen.

"I was having a pretty bad block this morning. I sat at the dining table with my laptop and just stared and stared at that stupid blinking cursor." She sighed as she traced the pattern on my shirt. "I don't know. My head feels muddled, like I could do everything else but write. Does that make sense?"

"It does." I nodded.

"If I don't at least get some kind of progress done today, I'll feel useless. Like that's one day I could be getting closer to publishing, but instead decided to waste it by doom scrolling, organizing, or cleaning. For fuck's sake, what am I doing? Dean, I have no income. I can't even write. My friends are relying on me for guidance with this content. I- I don't know what I'm doing with myself, how can I create new content with fresh ideas or write fifty thousand plus words."

I gripped her tight as I put my hand to her cheek. "My love. Look at me. You are not useless. Alright?" I shook my head. "I don't want you to ever think you're useless. You are amazing, you are talented, you are gorgeous in every sense of the word. *I* know you can do this, *you* know you can do this." She moved her hands up to my cheeks and I pressed a kiss to her palm.

"Think of it this way." I continued. "It doesn't matter if your publishing date is tomorrow or five years from now, either way you're going to have a publishing date. I know my girl better than anyone, and I know you're going to get published. The site has multiple brains for a reason, if you need help, or need a brainstorming session you have some amazing minds to bounce ideas with." I paused. "It's okay to take a day for yourself if you need it, it's okay to rest. I can't stress that enough Princess, if you feel like you need to doom scroll for a day to reset that's okay." I brushed my thumb over her cheek. "Remember, I will always be here for you no matter what. I make enough here to support both of us, alright? If you want to jump back into the 9-5 I'll support you every step of the way. If you're not ready, that's okay.

Hell, if you *never* want to go back to a 9-5 and want to become a full-time author slash content writer, I'll be right by your side. After the last place you worked for I'd be more than happy if you decided not to go back, but that's just my extremely biased opinion. I do love having you here all to myself."

She laughed as she looked down at me. "Are you sure?" She whispered.

"Of course, my love."

She laid her soft and addicting lips to mine. I held her tight as she wrapped her arms around my neck. Her tongue quickly found a way in deepening the kiss. I immediately stood picking her up with me and pressed her to the wall of the sound booth. Her body pressed against the panels as I slid my hands down into her shorts and dug my fingers into her hips making her grind on my now very hard cock. I released her legs only for a moment to take off her shorts revealing she had no underwear on and already soaking for me.

I rose back up taking her shirt with me as she peeled off mine in return. I kicked off my sweats and lifted her again. She moaned as I dove my face into her neck, sucking and biting as I rubbed my cock on her clit. Her nails dug into my back as she held on for dear life and I drove my cock in. She let out a small cry in my mouth that made me want to devour every single inch of her.

"No underwear, no bra, did you come in here expecting to be fucked, Princess?" I whispered in her ear. She threw her head back making more of those beautiful little cries of pleasure as I bit into her neck like a monster devouring its prey.

"Yes." She purred. "I wanted you to claim this pussy like a good boy, *like you fucking own it.*"

"Someone took a little reading break without me." I thrust all the way in again and stayed there. She attempted to grind her hips as if to try and get a smallest bit of friction. I pressed harder against the wall as I gripped one of the sound absorbers, almost ripping it clean off. I put my other hand to her throat and wiped my thumb over her bottom lip.

"Tell me Princess, did you finish 'House of Deviants' without me?"

She tried to hide her grin. "You narrated it, so it doesn't count."

"Oh." I raised my brows. "It counts. Now tell me," I put her wrists in my hand and slid my thumb down to her clit and pressed. Her breath hitched as she whimpered. Her eyes looked at me as she begged for even the slightest friction. But, I remained still.

"Did you finish it without me?" She stayed silent. "Answer me, Natalie." I moved my thumb ever so slightly to make her jolt.

"No, I promise. I just listened to a few chapters." She gasped. "I swear."

"Hmm." I kept my grip on her wrists above her head and I slid my thumb down as another jolt and feeling of pleasure reeled through her body.

"Please... " She panted. "I swear it was only a few chapters."

"I believe you, Princess. However, you still had reading time, with *our* book, without me. Therefore, you're not allowed to come until I tell you to." She nodded begging me to continue what we started. "Do you understand?"

"Yes." She purred again. I took her down off the wall and flipped her to where chest and torso were pressed against my desk. "Lift those hips for me, Princess." She does as she's told allowing me for better access as I put her hands behind her back and fucked her from behind.

"Good girl." I growled into her ear.

Her entire body shuddered at the sound.

"Fuck, Natalie. God, you're so wet for me." I could feel her tighten around my cock and stopped in my tracks. "Nuh uh. Not. Yet."

"Dean please." She begged.

"Please, what?"

"Please let me come." She whimpered.

I leaned down to her ear. "You know the rules. You don't come until I say so. That's your punishment." I slipped my fingers in between her folds to give her the slightest bit of friction. "And I'm far from finished with you."

"Fuck..." She breathed.

I brought her back to my chest and flipped her around again. I slipped my wet fingers into her mouth and she sucked and licked them clean. After I pressed my lips to her for a sloppy kiss I tugged at the nap of her neck by her hair. "On the chair and spread your legs for me."

She did as she was told and spread her legs as wide as she could. I stared down at the beautiful glistening mess I've created. My cock twitched as I knelt down in front of her, wrapped my arms around her thighs, and pulled her closer to the edge of the chair.

"Keep your hands attached to the top of the chair. If they move, I'll stop. Do you understand?"

"Yes."

Without warning I licked from her opening all the way up. Making her entire body shutter as she resisted the urge to put her hands in my hair. While I love it when she does that she's being punished right now, and I can't have her breaking the rules. My arms around her thighs tightened, gripping her tattoos, to keep them open as I licked, sucked, and tongue fucked her. The taste of her is so addicting, I could have her for breakfast, lunch, and dinner and I'd still be starving for more.

I reached my hand up her stomach as she writhed and threw her head back into the chair hanging on for dear life. Just when I feel *I'm* about to burst I feel her tighten again and I stop.

"Dean, please!" She cried out.

I licked my lips and wiped up the rest with my thumb and licked it off like she was a divine dessert. I switched our positions to where she's now sitting on my lap. She looked down at me with lustful eyes practically already grinding herself on my painfully hard cock.

"You've done so well, Princess. Now, lift your hips for me, I want you to ride my cock until you come, and don't stop. I want you to ride on that pleasure as long as you can. Can you do that for me?"

"Yes." She does as I ask and as soon as I centered myself she slid on with ease as if we fit perfectly together.

"Fuck." I let slip. I brought her close as she rode my cock with ease and took one of her nipples into my mouth and sucked hard.

She held the back of my head as she let out more cries of pleasure. I could feel her tightening around me as she continued her pace.

"Come for me, Princess."

As if right on command, she's falling apart around me. Letting out the most beautiful cries of pleasure. I felt her coming again, and again as she continued to ride me. Her body trembled as she held me close, still continuing to roll her hips.

"Fuck, Natalie, you feel so goddamn good." I whispered as I gripped her hips so hard my prints were etched into her skin.

"Come for me, Heartthrob." Her lips traced my ear as I buried myself into her neck and bit down as the pressure built. Her breath hitched as she rode me with an even and smooth pace as if she wanted to stretch out my orgasm until I was seeing stars.

We're both a heavy breathing sweaty mess, as she pulled away to hold my face in her hands. She laid a single soft kiss to my lips as we stole each other's breaths. "I love you, Natalie." I whispered against her lips.

"I love you too, Dean." She whispered back. My heart was practically beating out of my chest as she wrapped her arms around my neck with mine wrapped tightly around her back.

This woman is mine. Now, and forever, this beautiful, kind, and loving Princess, is solely and unequivocally *mine*.

Epilogue - Dean

When you said you were moving this was the last place I expected you to pick." I hopped out of the moving truck and tossed Teddy the keys.

He shrugged as he looked back at his luxury home he had renovated out in the middle of nowhere Indiana right down the road from our new house. At least he's not going to be living in our basement anymore. Thank fuck for that.

Natalie is a saint and I still can't figure out how she does it. I, on the other hand, was about to lose my goddamn mind all over again and counted the days until the renovations were finished. He took in a deep breath of fresh air and relaxed his shoulders at the sight of neighbors' country blocks away.

"Eh. I guess you could say it grew on me."

"More like *someone*." I cleared my throat as I opened the door to the truck and hopped in.

"Absolutely not." He scorned. "Don't ever tell that lunatic where I live."

I gave my little brother an obvious look. "You know she's coming to the party tonight right?"

His eyes widened. "Dean what the fuck?"

"She's Natalie's best friend, what am I going to say, no?"

"Yes!" He hopped up into the truck with me.

"C'mon! Just admit it." I picked up one of the boxes and set it on the lift. "You like her, you're just too goddamn stubborn to admit it."

"Please." He threw another box. "She's the last thing on my mind."

"Who is?" Mum said excitedly as her and Dad rounded the corner. "Are you talking about Kayley?"

"How did-" He turned to me as I tried to suppress the grin on my face. "Goddammit, Dean! I'm gonna kick your arse!" He swung his arm at me as I dodged and smacked upside the head.

"Boys!" Dad elevated his voice. "Knock it off before I have to kick both your arses." He looked over at Mum with a scowl on her face. "And before your mother beats me to it."

We pushed each other one more time before we hopped out of the truck and greeted them.

"Teddy, help your father with the bags and show him around the place. He's been itching to make sure the renovations are up to his standards." She turned and muttered to me. "The whole damn flight."

"Dad," Teddy gave him a confused look. "I called Uncle Tommy, he was *your* recommendation."

"So? Just because he's done some good work over the past 30 years doesn't change the fact that I watched that man superglue his fingers together. *Twice.*"

"The first time he was drunk." Mum retorted.

"That doesn't give him an excuse for the second time. If there's one screw loose I'm giving that fucker an ear full."

We rolled our eyes as Teddy helped him pick up the bags and headed towards the entrance.

"So." Mum turned to me. "How's Natalie?"

"I'm fine Mum thanks for asking." I joked and gave her a reassuring look. "She's great. She's on her way with Kayley and a few of our friends to help unload the trucks." I sat up on the lift as Mum stood next to me.

"Oh good, how'd her book signing go?" She asked excitedly.

"Really well, she's already half-way through her second book." I stated proudly. "And 'The Real Take' content is gaining a lot of traction."

She gasped. "That's fantastic. I can't wait to see her. I've missed her so much."

I raised my brow at her. "You're on the phone with her more than I am."

She lifted her shoulders. "Only because you two live together." She paused as she smiled. "I'm so glad you found someone who makes you so happy, sweetheart."

"Thanks Mum."

"Oh, that reminds me." She reached into her pocket and handed me a small navy blue felt box. I opened it and revealed my Mum's emerald engagement ring with small white sapphires on the sides. Passed down for generations on my dad's side. I took a deep breath as I stared at it. "We'll be traveling for the next eight months. So I brought it over for you just to hold on to when you're ready."

"It's even more beautiful than I remember. I thought you gave this Teddy?"

She scoffed. "Please. I love Teddy but from the minute I met Ell I locked this thing away at the bank. There was no way in hell she was getting her slimy little fingers on this ring." I laughed as she went on. "She was a witch from the beginning."

I nodded as I continued to stare down at the ring. "How did you know I was thinking about proposing?"

She lifted her shoulder. "I saw the way you two were looking at each other during the holidays. It reminded me of the way your father looks at me. The way your grandfather looked at your grandmother. And in those moments I just knew, you two were made for each other. That ring has been at the center of many beautiful marriages, and I have no doubt you two will continue that tradition. She loves you so much, sweetheart. And I'm so happy you found the person you want to spend the rest of your life with." Tears began to fill her eyes.

I hopped down off the truck as I gave her a hug. "Thank you, Mum."

"Of course." She pulled away and wiped her tears. "Oh god. You're not even engaged yet and I'm blubbering like it's the wedding day. Tell Natalie to call me as soon as she can afterwards."

I laughed. "I will."

She nodded. "Good. So," she took in a breath, "What about Teddy? Is Kayley going to be here tonight? The one you told me about?"

I clicked the box closed and put it in my pocket. "Yeah, she'll be here. She grows on you and Teddy can deny it all he wants but I've seen the way he looks at her."

Mum thought for a moment. "She was the one who recorded the video, right? The one that got Ell sent to jail?"

I nodded. "Yup, and she ran in to try and help us, even though she didn't have to. She tried her best to rip Ell's hair out."

"Hmm." She grinned. "I think I like her already." She sighed while taking in the fresh air. "I must admit, I was a little surprised your brother picked *this* of all states but," she looked out at the open fields and listened to the trees rustling in the background. "It is peaceful out here."

"Yeah. I guess he wanted to be as far away from paparazzi as he could. After Ell's trial and 'The Deal Breaker' dropping him, I don't blame him."

"And to be closer to his brother." Mum looked through her brow at me. "He's really going to need you, sweetheart. This Ell bullshit is going to follow him around for the rest of his life. Promise me, you'll always be there for him. Just like you were last year."

I nodded. "I promise."

She pulled on my face and kissed the top of my forehead. "Good."

She tapped my cheek.

"To tell on him when he's being a prick." I smiled.

"Oh." She whacked my arm. "And here I was about to compliment you two on being all grown up." She waved her hand. "You two are going to be the death of me one day, I swear it."

We both turned to see two cars making their way down the drive. Once they parked Natalie stepped out of the car and my heart immediately began to quicken. Dressed in her workout attire I can see every single delicious curve of her gorgeous body. She smiled as she saw me from across the drive and I felt like my heart's about to burst all over again. Seeing her smile never gets old, and I can't wait to see it for the rest of my life.

"There's my girl." I picked her up as she wrapped her arms around my neck and I gripped her waist.

"I've missed you too, Heartthrob." She giggled as she laid a kiss to my lips.

I set her down slowly when she saw my Mum and practically squealed. She was so excited to see her in person again it made me laugh and smile as I greeted Rob, Ben, Riley, and Kayley.

"Mindy! Let the poor girl breathe." Dad and Teddy came walking out to the cars.

"I can't help it Anthony." She continued to hug my girl as she hugged back. "Look at her, she's so beautiful. Do you know how long I've been waiting for her?"

"Hi, Anthony." She smiled and waved from my mother's arms.

"Hi, Natalie. I see you brought us some strong arms to help lift some boxes?"

"Hi! I'm Riley, this is my husband Rob, that's Ben, and that's Kayley." Mum and Dad went around shaking everyone's hands and greeting them.

Teddy shook hands with Ben as if to greet him again for the

millionth time. While Ben visited the house for meetings about content he and Teddy often found themselves hanging out afterwards. Eventually, they started meeting up on their own and became pretty good friends. Going to the gym, playing online games, and soon his very own stunt double.

I breathed a sigh of relief. Ben's a great guy and I couldn't be happier that it was him to help my brother renew his faith in friendships again.

Teddy and Kayley glared at each other, but as soon as Mum and Dad came over she turned on the charm like a flip of a switch.

"Hi, nice to meet you both." Kayley shook their hands and grinned.

"Don't let her fool you." Teddy whispered. "She's only here to get my address so she can stalk me."

"Oh, please." She shook her head. "As if I would waste my precious time stalking *you*."

"Then please, do tell me why you're here, Sunshine."

She shrugged. "I just needed to learn the layout so I know which vents are best for hiding rotting eggs."

"Sunshine?" Mum leaned over to Natalie. She quickly nodded and shared a knowing look with her.

I leaned down to my girl's ear. "My love, are you and my mother starting to develop a secret language?"

She lifted her shoulder. "Maybe."

"Dear god, what have I done?" I whispered back as she wrapped her arms around my waist.

After a long day of getting all the boxes into their respective rooms, and Riley keeping a close eye on Kayley after finding out she actually brought eggs to hide throughout Teddy's house like some foul Easter egg hunt. We all sat at the dinner table and played a few board games like we have once a month.

We all drank, laughed, and watched Teddy and Kayley go at each other's throats for either targeting each other or for cheating. I had my arm resting on the back of my girl's chair as she leaned into my side.

I don't know how I got so lucky.

A year ago I would go from project to project, posting content, then back to more projects. Now, I have game nights once a month, a renewed relationship with my brother, and a level of happiness I never thought I'd achieve. All because of her. I put my hand in my pocket with the ring box and pressed a kiss to the top of her head.

She'll always be my girl, but I can't wait to call her *my wife*.

About the Author

Hi K.C. here!

I've always had a love for writing and wanted to pursue it full time when I graduated high school.

After obtaining my Journalism degree I spent years in the online media industry and it sucked out my soul. The dream of becoming an author was still there, but when you have a 9-5ish job where you're attached to a screen and phone all day, it felt like it was ten times harder.

It wasn't until after two jobs that drained me, and my father passing away at a young age, I realized how much time flew by. I wasn't any closer to pursing my dream until one day I told myself that I was going to become a published author, like my father cheered me on to do, and I wasn't going to give up.

Now, here we are.

If you have a goal you want to reach, there will always be one excuse that will hold you back. Don't let it stand in your way. Don't wait. Do it before you look back and wonder what could have been. Most importantly, do it for yourself. Take that chance because I promise you it's worth it.

Thank you for being here, thank you for buying my first book, and I hope you enjoyed *The Narrator*.

With Love,
K.C. Barnes

Thank you so much to my amazing and supportive Husband, Mom, Mom & Dad In-Law, Family, and Friends. (And of course my cats Artemis and Shadow.) I love you all so much! I can't thank you enough for all of your love and support.

Make sure to follow me on TikTok & Instagram for more updates and more books that I have in the works.

You can connect with me on:

- https://www.tiktok.com/@kcbarnes_author
- https://www.instagram.com/kcbarnes_author